"Get away from me, you beast," Amber ordered the major whose arms were locked around her. "I am not one of your Southern belles. I detest Confederate animals."

Brant's eyes bored deeply into hers, a scant inch away. "When I arrived I was told there was a woman waiting for me—a woman who would satisfy my male needs." His gaze dropped to her mouth. "You never had any intention of sleeping with me. You only wanted to get inside to rescue your brother." His fingers twisted in her hair. "You may have played my men for fools, but you won't do the same with me."

Jerking her head still, Brant's mouth opened and closed over hers. His action had been unexpected, and Amber could not escape the punishing movement of his lips. Her body was crushed between his and the wall, and she was barely able to take a breath. His free hand glided along her thigh and waist to find her breast. Even though clothes covered her, Amber felt a jolt of electrifying awareness. His palm kneaded the flesh while his mouth plundered hers. His tongue heightened the intimacy at the same time he tore apart the buttons to reveal the petticoat beneath. Her legs trembled when his knuckles brushed her flesh and an involuntary moan escaped her throat.

It was bad enough that she was held helpless by this man and worse that she responded. Before she submitted to him completely, she protested weakly, "Take your hands off me, you filthy swine."

Then Amber wrapped her arms even more tightly about him and drew his head to her lips that were afire with passion . . .

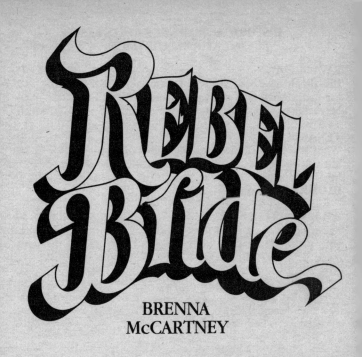

REBEL BRIDE

**BRENNA
McCARTNEY**

ZEBRA BOOKS
KENSINGTON PUBLISHING CORP.

ZEBRA BOOKS

are published by

Kensington Publishing Corp.
475 Park Avenue South
New York, N.Y. 10016

First printing: September 1984

Printed in the United States of America

*This book is dedicated
with love to Mom — a very special lady,
to the memory of my Dad,
and
love and thanks to Jojena.*

One

August 1862

The calm peacefulness of the early evening was shattered by the pounding of cannons. The acrid scent of gunpowder permeated the air with the stench of battle. Death and tortured cries of anguish were a chilling reminder of the war that waged between the North and South. In a few hours the darkness would slow the battle, but it would break fresh with the dawning of a new day.

Wounded Union soldiers were carried from the battlefield to the field hospital, but the injured far outnumbered the doctors and many died before they received care. Ten brave soldiers had given their lives that afternoon, and their covered bodies awaited burial.

Rising from the soldier's side, Amber Rawlins pulled a blanket over his body. It was an action done so many times in the past two days that her movements had become mechanical. Her chosen work put her in constant contact with suffering and death, but she did not let the depressing atmosphere reflect on her beautiful young face. Her smile was always quick, her eyes were a changing blue-green, and her amber hair, when not confined, tumbled over her shoulders. The helpless soldiers needed care, compassion, kindness and loving dedication and she eagerly provided it.

"Another one, Miss Amber?" a private asked, stopping at her side.

"I am afraid so," she reflected. "When will it end?"

The young man shook his head. "From the sound of them guns it's gonna get worse."

"Do you know if my father is back in camp?" she asked, concerned because he was overdue. Richard Rawlins was a medical doctor assigned to the camp, but he also worked as a spy, carrying the enemy's secrets to couriers for delivery to Union headquarters.

"Not yet," he said. "But I am sure he will be along soon." The soldier looked at Amber. If she was worried about her father, she had carefully hidden her anxiety. He, like many of his fellow soldiers, admired the strength and dedication he saw in this young woman.

Smiling, Amber excused herself and picked a path through the broken bodies to the area set aside for surgery. A few tables were inside tents, but most were outside. Darkness was becoming a problem and even the lanterns hanging on posts gave little light to the surgeon.

There were four doctors working on the wounded, and Amber's gaze stopped on the youngest, her blue-green eyes brightening in recognition of her twin brother's skill. Andy was only seventeen, but he had years of hard work behind him.

Amber's and Andy's medical training started when they were five years old. Their mother died and the responsibility of raising the children fell to their father. He didn't know how to care for his daughter, so he raised her as another son, unintentionally forcing her to subdue her feminine feelings in favor of the masculine values. He was most comfortable with his medicine and when the twins showed an interest in it he had been patient with their curiosity. As the years passed his explanations became more involved, and the twins showed promise of a future in medicine.

When Amber turned fifteen and started showing signs of becoming a woman, Richard realized he had a daughter and not two sons. Amber's medical studies ended and she had to dress in beautiful gowns and study etiquette. Her opportunity to return to medicine came when President Lincoln called for volunteers to squelch the uprising. Richard and his brother Hank enlisted in the Union Army. Hank was sent to Washington, and Richard went to the battlefield as a doctor.

Andy joined his father and continued his training. Amber abandoned her feminine teaching and followed. In the beginning all she was allowed to do was fold bandages and prepare the supplies. The Battle of Bull Run was all she needed to abandon the "useless" tasks, and she began following the men into surgery.

Richard's reluctance to have her at the operating

table vanished when he saw how competently she performed. Her skills became valuable and he encouraged her to learn all she could. Amber easily slipped back into the smooth companionship she had once shared with her father and brother.

Andy would be busy with the patient for at least an hour, and Amber would have to wait to tell him about Papa. She was worried about her father, but was careful not to let her concern show on her face. Her papa was a strong man and demanded the same of his daughter. Frowning, she walked toward the injured. Open wounds needed to be covered and soiled bandages changed to ward off pestering flies.

The thundering of horse's hoofs alerted her to an approaching rider, and she saw the guards lower their weapons in readiness. A sigh of relief broke from her lips when she recognized her father, but her relief was marred by concern when she saw the man across his horse.

Lifting her dress, she ran to his side. "What happened?" she asked breathlessly.

He ignored her question. "He will be dead in thirty minutes if we don't stop the bleeding."

"Surgery is full," she said, anticipating his next command.

Richard scowled. "We'll work on him here." He looked at the young man who had come to assist. "Private," he snapped. "Get me a lantern, fresh bandages, a blanket and medical tools. . . . Hurry." The man disappeared to do his bidding. "Amber, help me get him down." Richard slid off the back of the horse and Amber stepped to his side. "We have to be very careful. He has a serious head injury. When I pull him down, slip between him and the horse to take the weight until I can get a firm hold on him." Grabbing the man's upper body, Richard gently lowered him. When he was halfway to the ground, the horse moved, and Amber slipped between them.

The man sagged against her, and her arms surrounded his waist to offer support. She staggered under his full weight, her body feeling every hard muscle of his. Her breasts flattened against his chest, and her hips were pinned to the horse by his. His dangling arms brushed her thighs, causing an unexpected trembling in her limbs. Turning her head, she felt the man's warm breath against her cheek in an intimacy she had never experienced.

It was over in a few seconds, but the moment was burned into her mind and limbs in vivid detail. Never had she been forced into such close contact with a man and made to feel the dominant masculinity. This in no way resembled her first kiss at fifteen or the few that had followed. A total stranger, a man who was close to death, had showed her a world that had only been hinted at and the awakening was staggering.

"I've got him," Richard said and slowly lowered him to the dirt. Amber dropped to his side. When the supplies came, the lantern provided a clear look at his injuries. Blood soaked the left side of his shirt, but it was his head that was the most serious. His face was swollen from cuts and scratches and a deep slash marked the left side of his skull.

"He is lucky to be alive," she gasped.

"He won't be for long if we don't get busy." His

statement warned that it was not time for curious questions. "I'll work on the head wound. You take care of the side."

Amber nodded, her fingers automatically reaching for a knife to cut away the shirt. The man was not in uniform, so his loyalties were unknown and right now unimportant. He was a man who needed help and they would provide it regardless. The shirt fabric was blood-soaked and she threw it into a pile to be disposed of later.

The man moaned softly and Amber's gaze rose to his mouth. There was a trickle of blood oozing from one corner. Torn by an outward show of tenderness she rarely exhibited, she reached for a clean cloth to gently wipe it away. Her gaze lingered on the slightly swollen line of his lips in curious appraisal. What did his mouth look like without the puffiness? Amber's stomach rolled unexpectedly, and she felt the steady beat of his heart beneath the hand that rested casually against his hair-roughened chest.

"Amber," her father barked. "What are you doing?"

She looked up, unable to answer. She didn't know what was happening to her. This man was a patient, but something about him disturbed her.

"I — I don't know," she answered, the confusion showing in her blue-green eyes.

Richard appraised the softness on his daughter's face. It was an emotion he hadn't seen since she was a very small child. He hadn't known how to handle it then and he didn't know now. She had let her outward strength slip to display her vulnerability and pain over this man's agony. She could not let weakness interfere with her duty. He had taught his children that their strength and independence was important.

"Get hold of yourself and remember what you were taught. Get to work," he ordered. "There isn't time for softness."

"Yes, Papa," she said, reaching for a cloth to wipe away the blood.

The wound on his side was not serious, and she worked quickly to clean, close and bandage the flesh. Without being asked, she went to her father's side and assisted him with the head wound. The injury was almost in the hairline, and if he lived she suspected there would be minimal physical scarring.

Amber's eyes ran over the bruised face. In the semi-darkness it was hard to tell exactly what he looked like, but she was strangely curious what the light of day would bring. Nothing had come from his lips since they started, and she knew he was mercifully unconscious. A quick look at the man's chest confirmed that he was still breathing. He had never opened his eyes and Amber wondered what color they were. Unwillingly, her gaze followed the strong jawline to his mouth. What was there about his lips that captivated her? She had worked on hundreds of men before and none of them had ever affected her like this one. She had always been able to remain detached from her patients and exhibit the outward strength her father demanded. His nostrils flared with his breath, and his quivering lips forced a tightness in Amber's breast.

"Amber," Richard shouted impatiently. "Quit daydreaming and hold up that lantern so I can see what I'm doing."

Her cheeks reddened as she grabbed the light. The tone of Richard's voice warned that he wasn't happy with his daughter's behavior.

To keep the bandage in place he wrapped the stranger's forehead, then dropped it over one side of his face to come up behind his head. It concealed one eye and part of his cheek, but held the dressing firmly in place.

"Is he going to live?" she asked, unaware that something in her tone alerted her father.

"Amber, do you know this man?" he quizzed sharply. "Have you seen him before?"

"No, he is a stranger." She forced herself not to look at the man in the dirt.

"Amber," he said, a warning note in his voice. "Don't get involved with him. He will probably be dead by morning."

She brushed a loose strand of hair from her cheek. "He is nothing to me but a patient. . . . What happened tonight? Did you meet your contact?"

The stranger was so near death he was not a concern, but Richard scanned the area to make sure no one was within hearing distance. "I expected to meet William Boone, but he wasn't there." He pointed at the stranger. "This man was. I don't know if Washington sent a different courier, or if the Confederates learned about the transfer of information and sent this man to stop it."

"What do you think happened to him?" she asked curiously.

"The side was gunshot, but the head wound is from

a knife or bayonet. I don't think he was injured where I found him, so he probably got the scratches from stumbling in the brush."

"What are you going to do about the information you were supposed to pass?" she asked, knowing his messages were often crucial. He never told his children what he learned, but they recognized the importance of what he was doing.

"It is too important to ignore. It will have to be taken to another location." He looked into the darkness. "Where is Andy?"

"He was in surgery," she responded.

"I want to see him when he is finished," he said, and Amber suspected he shared more of his spying activities with his son. Andy had officially become part of the war two months earlier and was working as a doctor. "Cover him up and we'll check him in the morning." He gazed fondly at his daughter and put his arm around her shoulders. "Amber, I didn't mean to be so rough on you. You were only five when your mother died, and I didn't know what to do with a little girl. Perhaps I expect too many of the male values from you."

Touched by his concern, Amber smiled at him. "You don't have to apologize for the way you raised me. I am glad I can be independent. I can't stand to be around helpless, crying females."

Richard chuckled. "Neither can I." His blue eyes softened. "Your mother was an incredibly strong woman. Had she lived she could have smoothed out some of the rough spots I've created by treating you like your brother. I hope you can forgive me if I have cheated you."

Amber put her arms around her father's neck. She didn't know what "rough spots" he was talking about. She was happy with her life and grateful that her father had given her the freedom to experience things most women were forbidden. If something was missing from her upbringing she didn't know what it was.

"You have been wonderful." She fondly kissed his cheek in one of her few outward shows of emotion.

"You did a nice job on his side. I am very proud of you."

"Thank you," she said, smiling.

Rising, Richard walked into the darkness. His praise meant a lot to her, and his concern over her upbringing was touching. Raising two children had not been easy, but she had never doubted his love for his children. Amber's memories of her childhood were happy ones and held a special place in her memory.

Twisting sideways, she retrieved a blanket. It was a warm night and the man's flesh burned with fever, but the cover would help prevent the early morning chill. She put her hand down to shift her position and it fell against the stranger's lean fingers. Her initial reaction was to jerk it away, but something held her flesh against his. He was just another man and she had treated hundreds of them. What was there about the broken body of this man that fascinated her? Was it because she had felt every muscle of his body against hers? Or did she respond to the sense of mystery and adventure surrounding his appearance? Were they the same kind of people, sharing common values of independence and boldness?

Her magnetism for him was puzzling. None of her gentlemen callers had forced his way into her senses like this man had. Papa had seen her confusion and not liked it. Involvement, passion and desire hinted at weakness, and Amber had been taught never to let her defenses down and allow her outward strength to slip. Papa had said there was no room for it in medicine.

Just this once, she wanted to ease her curiosity, and gently ran her fingers up his arm to the broad shoulders. The lantern showed her very little about the man, but she felt a relaxed power beneath her flesh. Amber's fingers curved up his neck and her palm opened over his cheek, taking extra care not to disturb the fine cuts and scratches. Stopping, she lightly ran the tip of her finger along his lips. His warm breath tickled her skin and she jerked her hand free. It never made it to her lap. It caught and hovered uncertainly above the hair-roughened chest before dropping to the hard-muscled firmness of his chest.

She experienced an unexplained tightness in her limbs and wondered at its origin. This man, a stranger, aroused alien feelings—feelings that made her outward strength vanish beneath trembling vulnerability. Amber recognized the dangerous power a man like this could hold over her. He probably had the strength and dominance of her father, and she would always have to hide the feelings of vulnerability, or they would be viewed as weakness. The men in her life would have to have qualities opposite of the man who had raised her.

Amber pulled her hand back and gently covered him with the blanket. "You'll probably be dead by morning." There was regret in her voice. She did not like to see any man lose the battle with life. The back of her fingers brushed his cheek. "I don't understand my physical attraction for you," she whispered. "Even though you are unconscious, I sense you are a man with unbendable strength and confidence — like Papa," she murmured. "He told me that men with those qualities hate to see weakness. I have lived up to Papa's expectations, but I never had to fight the kind of vulnerability you make me feel. It is probably better if I never have to try." She rose to her knees and lightly brushed her finger along his lips. "Why am I so fascinated with your mouth?"

Did she secretly wonder what it would feel like against hers? She had experienced men's kisses, but none of them had physically aroused her. Amber was impulsive and usually went after what she wanted. Right now she needed something to shatter her magnetism to his man. Perhaps she could erase it if she touched his lips just once.

Amber quickly extinguished the lantern and was glad there were no other patients nearby. Still unable to understand what spurred her on, she bent over the man. "I don't even know your name," she whispered, her lips inches from his.

If Amber had any thought of drawing back without finding out what his mouth tasted like, it was forgotten. Her lips touched his tenderly and a hot rush of unexpected tingling raced through her body. It was more — much more than she expected and Amber scrambled to her feet. The man had been unconscious, unable to turn the desire into passion; nonetheless, it had been an electrifying jolt. Throwing her hand over her seared lips, she ran from the wounded man, certain that a man who could arouse such

18

strong feelings in her body would bring her nothing but heartache.

Amber's unanswered question had hung in the air seconds before she touched his mouth. "Brant," he said in a hoarse whisper. "M—my name is Brant."

Those few words caused intense agony for the man on the dirt, but the woman had eased some of his suffering. There was a question in his mind as to whether she was real or an illusion created by the intense pain. He didn't want it to be a trick of the imagination. She had shown kindness and compassion through the gentle touch of her hands. He had regained consciousness once while they worked on his body, and was certain she had tended to the injury on his side. Was it possible that a woman with such tenderness knew how to heal?

Brant tried to go back over her speech in his mind, but the pounding against his skull made thought very difficult. He was certain she had desired him, but he had sensed fear for that kind of feeling. What else had she said? Why couldn't he remember?

He tried to raise his hand to the bandage on his head, but his limbs were too weak and the arm just lay in the dirt. She had said he would be dead by morning. The pain in his body told him it was the truth. Brant knew he couldn't die. Besides the importance of his mission, there was a very desirable woman he wanted to get to know.

"Wake up sleepyhead," Andy called, poking his sister with his hand. "You've already had hours more sleep than I have."

Moaning, Amber threw her legs over the side of the cot and looked at her brother. The resemblance between them was remarkable. Both had the same amber hair, but while Andy wore his in the style of most men, just touching the collar of his shirt, Amber's flowed down her back. When they experienced their growing years, Amber did not lag behind, and she found herself taller than most women and only two inches shorter than her brother's six feet.

The bone structure of their faces was the same, their noses and mouths a replica of the other's. Their eyes hovered between blue and green and changed only to one color depending on their mood. Despite the similarities, Andy's features were bolder and more defined, and he had grown a moustache to sharpen his masculine image. Both were broad-shouldered, but Andy developed the muscular physique of a man, while Amber softened with the curves of a woman.

A faint smile touched Amber's lips as she reflected on the time Andy had cut her hair to the length of his and tried to deceive their father into thinking she was Andy. They had gotten away with the deception until he lost out on a chance to help Papa care for an injured man and gave away Amber's identity. Their father had been furious with his daughter and scolded her soundly for cutting her beautiful hair.

"What is so funny?" Andy asked.

"I thought we might try and trade places like we did when we were kids. You remove your mustache and I'll cut my hair."

Andy chuckled at his sister's daring and his eyes wandered down her ample curves. "Up close you might have trouble passing for me."

Amber pushed her lip forward in a pout. "I suppose you won't try?" she baited.

"Papa was mad enough the last time." He ran his hand through his hair. "He wants us to meet him by the wounded man he brought in last night."

Thinking of her behavior in the light of day brought a flush to her cheeks. How could she have been so brazen? What had gotten into her?

"Is he alive?" she asked, rising and hiding her uncertainty.

Andy shrugged. "I don't know." The twins stepped outside and walked toward their father. "Papa was upset things didn't work out for him. He is going to have to leave camp again soon."

"He is lucky he can come and go the way he does."

"Maybe that is why he is so successful with his work. The Confederates don't expect a medical officer to be a spy."

Amber looked at her brother so she could gauge his reaction. "Has Papa told you anything about what he is working on right now?"

Andy's eyes narrowed. "Papa doesn't want us involved. It is dangerous business."

"Somehow I don't think that bothers you." Amber stopped and touched her brother's arm. "Andy, are you involved in this? Are you carrying messages?"

He looked at his sister. They were as close as any two people could be and their love, trust and loyalty had seen them through a lot. "I carried a message last week, but don't tell Papa I told you. He couldn't do it, so I met the contact. If things work out, maybe he'll talk to Uncle Hank and let me get more involved."

Amber hadn't seen her uncle since they had left their adjoining plantations and enlisted in the Union army. "I think you'll have trouble convincing Uncle Hank to let you participate. From what Papa said, Hank didn't want him doing it."

"Papa is waiting for us," Andy said, and they walked the distance to his side. "Is he alive?"

Richard shook his head. "He made it through the night, but the pain must be keeping him unconscious."

"Do you know who he is?" Andy asked.

"No. If we don't learn something before I leave you'll have to try and get information out of him." He rose. "Andy, I want you to change the head bandage this afternoon. Let's get to surgery. Coming, Amber?"

Amber had stayed in the background, even more disturbed by this man now that she could see him in the daylight. Edges of his light-brown hair peeked above the bandage, but the swelling on his face made it hard to distinguish features. She experienced relief and fear that he had made it through the night.

"Yes," she said and quickly turned her back on the man who had upset her life.

Amber made sure she wasn't around when Andy changed the bandage on the man's head. She felt safer being away from him, and the reminder of the churning confusion he had aroused in her body.

His unconsciousness stayed with them for days and Richard warned that there was no way of knowing how much damage had been done inside his body. He might die without waking.

When it was time for Richard to leave, the twins walked with him to the edge of camp. "Keep track of the stranger's progress though I'm doubtful he'll survive." He put the reins over the horse's neck. "I'm headed for Antietam. I don't expect to be back for some time so don't worry about me." He looked at the twins fondly. "Take care of each other while I'm gone."

There was no more emphasis on Andy caring for his sister than there was for her taking care of him. Richard had raised them to be capable of handling whatever faced them and knew they would always be there for each other.

Richard embraced his children, then mounted his horse. Andy put his arm around his sister and they watched him ride away. "Are you going to make it an early night?" he asked.

"I want to work a few more hours," she answered.

"That is what I thought. I will see you later."

Amber spent two hours changing bandages and trying to make the wounded more comfortable. When exhaustion finally claimed her, she walked toward her tent. Halfway there she changed directions and strolled toward the stranger and knelt at his side.

His eyes were closed, but the slow rise of his chest told her he was still alive. Amber didn't want to get caught by the feelings she had experienced the other night and started to rise.

"Don't go," he whispered, his hand snaking around her wrist to keep her at his side.

Amber's trembling mouth matched her quivering

limbs. "How — how are you feeling?"

"Where is the man who found me?"

"My father is gone," she answered swiftly.

"Where?" he asked and even in his weakened state she recognized it as a demand. "Wh — where has he gone?"

Amber could sense his agitation and didn't want him to get upset. "He rode toward Antietam."

The man's eyes closed, but he did not relinquish his hold. His fingers laced through hers and pulled them to his mouth. The touch of his lips against her flesh was a sensuous gesture, and Amber's head spun.

"Don't," she said, snatching her hand away. Before he had time to speak, she scrambled to her feet and ran into the darkness. She didn't stop until she was in the tent. Stretched out on her bed she tried to forget the feel of his lips against her hand. The command he had over her body made her feel threatened. Why did she respond to him as she did? When she fell asleep that night her cheek was touching the place where his lips had caressed the flesh.

When Amber walked among the wounded the next morning, her eyes automatically sought out the stranger. The empty spot on the earth told her all she needed to know. An emotion unknown and unexplained knifed through her body. Was she disappointed she would never know more of the man? Forcing down her churning uncertainty, she walked to Andy's side and spent the day helping him save the lives of men who had bravely fought for the Northern cause.

When they had finished for the day, Amber told Andy the stranger had died. His disappointment was genuine, but he knew there was no point in dwelling on information he would never receive.

Days later word reached the field hospital that there had been a battle at Antietam. Casualty reports were not good and Andy was transferred to a hospital near the battlefield. Knowing they would be short-handed without him, Amber stayed behind to continue her work with the sick and wounded.

Two months passed before Andy returned. He found Amber at the supply tent getting things ready for the next day.

"Amber," he said and she turned.

"You are back," she called, smiling. She gave him an affectionate hug and stepped back. "How were things?"

Andy's blue-green eyes darkened. "Amber, Papa is dead," he said softly.

"No," she denied, the pain almost too incredible to bear. "How did it happen?"

"Something went wrong when he went to meet the courier. He was captured and shot."

Amber called upon all the strength Richard had instilled in his daughter and the weakness—the tears he had so despised—were locked away with the grief in her heart. Amber vowed to maintain that strength and always show her courage. The twins held each other and the special bond they shared drew them closer. Their father had asked them to take care of each other and in an unspoken agreement that was what they intended to do.

"Amber," Andy said softly. "I want to continue

Papa's work. He was doing something important and I want to finish it."

She looked at her brother and understood his need to avenge Papa's death and to aid the cause he believed in. She shared similar beliefs. "Promise you will keep in touch."

"I will," he said, kissing her cheek.

He left for Washington the next morning and Amber resumed her work at the hospital. Two weeks after Andy's visit, Hank found Amber at the field hospital counting supplies. There was a disapproving gleam in his eye, and Amber was glad he hadn't discovered her in surgery. He had never understood or approved of the freedom Richard allowed his daughter.

"Amber," he said. "I saw Andy last week. He told me you were working here." He shook his head. "This is no place for you."

Amber stiffened and pointed at the moaning men. "They need help."

"You are a lady," he reminded her angrily. "You do not belong here unchaperoned. You are going to return to Washington and live with me. Your father is dead. . . . You are my responsibility now."

"I'm fine," she protested. "Andy visits me whenever he gets the chance."

"Andrew has been sent to a hospital in the south. He won't be able to see you for months."

Amber knew her uncle was lying, but she couldn't argue with him. She wasn't supposed to know that Andy was a spy. He had been warned not to confide in anyone.

"I'll be fine."

"Nonsense," he said sternly. "You are leaving with me."

"What about my work here?"

"If you insist on folding bandages, you can help the women at the Washington hospital."

Amber had been at the City Hospital less than a week when she approached the doctors about helping in surgery. Their skepticism was something she had become accustomed to, but it vanished when they recognized her expertise. Sworn to secrecy because of their desperate need for help, the doctors welcomed Amber as their assistant.

As the months passed Amber tried to block her unexplained and unexpected response to the stranger in the battlefield hospital. He had forced her to recognize how easily desire could weaken the strength she had promised her papa. The stranger was gone from her life, but the memory of those firm, sensual lips was something she would never forget.

Two

Amber defiantly placed her hands on her slim hips and pushed her full lower lip forward in a pout. Her blue-green eyes turned a stormy blue, highlighted by green flecks of turbulence. Gently curved brows, the same color as the amber hair curling halfway down her back, narrowed in anger.

"You can't be so heartless," she protested. "Andy is my brother . . . your nephew. Are you going to let him rot in a Confederate prison?

Hank Rawlins ran his fingers through his graying brown hair. Ever since learning of his nephew's plight a few hours earlier, he had been expecting and dreading this confrontation with his headstrong niece. Once Amber took a stand on something she met the challenge with determination. Judging by the stubborn set to her jaw, she was prepared for battle.

"Do I have to remind you we are in a civil war?"

"Of course not," she snapped. Though she was living in Washington and away from the actual fighting, her work served as a constant reminder of the battle raging between the North and South.

"Then surely you understand how difficult, if not impossible, it will be to get Andrew out of a Confederate prison."

Amber's head bobbed forward in recognition of the difficulty. "I know it won't be easy, but I refuse to believe it is impossible. You are a high ranking officer in the Union army with ties directly to President Lincoln. I know you have been involved with prisoner exchanges."

"We have brought some men home," he conceded. "But it is a long, slow process. . . . Months of paper work are involved." He drew a tortured breath. It was not easy to know he was powerless to help his nephew.

"Will you start the paper work immediately?" she persisted, her hands falling to the soft fabric of her print gown.

"Amber," he said, striving for patience. "There are hundreds of men ahead of him. Many have been waiting months for a release. It would look suspicious if I requested his freedom so soon after his capture. I don't want to draw any unnecessary attention to your brother."

"You mean because he is a spy?" she shouted, and her breasts heaved with the quick burst of breath.

Hank's brows shot up in surprise, and he glanced uncertainly at the closed parlor door. "Lower your voice," he scolded. "Do you want the servants to hear your raving nonsense?"

"It is not nonsense and you know it," she declared in a determined tone. "I know you enlisted Andy as a spy for the North."

Turning, Hank walked to the parlor window overlooking the street. "Your brother was captured during a battle. You saw his name on the posted list of captured prisoners."

Amber took a deep breath. She was tired of her uncle's procrastinating. She had known the truth about Andy's job from the beginning, just as she had known her father had been on a spy mission when he was killed.

"We both know Andy wasn't taken prisoner after a battle," she argued impatiently. "There is no point in denying that Andy is a spy, so save the rebuttal," she said, refusing to let Hank convince her otherwise.

Hank turned slowly, the sun momentarily reflecting off the buttons on his officer's uniform. "You know the truth so I won't deny it any longer."

The verbal acknowledgment from her uncle was a victory, but until her brother was free, her personal war would not be won. "Then surely you must understand the importance of getting him out of prison. He could be hung."

Hank stared at his niece. She was not prone to hysteria, but there was fear and concern on her lovely features, and he was once again reminded of the close ties between the brother and sister.

"This may sound heartless, but Andrew knew the risks when he joined the army. None of us knows if we are going to survive the war, but we believe in the cause and are willing to surrender our lives for it."

Raising her hand, Amber waved her uncle to

silence. "You don't have to try and sell me on the war . . . unless you've started recruiting women for battle."

"You know we haven't," he replied with a scowl, "but I suppose you would be among the first to start toting a rifle. . . . I wish half my men shot as well as you," he muttered under his breath.

Amber smiled. She had been raised with emphasis on male skills and values, and was an equal match to her twin brother on many things.

Hank wished he would see some of Amber's boldness on the men in the battlefield, and he suspected her courage would put most of them to shame. She was meeting this crisis as she did the rest—with determined vigor and not tears of hysteria. She had never been one to stand in the shadows. If she believed in a cause, she acted on it despite public opinion. Hank was well aware of the whispering about his niece's activities at the hospital, and he was going to have to take definite steps to find out exactly what she did. He wished there was someone willing to take responsibility for curbing her wildness. He was rapidly losing control over her.

Hank's expression softened, and he had to stay the impulse to comfort his niece. Though he loved Amber dearly, she kept everyone except her brother at a distance and gestures of affection from others were seldom appreciated. She was fiercely independent and preferred to accomplish things on her own rather than ask for help. Hank believed the strong male influence had made her afraid to show her femininity.

Once again Hank blamed Richard for not providing Amber with an upbringing that had fewer masculine overtones. Her introduction to the world of a lady had been years late and had been interrupted and forgotten by the onset of the war.

"I promise to do all I can." Hank sighed. "I wanted your brother to stay at the hospital and use his medical skills, but he insisted on being a spy. Andy is young and inexperienced. He probably made a careless mistake."

"Careless nothing," Amber growled in an unladylike manner, her eyes sparkling her defiance. "Papa taught us to be careful. My brother . . . like my father . . . was betrayed by someone in the Union army."

Hank crossed the room and grabbed his niece's shoulders. "Why do you believe they were betrayed?" he demanded, his brown eyes narrowing on her face.

"Papa was trying to find the person responsible for giving the Confederates important information. He was going to relay his findings to the courier, William Boone. Andy continued Papa's work and asked William for his help."

Hank's eyes darkened and his arms fell. "Perhaps that was Andy's mistake," he remarked thoughtfully.

"What are you talking about?"

"Maybe it is more than coincidence that William was involved when your father and brother were captured."

"Do you suspect William of treason?"

"He is in an excellent position for passing information. It is possible William killed your father because he learned the truth."

Amber pondered Hank's accusation, and remembered the meeting William missed, forcing her father to ride to Antietam with the information. Had the stranger been a Confederate sent by William to capture her father?

Hank looked at his niece. "Did Andy suspect him?"

"I can't be sure, but he said his meeting with William was very important."

"I'll get Boone back to Washington and we'll question him. There is a strong possibility that he is involved."

Amber's face twisted in anguish. It hurt to know William might be responsible for her father's death and brother's capture. He had been a friend of the family for years.

"It will come as a shock to his father," Hank said. "He is one of our finest officers." His expression was distant and painful. "The war split many families and friends, but the time had come for change. . . . I believe the life we knew is gone. Thus far our homes in Virginia remain untouched, but will we ever be able to go back?" He sighed deeply. "I had a letter from the overseer of your plantation. There are some things that need immediate attention, but I can't leave Washington. He'll have to handle them himself."

Amber didn't offer to go in his place. She had responsibilities to her brother and the hospital.

"I want to get to headquarters with this new information on William."

"Are you going to try and help Andy?"

"You're a very determined young lady." Casting aside his earlier reservations, he fondly touched the tip of her nose with his finger. "My investigation is going to take a few days, so endeavor to be patient."

"I'll try," she promised, but knew it wasn't going to

be easy. "Can I ride to town with you?" she asked as Hank walked toward the door.

Stopping, he turned. "Why don't you stay home this afternoon? I know you spent yesterday with the casualties."

"There is so much work that needs to be done," she protested.

"Let one of the other ladies take your place."

Amber quickly moistened her lips. How could she explain to her uncle that the other women could not do her work? "It wouldn't be possible," she excused.

His niece's hesitation did not pass unnoticed, and the rumors he had heard about her activity at the hospital came to mind. Her father and brother were doctors, and he didn't know how much exposure she had had to medicine.

"Amber, are you doing more than fold bandages?"

She fixed a smile on her face, but her body tensed. If her uncle suspected how she spent time at the hospital, he would forbid her to leave the house. Women were very involved in the care of the injured, but they generally stayed with the basics. Amber didn't.

"I don't know what you're talking about," she said, twitching her small nose in confusion. "You visited the hospital last week and saw me packaging supplies."

"I know what I *saw* you doing," he said pointedly, "but what were you doing before I arrived and after I left."

"I read the men notices on the war and write letters for them. What else could I possibly be doing?"

"I heard there were some women tending to the personal needs of the men."

34

Amber's eyes widened innocently. "Do you believe I would do that kind of work?"

Hank's right brow arched in question. If he wasn't careful his niece would get control of the situation and easily wrap him around her finger. He had hoped to have this discussion with her, but wished the timing could have been better planned.

"Knowing your total disregard for public opinion, I'd say yes."

"But Uncle," she protested. "I am an unmarried maiden. It wouldn't be proper."

Hank sighed his exasperation. "Amber, we both know you are not one to stand on convention. You shoot, hunt, ride astride, and hold opinions on male topics. You are a woman, yet you refuse to participate in the feminine tasks."

"They are boring."

"A well-bred woman enjoys them," he said sternly. He folded his arms across his chest. "Are you tending to the men's personal needs?"

Amber refused to flinch under his scrutiny. She knew this encounter would come someday, and she had to break through his rigid thinking and make things work for her.

"On occasion I have shaved the men and washed their faces." She saw the uncertain shift of her uncle's eyes.

"Go on," he said, positive there was more. "I want to hear everything. I won't have my niece compromising her good name."

"My moral character is as strong now as it was when I started," she flung back, certain she had found a way to turn the discussion in her favor. "I am treating sick and injured men. Most are not strong enough to have a romp in bed. I have seen bare chests and naked limbs." She uttered a short gasp. "Are you suggesting that I have seen . . .?"

"Enough," Hank called, throwing his hands up in defeat. A reddish hue had heightened the color of his cheeks, and the sluggish droop of his lips told of his embarrassment. "We will finish this discussion later. Until then I expect you to conduct yourself in a lady-like manner. I will not tolerate gossip about your activities."

"Yes, Uncle," she answered meekly as he left the room.

Sighing her relief, she crossed the room and slowly climbed the stairs. If she were lucky weeks would pass before they could debate the subject; meanwhile, she would have to keep a low profile at the hospital.

It was true most of society would frown on her dedication, but it didn't matter to Amber. Her work with the injured was her way of helping the country she loved. Rebels had killed her father and threatened to take her brother's life. She wanted to see the Confederates defeated; she hated them.

Their home sat in the wealthy section of the city about twenty minutes from the hospital. An over-turned wagon blocked their route to the hospital, and they were forced to detour to Pennsylvania Avenue. When they passed President's Park, Amber admired the Executive Mansion blocked from the road by an iron fence. The War, State, and Treasury Departments surrounded the President's house and were bustling with activity.

Washington was a growing city. Buildings were being repaired and new ones built. Hotels, restaurants, and shops lined the cobblestone streets in the better part of town. Less than one mile away were ugly offices and shacks where poorer businesses were operated.

At the hospital Amber climbed out of the carriage with the promise to be home by seven o'clock. As usual there was a lot of activity around the building, and Amber went inside through the rear door. Going to a small room at the back, she discarded her cape and put on a clean white apron. Hoops were never worn in the hospital, but the dresses still contained yards of cumbersome fabric, and Amber fought the urge to discard the gown in favor of pants; her actions were already rebellious enough.

Looking in a small, cracked mirror, she secured her hair with a ribbon. Her blue-green eyes were wide with anticipation of the hours she would spend helping the sick and injured.

Most of the patients were grateful for her kindness and tender care. Amber viewed them objectively and refused to get personally involved. Her outward show of strength made it easy to remain aloof and only once that outward shell had cracked.

Amber's hand slowly crept up to her mouth, and she remembered the touch of the stranger's lips. He had been the only person to disrupt her equilibrium and throw her emotions into turmoil, and she did not want to examine the reasons she felt threatened.

Three days after learning of her brother's capture Amber was summoned to the parlor. There was tenseness in her slender body when she joined her uncle.

"You wanted to see me," she said, hiding her anxiety.

"Yes," he said, walking toward her. "William Boone is on an assignment and we can't contact him for a month."

"What about Andy?" she asked impatiently.

Hank took her slim hands in his. "Your brother was carrying treasonous papers when he was captured and charged with spying against the Confederacy." His brown eyes softened. "He has been sentenced to hang at the end of the month."

Amber paled. "Hung?" she echoed. "You can't let it happen. Use your influence."

Her blue-green eyes were dry, but a misty film covered her uncle's concerned brown ones. His decision concerning his nephew had not been easy. "I can't do anything. He is a spy. I can't try to save him at the cost of other lives."

Amber pulled her hands free from her uncle's grasp. With a straight backbone Amber turned and ran to her room. Slamming the door behind her, she paced the wooden floor, her hands closed into fists at her sides. Andy needed help and there was no one to help him . . . no one but her. Thrusting her chin forward in determination, Amber made the decision to get her brother out of the Confederate prison.

Three

A warm June breeze ruffled the delicate lace window curtains causing them to blow against Amber's sleeve. Neither the beauty of nature nor the occasional passing carriage registered on Amber's troubled mind. Less than two hours earlier she had received word her brother would be executed and had decided to try and rescue him.

From the beginning, the twins had been inseparable. As they grew their trust, love and respect for each other created a bond that made their relationship very special. It was because of their closeness that Amber knew she could not sit idle and let Andy hang without trying to help him. If they hanged him a part of her would die.

Sighing deeply, she reflected on the danger of entering the prison. If she got caught she would be in as much trouble as Andy, but it was a risk she was willing to take. Time was crucial and she refused to think of failure.

A light tap on her door drew Amber's head up and

forced her brows to narrow. She wasn't prepared for another confrontation with her uncle. She still needed time to formulate her plans.

"Come in," she called softly, a sigh escaping her lips when Myra, her maid since birth, stepped in and closed the door. She was the one person who would understand Amber's need to help her brother.

"Why are you still up?" the older woman asked. "Aren't you exhausted from the hours at the hospital?"

Amber shrugged. "I have some things on my mind."

Myra's graying brows came together and her lips drooped in a frown. "You've been pushing yourself too hard. . . . Some of the things you see aren't good for a lady. You should be surrounded by gentlemen and pretty things, not the horrors of death and suffering."

Amber took a deep breath. She would do anything to spare Myra the agony of what had happened to Andy, but she couldn't keep the truth from her, no matter how painful. In time she would need her help. Raising her eyes to Myra's face, she stepped forward and put her hand on the older woman's shoulder.

"It is not the hospital. . . . It is Andy." She took another breath to force away the tension. She had never been prone to female hysteria and did not cry in a crisis. She kept a tight rein on her emotions and always tried to show outward strength. Tonight was more difficult than usual.

"What has happened to my boy?" Myra wailed, her soft brown eyes clouding with moisture.

Amber tightened her grip on Myra's shoulder.

40

"Andy has been captured by the Confederates and charged with spying. They are going to hang him."

"No," Myra shrieked, her eyes widening in horror. "Tell me it's not true." She looked at the younger woman for some relief, but saw no mercy on the concerned features. Though her eyes were dry the color was clouded with pain.

"I'm sorry," Amber said softly.

Unable to control her grief Myra sobbed in the arms of her friend. Amber experienced the same hopelessness, fear and uncertainty, but her eyes remained dry, her head clear and focused on a way to help her brother.

"Myra," she said, guiding her to the bed. "I want you to listen to me."

When Myra was seated and had tapped her moist eyes with a handkerchief, she looked at Amber. "I am sorry child, but I love you and your brother like you were my own."

"Uncle Hank said there was nothing the army could do," she said bitterly. "I want to try and help Andy."

"You," Myra said, not surprised by Amber's willingness to tackle a problem of such depth. Over the years she had watched her overcome challenges that should have been too difficult. She had witnessed daring antics, but this went beyond everything else.

"I want to try and get him out of prison."

Shocked, Myra shook her head. "We are at war. Spying is a dangerous charge. Your brother is going to be under heavy security. If your uncle can't do anything for him, then no one can." Her voice cracked and heavy sobs shook her shoulders.

"Get hold of yourself," Amber scolded impatiently. "Your tears are not going to help Andrew. . . . We have plans to make."

Wiping her eyes, Myra looked at Amber. "I should have been a stronger influence over you in the years your papa was raising you. You have locked your emotions away. It is not wrong to cry when you hurt."

"Tears and hysteria won't get Andy out of prison, but hopefully a calm, clear head will. Are you through scolding me? We have plans to make."

"I am glad you are including me in this escapade," Myra stated. "Somebody has to keep you out of trouble. I won't let you risk your life pointlessly. I would rather have one of you than neither."

"Maybe we'll get lucky with Andy," Amber said on a positive note.

"Luck is what we are going to need."

"How are you going to get Hank's approval to leave the city?"

"I could just leave a note and disappear, but I think that would be cruel. Uncle Hank has been good to me, and I want him to think I'm safe."

Myra's eyes narrowed. "What are you going to do?"

"I am going to cause a ruckus that will make him want me out of Washington." Reflecting on the expression she would see on his face, she chuckled softly. "I am going to let him find out exactly what I do at the hospital."

Myra smiled at Amber's cunning. "He will be furious."

"I hope angry enough to send me home."

"But instead of going to Virginia, you will go to

42

Andy and devise a plan to free him." She nodded. "Amber," Myra said in a serious tone. "I love you for what you are trying to do, but I am scared."

Amber looked at her long time friend and knew this was a time to relax her outward toughness. It was time for honesty. "So am I."

Four

Amber was already seated at the breakfast table when Hank came downstairs. Despite her sleepless night, she felt exhilarated and hopeful for the day's events. She could not let anything spoil her plans.

Pulling out a chair, Hank sat opposite his niece. "You are up early," he commented casually.

"I want to ride with you to town," she answered.

Hank grunted his disapproval. "I thought you would be too upset about Andy to go to work."

At the mention of his name Amber sobered. "Are you sure there isn't anything you can do?" she blurted out. Any attempt Hank made at getting her brother out of prison would certainly be more successful than an attempt by a novice like herself.

"Amber, you don't seem to understand my delicate position. On one side I have my only living nephew. On the other side I am involved with a spy organization that is crucial to Union victory."

Amber saw the pain on his face. His responsibility as an officer and his love for his nephew pulled him in opposite directions.

"Do men ever escape from Confederate prisons?" she asked hopefully. She needed to obtain all the information she could if her rescue attempt was to be successful.

"It has happened," he admitted and glanced at his niece. "I wouldn't count on it happening with Andy."

Beneath the tablecloth Amber's hands curled into fists. With a melancholy expression on her face, she looked at her uncle. "Tell me about Andy's prison."

"What good is it going to do? Prisons are miserable." He couldn't understand why his niece was torturing herself for details about her brother's imprisonment.

"The hospital is not a nice place either, yet I am able to go there every day and work. I want to know how Andy's last days will be spent," she said with determination.

"You are torturing yourself needlessly," he argued.

"I want to know. If you won't tell me I will find someone at the hospital who knows."

His fork dropped to the table with a clang. "It is essential to the spy organization that your brother's activities be kept a secret."

His scolding did not deter her. "Then you will have to tell me what I want to know."

Hank scowled at his niece. He didn't know how she managed to do it, but she was skilled at getting the upper hand and making him look like a fool. Thus far he had been able to keep their confrontations private, but there was no guarantee her tongue wouldn't flare at him in public.

In the end there wasn't much he could tell her

45

about the prison except for the location and size. It wasn't the largest camp, but it was big enough for her to move around undetected once she got inside.

When he had finished telling her what he knew, Hank pushed back his chair and rose. "I have to get to headquarters. I have an important meeting this morning with President Lincoln." He pushed his coat aside and checked the time.

"Will you drop me off at the hospital?" she asked, rising.

Hank scowled his disapproval. "Very well," he said, ushering her to the door.

Though it was early the weather promised to be warm, and Amber lifted her face to the sun as she walked to the carriage. Fondly, she remembered sharing days like this with her father and brother, riding through the woods with her hair whipping out behind her.

Seated opposite her uncle Amber watched the people scurry along the streets on early morning business. She would not regret saying farewell to the confusion of the city.

"Amber," her uncle addressed, drawing her out of her pensive mood. "With Andy gone you are all I have. I've been a bachelor all my life, and I don't know how to handle a young lady with so much spirit." His graying brows came together. "In many ways I feel I have failed you. I have not been able to convince you to behave like a lady."

Leaning forward, Amber touched his hand. "I love you for taking me in after Papa died. You don't know what to do with me and neither did Papa. He did what he thought best and raised me like a boy. I don't blame him for not dressing me in beautiful gowns when I was a child. I was too happy to know the difference."

"You are so involved in your hospital work that you forget you're a woman." A gleam entered his eyes. "You need to be reminded of your femininity by gentlemen callers."

Amber didn't like the direction of the conversation and was glad when the carriage stopped at the hospital. "This is my stop," she called, pushing the door open. "I'll see you later."

"Goodbye," he called to her retreating back.

When the carriage pulled away, Amber sighed her relief and climbed the steps to the hospital. She didn't want Hank to decide she needed a husband. The building was filled with the same casualties she had seen in the field hospital in Virginia, and she was greeted by moans of anguish and the stench of death. She immediately went to one of the back rooms to wash her hands and don the white apron. Sighing, she knew before the day was over the whiteness would be splattered with blood.

Dr. Steven Monroe was already operating on a man with a severe case of gangrene in his leg. At thirty-five, Steven was the youngest doctor at the Washington hospital. His skills as a surgeon were excellent, and he worked with unwavering knowledge. When Amber stepped to the table across from him she found herself shorter than him by several inches. His blond hair brushed carelessly across his forehead, but wasn't long enough to hinder his vision. Blue eyes, a startling contrast to the fair coloring, glanced at Amber.

"I'm going to take his leg," he said, frowning.

Fortunately, medical supplies were abundant at the hospital. The man had been given something to make him sleep and had not heard the doctor's verdict. Many men who lost a limb felt their lives were over.

Amber did not question Steven's decision, and she reached for the instrument he needed. Using his professional skills, Steven severed the leg and closed the flesh. If the man was lucky the stump would heal and he would be able to return to a normal, if somewhat limited life.

"Take him away," Steven ordered, stepping back so the attendants could clean the table and instruments. He wiped a cloth across his forehead. "I don't know what I would do without you."

"We make a good team," she agreed.

Brushing aside his bloodstained coat, he pushed his hand into his pocket. "Have you ever considered becoming a physician?"

"I have always liked helping the sick and injured, but I don't know if I have the dedication to make it my life's work."

"Before we start another operation I want to warn you that some officers are coming here to prepare a report on the hospital. Your uncle will be with them." He checked his watch. "I expect them at noon, so you'd better plan to be in the bandage room with the other women."

She moistened her lips. "I want him to find me in surgery." She smiled at his surprised expression. "I can't explain why, but I need to leave Washington for a few weeks, and I think finding me here is the only way he will agree."

"I will miss you." Steven caught the bottom of her chin and tipped her face up. "When you get back, I would like to call on you."

Amber thought it was ironic that Steven would ask to deepen their friendship the same day Hank recommended she find a romantic interest. "I would like that."

Steven's gaze shifted to the table. "I think we'd better get to work. This one looks serious."

The man did not live through the operation. Steven sighed his exasperation and prepared for the next man. Amber carefully shielded her pain over the loss. A mysterious stranger with firm, sensual lips had taught her not to become involved.

They were finishing the third operation when the Union officers stepped into the operating room for their inspection. Amber's position across from Steven drew an immediate gasp from the men. Amber, busy aiding Steven with the final stitches, did not see her uncle's scowl of disapproval. It wasn't until the patient had been carried away that Amber looked up.

"Amber Rawlins," her uncle bellowed, and the men with him discreetly turned aside. "I want to talk to you immediately."

Hiding her smile, Amber glanced at Steven. His handsome face was marred by a frown of uncertainty. Even though she had warned Steven that she wanted this confrontation, he was still concerned by her uncle's rage.

Another man was placed on the table. "I am sorry Uncle Hank, but there is another operation scheduled." She smiled sweetly, denying that she had done any wrong. "Can't it wait until I get home?"

"It most certainly cannot," he argued, stepping forward to take her arm. "I am sure Dr. Monroe will excuse you."

"Uncle Hank, Steven needs my help. You know how desperate we are for medical personnel."

"Steven, is it?" he said in frank disapproval and cast an uncertain glance at the younger man. "I know how much we need help, but not yours."

Oblivious to the others in the room, Amber threw her hands on her hips and met her uncle's eyes. "Why not me? I am skilled in what I do. . . . Steven can attest to my qualifications."

"What do you know about medicine?" he scoffed.

"Quite a lot," Steven boldly inserted. "She is a valuable asset. She has steady hands and knows what I need before I ask. Unlike some of the men, the sight of blood doesn't affect her." He cast a praise-filled look at Amber. "Her father gave her an excellent background in medicine. I have been helping improve her skills."

Remembering the other men in the room, Hank took his niece's arm and directed her toward the door. "I want to see you in the next room, Doctor Monroe," he said over his shoulder.

Without waiting to see if his command was carried out, he pushed Amber out of the operating room and into the first vacant room. Steven, directly behind him, shoved the door closed to keep the discussion private.

Totally unconcerned by what was about to take place, Amber casually leaned against the table. While she didn't mind the confrontation with her uncle, she was sorry it had to include Steven. Certain her uncle wasn't watching, she gave Steven an apologetic look and mouthed the word, "Sorry."

Steven was relieved to see Amber's calm acceptance of what was happening and flashed her a generous smile. Though he was being confronted by his superior, he didn't balk when Hank turned his attention on him.

"Why did you allow my niece to help in surgery?"

"I already told you she is good in the operating room. She cares about the sick and wounded and treats them with compassion."

Hank's eyes widened. Compassion was a side of Amber he had never seen.

"Sir, if I thought Amber would be harmed I would have forbidden it. I hold your niece's welfare as my first concern."

"I find that hard to believe," Hank protested. "You saw that man they carried into surgery. He was practically naked."

Amber sighed and Hank turned to look at his niece. "Are you troubled because you think I am seeing men unclothed?"

"I am very concerned about your public image. You are . . . or I think you are . . . a young maiden." He threw an uncertain glance toward Steven before directing his attention back to Amber.

"Uncle Hank," she reproached softly, a reddish hue creeping into her cheeks. She liked Steven, but a discussion of her virtue was not something she wanted argued in front of another man, especially one who might be interested in her romantically.

"Are you embarrassed because I have raised the question of your innocence?"

51

"I only work at the hospital. I don't satisfy the injured men's desires in bed."

Her uncle turned a mottled red and Steven smiled at the way Amber had twisted things in her favor. If she continued her attack she'd be the victor.

"Enough Amber," Hank demanded, holding up his hand. He turned to Steven. "I want your assurance that Amber has conducted herself like a lady."

"Your niece's reputation has not been compromised."

"I would have your stripes if she had," Hank warned. "You are dismissed." After saluting, Steven gave Amber a wink of encouragement and left the room.

Hank swung around to face Amber. "I demand to know why you lied to me about your work here."

Amber calmly folded her hands across her chest. "I didn't lie to you. I wash the men and fold bandages. I didn't tell you about the surgery because you wouldn't understand. This is the way I aid the North. The war has taken my father's life and threatens to rob me of my brother. Do you expect me to do nothing?"

"You should have been a boy," Hank said, shaking his head.

"I am sorry if you are ashamed of me," she said defiantly.

"Oh," he groaned. "I'm not ashamed of you, but I don't want you to spoil your reputation. You are a beautiful young woman and it is time you started acting like one."

"Women have become an important asset to the hospitals. Any female can fold bandages, but few have the skills I possess. You know Andy is a doctor, but did you know I was studying with him? My learning was interrupted when Papa forced me to master the feminine skills, so I'm behind Andy in knowledge."

"I wasn't aware that your father was working with you."

"He knew you wouldn't approve."

"I don't. You are forbidden to return to the hospital," he said sternly.

"You can't do that," she gasped, secretly hiding her delight. "They need me here."

"I am sure we can find a *man* to replace you." He soberly regarded his niece. "You embarrassed me before my friends."

Amber wanted to be discovered, but she hadn't planned to shame her uncle. "You have my apology." She carefully removed her blood-splattered apron. "What do you expect me to do now? I have to find something to occupy my time."

Hank frowned. Amber would make his life miserable if she didn't find something to do. As long as she remained in Washington they would battle over her dismissal from the hospital.

"I am sending you back to the plantation for a few weeks. I know for a fact there aren't any hospitals in the area, and you can take the time to think about your behavior. You are to remain at the house and conduct yourself as a lady. Myra is to accompany you."

It was exactly what Amber wanted and she had to suppress her joy. "It will be good to get back home. It might help take my mind off Andy and the hospital."

53

"You can return in a month and resume your life here as a lady. You will attend social functions and meet eligible men." Hank's eyes narrowed. "Is there anything between you and Steven?"

"He asked this afternoon if he could call on me. Would you object?"

There was an obvious relaxing of Hank's shoulders. "I encourage it. Despite his indiscretion of letting you work here, his work is excellent, and I understand he is a very conscientious man." Hank grinned. "Steven might be the answer to our problems."

"What do you mean?" she asked, suspicious of his sudden interest in her relationship with Steven.

"If he reminds you of your femininity you might start acting like a lady." He guided her outside. "You are forbidden to return to the hospital. Do you understand?"

"Yes," she said meekly. Hank would be suspicious if she acted unconcerned over his order.

"There is a train out of town this afternoon. You still have time to go home and pack." Leaning forward he kissed her cheek. "Send me a telegram when you arrive at the plantation. I will trust Myra to keep you out of trouble."

Amber didn't like deceiving her uncle, but it was the only way she could help Andy. She would explain it to him when she returned and hoped he would understand.

"Goodbye," she said. "Take care of yourself while I'm gone."

Amber walked to the train station and purchased two tickets, then made a quick stop at the gunsmith

54

to buy a derringer for her purse. When she had come to Washington, fighting had made travel slow. Over the past months the war had intensified; it would be a dangerous trip.

Everything had gone the way Amber wanted except Hank's attack on Steven. Dr. Monroe had encouraged her work, and she wanted to apologize for getting him in trouble with Hank. She returned to the hospital and entered the back way. Making sure she wasn't seen, she went to a tiny room at the end of the corridor and knocked on the door.

"Come in," a voice called, and Amber quickly stepped inside. "Amber," Steven exclaimed, turning at the sound of the door closing. She had expected to find him working on papers and was totally unprepared for the sight of his partially clothed body. She had seen dozens of naked chests, but she had not expected him to be so broad or muscular. "What are you doing here?" he asked, walking to her side.

"I came to apologize for getting you in trouble with my uncle."

"I was more concerned for you. Did he give you permission to leave town?" She nodded. "I am not going to ask what you are planning, but is there anything I can do?"

Amber would have liked an ally, especially a male one, but it was too risky to trust anyone. She had learned from her father and brother that when too many people were involved it usually went astray.

"Nothing." Her eyes softened. "Thank you, Steven."

His blue eyes wandered over her face, noting the soft complexion that gave her face a smooth beauty.

"I am going to miss you," he whispered. "I — I would like to kiss you farewell."

Amber's limited experience with men had included kisses — some of them fumbling attempts at creating desire, others warm and passionate. None had made her melt with desire, and only one — the brief touch from the stranger's mouth — had made her tremble in breathless uncertainty and wonder if there were more. Would Steven's kiss spark the flame of passion she had yet to experience? He was an attractive man, and she felt no revulsion to feeling his lips against hers.

"I don't object," she said, meeting his eyes.

Smiling until dimples marked each cheek, he stepped forward and placed his hands on her shoulders, drawing her against his body, close, but not close enough to touch the naked chest.

Because he was taller, Amber was forced to raise her chin. Her eyelids fluttered down at the touch of his lips against hers, soft and gentle like the man he was. They moved with confidence over her mouth, sending tiny shivers through Amber's limbs. She enjoyed the feel of his mouth and sensed the controlled desire he held in check. Within seconds it was over.

"That was everything I thought it would be," he whispered. "You are a beautiful woman."

Amber was caught by the smoldering passion she read in his blue eyes and knew he saw her as a woman and not just an aide in surgery. He was a gentle man, not overbearing or demanding, and she did not feel threatened by him. Steven would always let her be the woman she wanted to be, and she would never have to be guarded in her actions or emotions. He was the kind of man she needed—a man opposite of her father.

Steven smiled. "I want to see more of you when you get back to Washington."

"I would like that," she confessed with genuine interest.

Smiling his joy, he opened the door and checked the hall. Certain it was clear, he stepped aside and Amber tiptoed into the corridor and walked quickly to the exit.

When she was two streets away from the hospital, she hailed a carriage and gave directions to her home. Settled against the plush seat, she pondered her future. Leaving the hospital was the end of a very important chapter in her life, but she was willing to surrender it out of love for her brother. If he died a part of her would die with him, and she was too full of life to want that bond to end.

Smiling with the challenge, she thought of the trip ahead, firm in the knowledge that she would be on a train headed out of Washington by evening.

Five

Major Brant Faulkner reined in his horse and sat looking at the town in the valley below. Removing his hat, he wiped the sweat from his brow. It had been a long, hot day and he was anxious to find a bed for the night.

Without his hat the wind ruffled his light brown hair against the collar of his gray jacket. Dark brown eyes narrowed as he surveyed the town. He was in the heart of Confederate territory, but a man with his rank couldn't be too careful. He would make an excellent target for a Union sniper.

Satisfied the town was unoccupied by Union soldiers, he put on his hat and nudged the horse forward. He remained alert as he rode through the street, his tall body straight. Spotting a hotel, he urged the animal to the side and dismounted. If he was lucky he would enjoy a nourishing meal, a soft bed and hopefully put the importance of his current assignment to the back of his mind.

He stepped to the planked sidewalk and strolled toward the hotel. A woman stood in the doorway blocking his entrance. Her green eyes locked with his brown ones and her full lips curved in a smile.

"Stayin' the night, Major?" she asked.

Brant shrugged. "I am here for food."

Her gaze wandered over his strong jaw and down to the gray jacket stretched over his broad shoulders. Boldly, she dropped her eyes to study the muscular thighs beneath the coat.

"Would you like a lady to join you?"

Brant's brow arched in reference to her feminine standing. "Maybe later," he said and walked past her.

The dining room was small and crowded, but Brant got a table near the wall. He ordered a hearty meal then sat back to wait for the food. He had not intended to eavesdrop when he sat down, but the table behind him was close, and he couldn't avoid hearing the woman's sniffles. Brant had nodded to the enlisted man when he sat down, and he assumed her anxiety was over the war.

"Why don't you desert?" he heard her say. "We can go away. How will I live without you?"

Brant scowled. He doubted the woman could survive on her own. Instead of being strong and proving how brave she could be, she was showing him her insecurity. Without realizing it she was creating anxiety in her husband that he would carry into battle and possibly get him killed.

Brant sighed. Why couldn't women show strength and still be soft and feminine? Why did they always crumble when faced with a crisis? Flashes of his childhood clouded his thoughts, and he remembered the women in his life. His mother had died in childbirth, and he had been surrounded by helpless nannies. He had grown up hating their incompetency. When he became old enough to appreciate women, he usually found them beautiful but stupid, totally lacking in courage and imagination.

His meal was placed before him, but he was no longer hungry. Scowling, he pushed his plate aside. Perhaps it had been the reminder of the women in his life that had spoiled his appetite, but he also knew it might be his current assignment. He had been troubled by it since he had received the orders. Brant had not gotten to the rank of major in the Confederate army without proving himself capable of tackling anything they gave him to do. A lot of attention would be focused on him and the success of his mission. He could not fail.

A shadow passed over the table and Brant looked up. The woman he had talked to outside smiled down at him.

"Interested in comin' upstairs?" she coaxed.

Brant had had plenty of offers in his twenty-six years, but only one woman had remained in the front of his thoughts, and she had done it with the touch of her lips when his body had been torn apart in pain. He wanted a woman who could be his equal—a woman who wasn't afraid to meet the challenges of life. His loins ached to feel soft naked flesh against his, but this whore wasn't the one. He wanted the woman who had eased his agony at the battlefield hospital and promised everything in the brief touch of her lips. If he found her he would never let her go.

"Come on," she coaxed. "I like you Rebel boys. Why not let me show you how proud I am of the work you men are doin'?"

"I don't have the time," he said, rising and tossing coins on the table.

"You have rank. Can't you do what you want?"

Her stupidity was another flaw against her. If women were attractive they lacked intelligence. Her statement proved her naivete.

"I have my superiors," he answered briskly. "I have to leave town."

"Are you gonna travel all night?"

Brant shrugged. He had intended stopping for the night. Now he couldn't wait to get out of town.

"I might," he answered, reaching for his hat.

"All you soldiers ever think about is the war." She pushed her lip forward in a pout.

Brant scowled. Her complaining would drive most men right out of her bed.

"What is so important?"

He picked up his hat and settled it on his head. "I'm on my way to a hanging."

Six

Amber pushed open the door at her uncle's home. "Myra," she called, racing up the steps. She found Myra in her bedroom closing a small traveling bag.

"I packed a few things in case you were successful."

Amber tossed her reticule on the bed and searched the closet for a clean dress. "I was. Uncle Hank was furious." She laughed. "He is trusting you to keep me out of trouble."

"That is not going to be easy. Amber," Myra said seriously. "Maybe you should reconsider. I love Andy too, but I don't want you to be hurt."

Amber removed her soiled gown. "Andy is worth the risk. Papa raised us to make things happen, not to sit idle and do nothing."

"You are too headstrong and independent. It is going to take a strong man to tame you."

Amber instantly thought of the man at the field hospital. Had she felt threatened by him because she recognized a hidden power? Would she always feel threatened by a man with the same qualities as her father? A strong man might tame her feistiness and she didn't want to be smothered beneath a man's dominance. Amber knew it was not a question she could answer until she fell in love. Love could change people, and she accepted the possibility that it could happen to her.

Amber thought of Steven. He was not an aggressive, masterful man, and he made her feel good about herself by encouraging and supporting her work. Amber recognized how different he was from her father. Papa had been a strong, forceful man, and he wanted the same qualities for his daughter. Amber could never show weakness through tears, and the emotions that made her a vulnerable woman were locked away and afraid to surface. Because Steven was the opposite of her father he might be the man to find her womanhood.

Myra watched the confusion on Amber's face. Something that was said had put her into deep thought. Since the death of her father, Myra had hoped Amber would let more of her femininity show. Richard had loved his daughter deeply, but he had been wrong in trying to impress the male values on her. The twins were sensitive and caring, but Richard had forced Amber to suppress her feminine emotions and as a result, she was afraid to let a strong man—a man like her father—see her weaknesses. Andy had seen what was happening and tried to show his sister that fears and uncertainties were not a shortcoming but a part of life. Myra hoped that one day a special man would enter Amber's life and shatter the barrier she had erected.

"Myra," Amber said, finally breaking out of her

reverie. "Uncle Hank thinks I should start taking an interest in men."

"I agree. You are a beautiful woman."

Frowning, she said, "Uncle Hank admitted that he couldn't control me." She paused. "I think he would like to find me a husband so he won't have to be responsible for me any more. Steven, a doctor from the hospital, would like to call on me when we return."

Myra wisely remained silent. She recognized the possibility that Amber was finally ready to let some of her femininity shine through and did not want to upset the delicate blossoming of her character.

"I think I would like to see him." She looked at Myra, her eyes mirroring uncertainty that held a flicker of hope.

Myra smiled warmly. "Then let's make this a quick, prosperous trip. What time does the train leave?"

"Five this afternoon."

"I'll take the traveling cases to the carriage and meet you downstairs."

Amber styled her hair then dressed in a deep blue gown with a modest neckline that would discourage unwanted attention. She left off the cumbersome hoops in favor of a full skirt marked by tiny flounces of contrasting fabric. Thick layers of petticoats added a fullness to the gown and accented her tiny waist. She had chosen her dress with the hope of traveling inconspicuously, but had no way of knowing the beautiful picture she presented. Picking up a bonnet, she dropped the cut-away back over the chignon and secured the ties beneath the chin. After a final check in the mirror, she stepped into the hall.

Halfway down the corridor she stopped and

opened a door. Andy's possessions were just as he had left them, and they awaited his return. The sight of his belongings stiffened her backbone. This had to be a successful mission.

On the first stop out of Washington, they changed trains and started their journey south. Days later, when they were forced to seek alternate transportation, Amber bought a wagon and horses while Myra purchased needed supplies. Rather than risk traveling after dark, they found lodging and had a warm meal. Armed with the knowledge that they would soon be near her brother, they retired for the night.

Travel was not easy. The roads were poor, and the land had been ravaged by the hardships of war. Myra averted her eyes from the dead men littering the roadside and grazing land. Amber walked, hoping she would find life in one of the torn bodies. Groups of mounted riders, mostly Confederate troops, passed in the distance, and they had to move cautiously to avoid suspicion.

After three long days of travel, they rented a room in the town near the prison camp. They were in Confederate territory and no one could be trusted. Their success depended solely on their own inventiveness.

In the privacy of their room, they huddled in a corner and whispered plans for seeing the prison. The camp was located on the fringe of the city near some of the poorer merchants. Once Amber got a look at it she could make plans.

Rising at dawn, she dressed in an old everyday frock and combed her hair in a severe, unattractive style, hoping to hide the beauty most men enjoyed. Despite the early hour there was a stickiness to the air, and beads of perspiration formed around the collar of her high-necked dress as she briskly walked down the street.

Based on her uncle's description, the prison camp was the size she expected, and she believed once inside she would be able to move without detection. The prison was longer than it was wide, the total camp contained by a high stockade fence. Two guardhouses, overlooking the central complex, served as the main security, and Amber knew they would be the biggest hindrance to their escape.

Amber used the cover of buildings to watch the camp unnoticed. The main gate was open and she saw soldiers working with supplies. A fenced structure sat off to the left, and she decided it was where the prisoners were held. Once inside she would still have the problem of getting past the second barricade to locate Andy. Amber crushed the uncertainty that crept into her thoughts. She was going to take a dangerous risk that would involve a complex plan; she could not fail.

Shortly before the noon hour eight ladies strolled toward the door on the right side of the main gate. They stopped briefly then entered the prison. Amber's heart quickened and she experienced a surge of hope. If the women made regular visits to the jail she was determined to use them to get inside. She didn't know what they were doing, but she would make them fit into her plans.

She waited almost two hours before the women filed out and walked back up the street. Amber followed on the opposite side, not crossing the dirt road until they turned down a narrow street and entered a house. Making sure she was unnoticed, she walked to the dirty windows and peered inside. Amber had never seen a brothel, but suspected the women were whores. The realization stunned her. How could she make them fit into her plans? She had been kissed, but she had never lain with a man or had her body touched intimately. If she was going to make them part of her plan, she would have to be one of them. A tight knot of fear caught in her throat. She loved Andrew, but could she sell herself to save his life?

Squaring her shoulders, she walked past the establishment and turned the corner. Stopping where she would be unobserved, she sagged against the building and raised a trembling hand to her brow. If she didn't help Andy she would have to live with her failure. If she agreed to work as a harlot, it was possible she would be sacrificing her maidenhood for nothing. She was caught between fear for herself and fear for Andy. With a shake of her head, she wondered why she had stopped to consider the problem. There was only one solution and that was to help her brother, regardless of the sacrifice to herself.

She stopped at a small shop and purchased two secondhand dresses. Hers were too expensive and modest for a poor whore. Myra jumped to her feet as soon as Amber stepped into the room.

"What did you learn?" she asked anxiously.

Amber put her packages down and raised her finger to her lips in a motion of silence. If there was one thing Amber had learned, it was not to trust the strange environment. She put her arm around Myra's shoulders and led her away from the door.

"I got a good look at the prison. It is big."

"You have been gone for hours. I was starting to worry," Myra chided softly. If anything happened to her young charge, she would never forgive herself. She was having strong doubts about Amber's impulsiveness to free Andy. She knew Amber tended to view obstacles as stumbling blocks rather than major deterrents. Myra blamed it on the male influence in Amber's life, knowing how men often refused to admit defeat in a given circumstance.

"I wanted to watch the prison and figure out a plan."

They stopped before a tiny window, the only light in the room. Amber looked down the street, her expression thoughtful.

"What are you going to do?" Myra prodded.

Amber shrugged her thin shoulders. "I am going to walk in the main door."

Myra threw her hands on her hips. "Just like that!" she exclaimed doubtfully. "We both know that is not possible." Her eyes swept Amber's face, noting the determined jut of her chin. She had seen that familiar expression, and knew Amber had decided to proceed with her plan regardless of Myra's protests. Arguing wouldn't do any good, but she had to know Amber's plan. If her impulsiveness got her into trouble, Myra would have to get word to Hank.

"I know you have already made up your mind, but I demand to know what you are going to do."

Myra was right. If Amber failed she needed an ally. "I saw eight women go into the prison today. I'm going to get a job with them."

"Amber," Myra said cautiously, her graying hair

68

bouncing with the motion of her head. "What were the women doing?"

"They were harlots," she stated matter-of-factly.

Myra's eyes widened in shock. Amber had never been one to look down her nose at any profession, but her calm acceptance was totally unexpected.

"Whores! Strumpets!" she said horrified. "Amber, you can't go to work with them. Andrew would never approve."

Amber turned her blue-green eyes on the older woman. "If I don't do something Andy will hang. I have made my decision."

Scowling, Myra said, "I don't like it. Think of another way."

"There isn't one." Amber turned from the window and opened one of her packages. "I want to look pretty but in desperate need of work." She unfolded a sea green dress and laid it on the bed. "I'm going back as soon as I change. I suspect they get a regular flow of customers after dark, and I want to get myself in position for tomorrow morning."

Myra's eyes widened. "What if you have to start work tonight? Amber, you can't sell yourself. . . . I forbid you to do it."

Amber raised her hands to her hips, a gesture to mark her defiance. "I'll think of a way to get out of work tonight. I am determined to make my plan work." She turned her back to Myra. "Will you unfasten the hooks?"

Reluctantly, Myra aided Amber's dressing. Her fear for Amber was real but she knew nothing would stop the headstrong woman from achieving her goal. If she protested too much, Amber might alienate her from further plans, and Myra had to know what she intended to do. She was Amber's only safety factor.

"Well, how do I look?" Amber asked, standing back for Myra to study her appearance. The dress, though out of date, was a striking garment. It had been made for a smaller woman, and as a result, the bust was tight and the low neck added emphasis to her swelling breasts. Her hair had been twisted up to make her attractive without presenting the pure image of a maiden. Amber had to look hard and be hard to fill the part of a whore.

"If you don't get the job, the woman is crazy," Myra said, putting the second dress in a traveling case. "I know you are a lady, but this isn't the time to show fine manners. Forget the feminine things you learned and remember the hard truths your papa taught you. Your life might depend on it."

Amber straightened and turned toward the door. "If you don't hear from me in two days, go back home and tell Uncle Hank what happened. He won't like it, but he'll know what to do."

Myra touched Amber's shoulder and she turned back. Tears brimmed in her eyes, but the younger woman remained unmoved by their parting. "Promise to take care of yourself. I don't want to lose both of you."

Touched by Myra's affection, Amber leaned forward and lightly kissed her cheek. "Thank you for understanding why I have to do this." Unable to speak, Myra nodded. Amber picked up the valise and silently let herself out of the room.

Amber was not as unaffected as she had appeared. While she was not prone to outbursts of tears, she still had very deep feelings for Myra. Despite Amber's strength and determination not to be afraid, her heart pounded against her breast in fear.

She took a direct route to the whorehouse, her brisk pace slowing as she neared the entrance. Taking one last deep breath, she pushed the door open and stepped into the dim interior of the richly decorated building. Remembering not to act frightened, she walked into the empty room and shouted, "Anybody here?"

Dropping her bag, she put her hands on her hips. It was less than a minute before someone appeared at the top of the short flight of steps. Amber immediately recognized the woman who had led the ladies into the prison.

The woman was older than Amber first thought, her hair tumbling around her shoulders in disarray. Her robe, though adequate covering, hinted that there was nothing beneath. Her brown eyes flickered over Amber in appraisal.

"Are you the lady in charge?" she asked, sauntering forward. "I'm lookin' for work."

The woman arched one of her brows. "Really? What kind of work do you have in mind?"

"Pleasuring men," she stated bluntly and watched the lady step off the stairs. "I got to town yesterday and I need work." Amber raised her hand to her forehead and wavered. "I'm broke. I ain't eaten for three days."

"What makes you think this is a brothel?" the woman asked, amused.

"I bedded a Confederate soldier last night." Her lips curved in a sneer. "After he had his way he said he

71

was broke. He told me about this place, and I decided to get a job."

The woman's eyes carefully studied Amber. "You are a fetching female. What is your name?"

"Amber."

"How many men can you take each night?"

"Whatever you give me," she said flatly, not knowing how many men a whore bedded a night.

"We split fifty-fifty and all the girls stay here." The older woman stepped forward and held out her hand. "The name is Alicia and you're hired. Our evening crowd should start arriving in about two hours. Can you be ready?"

Amber moistened her lips. She couldn't start work tonight. "I've been travelin' for days. I—." She crumbled to the floor in a faint, and forced herself to relax in an attempt to make her unconscious state look real. She waited several minutes before slowly opening her eyes.

"Wh—what happened?" she asked weakly.

"You fainted," Alicia said, helping her to her feet. "Rest tonight. Tomorrow is time enough to start." Alicia chuckled. "Your arrival has solved a problem I was going to have at the prison in the morning."

"How?" Amber asked curiously.

"We all have our regular men, but tomorrow a major is arriving and I need an extra girl."

"Sounds fine with me," she said casually. "What is he coming for?"

"To hang a Yankee spy. I guess he's got high connections." She linked her arm through Amber's. "I'll show you your room."

Because of their trade each woman had a private

72

room. The accommodations were small but nicely furnished. The ravages of war had touched many areas, but in this house there wasn't any hardship. Alicia promised to send her dinner and warned her to stay in her room unless she wanted to start work that night.

When she was alone, Amber walked to the window, her mind mulling over the new information. Andy was alive, but a major was being brought in to take charge of his hanging. Had they made the connection between Andy and a high-ranking officer? Amber was supposed to satisfy the major's physical needs. What kind of man was he going to be? Would she have to sacrifice her virtue?

Turning, she walked to the bed and flopped on the mattress. Amber lay in the darkness, her thoughts on the next morning. Their lives depended on her action. She could not fail.

Seven

The day dawned warm and sunny and Amber's hope soared. If everything went according to plan she would get inside the prison to see her brother. After a quick breakfast in her room, she joined Alicia and the other women.

Amber uttered a greeting, remembering not to act too refined. She waited patiently while introductions were made.

"We're ready to leave. The girls all have their regular men. You get the major." She studied Amber's figure in the tight-fitting gown. "I think he'll like what he sees."

Straightening, Amber thrust her bosom forward. "Ain't ever had many complaints."

When they left the alley for the short walk to the prison, Amber's heart raced. Thus far her plan to get into the fort had held minimal danger, but the time had come when she would be putting herself in a threatening situation. She had to stay calm and alert to anything that might happen. Her life and Andy's depended on it.

The door to the prison was open and the guard was waiting for them. "Got yourself a new gal?" he asked, pointing at Amber.

"She is for the major. Has he arrived?"

"Nope. But he is expected anytime." He shifted to get a better look at Amber. "He is sure gonna like her. Maybe I can have her when he's done."

Alicia laughed. "She is yours for a price."

The soldier scowled. "You know we don't git much money." His eyes switched to Alicia. "How's about lettin' me have a little free time with her before the major arrives?"

Amber's stomach curled in a knot. What if Alicia offered her to this man? He was young, not unattractive, yet she trembled at the thought of allowing him intimacies. What would happen when she was confronted by the major? Was she going to be able to make the plan work?

"Sorry honey, she is taken." Alicia threw her hand on her hip. "Are you gonna let us in? My gentleman is waitin' for me."

Scowling, the soldier stepped aside. Amber's relief quickly disappeared as she got a clear look at the inside. The Union prisoners were held inside a fenced area. A putrid odor of unwashed bodies and waste filled the air, almost gagging her. They walked along the fence and the prisoners crowded the wooden partition to hoot at the women. They called back to them, teasing the men with their voices and bodies. Amber kept her eyes on the captured soldiers, hoping for a sign of Andrew.

Alicia stopped at Amber's side. "We meet at the gate in two hours." She pointed to a building where the Confederate flag blew in the breeze. "You can wait for the major over there."

Amber watched the women walk to different parts of the compound, surprised by the freedom they were allowed inside the restricted area. She continued along the prisoner compound and her heart ached for them. The men shouted crude remarks, but Amber didn't fling insults or use her body to tease them. It was too cruel, and they had no way of knowing she was on their side.

The compound ended and Amber started across an open area. Her attention was immediately drawn to the guards surrounding a group of shackled men. They were offered no protection from the weather and heavy iron chains kept them from moving freely. Amber knew with certainty that these men were special prisoners, and she wondered if Andy was one of them. She scanned their faces—young, old, sick, beaten faces, and her hatred of the Confederates increased. If she wasn't successful, her brother would become a victim of the war—hanged because of his beliefs. When Amber was certain Andy was not among them, her heart sank.

She noticed a man sitting in an isolated area, his head hanging between his propped up knees. His amber hair reflected red highlights as the sun touched it and something stirred inside of Amber.

Her curiosity about the man had drawn the attention of the guard. Taking a deep breath to push her breasts forward, she smiled at him. His interest was immediate, and he rested the stock of his gun on the ground. Swinging her hips provocatively, Amber sauntered toward him.

"Ain't never seen you before," he said. "Are you one of them whores that come for the officers?"

"That's right, but the man's rank don't matter. If I like what I see. . . ." Stopping before him, she boldly placed her hand on the front of his shirt. "You look like a man who could really please me."

The sergeant grinned a toothless smile. Amber wanted to turn and vomit, but forced herself to continue the act. His hand rose to her tiny waist, and her shiver of revulsion was mistaken for one of desire.

"Can you leave?" she asked, moistening her lips.

The man scowled. "Can't. I got to guard this prisoner until the major arrives."

Amber looked at the man he indicated, certain it was Andy. "He don't look dangerous with all those chains on him," she said, trying to ignore his hand as it curved over her buttocks. "Surely you can leave him for a few minutes."

"If I did I would probably be hung in his place." He shook his head. "He's a spy. They want him real bad."

Amber's heart quickened. It had to be Andy. The prisoner hadn't moved, and she wondered if he were alive.

"What is the matter with him? Is he sick or something?" she asked, beginning to worry about his health.

"Could be. They ain't been feedin' him too good."

Scowling, the sergeant walked over to him and nudged his knee. The prisoner swung at the boot and missed. Slowly, he raised his head and Amber's heart lodged in her throat. Andy looked worse than she had expected. His clothes were in rags, his bearded face swollen and discolored, and his blue-green eyes were sunken and dull. The Confederates had not been gentle with him.

It had never occurred to her what Andy's reaction would be when he saw her, and Amber felt the initial stirring of panic when he looked at her. Had his face been unmarked the resemblance between them would have betrayed her as family.

She bit her lip to keep from crying out when she saw a flicker of recognition in the blue-green eyes. "He ain't more than a boy," she spouted, walking to the prisoner's side. "I think you are afraid of me. Ain't you never had a woman before."

She had never made such a bold statement to a man before and was certain her query had shocked her brother. But when she glanced at him, he was expressionless. Both of them knew if he responded to her presence, she could be taken as a spy.

The Rebel soldier's chest puffed. "Of course I've had women, but I got a job to do here." He stroked his jaw. "I get off duty in two hours. I could meet you at the shed over yonder." He pointed to a shack behind Andy.

"What is it?" she asked, wondering if it could be used for their escape.

"It is where he gets locked up at night."

Amber knew from the man's tone it was the best she would get. "I got an appointment with the major. If he is done with me, I'll meet you."

Amber turned and walked away, her hips swinging. Glancing over her shoulder at the soldier, she said, "Don't worry. I'll be seein' you soon." The message was intended for her brother, but the soldier grinned. There was a slight movement of acknowledgement from Andy's hand, and Amber was smiling as she strolled away.

One of the guards outside the command post headquarters showed her to the captain's office. He gave her a leering glance before leaving her alone. Amber uttered a deep sigh of relief. Thus far she had been lucky with her plans. She had not thought to hide her gun in her clothes and decided to search the room for a weapon.

The closet and cabinet contained clothes and papers. Frowning, she turned to the desk and pulled open a drawer. The map on top of a pile of papers caught her attention, and she studied the markings for troop positions. Further searching uncovered a letter from General Lee listing troop activity near Gettysburg. This was important information.

Refolding the map, she returned it to the drawer. Verbal warnings about the Confederate activity near Gettysburg would be doubted, but Lee's letter was proof. Lifting her skirt, she tucked it into the waist of her undergarments, then smoothed her dress into place.

An hour had passed since her arrival into the fort and time was running out. She had not found a gun, but the desk top paperweight was heavy and small enough to be hidden in her hand. Lifting the object, she turned and walked to the door. Opening it a crack, she made sure the hall was clear then walked toward the exit and into the sunshine. There were few guards, and she decided it was because the men stationed on the walls could almost see the entire compound. They would make escape risky.

Keeping the weight in her hand, she strolled toward the man guarding Andy. He watched her approach, his eyes hungry.

"The major never got here," she explained, stopping close enough to him to feel her body against his. "Are you ready?"

His gaze dropped to Amber's breast. "Let's go to the shack." He waved to the sentry in the closest tower and the guard hooted back. Taking her arm he led her toward the two-room shack.

Amber stopped. "What about him? Ain't you worried someone will see him sittin' by himself?"

The soldier nodded. "You're a smart gal. I'm supposed to keep him in sight at all times."

Hauling Andy to his feet, the guard dragged him toward the shed. Happy, yet apprehensive, Amber followed. The guard secured Andy's chains to iron rungs protruding from the wall. Grinning, he turned to Amber.

"Get your clothes off. We ain't got much time."

Trembling, she reached for the hooks on her dress. Out of the corner of her eye she saw her brother's uncertain gaze. She clutched the paperweight tightly against her skirt.

"Why don't you help me?"

"Sure," he said, putting his rifle against the wall out of Andy's reach. His fingers fumbled down the fasteners until the dress fell open. He stripped to his underwear and stood grinning while Amber pulled her dress over her head.

"Hurry up," he ordered. "I can't wait much longer. You're too pretty."

There was a tightness in her throat as she put the hand holding the weapon behind her back and let her dress fall. Andy had seen her in petticoats, but the man's leer made her stomach knot.

"I don't like givin' *him* a show. How about goin' to the back room?"

Eager to comply with her wish, he turned to the second room. Clutching the paperweight, she raised her hand and slammed it against the side of his head. He dropped at her feet. Amber knew he wasn't dead, but she didn't like seeing the blood that darkened his hair. Thanks to her father, she knew how to render him unconscious without killing him. She ran to Andy's side and dropped to her knees.

"I've been so worried about you." He looked sick and his flesh was too warm.

He raised his manacled hands to her face. "What are you doing here? Don't you realize the danger?"

"I couldn't let them kill you," she said honestly.

Andy grinned. "My unpredictable sister."

She met his eyes briefly then turned to search the unconscious man's clothes for the key to free Andy. She located it and released the shackles.

"I suppose you have a plan," he said, rising.

"Your face is too messed up to wear the uniform without drawing attention. I will wear his clothes and try to get you out."

Andrew looked at his sister in surprise. "You aren't planning to walk out the gate!"

"Of course not. Help me get him into the other room."

They dragged the Rebel to the adjoining room, then Amber grabbed his clothes and slid her legs into the pants. They were large, but she was able to secure them at the waist without making them look baggy. Taking the letter from the place in her undergarments, she tapped her brother's shoulder.

"Look at this. It is a report on General Lee's troop activity near Gettysburg."

His eyes widened. "Where did you get this?"

"Out of the commanding officer's desk."

Andy scanned the contents. "This is important information but dangerous for you to have." He tucked it into the band of his pants. "It is better if I keep it. They can only hang me once. I don't want you caught with incriminating evidence."

Amber held out her hand. "I stand a better chance of getting away because I'm a woman. If something goes wrong and we can't escape together, this information must be turned over to someone in the Union army immediately."

"You're right," he agreed reluctantly. "But I don't like turning you into a spy. It is too dangerous."

"I know the risks."

Andy put his hand on her shoulder. "I know better than to argue with you. . . . Thanks for coming to help me." They exchanged a look that told of the special bond they shared. Andy handed her the paper, and she tucked it back into her bodice before putting on the shirt and buttoning it.

"How do I look?" she asked, turning for inspection.

"What about your hair?" he queried, admiring the amber tresses.

"Cut it," she ordered, willing to surrender the beautiful hair to aid her brother's escape.

"I don't have a knife and there isn't a bayonet."

Frowning, she piled her hair on top of her head and reached for the oversized hat, hoping it would not fall out. She strolled toward the door.

"This side of the building can't be seen from the towers." Opening the door a crack, she peeked out. "Let's not waste any more time. There is a major coming to take care of your execution."

Andy gathered the chains and walked toward the back room. "I'm going to chain the Rebel in case he wakes."

Amber saw her dress on the floor and knew it couldn't remain where it would give away their plan. Crossing the narrow room, she bent to retrieve it.

"Sergeant, where is the prisoner?" a deep voice asked.

Amber froze. The enemy had arrived to block their escape.

Eight

Amber was trapped. She forced the knot of fear down her throat. Andy was still in the back room oblivious to the danger.

"Sergeant, where is the prisoner?" the man repeated, his voice filled with impatience.

She heard booted feet on the floor and her muscles tensed. "In the back room," she muttered, trying to keep her voice low.

"Is he injured?" the man asked.

"No, sir," she answered gruffly, puzzled that he would make such an inquiry.

"Where did the fresh bloodstain come from?" He eyed the soldier suspiciously. "What are you doing?" he demanded.

His voice sent shivers through Amber. It was deep and commanding, and she was sure he wasn't a low-ranking officer. Footsteps came nearer and Amber took a deep breath. He was already apprehensive; she couldn't wait to be taken. When he was directly behind her, she turned and lunged at his knees. It was

84

like hitting a rock and the breath was zapped from her body. The man staggered but did not fall, and Amber felt his hands on her arms as he hauled her to her feet.

"What is the idea?" he demanded.

Amber looked up, her blue-green eyes shadowed with uncertainty. Although she was tall, the man was several inches taller, and she felt dwarfed by his size. His dark brown eyes narrowed and raked her face—a light of uncertainty clouding their depths. His mouth was wide, his thin upper lip resting over a full lower one. A muscle in his jawline twitched to mark his irritation. Locks of light brown hair fell across his forehead to touch the edge of his brows. The light hair and dark eyes offered an attractive but dangerous combination.

Amber knew she should speak but what could she say? Her gaze dropped to his broad shoulders then traveled down his chest. Her horror intensified when she recognized the official insignia of a Confederate major.

"Who are you?" he demanded, reaching for the hat. Amber's hair tumbled over her shoulders. "A woman," he snarled. "What are you doing here?" She didn't respond and he shook her.

He stopped suddenly, his gaze very intent. The gleam in his eyes changed from a close scrutiny to one of astonishment and finally relief. Slowly, he raised his finger to follow the outline of her lips.

Amber was puzzled by his actions and unwillingly her gaze fell to his mouth. Something shot through her veins and she remembered another man's mouth a long time before. Tearing her gaze from the firm line of his lips, she struggled for control.

"Take your hands off me," she ordered, refusing to be intimidated by him.

"*You* are ordering me around," he said in irritation and all earlier tenderness vanished. "What are you doing here? Who are you?"

"I won't answer your questions."

"We'll see about that," he said, his eyes narrowing. "There was supposed to be a prisoner in here. Where is he?"

Forgetting she had told him the prisoner was in the back room, she said, "Gone." She wanted to give Andy every chance to escape.

"We better make sure," he said, nudging her toward the rear.

"He left," she argued, refusing to move.

The major grabbed her arm and jerked her behind him. "One of the guards saw him come in here." Reaching the back room, he pushed her inside.

Andy, oblivious to what had happened, looked up uncertainly at his sister's sudden appearance. A sick expression clouded his face when he saw the Confederate officer.

"Are you all right?" he asked.

Amber walked toward her brother. "I'm sorry," she whispered. "He surprised me. There wasn't anything I could do."

He squeezed her hand. "You tried," he said softly.

"Is he dead?" the major asked, motioning to the injured man.

"Just unconscious," Andy supplied.

"What did you hit him with?"

"I did it," Amber said, her eyes stormy with

defiance.

The man arched his light brown brow. "Our army isn't recruiting women. Thus I can assume you are here to help him." The man's voice was deep and merciless, and Amber saw no pity in the dark brown eyes.

Unwelcome terror seized her thoughts and she struggled to throw them off. This was not the time to panic. She had known rescuing Andy would be a risk, but she had refused to dwell on how she would feel if she were captured.

"Looks like we have two spies. It will be a double hanging."

Amber trembled and Andy slid his arm around her waist. The color washed from her face, and she bit her lip to control the surge of emotions. As uncertain as she was about her future, she wouldn't break in front of the enemy. She made a vow to Papa's memory to always be strong.

"Be strong," Andy whispered, mirroring her thoughts.

"I'm fine," she said, straightening her slender form.

Andy met the major's probing glance. "Sir, she is not responsible for anything. I take sole blame."

"You do not," Amber sputtered. "I came here of my own will. I wanted to get him out of prison and safe from the hangman's noose."

"Shut up," Andy warned, nudging her with his elbow.

The major leaned against the wall. "Let her continue. Most of our spies aren't this informative."

Amber shot him a hate-filled look. "I am not a spy. I came here to help my—him get out of here." She decided not to volunteer their relationship. If he saw the facial similarities, he could draw his own conclusions.

"All by yourself?" the major quizzed, throwing her a doubtful expression. "What did you—a woman—think you could do against a prison full of soldiers?"

Amber clenched her hands into fists. "I got in past the guards, didn't I?" she said smugly. "I don't think much of your security when a *woman* can get inside."

The major's eyes narrowed. "How *did* you get in here?"

Amber smiled sweetly. "Figure it out for yourself. Spies don't give out information."

A muscle in his jaw tightened. "There are ways to make you talk." He looked at Amber and Andy. "I want some answers."

Reaching out, Andy covered Amber's hand with his. He was offering her reassurance, but she wasn't afraid. Her father had taught her to be strong, and she needed that strength now.

The major looked at Andy. "I know who you are. I'm here to hang you for spy activity against the Confederacy." His gaze switched to Amber. "Who are you?"

Amber clamped her jaw tightly and glared at him. She wasn't going to answer his questions. The less he knew about her the safer she would be. When Amber didn't return, Myra would go back to Washington and tell Hank what had happened.

"What is your name?" he demanded in a tone that warned his patience was beginning to wear thin. "I want answers."

"We don't have to tell you anything. I have already been sentenced to die."

"What about her?" the major asked. "Are you will-

88

ing to let her hang at your side?"

"Amber isn't a spy. She came to free me."

Brant was mulling over her name when two guards joined them. "Get the wounded man out of here," he ordered. "And chain the prisoner in the outer room. I want to talk to the woman."

Amber stiffened. She knew it wouldn't be a simple interview. The man was frightening, and she sensed a toughness about him she had yet to see. Before the guard could grab Andy's arm, he had stepped in front of his sister.

"I won't let you touch her."

The major's expression darkened. "Who are you to give me orders?" Stepping forward, he grabbed Andy by the shirt front and pushed him toward the door. "Get him out of here."

The wounded man was dragged out and Andy was shoved behind him. The door slammed leaving them alone, and Amber knew they had been locked in their private battlefield.

Enraged by the attack on her brother, Amber sprang forward and jumped on the major's back. Keeping one hand against his throat, she punched at him with her free fist. Her legs curled around his waist, holding her tightly against his body. Her thigh pinned his gun to his waist, and he was unable to reach it.

The major's hand clamped around the arm choking him. Amber was no match for his strength and she felt her grip loosen. Afraid of being thrown aside, she renewed her attack on his face. Moving her leg, Amber tried to kick him in the groin, but he anticipated her attack and clamped a hand around her ankle.

Throwing her leg out, he pushed it behind him and twisted sideways. Her body slid around the side to his hip. Amber's eyes matched the stormy sea when she looked into his dark ones. He caught her flailing arm and easily pinned it to her side. The other arm could do nothing but hold on to keep from falling.

"Haven't you had enough?" he asked, inches from her face.

"You Confederate pig. I will kill you if I get the chance."

The major chuckled. "I have no doubt you would, but you aren't going to get that chance." Crossing the room, he put Amber's back against the wall and forced her legs to the floor. Her hands pushed at his chest, but they were pinned between them when he pressed his body against hers to stop the attack. "Who are you?"

Amber didn't respond. "I don't have to tell you anything. Just hang me with my brother," she said, then realized she had provided him with the information she needed.

The major's mouth curled in a smirk. "I thought I noticed a resemblance under all his mud and bruises." He chuckled. "Since when has the Union started sending women to do men's work?"

"How dare you!" she sputtered. "I'm not in the Union Army, and they don't know I'm here."

He regarded her thoughtfully. "You were foolish to think you could succeed."

"I had to try," she said, refusing to offer excuses for her failure. "I couldn't let him die."

"Your dedication is admirable, but your actions were foolish."

Amber couldn't say anything. She had failed in her attempt to free Andy and gotten herself a sentence of death. She had yet to feel the hopelessness of the situation and was determined to fight.

"Let go of me," she commanded.

"How did you get in here?"

Amber smiled. "You want to know how a mere woman tricked the soldiers." She laughed. "I made all of you look like fools. A man's lust is his weakness."

The major's eyes narrowed in confusion. "What are you talking about? What does lust have to do with your getting in here?" His gaze raked the upper part of her body. "From the way you are dressed, you wouldn't get a second look."

Amber had always been considered attractive by the gentlemen she knew and to be put down by a Confederate pig was the last straw. "You wouldn't know a real woman if you saw one."

Chuckling softly, he said, "And I suppose you are a real woman."

The lower part of her body was pressed against the wood by his thighs. She usually had the buffer of her skirt between her and the gentlemen she had known although none of them had ever gotten so intimate with her. Despite the antagonism she felt toward the man who held her captive, she could not stop the stirring awareness in her limbs.

"Get away from me, you beast," she ordered. "I am not one of your Southern belles. I don't like Confederate animals."

His eyes bored deeply into hers, and she noticed the tiny lines fanning from the edges of his eyes. She was once again reminded that he was a dangerous man, and he held the power to destroy her life.

"When I arrived I was told there was a woman waiting for me—a woman who would satisfy my male needs. I went to the office, but she wasn't there." His gaze dropped to her mouth. "You never had any intention of sleeping with me. You only wanted to get inside to rescue your brother." His fingers twisted in her hair. "You may have played my men for fools, but you won't do the same with me."

Jerking her head still, his mouth opened and closed over hers. His action had been unexpected, and Amber could not escape the punishing movement of his lips. He was brutal in his attack, his mouth bruising her flesh, her lips ground forcibly against her teeth. Her body was crushed between his and the wall, and she was barely able to take a breath. His free hand glided along her thigh and waist to find her breast. Even though clothes covered her body she felt a jolt of electrifying awareness. It was the first time she had felt the weight of a man's hand. His palm kneaded the flesh while his mouth plundered hers. His tongue heightened the intimacy at the same time he tore apart the buttons to reveal the petticoat beneath. Her legs trembled when his knuckles brushed her flesh and an involuntary moan escaped her throat.

Although his actions were intended to make her feel cheap and to satisfy a need in his body, she could not stop the slow awakening of her body. Her fingers trapped between them curled against his shirt. Her breath left her body, yet she refused to surrender to the lethargic feeling he was creating.

His lips left her swollen mouth and glided across her cheek. His breath warmed her flesh and sent a tingling up her spine. Her aching lips parted, her tongue gliding over the tender flesh. Brushing aside the shirt, his mouth nibbled her neck. His tongue tickled the hollow of her collarbone, creating an unbidden response. His body pressed closer to her, his leg pushing between her thighs to fit them together in an embrace that told of his desire.

It was bad enough that she was held helpless by this man and worse that she responded. No man had ever taken such intimate liberties with her, and she was shocked by the sensations she had experienced. She hated knowing the man responsible was an enemy — a man determined to kill her brother, violate and kill her.

"Take your hands off me, you filthy swine."

"This is what you came here for. I am the major you were waiting for," he muttered against her amber hair.

"I would rather die than go to bed with a Rebel."

He pulled back. "That is exactly what you are going to do. Wearing a uniform of the Confederate Army, entering this complex and trying to free a spy, all points toward treason against the South."

Amber pulled her shirt together and tried to force off the feel of his body against hers. "The only thing I am guilty of is trying to help my brother. He doesn't deserve to die."

"Neither do any of the other men caught up in this battle." He regarded her innocent face thoughtfully. "You must love him very much to sacrifice your own life."

Amber straightened. "If you had a twin you would understand the bond we share. There isn't anything I

93

wouldn't do for him."

"You have proved that," he conceded, "but I wonder how far you would be willing to go." Reaching out, he placed his hands on her waist. "Most men would find your loyalty very touching."

Amber tipped her head to the side. "Does that include you?"

"Yes. I admire that quality."

Amber was stunned by his admission, but delighted that the enemy would praise her dedication to Andy. She studied the tall dangerous man. Was there some way she could use his sympathetic nature to her cause?

"Does that mean you'll consider letting me go?"

His thumbs caressed her flat stomach. "I don't believe you're a spy. I think your loyalties belong with your brother."

Amber felt a surge of hope. If she could use this man to gain her release, perhaps she could also get Andy's freedom. It was certainly a risk worth taking. Unconsciously, Amber raised her hand to cover his.

The major watched, the light of uncertainty in his eyes. He was certain she was not a whore. When he'd held her in his arms, she'd expressed an immature passion—a passion not yet developed by a man's desire.

"How far would you be willing to go for him?"

She moistened her lips. "What do you mean?"

"I mean would you really play the whore for me."

"I—I." She found herself unable to answer. She had willingly accepted the possibility when she'd entered the fort, but standing before a man who had exhibited animal-like passion she was unsure. She'd always been able to handle men because she'd only become involved with those who would let her manipulate them. This man was too dangerous for games, and the prospect of doing battle with him was frightening.

His brown-eyed gaze was penetrating as he watched and waited for an answer. His lips parted and a soft puff of air escaped his mouth as a sigh. Unable to bear his gaze, Amber turned sideways. He was reluctant to let her get away, and his hands pulled against the shirt. It broke free of her pants and a paper floated to the floor.

For several seconds neither of them moved. Amber wanted to pick it up, knowing it was the letter from General Lee about Gettysburg, but her limbs were locked in horror of what her enemy was about to discover. Bending, the major lifted the parchment. His eyes briefly flickered over her as he unfolded the paper. The tensing of his jaw, something Amber already recognized as a common trait, marked his anger.

"You lying traitor," he said, waving the paper in her face. "This evidence convicts you as a spy for the Union Army."

Amber could not deny the existence of the document. It had been found on her person and no one else could have put it there. Her father had instilled pride in his children, and Amber could face her present crisis in one of two ways — with her head down in shame or raising her chin and accepting whatever happened. Squaring her shoulders, Amber's stormy blue-green eyes met the major's dark ones.

Folding the paper, he tucked it into his pocket.

"This is important proof of your guilt. It will easily convict you with your brother." Reaching out, he grabbed her arm. "We are going to the main office. We have some things to discuss."

Amber was pulled to the outer room. The major looked at the private standing guard over her brother. "Bring him to my office in one hour."

With the major's arm firmly around hers, he escorted Amber across the yard. She walked proudly, determined not to let him think she was afraid. She entered the commander's office at his side and he gently pushed her into a chair.

"I'm Major Brant Faulkner. I believe you were expecting me."

The man behind the desk rose and saluted. "Yes, sir. I'm Captain Edgar Mason. I am sorry I wasn't in my office when you arrived. I was taking care of important business."

The corner of Brant's mouth curved in a smirk. "Did your 'business' wear a skirt?" he inquired.

The captain shuffled in embarrassment. "Yes. The ladies come over several times a week to take care of our needs. We are shorthanded and can't get away."

"You don't have to explain. I am fully aware of a man's needs." His gaze rested briefly on Amber. "We all have our weaknesses and needs. . . . I understand fully."

Turning, he walked toward Amber and stopped before her. She met his eyes without flinching, but sensed he was more wrapped up in his thoughts than he was in looking at her. She could see the indecision in his eyes and wondered what puzzled him. His lips thinned, and his gaze suddenly changed to an intent study of her body. Amber blushed under the intimate scrutiny as he mentally stripped the clothes from her body. To her horror she responded to the inspection, her nipples hardening against the gray shirt.

Brant noticed the involuntary betrayal of her flesh and tensed. She had sputtered insults, but her body responded to him. He had not been immune to her curves, and a hungry desire licked through his limbs. He turned. If he didn't look at her, maybe he wouldn't want her.

"What I don't understand is your lack of security. You let women waltz in and out of here like it is a whorehouse. Your men are so influenced by a pretty face you risk the security of the prison."

"Major Faulkner, we have never had a man escape or enter our facilities unless it was with our approval."

"What about a woman?" Brant asked, throwing one of his hands on his hip.

"Why would a woman want to get inside the fort? The very thought is ridiculous. We had an extra whore brought here for you this morning. Didn't she satisfy you?"

Brant's brown-eyed gaze swung to Amber. "A female came in for me, but she was *not* a whore."

Amber didn't flinch, but she wondered what kind of game Brant was playing. Whatever happened, he was making the rules.

"I don't understand," Edgar said. "Alicia told me she had brought you a woman." His eyes narrowed suddenly. "What is going on here?"

Brant folded his arms across his chest. "That is exactly what I intend to find out."

"Why is this woman wearing a Confederate uniform?" Edgar demanded. "I don't remember hearing that we are enlisting women."

"This lady came into the fort *posing* as a harlot," Brant said, emphasizing the fact that Amber was not a woman of the streets. "I want to know where your security is. This is a prison camp. You have a dangerous spy here — a spy I have been sent to execute. Headquarters wants the Yankee dead."

Edgar shook his head. "I don't see what the women who entertain us have to do with the spy."

"I don't object to your need for whores, but you have let them overshadow your judgment as a commander of this compound." Brant pointed at Amber. "This woman was brought to your office and left alone to wait for me. She had access to all your papers." The captain paled. "She talked the sergeant, who was supposed to be guarding the spy, into a romp in bed. All he received was a nasty cut on the head."

Edgar's hand crashed against the desk. "She will hang for treason. Lying about her identity and trying to help a prisoner escape is punishable by death."

Brant cast a quick look at Amber, then stepped in front of her and threw his hands on his hips. "No. She has exposed a serious weakness in the prison system. She deserves a commendation."

Edgar's eyes narrowed. "That is ridiculous. Now you are the one who has been influenced by a pretty face. You don't have to lie about her to save her life. You have time to bed her before she is executed."

"Are you questioning your superior officer?"

"I am questioning your right to come in here and

try to pass a whore off as someone she isn't."

A muscle in Brant's cheek tightened and his hand curled into fists. He had not meant this incident to become so complicated, but something in him wanted to protect her from the fate of a spy. He knew he had thrown out his military judgment as a Confederate in favor of personal needs, but the woman took priority. She was more important than the Southern cause. He would take time to examine his feelings as soon as he had protected his position as an officer.

"The lady is not a whore and I will not allow you to insult her. She came here on my invitation to see if she could get inside."

Had Brant not been standing in front of Amber, the captain would have seen her shock. Stunned, she clutched the side of her chair. Had she heard correctly? She had been caught in a treasonous act against the Confederate Army, and Major Brant Faulkner said the whole plan had been executed to test the weakness of the prison system. He had led the captain to believe she was working for the Rebels.

Edgar was flabbergasted. "Headquarters would not use a woman to test the security," he said in a hostile tone. "I think you are lying."

Brant's eyes narrowed. *"Captain,"* he said with emphasis. I don't need headquarters' approval for my actions. They accept my loyalty without question. I may be fifteen years younger than you, but remember I am the major and you are the captain." There was authority in his voice that made Edgar hesitate.

"Have you known her longer than a few hours? Where did you meet this wh — woman?" Edgar asked, still convinced that she was a tramp and Brant's story had been created because he desired her. There was no denying her beauty, but she had used it to make a fool of him. Edgar fought back a surge of hate. There had to be a way to prove Brant's poor judgment. If he did there might be a promotion in it for him.

Brant didn't like Edgar's probing. He had made it very clear he didn't believe the fabricated story, but there was no backing down now. His gaze shifted to Amber, his eyes devouring her beauty. Even now with everything in turmoil, she remained cool and he suspected poised for action. She was a special lady — a woman who could become very important to him. He would do whatever necessary to protect her.

Brant caught Amber's hand and pulled her to his side. "The lady you are insulting is going to be my wife."

Nine

Brant's news was an unexpected blow and while Amber had tried to brace herself for anything, she had not expected a marriage announcement. Surprise briefly showed on her face.

When Brant made the announcement, Edgar switched his attention to Amber and witnessed her shock. There was no question in his mind that Brant had fabricated the story, and he recognized his chance to expose Brant as a liar.

"When is the wedding?" he asked smoothly, looking at Amber for confirmation.

She searched the foggy recesses of her mind for an understanding of what was happening. Weak legs made her lean against Brant for support when she wanted to stand independent of him. Her helplessness added validity to their forthcoming marriage.

"As soon as it can be arranged. We are eager to have the ceremony."

A smirk appeared on Edgar's lips, and when he looked at Amber, there was a gleam in his eye. She

101

knew this man had not liked being made a fool of, and it wasn't likely he would forget it. Edgar was more than just a Rebel. He was an enemy who hated her.

Brant didn't like the way Edgar was looking at Amber. This man could be trouble. "Captain," he said. "I could have you demoted to private for your negligence and insubordination, but until now your record has been beyond reproach. It is my recommendation that we forget the incident on the condition that you reinforce security. The war is escalating and the prison camps are going to become crowded. We must learn to control the men we have guarding them."

Though still angered at being made a fool of, the captain was relieved the incident would not result in the loss of his stripes. His family, prominent members of society, would not be humiliated.

"Thank you, sir. I will do *everything* I can to make your time here memorable."

There was promise in his words that left Amber feeling very unsure. He was going to plan some kind of retaliation, and she would probably bear the brunt of his vengeance.

"I would like some time alone with my fianceé, then I am going to question the spy. I will send someone for you when we have something to discuss."

Scowling at the dismissal, Edgar crossed the room. The door closed with a bang and Amber jerked free of Brant.

"Why?" she asked, covering all her questions with one word.

"Why what?" he parried, pretending ignorance to her confusion.

She ran her hand through her thick amber hair. "Why did you lie about me? Why did you tell him I was going to be your wife?"

Brant shrugged his broad shoulders. He had to admit that things had happened very fast and some of his actions had been on the spur of the moment, but he knew he could not let Amber fall prey to the Confederate Army. She had been caught with incriminating evidence that would convict her as a spy, but Brant didn't believe she had entered the fort with that intent. She had come after her brother, not to wage war against the Confederacy and kill the enemy.

"Don't just stand there. Answer me," she demanded.

"If I hadn't lied, your pretty neck would be stretched from the nearest gallows."

"But I don't understand. In the shack you said I would be hung. Why did you change your mind?"

He smiled sardonically. "I think you referred to it as 'male lust'. I want you."

Amber's eyes widened. In the past men had looked at her with interest, but none had the same intensity and none had ever propositioned her. She was flabbergasted.

"Don't look so surprised. Even if you chose to wear men's clothes, you are a beautiful woman. I got a sample of what you had to offer and I am interested."

"Well, I'm not," she argued, throwing her hands on her hips. "That assault on me in the shack was brutal and without feeling." Tossing her head, she stuck her nose in the air. "I prefer men who know how to make love."

Brant threw back his head and laughed. "If you are

103

trying to hurt my male pride, it won't work. I'll admit you made me angry, and I wasn't as gentle as I should have been with a novice, but you are beautiful and very desirable."

"What do you mean, a novice?" she sputtered. "I have been in a man's arms before." She briefly remembered how she had felt when held by Steven. His embrace had not been as crushing as Brant's, but nonetheless fulfilling.

He arched one of his brows. "Ah, but have you ever been in a man's bed?" He glanced at her horror-stricken face. "I suspected not. There is a lot of passion locked inside of you, and I intend to be the key."

Amber could not remember doing anything that could have been interpreted as a response. She had struggled against his advances and felt like a trapped animal.

"You have an inflated ego if you believe you can teach me something I only want to share with a man I love." She viewed him with disgust, her blue-green eyes sweeping the Confederate gray coat. "I could never respond to a Rebel. I hate you too much."

"Is that any way for a woman to talk to her future husband?" he mocked.

"You could never be my husband. Why did you tell Edgar Mason we are getting married?"

"It gave credibility to my story."

"I would rather tell Mason the truth," she lied. She owed this man her life, but she felt threatened by him. He did not back down from her challenges, and his strength and power reminded her of Papa. She had decided long ago that type of man was not for her.

"Watch your tongue," he cautioned. "I managed to save you once, but don't expect me to do it again. I won't jeopardize my position for you. As long as your brother is alive I can and will dictate your life."

Recognizing the truth of his words, Amber remained silent. Puzzled and bitter by the new restrictions placed on her life, she turned and walked across the room.

Brant hated to use her brother as a weapon against her, but it was the only way he could control her actions. He had called her his fianceé to protect her, but he realized it was not an abhorrent thought. She was the woman who had eased his pain with the touch of her lips, and he had been searching for her ever since.

Never in his life had he wanted a woman more. Her beauty was unmistakable, and he had the urgent need to unlock her passion. He wanted to lose himself in her body and revel in the feel of her limbs against his.

Her attack had been totally unexpected and he had never expected to find a woman beneath the Confederate uniform. From the beginning her pride had been evident. There was a haughty tilt to her chin, and a determination in the green eyes usually reserved for men. She was not a woman to let her femininity stand in the way, though he was certain she would use it to win her way. Her love for her brother was strong—strong enough that she willingly risked her life to save him from hanging. Trying to free him from a Rebel prison was a dangerous risk for a man, an impossible risk for a woman, yet she had almost succeeded.

She was not the kind of woman you hanged for

spying. She was a woman who could stand at your side and fight with you. Most men did not possess the courage he had seen in the young woman, and he admired her for it. In his travels he had seen cowardice and bravery, and he recognized the strength she displayed. The color of his uniform kept them from being on the same side, and he wondered if she could be convinced to side with the South. Scowling, he dismissed the idea. She had called him a 'Confederate pig' and harbored strong bitterness. If he could save her brother would she find sympathy for the Rebels . . . for him?

Looking across the room, he noticed the determined set of her slender body. She was a fighter and would never succumb to a cause she didn't believe in. Her blue-green eyes changed in the few minutes he had watched her, and he realized it was a way he would learn her moods.

Amber regarded Brant warily. There was indecision on his face—a face she recognized as attractive. His size was frightening—inches higher than her tall figure. The gray uniform stretched across his broad shoulders and his pants hugged his muscular thighs. He was by no means slender. His body was thick and strong without being heavy. She had no doubt he was an active man and his clothes hid his power. Fleetingly, she wondered what he would look like without his uniform. Appalled by her thoughts, her cheeks reddened. The edge of his mouth curved in a smile, briefly detracting from the brooding expression. The light-brown hair flopped carelessly across his forehead in defiance of conformity and gave him a rugged look. She decided he was probably in his late twenties and not early thirties as she had first thought.

Despite his young age, she was wary of the maturity and experience she was certain he possessed. He was not a man who would bend to her will and that made him dangerous. Amber suspected her strength could never match his power. He was a man like her father, a man she had to hide her weaknesses and emotions from. He wanted her body and she had seen the lust in his eyes. There was something about him that troubled her and sent shivers racing along her spine. This was one man she didn't know how to handle.

"Do we have a truce?" he asked.

"What do you mean?" she asked uncertainly.

"Are you going to stop fighting me and do things my way?"

Amber ran her fingers along the edge of the desk. "I am not sure I understand."

The major's booted feet sounded on the wooden floor as he crossed to her side. "I think you do." He looked into her eyes and she felt choked by his nearness. "I said I want you."

Her fingers curled around the edge of the desk, suddenly wishing the paperweight was within reach. "You can't expect me to bow to your commands."

"I expect it of the men I supervise."

"I am not one of your soldiers," she reminded him.

Brant grinned, his brown eyes wandering over her clothes. "You are dressed like one. . . . Actually, you should be saluting me. You are only a sergeant."

"Don't be ridiculous," she snapped. "You know why I am dressed like this and I would never salute a

107

Rebel."

"You certainly aren't choosy about wearing our uniform."

Amber looked at the outfit with distaste. "I only put it on to help my brother." She shuddered. "It makes my skin crawl."

"Take it off," he challenged.

"I will as soon as you get me my dress."

Lean fingers reached for one of the buttons, and he deftly flicked it loose. A second one followed. "I agree you would look better without it."

Amber slapped his hand. "How dare you touch me!"

"I am going to do more than just touch you. I am going to make love to my future wife."

Amber drew a sharp breath. She was stunned by his bluntness and found herself floundering in unfamiliar territory. She wasn't certain how to meet this man in battle because he wanted something she knew very little about.

"No," she said, backing away. "Stay away from me."

He advanced on her, his tall body tracking her like a predator. Amber's eyes widened and she felt like a frightened animal before the hunter.

"What happened to all the bravery you were spouting about?"

She stopped when the edge of the cot pressed against her legs. She was trapped.

Brant paused inches from her and looked into her eyes. The stormy sea of green had been replaced by a flicker of indecision and possibly fear. He felt a tightening in his loins when he looked at the creamy skin exposed by the open shirt. He didn't know why she affected him so strongly. He had not had a woman for a long time, and he needed to satisfy himself in her softness. Her physical body was attractive, but he suspected he was also responding to the other qualities he had seen in her and admired.

Raising his hand, he ran his fingers over her shoulder until his knuckles brushed her neck. His other hand touched her fingers, gently caressing the flesh exposed below the cuff of the shirt. He teased away the hair at the nape of her neck, the soft, silky strands tickling his skin. Gently cupping her cheek, he let his fingers caress her jawline.

Amber felt trapped. She wanted to run from him, from the closeness of his body, and from the unfamiliar lethargic feeling creeping through her limbs. His brown eyes touched every part of her face, memorizing the details of her beauty. The finger stroking her flesh brought an unbidden response she didn't know how to handle. She was rapidly losing control of her body, and the warnings in her mind were sluggish.

Brant's thumb touched the corner of her mouth and an involuntary gasp escaped her parted lips. The tip of his finger glided slowly across the lower lip, and Amber was appalled by her actions when her tongue darted out to touch the foreign object. Brant drew a quick breath, his body becoming rigid. Suddenly, he jerked her against his chest, his hands resting against the small of her back to trap her arms uselessly. He held her tightly, her body fitting intimately against his.

Amber felt the muscles in his thighs contract, and she took shallow breaths so their bodies would not have to come into closer contact. She felt like she was one with him, and the nearness was an awakening experience. Her eyes focused on the shiny buttons on his uniform, afraid to look into his eyes. She was too shaken by the sensations he was arousing in her body. She had not felt the same awareness in Steven's arms and he had been half naked. What would it be like in Brant's arms when he was half dressed? Her thoughts shocked her!

His breath fanned the top of her head, and she knew he was watching her. She tried to moisten her lips, but her throat was dry.

"Amber," he whispered. "Amber."

Her stomach somersaulted at the soft caress of her name. It had as much effect on her as the nearness of his body. She wanted to break free of his hold and run, but there was no place to go. This man was slowly, deliberately, awakening her senses and she was totally helpless. She could have fought his rape, but she was powerless over the betrayal of her body. He had made her his prisoner as if he had chained her.

She raised her head and looked into his eyes. The dark brown color was consumed by the fire of his desire. Her gaze wandered over the loose hair on his forehead, then down the bridge of his straight, narrow nose to the excited flare of his nostrils. His mouth, curved and sensuous, hovered inches above her face. Amber swallowed thickly, trying to force away the knot in her throat. She had been mesmerized by a mouth once before, but she blocked the reminder. That man was dead. This was another time and place.

She found herself waiting, wanting to feel the touch of his lips and hating her feelings for being a traitor to her. This man had aroused her body, and she would never again be satisfied with teasing, cautious kisses. She had been introduced to the passions of a woman and she could never look back. The arms trapped at her sides ached to be free to draw him closer and run her fingers through his brown hair. Unknowingly, her body moved against his, and Brant's hands glided over her buttocks to fit her more intimately against him. The shock of his arousal was a jolt to her already tingling nerves, and her palms spread over his thighs.

He felt the touch of her fingers through his pants, and the pulse in his throat throbbed. She was even more than he expected her to be, and he ached with desire. He longed to toss her on the bed, throw aside their clothes and make her his, but he first wanted to be assured of her total submission. Her reactions to his nearness were like a bud opening to the sunshine, and he knew he had to let her feelings grow or they would be squashed by the chill of reality. He could feel her limbs tremble against his, and her gaze continually strayed to his lips. She wanted more and he was willing to be her teacher.

Parting his mouth, one of his hands tangled in her amber hair to tip her head back. There was a sultry glaze over her eyes as she watched the descent of his mouth. The touch of his lips against her forehead sent her grabbing at him for support. Her flesh warmed beneath his caresses. As his mouth glided along her jaw, his hands slid under her shirt to curve around her waist.

Amber was consumed by a desire so intense it left her breathless and aching. It had never seemed possible to feel such strong emotions, but this man, a stranger, a Confederate officer, had shattered her defenses and left her awakened as a woman.

His lips nibbled her ear lobe then dropped to the sensitive skin lining her throat. Rays of sensation shot through her limbs, continuously supplying her with the erotic pleasures of her body. Brant's mouth covered her face with kisses, but he never got near her mouth where she ached to feel their touch. His deliberate avoidance of her lips only excited her more, and she clutched at him, her body arching against his.

"Brant," she whispered, turning her head toward his searching lips. He kissed the corner of her mouth, his tongue sweeping over the warmed flesh. She was ready to cry out her surrender to the enemy, her hatred swallowed by the passion he had aroused.

The sharp knock on the door brought an abrupt awareness to Brant's body. As though doused by cold water, his hands fell to his sides. Amber, still under the effect of his love-making, found her legs unable to support her, and she sank to the cot.

Brant's hands closed into fists at his sides, his body trying to fight off his arousal. He ached with the need to satisfy himself, but it was a desire he would not see fulfilled—at least not now. His lust had been kindled by the feel of her body against his, and it had heightened his need. One day soon he would hold her in his arms. There was so much he wanted to teach her, and he suspected her passion would teach him something as well. It would be a welcome exchange. No woman had ever aroused him like this beauty. Standing with his legs apart, he regarded her flushed features. Had they not been interrupted, he would have filled her with his desire, and they could have ridden to new heights of awareness. Amber would never be able to walk away without remembering the moments she had shared in his arms, and he was determined to use that knowledge in his favor.

Someone knocked for a second time, and Brant ran his fingers through his light brown hair. He had not fully regained control of his emotions, but enough that his hcad was clcar.

The interruption had been Amber's safety valve, but she found herself hating the interference. Her toying with men had never aroused the kind of response Brant had evoked, and she was appalled by her wanton desires. She wanted him, but hated herself for the alien feelings. He was the enemy and she had to remember her position. The ache in her body for something she had never experienced was undeniable, and she was convinced if a man could use his lust to gain a response without love, the same was true of women.

Fortunately, their encounter had not resulted in ultimate, intimate commitment, but she knew it could have occurred, and she would have welcomed the exchange. What had happened to her? Where was the strength she had been taught to possess? Where was the sound judgment her father had instilled in her? In a few moments all of it had been thrown out the window and discarded as useless. Raising her eyes, she watched the Rebel reach for the doorknob. He was to blame for her turbulent feelings, and she hated him for it.

"Bring the prisoner in," she heard Brant order.

"Would you like me to stay?" the private asked.

Brant noticed the heavy shackles. "It won't be necessary, but stay outside the door."

The man looked at Amber. "What about the lady? Is she coming with me?"

Brant's gaze flickered over Amber. She had regained some of her composure, but the unusual color in her cheeks warned of her anxiety. "My fianceé will remain."

The door closed behind the soldier and Brant turned. Andy's chains rattled as he rested his hands on hips and looked from Amber to the Confederate officer.

"Your fianceé," he said, his eyes, a copy of his sister's, widening. "What is going on here?" he demanded, noting Amber's flushed appearance. "Are you going to marry this man?"

"Of course not," she argued, disappointed he would even consider her capable of a relationship with the enemy—a man fighting to keep people in bondage. Tossing her amber hair over her shoulder, she rose. "How could you think I would marry a Rebel?" she growled, walking to his side. "You know what they stand for."

Andy didn't know what to think, but he shook his head. "Sis, you don't have to be afraid to admit the truth. I can understand that you love the man and not the side he represents. There is a difference," he said softly.

Amber stared at Andy in disbelief. He was certainly more sympathetic than she. She could never separate the man from his loyalty to the Confederacy.

Brant was and always would be the enemy because of his belief in the Southern cause. More than that, he was the enemy because of the threat he presented to her emotional state. In a short time he had thrown it into turmoil. Only one man had not backed down when she challenged him and that was her father. Brant had showed the same power and strength, but he was definitely not a father figure.

Realizing he wasn't going to get an answer from his sister, he turned to Brant. "Why are you calling Amber your fiancée?"

"To save her life."

Andy's eyes narrowed. "You are here to hang me. Why do you want to protect her?"

"Ask your sister," he suggested, his eyes roaming over her face.

Raising his chained wrists, Andy put his hands on her upper arms. "What does he want from you?"

She couldn't explain even to her brother what Brant wanted from her. It was too humiliating to consider.

"Nothing," she supplied.

"Not quite true, but we'll leave it for now," he said, pushing away from the wall and walking toward the twins. "The resemblance between the two of you is remarkable. Without the dirt and beard the relationship would be obvious."

Andy was wary of the major. He was not like the captain who ran the prison. This man was more ruthless and capable of results. "You've got nothing on her," Andy defended. "Let her go."

Brant's eyes wandered over Amber's face, reminding her of the intimate embrace they had shared. A

115

newly awakened tingling swept into her limbs. He slowly shook his head. "That is not possible. She was caught in this fort wearing a uniform and carrying an important document from General Lee."

Andy had forgotten the paper and fear crept into his eyes. "If you believe she is guilty of spying, why did you lie about her involvement?"

"I already told you," he said, sitting on the edge of the desk. "She is not useful to me dead."

"Useful," he said, the light of Brant's actions suddenly coming into focus. "Amber, don't let him hold my life over your head. I'm a dead man."

She could not add to her brother's anxiety. He looked too pale and she didn't like the warmth of his flesh. If she could use her power over the major, she might gain Andy's release.

Softly, she said, "Don't antagonize him. I will try to convince him to let you escape."

Andy's eyes narrowed suspiciously. "How do you propose to do that?"

She threw a quick glance in Brant's direction and saw him watching her. "There is a way." She knew what it would take to control this man and hoped she would have the strength. Moments before, when they had been in each other's arms, he had held all the cards. Could she manipulate him in her favor?

"I don't like this. You should not have come here. It was too dangerous."

"It is going to be fine," she falsely reassured him, wishing she could believe her words. "Trust me."

He grinned. "I don't have any choice. Want to tell me what you are planning?"

"No," she answered, an embarrassed flush spreading over her cheeks.

The suspicions in the back of his mind raced forward, and he stiffened. "I won't allow it," he said gruffly. He shook her slim shoulders. "Do you hear me? I won't allow it."

Brant was alerted to Andy's anger and came to his feet.

"Stop it, Andy. It is my life. I will do whatever is necessary."

"No. I forbid it," he shouted.

"What won't you allow?" Brant asked.

"I won't let you rape my sister."

Chuckling, Brant remembered the minutes before. "I can assure you it would not be rape."

Amber trembled, her rage at Brant mounting. It was enough that he had humiliated her, but now he was going to drag her down in her brother's eyes.

"My sister is not going to exchange her body for my life."

"I never asked her to," he announced and Amber's mouth dropped. She was certain he had implied that something might be worked out between them. "You are going to hang for spying against the Army of the Confederacy."

"Then I'll have the satisfaction of trying to protect my sister against a filthy swine."

Lunging forward, Andy raised his chained hands and jumped behind Brant. The attack was totally unexpected, and the officer didn't have time to prepare himself. The chain caught him in the chin then dropped to his throat. Crossing his hands, Andy pulled the chain tightly, forcing the air from Brant's throat. Brant's fingers clawed at the metal strangling the breath from his body, but Andy's grip was too tight. Flashes of blackness shot before his eyes.

Amber stood immobile and watched her brother choke the life out of a man she had responded to with surprising ardor. A part of her wanted to stop the killing, but his death could only aid her brother's freedom and that was the first consideration. She had hunted and seen animals die, but she had never seen a human fight for survival. This was what war was all about — killing the enemy.

The element of surprise had been on Andy's side, but he was weak and his arms ached from the torturous hold in the chains. Brant, however, was not about to succumb to the death his attacker sought. Pulling his arm forward, he let his elbow fly into Andy's stomach. A startled puff of air erupted from Andy's throat, and he momentarily lost his grip. Ducking beneath the chains, Brant swung around, his fist doubled up as it connected with Andy's chin. His head snapped back from the impact, his body falling against the desk. Brant's fist found a home in Andy's stomach. The younger man tried to hit Brant's head with the wrist chain, but the major ducked out of the way.

It was one thing to watch Andy defeat his enemy and another to watch her brother be beaten. Springing into action, she picked up a chair and advanced on Brant. Sensing Amber's presence behind him, Brant agilely ducked out of her path, and the chair uselessly hit the floor. Knowing he could control the brother through his sister, her grabbed Amber's arm and pulled her to his side. Andy started after him then stopped, his eyes widening.

Brant's hair had fallen away from the left side of his head, and Andy stared at the scar in the hairline. His mind flew back to the stranger in the field hospital and tried to picture that man's face without the bruises and cuts. The stranger had not died.

"I know you," he accused.

Brant smiled. "I wondered when you would remember. Guard," he called, smoothing his hair into place. The door opened and the private entered, his eyes widening at the sight of the overturned chair. "Chain this man and put a double guard on him. He is going to hang."

Amber's legs sagged and Brant's arm tightened around her waist. Dry-eyed she watched the private drag Andy from the room. They had gambled and lost, but until her brother was executed for his crime there was still hope.

"You can't hang him," she said, looking into Brant's face.

"I am an officer in the Confederate Army. I was ordered to hang him," he stated indifferently.

"Hang me at his side," she pleaded, "or let me go."

"Until your brother is dead, you are not leaving my side."

Amber's eyes narrowed. "How does my brother know you?"

Brant smiled and Amber's gaze was drawn to the curved line of his lips. "Don't you remember?"

"Remember what?" she asked, certain she didn't know him.

"I was the dying man who felt the touch of your lips."

The dryness in her throat nearly choked her. Unwilling to believe what he said, she brushed aside his hair to

119

reveal the scar.

"Would you like to see the way the wound on my side healed?"

Amber's hand fell. "I thought you had died."

Her mind flew back to the wounded stranger. He had thrown her life into turmoil. She had never understood her response to him or wanted to search for the reasons. She had felt threatened by him and recognized him as a man like her papa. The reminder of her father put a sneer on her lips.

"What is the matter?" Brant asked.

"I just realized the Confederates knew about my papa's meeting place. You had been sent to kill him," she accused.

"I was ambushed a short distance from where your father found me. I can't recall most of the next few hours, but I do remember the feel of your mouth. You gave me reason to live. I wanted to get to know you."

His confession made Amber tremble. Why had she acted so foolishly? Why hadn't she maintained her strength and remembered not to get involved. She had kissed him to erase her attraction and not to stir his interest. When he had regained consciousness and asked about her papa, she had not seen any reason to lie to a weak, wounded man. Had he been pretending to be weak so he could get information about her father? She had to know.

"If you were interested in me, why did you disappear?"

His eyes narrowed in response to the pointed inquiry. "I didn't want questions."

Amber backed away. "You went after my father. You killed him."

Stepping forward, Brant grabbed her arms. "I didn't have anything to do with his death." There was strong emphasis on his words; he wanted her to believe him. "I couldn't make it to Antietam. I collapsed a day's ride from the hospital. I woke weeks later in a Confederate hospital."

There was sincerity in his voice, but Amber refused to be tricked into trusting a Rebel. "I don't believe you. Let me go."

"Never. I have learned you can't be trusted. You are dangerous to the Southern cause."

"I can't believe you are afraid of a woman."

Brant chuckled. "You are not just any woman. You are passionate, beautiful and dangerous—an enticing combination." Even now his body burned to hold her, and he was determined to know her in every way.

Amber's mouth felt dry. She didn't like the intent look in his eyes. He was a man with a purpose.

"What do you want from me?" she whispered.

"I want what you offered me in the field hospital. . . . I want you. You are the woman I want at my side."

Ten

"Private," Brant called. "Take my fianceé to my quarters." He took Amber's fingers in his. "We will talk later."

She pulled her hands free and numbly followed the private outside. She scanned the compound for Andy, but he wasn't in sight. Her brother had recognized Brant and probably surmised that he had been at the meeting place to kill their father. Brant wanted Amber to believe he had nothing to do with Richard's death, but evidence indicated otherwise. His sudden departure the same night as her father was highly suspicious. Assuming he had been sent to kill Richard, who had told the Rebels her father's plans? The leak in the Union organization had to be found and stopped.

Brant's room was in a small building on the far side of the compound. Amber looked out the only window and scowled. Nothing had gone as she had planned. Andy was still a prisoner, and she was captive of a man who had turned her life inside out.

Brant was no fool and he would be on the alert for her attempts to help her brother. Her only weapon was her body, and she wasn't sure if it would be useful against him. Brant had brought out a passionate side of her nature that she had never suspected. If Brant took her maidenhood, it would be a mutual coaxing of their needs and not rape. She could not manipulate him physically, and she would only humiliate herself by responding to a Rebel. Could she swallow her pride to save Andy's life?

She could try to kill Brant but knew it would gain nothing but personal satisfaction. He had not gotten to his position in the army by being a fool, and she already knew him to be a man capable of protecting himself.

She looked at the prisoner pen, and her heart ached for the men trapped in the unsanitary confinement like animals. Many had been sick or wounded and she wanted to ease their pain. Perhaps by soothing their agony she would find relief from her helplessness.

Crossing to the door, she stepped outside and walked across the compound. As before there was no sign of Andy and her brows came together in concern. She was certain he had been sick, but she didn't know how serious it was. Every hour they delayed their departure could mean trouble. She felt bitterly disappointed in her failure thus far, but was determined not to give up.

As she neared the prisoner compound, she realized her actions were spontaneous. She had no authority to help the soldiers and didn't know how the Confederates would view it. Edgar already resented her presence in the compound, and this would probably strengthen his need for vengeance. Brant's thoughts were a mystery to her, and she wasn't sure if he knew she had treated his side and was qualified for medical work.

She approached one of the guards and smiled. "There are sick and wounded men in the prison area. I would like to examine them."

The soldier ran his eyes down her male-clad figure. "I don't know," he sneered. "Them's Blue Bellies. Ain't right fer a lady to go among them. Our doctor will return in a few days."

Amber glanced past him to the men. They were ill fed and clothed and many were weakened by illness. She desperately wanted to help ease their suffering. "If we wait some of them will be dead," she argued, throwing her hands on her slim hips.

"What do you care? They are Yankees." He regarded her suspiciously. "Who are you anyway?"

Amber knew if she was going to get into the compound she needed leverage. "I am the major's fiancée," she answered swiftly, intending to use the lie to influence him.

"Are you having trouble, darling?" someone asked.

Amber stiffened at the sound of Brant's voice and forced away her anger at his use of the endearment. He had obviously heard her admission and intended to use it in his favor. She didn't like his game, but as long as she was in the prison camp he made the rules.

Amber turned, surprised and uneasy to find Edgar at Brant's side. The hostile look in the captain's eyes put her on edge. He was probably the most frightening man she had ever met, but she would never show him fear.

"What is the problem?" Edgar asked, not waiting for Brant to take control. This was his camp and he would make the decisions.

"This lady wants to treat the sick and wounded Yankees."

"Are you a doctor?" he asked, a smirk on his lips. Women didn't know anything about doctoring—at least the kind of care these men needed. Letting her care for them might be the way to make her look like a fool. He desperately wanted to humiliate her.

"No," she admitted, "but I have enough skills to make some of them more comfortable. These men are human beings and deserve proper care."

"Why are you so concerned for the enemy?" Edgar asked.

Brant had not spoken and his silence put Amber on edge. She was the infiltrator and didn't know how far he could be pushed before he would expose her.

"The men are a concern to all of us. If I'm not mistaken some of them have an illness that could threaten everyone in the complex." Edgar stiffened and Amber knew she had hit on a sensitive area. "We can't let their poor health jeopardize our soldiers," she said, pretending to be a Rebel.

"Amber is right," Brant said smoothly. "Disease is a problem in most of our prisons. It must be controlled."

Fear heightened the color in Edgar's gray eyes. Sickness was a threat he couldn't fight and it terrified him. "You have permission to enter the compound. I want a full report."

Turning, the guard unlocked the gate and pulled the door open. "Excuse me," she said to the gentlemen. Both men troubled her in different ways and she wanted to escape them.

The male clothes allowed Amber freedom of movement, but she was conscious of leering gazes from the prisoners. The smell of unwashed bodies and human excretion was overpowering and Amber's hand went to her nose.

"Are you sure you want to do this?" Brant quizzed.

She looked up, surprised to find him with her. "I've seen and smelled worse," she replied and dropped her hand.

Ignoring the stares, she walked toward a sleeping soldier and put her palm against his forehead. His flesh burned with fever. The men on either side of him were in the same condition. Conversing with two healthy prisoners, she learned the men's symptoms. Rising, her brows creased in a frown. She turned to Brant.

"The men have typhoid fever."

He nodded grimly. "I agree. This place is nothing but a breeding ground for infection," he said in distaste.

"Then why don't you give these men decent care," she countered. "They are being treated like animals."

Brant's eyes narrowed. "We are in a war. Money and personnel aren't always available."

"The sick men should be separated from the healthy ones. Fortunately, I have had the sickness," she said, reflecting on her father's attempt to save her life.

"Did your brother have it?"

"No. Papa kept us apart." She met Brant's gaze squarely. "You might get ill."

126

"Are you worried about my health?" he baited.

"Only because it is a way I can get rid of you." She would not wish the fever on anyone, but she flung the barb because she hated him.

Bending forward, he whispered, "Have you forgotten I am the only buffer you have against being discovered as a traitor?"

Amber didn't have a suitable retort, so she directed her attention to a man with a thigh wound. He was in desperate need of a surgeon. She had seen a small medical facility and hoped to find the necessary supplies.

"I can't work on him here." She carefully probed the torn flesh. "He needs to be taken to the hospital."

Brant crossed his arms over his chest. This woman was full of surprises. She had come to the prison to save her brother, a feat almost certain to fail, yet she had met the challenge with determination. He admired her spunk, courage and loyalty to her brother. She was an outsider, but had stood before the commanding officer and demanded care for the wounded.

Watching her work with the sick showed him another side of a complicated, fascinating woman. He vaguely remembered her helping with his injuries, but he had not realized the extent of her ability. She had admitted she wasn't a doctor, yet she possessed knowledge of medicine. Where had she gained her skills? She was becoming a captivating challenge.

Brant signaled the guards and told them to move the man to the hospital. When they were gone, Amber issued directions for separating the sick from the wounded and healthy.

She had hoped to go to the hospital alone, but Brant remained at her side. Unfortunately, there were few supplies and no medicine. She found a knife on the work table and cut the pants from the bloody thigh. It was a nasty injury and needed cleansing to avoid infection. She looked at the wound uncertainly. She wanted to help the man, but he needed the skills of a surgeon.

A movement by the door reminded her Brant was watching, and she wondered if he intended to stay the entire time she worked. "This man needs a doctor. My brother could save his life."

Brant's eyes narrowed. "Is your brother a doctor?"

She carefully inspected the injury, looking for the best way to repair the damage. "Yes. My father trained both of us, but my studies were interrupted for a time, and I never performed an operation."

He frowned. "How did a surgeon get captured as a spy?"

"That is not important."

"What interrupted your studies? I can't believe you let something stand in your way."

Amber remembered how she had hated giving up medicine for the feminine things. "I don't need your snide comments. A man's life is at stake."

Crossing the room, Brant got a bowl of water and stepped to her side. "I can't get your brother. You'll have to put up with me. I promise not to faint," he teased.

Amber worked diligently over the injured soldier. His wound was serious, and she knew most surgeons would amputate the leg. Steven had believed in trying to save the damaged limbs, and Amber had adopted his beliefs. In this man's case it was the only option. She had never done the procedure and wasn't sure she had the skill or strength to perform the delicate operation. Hopefully, the man would survive if she kept the wound clean and didn't let it get infected.

Working quickly, she removed the gunshot and stitched the broken flesh. Amber was relieved when the soldier lapsed into unconsciousness and she was able to work without hearing his tortureds cries of pain. She never liked to be the cause of agony even if it was to help.

"Aren't you going to remove the leg?" Brant asked, stepping to her side.

"No,' she said, refusing to let him know she was unsure about operating. She checked the leg awaiting the final bandage. "Don't you agree?"

He studied her neat work. "You're the doctor," he mocked. "If he doesn't get an infection, I'm sure he'll thank you for leaving him whole." Amber bandaged the thigh. "You did an admirable job," he praised. "Most women would be afraid to tackle what you just did."

"I don't like being compared to 'most women'. I only did what I was trained to do."

Her tone was icy and Brant wondered what had happened to the warm, compassionate woman who tenderly cared for the wounded and loved her brother. Why did she become hard and emotionless whenever she talked to him? Why wouldn't she let him see her softness?

"You are definitely not like any woman I've ever known," he said, reaching up to catch the silky strands of her long hair.

Amber didn't know if she should take his statement as a compliment or insult. She didn't like the way he was trying to pry into her life and thoughts. She slapped his hand away and bent over the soldier. His breathing was shallow but regular. Relieved, she tenderly brushed the hair from his forehead.

Brant watched the gentle caress and the way her expression softened when she gazed at him. She really cared about the stranger. His life was important to her. Brant felt a tightening in his loins. He wanted the same tenderness. He wanted her to look at him with gentle eyes and caress his face.

Reaching down, his fingers closed around her upper arm. He felt her muscles tense in protest as he pulled her toward him. The heat from his body reached past their clothes to touch her flesh.

"Don't fight me," he whispered. "You want this as much as I do."

Amber was speechless. In the past she had flirted to interest a beau, but only when she could maintain control of the situation. Brant was too dangerous and experienced for her tricks.

"No — no," she stammered. "You are mistaken."

"No," he whispered softly. "I'm very receptive to the signals your body is sending me."

Amber's eyes widened. "I hate you." She shook her head in disbelief. "I came here to rescue Andy, not to jump into bed with you. . . . *You* have an over-inflated ego." She didn't like the hungry look in his eyes. "You are going to hang my brother and I believe you killed my father. I can't feel anything for you but hate."

"You have very strong feelings," he whispered,

"and they are not hate. I am going to prove it to you."

He pulled her into his arms, and his hand slid along her neck to tangle in the soft amber hair. His closeness had not yet succeeded in weakening her defenses and she was determined to erect a barrier against his sensuous love-making. She already knew he possessed skilled techniques in arousing a woman's passions, but she was not going to be a pawn.

His mouth glided along her hairline, his lips barely brushing the flesh. The intimacy was enough to send a shiver down her spine, and she realized the need to build stronger defenses. In a matter of seconds this man would render her weak and helpless. She had to get away.

Throwing her head back, she allowed him access to her throat, and he eagerly accepted her invitation to slide his mouth to the throbbing pulse. Bracing her hands against his forearms, she planted her feet firmly on the ground and shoved him with all her strength. Brant, completely engrossed in his lovemaking, was caught off guard and fell back. Without waiting to see his reaction, Amber raced to the door and ran outside. When she was a safe distance away, she stopped and glanced over her shoulder.

Brant stood in the doorway, his hands curled into fists. There was a determined gleam in his dark brown eyes, and Amber recognized him as a dangerous man—a man who would not be pushed too far. She threw her head in the air and defiantly marched to the prisoner compound.

Brant chuckled softly at her rebellion. She was a very interesting woman and he enjoyed their verbal sparring. What he did not enjoy was the way she made his body ache with desire. Thus far he had not had trouble getting a reaction from her physically, but he wanted the emotional response as well. Before he could get that he would have to erode the hate she felt for him. He frowned. That was not going to be an easy battle. She hated him because he was the enemy, and already believed he had killed her father. Once he hanged her brother her spite would blossom. He knew he would still be able to make her body respond, but her bitterness would thicken the emotional barrier.

She had never shown him anything but bravery and determination. He wanted more than her icy strength; he wanted her softness too. Perhaps if he went slowly and carefully aroused her sensual desire, he could shatter her exterior shell and force her to open to him as a soft, vulnerable woman. Brant was going to find the way to unlock her heart.

Amber's day had been long and exhausting. Two men had died during the afternoon and several more hovered on the brink of death. Amber had sat with them, wiping their fevered brows with a soft cloth and trying to make them more comfortable. One of them had regained consciousness and whispered his appreciation for her tender care. She had smiled down at him, aching inside because there was no medicine to ease his suffering.

Throughout the day she had watched the shack where Andy was held. Brant had spent two hours with him, but her brother did not appear outside and she worried for his safety. Brant wanted her body, but he had made it clear that his duty to execute her brother would not be confused with his physical desire. She would have to make another attempt to free him.

When darkness offered cover for her plan, she left her patients and slipped a surgeon's knife into the band of her pants. The sentries allowed her free access to the compound, and she easily disappeared into the darkness. Andy's shack was unguarded, and she cautiously pushed the door open and stepped into the darkness. She hadn't taken two steps across the room before she was grabbed from behind and spun around.

"I have been waiting for you." Brant whispered, clamping his arms around her waist.

She started to twist out of his grasp, then remembered the knife in the band of her pants. The blade was uncovered and could inflict a nasty cut.

Grabbing her hair, Brant jerked her head back and pressed his hips against her stomach. The reaction to pull free from the intimacy was spontaneous and a startled gasp flew from her lips as the knife shifted and sliced her skin. Brant recognized the sound of pain and pushed her away to light a lamp. His eyes were a dangerous brown as they surveyed Amber's hand protectively shielding her waist. Crossing the room, he pulled the shirt from her pants. The knife dropped to the floor.

He bent to retrieve it. "Not a large weapon, but suitable to cut a man's throat. You can't have him, Amber. He is going to hang." His eyes narrowed. "I warned you to stay away from here."

"I have no intention of listening to you." She

looked at the open door to the back room. Why didn't she hear any noise? Something tightened in her chest. Had Andy already been executed?

Panic drove all reasonable thought from her mind, and she lunged at the door. "Andy," she called.

Brant stepped into her path and she plowed into his chest. "You can't see him."

"Let me go," she hissed. "He's my brother." Brant didn't move. "I hate you."

"Your body is speaking another language," he whispered against her ear. His tongue teased the tip as his teeth nibbled the flesh. It was a shot of awareness Amber had never experienced and her limbs trembled uncertainly. Brant was starting over again, slowly awakening her body in an attempt to force her to admit her needs. His mouth expertly ran down her throat and across her collarbone to the hollow of her throat. Her skin prickled beneath his touch and a warm flush spread over her flesh. Brant fitted her against his body until she felt the hardness of his loins through her clothes. Being made aware of his desire was a warning to her senses, and she struggled to break free.

"Surrender. . . . Don't think of me as the enemy. . . . Think of me as a man," he coaxed.

In Amber's mind the man and enemy were one. She hated the Rebel and feared the sensations the man aroused in her body. His warm breath sent a shiver down her spine. He was dangerous because he knocked all sensible thought from her mind and made her feel weak and helpless. She didn't like it. There had to be a way to escape his grasp, but with her body pinned against his, her limbs were ineffec-

134

tive.

Reflecting on her past experiences with men, she remembered a few times when she had been forced to stop a gentleman's advances. Her methods had always been effective, but she had never had such a strong opponent. Turning her head to the side of Brant's chin, she opened her mouth and bit his collarbone. Fortunately, he was only wearing a thin shirt and her teeth clamped around the bone.

Brant's muffled exclamation of surprise forced him to lose his grip. Amber stepped back and shoved her knee into his groin. She moved away uncertainly when his head snapped up and his brown-eyed gaze locked with hers. She saw a dangerous warning glint in their depths and all thoughts of her brother fled her mind. Brant's jaw was set in vengeance and she knew she had to escape. Backing toward the door, she watched the agony on his face as he slowly stood.

Amber turned and fled into the night. Her attack had caused him pain, but the blow had not been hard enough to cause permanent injury. His expression had warned her that he would never be taken as a fool again.

As the pain in Brant's groin lessened he shook his head. Amber exhibited male courage and daring and was not a woman to toy with. Scowling, he walked toward the back room. He needed some answers to her complicated actions and emotions. Andy was the key to getting inside Amber, but would he talk to a Rebel?

Eleven

News of the war came in the early morning hours. The Confederate Army had met the Union soldiers at Gettysburg and the war raged. Amber had gotten the sparse details when she left her all-night vigil with the prisoners to have breakfast. The dead and wounded were estimated to be in the thousands.

She was on her way back to the prisoners when Edgar stopped her. "Still playing doctor?" he baited.

A shiver of apprehension ran down her spine. She didn't like anything about this man and knew the feeling was mutual. He wanted to expose her as a liar and discredit Brant as an officer.

"I don't have time for this," she said and walked past him.

Edgar grabbed her arm. "Not so fast. Where is your fiancé?" he sneered.

"I don't know. He doesn't tell me every move he makes."

His eyes bored into hers. "I suspect you are glad. I don't know what he sees in a whore like you. You're pretty, but there is always a pretty face."

"I am not a whore," she said, pulling her arm free.

"I also know you are not his fiancée," he accused. "I think you came here for an entirely different reason."

Amber didn't like Edgar's probing. "I have work to do."

"You are coming into my office first," he said. Amber was wary of the way he smiled. Something was going on and she did not like it. "I have a surprise planned."

"I will wait for Brant," she said, not wanting to be alone with this man.

"He has already been summoned."

Amber had no choice but to follow him. Apprehension tugged at her thoughts. Edgar was not a man to be trusted, and she suspected whatever he had planned would not be pleasant. Brant was not in his office, but there was another man waiting. Brant's appearance a few minutes later calmed some of her uncertainties and strangely gave her relief. He walked to her side and put his arm around her waist.

"Why have you called this meeting?" he asked, his tone agitated. "I want to question the prisoner again."

Edgar smiled slyly. "I told you on our first meeting that I would do everything I could to make your time here *'memorable.'* Today I am going to complete that promise." He pointed to the other man. "This is a preacher. I have called him here to perform your marriage ceremony." Edgar's eyes gleamed with vengeance. "I believe you wanted to marry as soon as possible."

Brant reacted swiftly to Edgar's comment. Anticipating Amber's shock, he pulled her into his arms and pressed her face against his shoulder. The tension in her limbs relayed her anxiety.

"The lady and I are honored," he drawled. "I am eager to make this woman my wife." He stroked her amber hair. "Are you ready, darling?" he asked softly.

Everything was happening too fast and she struggled to still the rapid pounding of her heart. Edgar had seen through their contrived engagement and had arranged the ceremony to trap them in a lie. He believed he had found a way to catch them in their own game.

Amber knew her life and credibility rested with her next actions. If she refused to go through with the wedding she would be admitting that she was a fraud. As long as Andy was alive she had to protect her reason for being at the prison.

Raising her head, she looked into Brant's eyes. His reputation was at stake, but he gave no indication of his inner turmoil. If he objected to what was happening, he was not going to betray the truth. As her blue-green eyes searched his brown ones, she made the decision.

Staying in the protection of his arms, she turned slowly. "Captain, that was very nice of you to make the arrangements."

"Shall we get on with the ceremony," Brant said swiftly.

Amber spoke her vows in a daze, still unable to believe that she was marrying this man—her enemy. She knew when she entered the prison that her life might undergo a change, but she had never suspected this.

Brant's vows were spoken in a deep, strong tone,

and Amber trembled when he accepted her as his wife. The ceremony was over swiftly and the preacher congratulated them. Edgar's eyes were hostile when he acknowledged the married couple. His plans to expose them had met with failure and his anger intensified.

"If you gentlemen would excuse us, my bride and I would like to be alone." Before Amber could protest Brant had swept her into his arms and carried her out of the room.

"Put me down," she hissed when they reached the sunlight.

"Stop squirming," he threatened. "If I put you down you would disappear, and I want to spend some time with my wife." He reached their cabin and pushed the door open. After kicking the door shut, he put Amber on the bed. Straightening, he reached for the buttons of his shirt.

Amber scrambled to her feet. "What are you doing?" she asked, catching a glimpse of his naked chest.

"Undressing," he said flatly.

"I have to get back to work," she said, walking toward the door.

Brant stopped her by putting his body in her path. "You are not leaving. We were just married and it will look suspicious if we don't spend some time together."

Amber threw her hands on her hips and her blue-green eyes flashed her defiance. "I don't care how it looks. This marriage is meaningless. I don't recognize it as valid."

"It is very real," he said, his gaze dropping to her mouth. "You are my wife in name . . . and soon in body."

"Never," she argued, frightened by the intensity of his gaze. Having the stigma of marriage attached to their relationship added an intimacy that made her pulse race. In the eyes of the law he was her husband, but she would not recognize the marriage and intended to do everything in her power to dissolve the association once she returned home.

He smiled and Amber's gaze was drawn to the firm line of his lips. A wisp of breath blew from between his teeth to tickle her cheeks. Raising his hands, Brant tangled his fingers in her hair and pulled her head back. His mouth hovered above hers and moved with feather-light caresses over her trembling lips. He increased the pressure only to draw back and leave her uncertain, trembling, confused and wanting. A low moan erupted from his throat as he pulled her against his aroused body.

Involuntarily, Amber's lips parted in expectation. There wasn't an inch of her skin that was left unaffected by his touch and nearness. Her limbs trembled and tingled in expectation.

Brant's lips closed her sea-green eyes with his kisses. Amber didn't have to look at the man arousing her senses; she was acutely aware of every fiber of his being. He was playing with her, deliberately exciting her body to her passionate needs. She fought for control, but he was successfully shattering every barrier she had erected against him.

Holding her against his body, Brant walked to the bed. Taking her weight, he twisted and dropped against the softness. Their limbs were tangled and the more they struggled the more intimately entwined they became.

"Stop squirming and enjoy this," he whispered, nuzzling her neck. "You were meant to be loved."

Amber fought for breath, her hands unable to push him away. He was her husband and had every right to touch her body, but he was also the enemy and Amber had to drag the reminder to the front of her thoughts. He was going to kill the person she loved most in life. She could not love or give her body to a man who would destroy her happiness.

Rolling her head to the side, she said, "This isn't love. It is pure, simple lust."

Brant's hand curved over her shoulder to the neckline of the shirt, seeking entrance to the flesh beneath. He was tenacious in his pursuit and his body curved closer to hers.

Amber couldn't let the assault continue. She felt confused by her feelings. She was supposed to show this man strength, but she was displaying a vulnerable weakness. She couldn't allow him to have this power over her. It was not what Papa would have expected, and this man was her father's equal in strength.

"Let me go." She pounded her fist against his back. "I hate you," she screamed. "Let me go. You are responsible for my father's death and you are going to murder my brother."

Her accusations and the tone of her voice relayed fear and hate, and Brant knew he would never get the response out of her he craved. He wanted their lovemaking to be a spontaneous nurturing of their desires. The bond of marriage had made her his, but they had obstacles to overcome before she would recognize the relationship.

Scowling, he rolled to her side. "Why are you

141

afraid of your natural emotions? It isn't wrong to experience desire."

Amber was too embarrassed by her response to look at him. He had aroused her femininity in a way that made her feel threatened. Steven's kiss and closeness had not brought out the same fear. He was a gentle man and in his arms she had known a calm peace. Brant constantly made her feel like a woman, but with a hot passion that made fire lick through her veins.

"I don't desire you," she said heatedly. "I could never feel anything for the man who kills the people I love. You are a Rebel and on the side of slavery. I believe in freedom for all people. . . . There can never be anything between us." Her earlier passion forgotten, Amber glared at Brant. "This marriage was forced on me. I do not recognize it as being valid. As soon as I can escape I'll take legal measures to have the relationship annulled. There will be nothing to bind me to you."

The muscle in Brant's cheek tensed. From the beginning he had decided he wanted this woman for more than just the physical pleasures. She was special and he could not let her escape. The marriage had provided a permanence he found calming, but Amber's threat to dissolve it sparked his anger. He could not let this woman out of his life. They were on opposite sides of the war and she hated him because of her father and brother. He believed time would heal her mental wounds, but he had to break through the emotions she had locked away. He had to make her need him.

Brant was not driven by desire but by fear that he

would lose her. "This marriage is valid. We are enemies in this war. I had nothing to do with your father's death and there is nothing I can do about your brother's life." He looked into her eyes. "I won't let you go. We are bound together by our vows and will be by the flesh.

Brant fumbled with the fastenings on her pants and pulled them over her buttocks. Amber fought him, pounding at his body with her fists. After loosening his trousers, he caught her flailing arms and pinned them above her head. His pants had caught someplace at his thigh, and Amber felt their roughness as his body settled over hers.

Amber's struggles ceased. She knew she lacked the strength to battle this man. He had decided to make this marriage real and there was nothing she could do about it. Clamping her teeth together, she glared at him, her eyes green with hate. The horror of what was about to happen was locked away inside, and there was no outward show of fear—only hate and spite for the man who was about to steal her maidenhood.

Brant looked at the woman beneath him, knowing she was hiding her real feelings from him. He slowly joined their bodies, his own pausing when she flinched in pain. And then it was over and Brant's weight was lifted from her. Without looking at her nakedness, he pulled a sheet over her body. Lying at her side, he fastened his pants and looked into her eyes. They had changed from the green of hate to a smoky blue of confusion. Raising his hand, he lightly stroked her cheek.

"I didn't want to hurt you," he whispered softly.

"You are my wife now in name and body. We did not make love; we consummated the marriage. When we finally make love, you will want it as much as I do."

"It will never happen," she said.

Brant rose and looked down at his wife. His brown eyes were soft with emotion. His action had not fulfilled him physically and his body ached for release. He didn't know how this would affect their relationship. She already hated him, but he was determined to work to break down the emotional barriers she had erected against him. He would make her crave the physical bond he intended to introduce slowly.

Amber heard the door shut a few seconds later, and she raised her hands to cover her face. Why had everything gotten so complicated? She belonged to Brant in the most intimate way, yet she had not made love or felt the weight of his naked flesh. She could not even call it rape. She had not wanted it, but he had been gentle and considerate of her pain. Why had Brant wanted to make the marriage real? It was puzzling.

Rising, she fastened her pants and walked to the door. Perhaps work would help ease her troubled thoughts. Stepping outside, she walked across the compound. Her attention was captured by the activity near her brother's place of imprisonment. Driven by curiosity, she changed direction and watched with uncertainty and apprehension. A wagon pulled up before the hut and two men went inside. Amber stopped near Brant and Edgar, her eyes searching her husband's face for an explanation. The two men reappeared in the doorway and stepped outside. Stretched between the men was the limp body of her brother. A deep trembling began in her stomach and raced through her limbs. A knot of grief rose in her throat. There was no gentleness as the men tossed him into the wagon. She stepped forward, her eyes fixed on her brother.

Edgar's voice landed heavily on her ears. "There won't be a hangin'. We're lucky the fever took him."

"My trip here was worthless," Brant growled. "He wouldn't tell me anything."

Amber staggered. Andy was dead. Grief bubbled through her thoughts and emotional pain swelled in her body. Not wanting to show these men her agony, Amber blocked the outward show of her grief. But even for Amber, who had always been able to control her emotions, this was too much. Her body responded the only way that was left. She slumped forward in a faint.

Exhaustion and the loss of her brother kept her in the depths of unconsciousness, and she didn't want to surface and face the realities of life. She ached inside and the constant throb of grief pounded in her mind. The bond with her twin had been strong and she felt empty and alone.

Finally, unable to remain oblivious to her surroundings, she woke. Throwing aside the blanket covering her, she sat up and swung her legs over the side of the bed.

"I'm glad you are finally awake," Brant said, coming to sit at her side. "How are you feeling?"

"Does it matter?" she asked flippantly. Nothing seemed important with Andy dead.

Brant scowled. "Yes, it does," he said gently. She had received a tremendous shock and he wanted to help her through it.

"Why didn't you tell me he was sick? Didn't you think I would care?" she asked, reflecting on Brant's deceit.

"You know medicine. You must have guessed he wasn't well."

"I suspected, but I didn't know it was serious."

"He loved you," Brant said simply. "He asked me to tell you."

Amber lunged at Brant, her fists flying at his face. "I loved him and I'll never forgive you for not letting me see him."

He caught her flailing wrists and looked into her eyes. Everything about her mirrored hate, not grief. She had been through a lot, but her actions were not normal.

"Why don't you cry for him?" he asked softly.

Amber stared at him. There may not be an outward show of grief, but she was sobbing inside. "Why don't you mind your own business?"

"You are my business," he warned. Her grief had to be tearing her apart. Why couldn't she be soft and open with her emotions? She had shown others her vulnerable side. Why wouldn't she let him see it? As a rule he hated sniveling females, but there were times when tears expressed a very deep pain and offered release from inner agony. This was one of those times.

"You don't have to hide your emotions. I understand your pain."

Amber's eyes darkened. "The only emotions you will ever see from me are anger and hate."

Brant knew there was no point in arguing, and he slowly rose from the bed. She was coping with her grief the only way she knew how. What had happened to bottle up her emotions? He desperately wanted to break down that barrier.

He picked up a dress and tossed it to her. "Put that on. My reasons for being here no longer exist. We are leaving."

"What is wrong with pants?" she asked. "They are more comfortable."

"You are a woman and will dress like one." Amber didn't move. "Are you going to change, or do I get to hclp?"

Scowling, she turned her back and put the frock on. The hooks up the back proved to be a problem, and Brant pushed her hands away to complete the work.

"Let's get out of here. I can't wait to get you out of my sight."

Brant threw back his head and laughed. "Have you forgotten you're my wife?"

"How could I?" she asked dryly. She had married him because she believed it would help her brother. Her hope had been shattered and she was bound to an overbearing man.

Edgar was waiting by the horses. His farewell to Amber was hostile and she was glad to be leaving. He was one man she never wanted to meet again.

Her stallion wore the Confederate blanket and saddle, but all weapons had been removed. Brant was not taking any chances with her.

"Will the prisoners be given care?" she asked as they galloped out of the compound.

"The doctor will be back today."

"Where was Andy buried?" she asked, hoping he

would allow her to see his final resting place.

"He was put in an unmarked grave. I personally took care of it."

Amber flinched at the sharpness of his words. His coldness showed his spite for the enemy, and her hate for him deepened. Turning, she looked at the street through the center of town. Myra had probably returned to Washington to tell Hank what she had attempted.

"Forget it Amber," he said. "I won't let you go."

A chill ran down her spine. This was a man with a purpose, and she would have to be prepared to meet him in battle. The North would meet the South in the war of husband against wife.

Twelve

Amber was uneasy about being pushed deeper into Confederate territory. Every mile they traveled south made it more dangerous and difficult to escape. They stayed away from the battle areas, and their travel was not interrupted by fighting. They followed the road as it wound around the mountains and hills, the lush green of summer offering occasional shade from the hot summer sun.

Until escape became possible, Amber was determined to remain alert to the movements of the Rebels and pass information if the opportunity arose. With the death of Andy her need to see the Confederates defeated was twofold.

"What are you thinking about?" Brant asked curiously.

"I'm sure you wouldn't be interested."

"I'm interested in everything you think and do."

Amber arched her brow and looked at him. "Really? Why?"

His gaze dropped to her lips. "I think you already

149

know the answer to that. . . . I have never met a woman like you."

"Is that a compliment?" she asked reluctantly.

Brant shrugged. "It might be."

"What you think doesn't interest me in the least," she said, brushing aside his remark.

"Always the cool, unruffled female," he remarked casually. "You have shown emotions of ice, but passions full of warmth and promise."

Amber laughed. "It is not my passion. It is your lust." She met his gaze, her blue-green eyes twinkling in mockery. "If you are not careful, you will let a woman be your downfall."

Amber waited until she heard the sharp intake of his breath before digging her heels into the stallion and letting him take his head. Brant's horse picked up the pace, but he stayed behind her. Amber was a shrewd, perceptive woman and could never be underestimated. On more than one occasion he had let his judgment of her cloud his thinking.

Scowling, he looked at her slim figure. He had never thought to ask her if she rode. It was something he had taken for granted, just like so many other things she did. He grudgingly admired the way she handled the stallion and wondered what other skills she possessed he hadn't even touched on.

When she was in his arms, he experienced excitement he had never dreamed possible. Her desire was real, but he sensed an immature passion that was slowly awakening under his careful arousal of her senses. Her work with the sick had given her an undeniable awareness of the male body, but he knew she had not felt a man's naked length. He had broken her

150

maidenhead, but had not filled her with the driving passion of love-making. Brant was determined to be the man who would stir that need and make her dependent.

He scanned the sky. It was almost time to stop and make camp. Thus far they had avoided the fighting, but they were nearing a trouble spot and he would have to be on his guard. He knew Amber would seize the first opportunity to escape and wondered if he had been right in forcing her to remove the Confederate uniform. It might have made her more cautious about running toward the Union soldiers. From a distance they wouldn't know her from a man.

"Hold up," he ordered, riding to her side. When she didn't stop, he grabbed her horse's reins and slowed the stallion. "It is time to rest. We will make camp in that stand of trees."

Amber regarded him with a smirk on her face. "Are you sure we can't continue?" Her eyes twinkled mischievously. "Of course if you are too tired . . ."

"I'm not," he growled. "But I thought you might be."

"I could go on all night," she said, brushing the amber hair from her shoulders.

Brant's eyes narrowed and he wondered at her teasing mood. "The animals need rest."

She shrugged. "If you want to use them as an excuse, it is fine with me."

His hand clamped around her wrist. "What game are you playing?"

"Game?" she asked innocently and without fear. "I definitely don't consider this war a game."

Brant tipped his head to the side. "Never underestimate the enemy. They are as sure in their beliefs as you are in yours." His eyes darkened. "Especially don't underestimate me. I'm wise to your tricks and I won't let you make a fool of me." He reflected on the two times she had freed herself from his embrace using physical tactics.

Amber laughed. "Thus far it hasn't been too difficult. I believe I could wrap you around my little finger and lead you around like a dog."

Reaching over, he grabbed Amber's arms and dragged her onto his horse. She felt the powerful thighs against her buttocks and the ironclad grip around her waist. Brant's lips were thinned in a dangerous line and the muscles in his cheek were tense. Amber knew they would meet in battle—two strong foes fighting for what they believed. Who would be the victor in their war?

"You are pushing too far," he warned.

"Am I?" she dared, refusing to let him bully her. "You don't frighten me."

"So you think I'm a brute." The line of his lips curved into a smile.

"Brute or bully, take your choice. You think because you're strong that you will be able to bend me to your will." She smiled confidently. "It won't work. Just because you violated me doesn't mean I will fall into your bed."

"No?" he quizzed, drawing her against his chest. "I believe differently." His gaze dropped to her lips. "When it happens, you'll want me as much as I want you."

"You are going to be disappointed. I don't find you attractive."

Brant chuckled softly and said confidently, "When the time comes you will respond."

She looked him straight in the eye. "I'm bored. Would you put me down so I can get on my horse."

His hold on her tightened as he reached for the reins of her stallion. "You can ride with me. . . . Not scared, are you?" he baited.

"Of course not, but I would rather ride my stallion."

"I prefer it this way," he countered and urged the animal forward.

Brant stopped the horses beneath a cluster of trees, and they dismounted. After surveying the surroundings, he reached for the small bundle of supplies strapped to his saddle. Opening his blanket, he spread it on the ground and sat down.

"We'll eat a cold meal. A fire might draw the attention of the enemy."

"In my case you wouldn't be warning the enemy," she argued, wishing a Union troop would come along.

She removed her blanket and tossed it to the ground. Hunger gnawed at her stomach and she reluctantly accepted the food. Sitting a safe distance away, she studied the countryside in the hope of finding a way to escape.

"You are not leaving," Brant said casually.

"I don't know what you are talking about."

"I'm learning to read your thoughts."

Amber glowered at him. Predictability was something she couldn't risk. It would hamper her eventual escape attempt and keep Brant constantly on guard.

"Really?" she said innocently. "What was I thinking?'

"You were plotting an escape."

Amber laughed, her voice a low melodic sound. "I would be foolish to escape."

Brant regarded her thoughtfully. "A few minutes ago you were making sure I was aware of your contempt. Are you ready to surrender to me?"

"Who is talking about giving up? Perhaps I have decided I want to go with you to Confederate headquarters."

"Is this another one of your tricks?"

"No, but I am going to make this forced captivity work to my advantage."

"How?"

"You said you can read my mind. Figure it out for yourself."

Angrily, Brant rose and crossed to her side. Reaching down, he grabbed her arms and hauled her against his chest. "I don't need your snide comments. I don't know what you think you are going to do, but don't try anything foolish."

"Who is the fool?" she flung back. "You could have hanged me as a spy, yet you let your physical desire override your responsibility as an officer. You were forced into a marriage with a woman who hates you."

"Who said I was forced?" he said, looking into her eyes. "I was the highest ranking officer. No man there could tell me what to do."

Amber had expected some retort, but not one with so much frankness. Stunned, she stared at him. What possible benefit could their marriage have for him?

"I won't believe you wanted to marry me."

Brant smiled and his eyes roamed down her body.

"Having you for my wife has its benefits. You are a very desirable woman and I enjoy the prospect of sharing my bed with you and experiencing a night of passion-filled love."

Amber's mouth went dry at the implications of his verbal love-making. Why did he have the power to stir her body with mere words?

"I would rather hang for treason."

"Have you ever seen a man hanged?" he quizzed, his hand sliding to her throat. "The noose catches you about here." His fingers pressed against her throat. "You wait, wondering when the door at your feet will fall away, or the horse you are sitting on will vanish beneath you." Amber looked into his eyes determined not to show fear. "Suddenly, the rope tightens. If you are lucky your neck breaks. If not, the rope closes off your air supply until your body feels ready to explode." His fingers tightened to block the precious supply of air to her lungs. Amber's mouth went slack as the pressure increased. Her fingers clawed at the hand against her throat. The pain was intense, his features blurring into blackness as she slumped against him.

Her breath returned in a gasp, but she was unable to control the weakness in her limbs, and she was forced to rely on Brant. Her hand protectively covered her bruised throat, frightened for the first time of the physical strength this man possessed. Had he wanted to kill her, she would be dead. Her head rolled against Brant's shoulder as he lifted her into his arms and carried her to his blanket. Gently placing her on the fabric, he stepped away to retrieve her bedroll. Back at her side he stretched out and pulled her

155

against his body. Amber still felt too weak to protest, but when his body fitted against her back and buttocks, her senses were alerted.

"No," she muttered, trying to break free. "Let me go."

"I am not going to let you escape."

His hand flattened across her stomach directly below her breast. "Tie me up," she said breathlessly. She couldn't remain this close to him all night. She never knew what he might try to do, and if he imprisoned her with his weight she would be helpless.

Not wanting to mock what he knew would be a sensitive area for her, he queried softly, "Are you frightened of me?'

Amber feared this man, but his physical strength was just one of the reasons. She was also frightened of the power he had over her.

"Do you finally believe that I am in control of the situation and don't intend to let you go free?" His hand slid to her throat. "When we get to headquarters, don't try spying. You are my wife, but my protection can only go so far. I am an officer first and I won't hesitate to betray you."

Amber knew he spoke the truth. The marriage had been forced on him, so there was no emotional bond, no sense of commitment to make the marriage a success. She had not been able to use her physical attraction to manipulate him with regard to Andy's life and doubted it would work with spying. If he got her to the headquarters, she would live in fear of being betrayed. She had to escape him and the confusing complication of their marriage.

Amber stirred restlessly during the night and Brant

continually tightened his grip. As hard as she tried to ignore the body fitted against the curve of hers, she was unable to do it. She had never spent the night in the arms of a man, and the experience was shattering. At dawn Brant left her side and she scrambled to her feet.

"Are you always so restless when you sleep?" he complained. "Or aren't you used to sleeping with a man?"

"That," she said pointedly, "is none of your business."

Brant chuckled. "You just answered my question."

She threw her hands on her hips. "Don't be too sure. You don't know anything about my past association with men."

Brant couldn't resist baiting her. He wanted to know how much fire was underneath that amber hair. "I know you were untouched," he said, reminding her of the brief intimacy they had shared. "With the exception of that one incident you have always melted in my arms."

"I was held there against my will," she reminded him.

"I don't want to use my strength with you. . . . Amber, you were where you wanted to be . . . Where you belonged."

"You certainly have an inflated opinion of yourself." She glared at him. "You used your strength when you violated me."

"Only in the beginning. You stopped fighting me. It wasn't rape," he whispered.

Amber was inexperienced, but she knew there had to be more to the physical side of a relationship than

157

what had happened. Everything was so quick.

"Brant," she began. "Why did you stop?"

He was surprised by her question, and it proved she had been giving the incident some thought. Had it sparked her curiosity? Was she possibly ready to start accepting their passion?

"You were afraid." He saw the angry flash in her eyes and knew she was going to deny her fear. He raised his finger to her lips. "I didn't want our first time to be without feeling. We will have our marriage night and you will eagerly accept our coupling. You are a woman awakening to her desires."

She brushed away his finger. "Is that what you think I'm doing? You are driven by lust. You want me, but I don't want to make love to you. I have too many reasons to hate you," she said sadly.

"Do you know how to make a man want you?" he teased.

Amber's lips curled in a smile. "I must. You want to crawl into my bed."

Brant whistled between his teeth. She had successfully made him look like a fool. His eyes narrowed and Amber knew she had wounded his pride.

"I want to know if you can lure a man to your bed. Do you have the skills?"

"Of course," she remarked. "But you are not going to see them."

"We are married. It is perfectly all right to seduce your husband."

Amber glared at him. "I don't recognize you as my husband. Our marriage was forced."

"But nonetheless valid. Can you pretend to be in love with me?"

"I choke on the thought," she said crisply. "I can't see any reason to pretend affection for you."

"What if I told you it might make a difference to my—."

The sound of horses' hoofs propelled Brant into action. Seizing Amber around the waist, he grabbed the bedrolls, tossed them over the horses' saddles, picked up the reins, and led them into the woods. Wrapping the reins around a bush, he turned to Amber.

She had finally realized what was happening and struggled for freedom. Before she could scream a warning, his hand clamped across her lips and his arm tightened around her waist. Her eyes widened and her shoulders sagged in defeat when Union troops rode past. Amber bitterly regretted that she had not heard the soldiers first. A Confederate officer would be an important capture.

The group had long since passed when Brant let her go. "We better get moving. I didn't expect Union activity this early." His mouth drooped in a frown. "I hope we don't run into a battle."

Amber hoped the opposite but didn't bother to voice her opinion. From now on, she would have to stay alert and hope for the chance to escape. Brant, however, intended to be prepared, and he tied her horse to his so she couldn't flee.

There was no trouble until early afternoon when someone took a shot at them. Although Brant had been the target, she was in his company and had to be very cautious. Urging the horses into the brush, they dismounted. Brant dragged Amber into the bushes and kept his hand tightly clamped around her wrist while he scanned the terrain. Amber had not seen anyone and didn't know where the shot had come from. After fifteen minutes of silence, Brant nudged her arm.

"Unless you want to force me into killing him keep your mouth shut." He pointed to a tree and Amber saw the man high in the limbs. His position gave him an excellent view of the road, but the brush kept them hidden from sight. If Brant got closer he could easily shoot the man. A knot rose in Amber's throat. She didn't want a senseless killing.

He pulled on her arm. "Are you ready?" he asked, reaching for the horse's reins.

"No," she pleaded. "Don't kill him."

"Afraid to see one of your soldiers die?" he sneered. "He tried to end our lives. Why should he live?"

"No," she argued. "Don't take his life."

He stared at her for several seconds. "I won't hurt him unless it is necessary."

Amber eyes widened in surprise. She never suspected her pleas would be considered by him.

Brant laughed. "I am afraid you might get hurt if there are shots fired." His gaze dropped to her lips. "I am not finished with you."

As long as the man lived she didn't care what his reasons were. "He will never see us if we cut through the trees. There might be more soldiers around, so stick close." His gaze dropped to her breasts. "I don't have to remind you that you are a target for scavengers and men who haven't been with a woman for a long time. It is something you would be wise to remember before you decide to run away."

Keeping a firm grip on her wrist, he led them slowly and cautiously through the dense brush. When they were a safe distance away, they mounted the horses. Brant held Amber's reins, unwilling to give her the chance to flee.

Gunfire was heard late in the afternoon and Brant changed directions to avoid a confrontation with troops from either side. They stopped at dusk and ate another cold meal. After checking the horses, Brant spread the blanket on the ground.

"It is time for bed," he said, waiting for her to stretch out on the blanket.

"I'm not tired," she argued. "You can go to sleep if you want," she said, shrugging. "I'll sit here for a while."

Growling deep in his throat, Brant crossed to Amber. Anticipating his intention, she jumped to the side and got behind him. Brant faced her, his hands on his hips. "So you feel like playing," he said, a smile parting his lips. "You know I will be the winner."

"I am not tired. I will make my bed on this side of the fire."

"No you won't," he said lunging for her. He caught her arm at the same time Amber twisted. Her movement threw them off guard and they fell. Brant chuckled when they landed on the blanket. "This is where I wanted us to be though I never expected my tactics would be quite like this."

Neither had Amber. She had landed flat on her back with Brant's body stretched across hers. He was a big man and his weight pressed her firmly against the earth. The corner of his mouth curved in a smile.

"I wonder if you expected this to happen."

"Certainly not," she spat, "or I would not have resisted."

Brant shifted his position to bring his weight onto his arms; nevertheless, Amber still felt his body from breast to mid-thigh. If she thought their position had been compromising last night, this was doubly so, and she felt every muscle in his lean torso.

"Move," she demanded. "I want to get up."

He chuckled deep in his throat. "I think this is very comfortable. It might be a nice way to sleep."

"If you don't mind being crushed to death," she sputtered sarcastically.

Once again Brant shifted, forcing his weight onto his hip and pushing his thigh between her legs. Amber felt the hard thrust of his body and experienced a strange flutter in her stomach. If Brant had intended to make her aware of his body, he had been successful, and Amber found the awakening very disturbing. She tried to slow her breathing so she would not give away her uncertainty. How did their brief intimacy at the prison fit in with their passion? What had she missed by his quick withdrawal? The aroused part of her body wanted to know.

Pulling her against his side, he cradled her head in the crook of his shoulder. His free arm lay heavy across her abdomen, his hand curving just below her breast. Every place his body touched hers she experienced unexplained tingling. His warm breath caressed her cheek. Unconsciously, her head turned and found his face inches from her. Raising her eyes, she looked into the brown depths of his gaze. She had his complete attention and she nervously moistened her lips.

Unable to keep meeting his eyes, she dropped her

gaze and found herself staring at his mouth. She had been fascinated by the firm sensual line of his lips from the beginning. Her heart surged in an unexplained flutter, and she breathed deeply to calm herself. Her breath, however, only forced her breast against the side of his chest, and she felt the soft flesh compressed by his muscular torso.

Amber wanted to move, but her limbs felt weighted by a languorous sensation of awareness. She hated the craving need and hated herself for responding to this man's nearness. She suddenly felt weak, powerless over him and herself. Her thoughts had wandered to forbidden territory. She wanted more than he was offering; she wanted her husband.

Amber shook her head. Where was her imagination taking her? This man was the enemy and she could never weaken her defenses against him. He had not helped Andy and her brother was dead. She could never look past that incident and see him as a trusted lover and friend. There was also the fact that the passion he stirred in her made her feel weak, and that was something this man must never see.

"Go to sleep Amber. We have a long day tomorrow."

She muttered an exasperated sigh. Did he expect her to sleep when her body was in a knot of turmoil? She didn't know if she wanted to run or press closer. Turning her head, she closed her eyes. She could never let him see her conflict. They still had to meet in battle and she wanted to be the victor.

When Amber's head turned, Brant let a sly smile part his lips. Things had gone better than he had planned. He had watched her face and witnessed her confusion. She was physically aware of him, but she fought her response. At one point he believed her young body had pressed closer to his, but he had fought his desire and remained noncommittal. He had not stirred enough of her passion to make her his. She was too willing to fight and when he made love to her he didn't want it to be a battle.

He suspected her emotional awareness was blocking her free response. She blamed him for Andy's death, their marriage, and for some reason she would not show him her vulnerability.

Amber's breath returned to normal and she slid into a deep sleep. Brant joined her soon after, their bodies as close as lovers, but divided by the barrier of hate that kept them on opposing sides. Amber could not—would not—feel anything for the enemy. It would be like betraying her father and brother.

Thirteen

Unwilling to surrender the lethargic feeling holding her limbs in a steadying peace, Amber kept her eyes closed and burrowed toward the enjoyable stimulant. She had been able to forget her troubles, and her dreams had been pleasant and filled with security and arms of strength. If she could feel like this forever, she never wanted to wake and remember the harsh realities of war.

Brant's brown eyes opened slowly to focus on the amber strands of hair against his shoulder. He had spent one of his most restful nights, but he had awakened longing for the woman at his side. His attention switched to her face. She was one of the most attractive females he had ever seen, and he was amazed by her beauty. He not only found her physical beauty alluring, but he admired her boldness, spunk and skills.

Amber snuggled closer to him and Brant tightened his arms around her. Did she know what she was doing? Or was she reacting to the warmth of his body? He sighed, his breath teasing the thick strands of hair.

He was already aroused by her nearness, and he experienced an aching need to lose himself inside her body and make her his.

By tonight they would reach their destination, and Amber would join him in his bed. Would she be ready to respond to his teasing caresses? Or would she brush him away? He knew it was risky taking her to headquarters and hoped she would behave herself. If anyone learned she was a Northerner, his credibility as an officer would be questioned. Despite the risk, he had to take her with him. He couldn't let her out of his life.

Brant watched her eyes open and dart around uncertainly. Slowly, she met his gaze. His lips curved in a sensuous smile, reminding Amber of the night in his arms. There was little space separating them, and she felt the muscles in his body pressed against hers. It was a feeling that made her weak and uncertain. Her awareness of Brant was steadily increasing, and she noticed everything: the flexing of a muscle, the attractiveness of his face, the firm line of his mouth, and all the mannerisms that made him Brant. She didn't like the feeling of power he had over her and knew she had to fight it. He was the enemy—a man she couldn't trust.

Her lips parted to ask him to move, but nothing came from her throat as his hand tangled in her hair, and his fingers threaded through the silky strands. There was something teasing in the sensuous caress and her pulse surged uncertainly. His palm spread over her cheek with a tenderness that made her quiver. Upon reaching her mouth, his fingers lightly stroked her lower lip until it trembled. His face was close to hers and besides feeling his warm breath on her cheeks, she saw the rising need in his brown eyes. Brant wanted her and the knowledge took her breath.

Shifting, he covered her body and held himself up on his elbows. His eyes slowly roamed her face, touching every inch of her flesh with a heated caress. His gaze dropped to her breasts, and she felt their thrust against the fabric of her gown.

Amber's hands pressed uncertainly against his forearms, powerless to push him away. There was a tightness in her chest she couldn't explain, a breathlessness caused by his nearness. Brant had stimulated her desire and she had surrendered. He wasn't like most men she had known. His kisses had been drugging, yet he had not plundered her lips since the prison. Several times he had aroused her, but he refrained from caressing her mouth, and Amber found herself craving his touch.

Brant's head dropped, his lips brushing her cheek. One of his hands dropped to her shoulder, kneading the skin with sensuous expertise. Gently, his teeth nipped the lobe of her ear while his tongue tickled the flesh. His hand curved between the valley of her breasts.

Amber's heart surged against her chest, and she wondered if he could feel the excited pounding. Her eyes became a sultry green, her lids dropping from arousal. A faint flush covered her creamy cheeks, and her breath no longer came in regular pace. When Brant's hand curved over the roundness of her breast, his lips dropped to her neck. Even through the clothes she felt the betraying peak harden against his palm. In the past Amber had repelled the men who had tried

167

to touch her intimately, but now found herself unable to rebuff the caress.

Turning her head, she found her lips against his sun-bronzed cheek. His skin had a pleasant male scent that added to his masculinity. His lower body pressed against hers and she felt his arousal against her thigh. She remembered the time she had felt his desire without the barrier of clothes, and a strange flutter rolled her stomach.

"Amber," he muttered. "I want you." His thumb caressed the tip of her breast. "My beautiful wife. . . ."

She turned her head and searched for his lips, wanting to feel them against hers. Throwing her caution away, her hands slid to his shoulders to pull him closer. Brant's mouth followed the line of her jaw to her chin. Amber's excitement heightened as she waited for the touch of his lips against hers.

The explosion of a cannon followed by gunfire put an abrupt halt to their love-making. Brant, once again the soldier, rolled off Amber and rose. Grabbing his rifle, he ran across camp. Amber, drugged by the nearness of his body, slowly sat and tried to collect her scattered sense. She had let her desire run away with her good senses. Had it not been for the interruption she would have made a commitment to the enemy and never forgiven herself for it.

Smoothing back her hair, she struggled for composure. She didn't want Brant to witness the confusion she felt. Glancing sideways, she saw him saddling the horses. The explosion had warned of troop activity and Amber knew Union soldiers meant freedom. Scrambling to her feet, she ran toward the trees. She had not gotten more than a few feet before Brant grabbed her around the waist and forced her against his body.

"Let me go," she screamed. "Take your hands off me."

"You are not going anyplace. Did you hear that cannon?"

Her eyes flashed hate. "I heard it and it means Union soldiers. I want to get away from you."

Brant slowly smiled. "I wouldn't have believed that a few minutes ago."

Amber's cheeks flamed. How dare he remind her of what had happened between them! He was certainly no gentleman. "How dare you!" she exclaimed and wished she could slap his face.

"With you I would *dare* almost anything." Amber swung her booted foot at his leg, catching him in the shin. "That is enough," he warned. "We have to get out of here. I don't want to get caught in a battle."

Amber was pulled tightly against his chest, and his nearness reminded her of their earlier contact. A familiar flutter started in her stomach, but she squelched it before weakness invaded her limbs.

"Let me go," she snarled.

"Let the lady go," a voice commanded, and Amber and Brant turned their heads. "I said let the lady go," he repeated.

Slowly, Brant's hands dropped to his side and Amber stepped back. The Union soldiers surrounding them made escape impossible. Amber's shoulders sagged with relief, and she shot Brant a smug look. His eyes darkened to a deep brown and the muscles in his jaw flexed in anger.

"Who is in charge?" she asked and a man stepped forward.

"I'm Sergeant McDonald," he answered.

"This man has been holding me prisoner with the intention of taking me to Confederate headquarters. I am the niece of Major Henry Rawlins currently stationed in Washington. I am sure you will receive special acknowledgement for getting me out of the hands of this Confederate pig." Amber sneered at Brant.

"We are glad to be of service. If you will come with me, I'll take you to the commanding officer."

Amber stepped to his side. "We heard cannon fire. What happened?"

"We met a small troop of Rebels." He motioned to two of his men. "Bring the horses and the major. Lieutenant Anders will want to question him."

Amber walked at the sergeant's side, totally oblivious to Brant. She didn't want to know what happened to him. From their first meeting he had been an upsetting factor in her life, and it was time to put him out of her mind. She wouldn't plead for him; he deserved whatever punishment they gave him.

They walked for nearly twenty minutes before they arrived at the temporary Union camp. Amber was introduced to Lieutenant Peter Anders. A moustache hid part of his upper lip, but Amber didn't miss the smile of pleasure when they were introduced. After taking her to the food tent for something to eat, he left to see Brant.

Amber ate quickly, then stepped outside. Unwillingly, she scanned the camp for Brant, wondering what had happened to him. She told herself it didn't matter, but the memory of his body against hers was hard to erase. A part of her was glad he was no longer a threat to her maidenhood. He was a man out of her league and despite her flirtatious times with men, she had been totally unprepared for his male dominance. The other part of her, the side she didn't want to admit, ached for the loss of not knowing what it would be like in his arms tasting the untalked of pleasures of her body. She was certain he could teach her everything she needed to know.

Suddenly, Amber straightened. Where was she letting her thoughts wander? Brant was her husband, but she could not — would not — allow even him intimate liberties when there was no love.

Amber's gaze slid over the soldiers sprawled in the grass and her thoughts strayed to Andy. His death was a vivid nightmare she wanted to block from her mind. Part of her had died with him, and she knew time would not heal the emptiness. She had the inner strength to continue with her life and would put his death, like her father's, in proper perspective. Too much had been taken from her, and she would continue with stronger determination to do all she could for the Northern cause. Amber knew the best way she could help was through medicine. There were too few good medical people and her skills were necessary.

Amber was determined to return to the hospital. Uncle Hank would have to understand and be patient. Amber frowned. Convincing him would not be easy. Myra had probably returned with the news of her capture and Hank would be furious that she had tried to free Andy.

One of the soldiers rode through the camp and ordered the men to take down the tents and pack the supplies. An enemy troop was headed their way and they had to move.

There was still no sign of Brant, and she decided he was still being questioned. His rank made him an excellent source of information though she doubted he would confess details. He would never bend to another man or woman's will. He was his own man— proud and confident. Reluctantly, Amber had to admit he was probably an excellent officer. Why had he chosen to battle against the North? The question hovered in her mind. If they were on the same side would her feelings for him be different? He would still be the same man—strong and threatening. How would she cope?

"Miss Rawlins," Lieutenant Anders said, interrupting her thoughts.

Amber turned, grateful for the interruption. Brant was the enemy and nothing was going to change that. "Is there going to be a battle?"

"I hope not. They outnumber us, and I'm not willing to sacrifice my men needlessly."

"A wise decision," she praised.

"I'm afraid it will delay your return to Washington for a day or two, but it can't be avoided." He frowned. "I cannot offer you accommodations befitting a lady."

Amber smiled. "I wouldn't expect it. I would like to help care for your wounded." Lieutenant Anders arched his brows in surprise. "I understand your hesitation," she said in a sympathetic tone. "I have worked with some of the best physicians. Until two days ago I was at a Confederate prison taking care of Union soldiers." She sighed. "They were in desperate

172

need of care."

"I've heard of the prison," he admitted. "It may not have been good, but it is better than most." He paused. "Our wounded have been transferred to a field hospital."

"Have you learned anything from Major Faulkner?" she quizzed, aching to know something about Brant.

"Not yet." Peter shrugged. "But we have our ways. I will get something out of him."

Amber's stomach clamped unexpectedly. Even her intense dislike for Brant had not prepared her for the possibility that he might be tortured. Amber shook off the uncertain feeling.

"Your horse is ready."

Thanking him, she walked toward the stallion and mounted. She wished she didn't have to wear a dress, but if she asked for pants the request would shock Peter. He had been surprised enough to learn of her medical work.

Amber guessed there were about one hundred men in the outfit. Four wagons loaded with supplies were waiting near two horse-drawn cannons. Travel would be slow because only the officers and infantry were given horses.

Her eyes stopped on the gray-clothed man less than fifty feet away. Brant's horse had been confiscated and given to a Union man, so he was on foot. His wrists had been secured to a long rope which was held by one of the infantry.

At that moment Brant turned his head and their eyes clashed. Amber's emotions churned uncertainly as she stared into the brown gaze. Slowly, a smile spread across her face. She would not feel desire for him, nor would she feel pity. He was the enemy and the harsh treatment was what he deserved.

Brant was in trouble, but she saw a mocking smile curve his lips. Amber clamped her jaw tightly. Brant was on the losing end, a prisoner, yet he had the nerve to find the situation humorous. Brant Faulkner was exasperating. Determined to put him out of her thoughts, she turned her head and nudged the stallion forward.

Gunfire was heard in the distance, but they didn't meet any resistance. Brief stops were made for food and rest, and each time Amber scanned the camp for Brant, hoping to find him exhausted. His uniform was covered by a thin film of dust, but his eyes and body were alert and untouched by the travel.

They made camp on a small rise near the river bank. It gave them an excellent view of the surrounding land and adequate protection from surprise attack. Tents were not set up because their stay was only for the night. Peter joined Amber for dinner.

"Feel free to walk around, but stay inside the camp," he said when they had finished eating. "Tomorrow you will start back to Washington. I hope you will give it serious thought before you leave the city again."

Amber ignored his suggestion. "I heard about Gettysburg. Were many lives lost?"

"We kept General Lee from advancing, but it was a bloody battle. Thousands of men died. Medical personnel were desperately needed." He shook his head sadly. "General Grant took Vicksburg. We now control the Mississippi River."

"When will it end?" she asked thoughtfully.

"I don't think it will be soon." He rose. "Excuse me. I have to meet with the officers."

Rising, Amber walked forward and scanned the flickering campfires. The soft, melancholy hum of a harmonica created a somber atmosphere. Sighing, she wondered how many of the soldiers would survive the next battle. How many more wives, mothers and sisters would grieve over the loss of loved ones as she had? How much longer before the barrier of hate would be shattered?

She stopped abruptly near a sheltered stand of trees. Was she any different from the men fighting? She hated the Confederates and wanted them brought to their knees. She had been unable to look past her hatred of the enemy and see Brant as a man responsible for introducing new feelings. Was it because she feared her response? It couldn't be the reason. She was never scared of anything.

Amber turned to start back to her bedroll, but stopped at the sight of Brant securely bound to a tree. She walked toward him, determined to prove to herself that she wasn't afraid of him.

Brant was the prisoner, but he had adopted a casual air that surprised her. His smile mocked the danger and her arrival.

"I am glad to see you are finally where you belong," she gloated, her hands on her slim hips. She stopped at his feet.

"I am surprised you feel that way," he said, his smile deepening.

"Why should I feel differently? You are the enemy."

Brant laughed softly. "You have a different ap-

175

proach for fighting your battles."

"What is that supposed to mean?" she snapped.

"Did you intend to defeat me by making love to me?"

Amber gasped. "No," she denied.

"No?" he repeated, his brow arched in surprise. "You invited my caresses and were eager for the touch of my lips." He moved his arms. "Why don't you get a knife and cut me loose? We can continue where we left off."

Amber stomped her foot. "You arrogant Rebel. I wasn't interested in your caresses or kisses. I don't even like you."

"I know," he said dryly. "I'm the enemy. You have told me often enough." He regarded her through narrowed eyes. "You are afraid to admit that you want me. You are using my loyalty to the South as an excuse because you are scared. . . . What if we were on the same side?"

She had asked herself the same question, but had not searched for the answer, and didn't intend to. She had never been called a coward. Her father had taught her never to show fear or weakness to a strong-willed man. "I'm not afraid of you."

"Then you are afraid of yourself," he taunted.

"I have never been frightened of anything in my life," she gritted, angered that he would challenge her. She glanced at the guard, grateful that he was out of hearing distance.

Brant had despised women who acted like cowards and cried over everything, but he expected some show of the soft emotions. Why did Amber refuse to exhibit any toward him?

"Who ever told you a woman couldn't be soft and have fears. Who made you so hard? Did a man hurt you?"

"No. Would you rather have me sobbing and clinging helplessly to men?"

"I would like a woman who wasn't afraid to admit the truth."

Amber laughed to hide her uncertainty. "You are dreaming up things in your free time."

Brant remained silent, but his brown eyes slowly wandered over her face. His gaze made Amber tremble uncertainly. Her flesh burned with an intensity that left her limbs shaking. His eyes dropped to her lips, his own mouth parting to give Amber the full view of his sensuous lips. Flashes of how they had caressed her body swam in her subconscious. Her breath quickened, forcing her breasts to strain against the fabric. Brant's gaze dropped and a smile of satisfaction curved his lips.

"Are you still going to tell me there is nothing between us, my dear wife?"

Rather than answer him, Amber turned and calmly walked away. Brant made her furious and she hated the reminder of their marriage. She didn't care what happened to him. Tomorrow she would return to Washington and he would be out of her life forever.

Fourteen

Amber rose at dawn and had breakfast with the soldiers before mounting her horse for the trip north. Twenty men had been assigned to accompany her to the nearest Northern-held train station. Her eyes locked briefly with Brant's brown-eyed gaze before she rode out of camp. Her face was expressionless, the vulnerable, confused emotions locked carefully away.

It took three days to reach a depot with trains running to Washington. Her escort made sure she had money and a seat on the train before returning to the battlefield.

The trip to Washington was long and tiring, and Amber had nothing to do but sit and think about what had happened. Andy's death would not be a shock to Hank. He expected him to die anyway and would probably tell her it was better he had not died at the end of a hangman's noose.

She was determined to keep her encounter with Brant a secret, but the marriage could complicate things. Brant had made annulment impossible and she would have to pursue the possibility of divorce. One thing was certain. He was out of her life, and she was determined to push him out of her thoughts. The passion they had shared was in the past, and when she was free, she hoped to find a man to block out the memory of Brant Faulkner—husband, enemy, and Rebel.

The Washington depot was bustling with activity. More than one hundred soldiers waited to board the train and Amber was caught in the confusion. Breaking free of the crowd, she hired a carriage to take her home. Despite her determination not to be put off by her uncle, she experienced apprehension as she dismissed the carriage and strolled toward the house. The door was unlocked, so Amber stepped into the hallway.

"Anyone home," she called after checking the drawing room and finding it empty. She was stepping back into the hall when she heard feet on the stairs.

"Who is making all that noise?" Myra called. When she saw Amber, her hand flew to her breast. "Amber, I don't believe . . . It is really you." She held out her arms, tears streaming down her cheeks. "I'm so glad to see you."

"Myra," she said, putting her arms around her friend. "It is good to be home." It was wonderful to be back with a woman who loved and understood her.

"Why didn't you telegraph and let us know you were coming?"

One of the Union officers had suggested it, but Amber had decided it would be better to arrive without warning. "I wanted to surprise you."

"You certainly did. I'm so happy to have you home." She stepped back. "What happened to you?"

Amber ran her hand through her hair. "It is a long story." Most of which she wanted to forget.

"I waited three days for you, but when you didn't return to our room I came back and told your uncle. Did you find Andy?" she asked anxiously.

"He was there," she said with a nod. "I got to see him," she said, her blue-green eyes clouding as she reflected on her brief visit with him. She would always cherish it.

"Is he here with you? Did you get him out?"

Amber sadly shook her head. "Andy caught the fever. He is dead."

"No," Myra wailed. "Not my boy." Deep sobs shook her shoulders. "I don't want to believe it."

Amber put a comforting arm around her friend. Andy's death was hard to accept and she ached with the loss. "It won't do any good to cry," she said softly.

Myra wiped her eyes and looked at Amber suspiciously. "Didn't you cry for your brother?" She didn't respond. "Amber, you have got to let go of what is in your heart. You can't keep everything inside. I blame your papa for the tight rein he expected you to keep on your emotions."

"We all have different ways of coping with grief. Don't blame Papa," she pleaded. "He was a strong man and taught me to be the same."

Myra shook her head. "That is the problem. You are not a man. You have feminine emotions he couldn't understand."

Their conversation triggered something in Amber's thoughts, and she realized Brant had accused her of the same thing. He had known she was afraid to show her emotions and let him see her vulnerable side. He had known she hated him because he was a Rebel, but he also knew the hate stemmed from fear of being a woman. No person had ever come so close to recognizing her inner feelings. That man had become her husband and the revelation was shattering. Amber realized there was nothing she could or wanted to do to change things. He was out of her life, and she would find a kinder man to take his place.

"I don't want to talk about it. Where is Uncle Hank?"

"He is expected home any time. He was furious with me for letting you try to free Andy. I am lucky to still be in the house."

"I am sorry you had to become involved."

Myra smiled. "As long as you are safe nothing else matters. I have to go see about dinner. Why don't you wait for him in the drawing room?"

"I want to change. Would you have someone send up fresh water?" she requested.

"I'll take care of it," she said, moving toward the back of the house.

Lifting her skirt, Amber took the steps two at a time. She passed Andy's room without stopping. Her pain was still too strong to look at his belongings. Nothing would ever be the same without her brother. The attempt to rescue him had made important changes in her life and had altered the simplicity she had known. Amber knew she could never go back.

After changing she went to the drawing room to wait for Hank. Memories of Andy flooded her mind and Amber knew the only thing that would ease the pain was work. The hospital needed her and she needed it.

Amber thought of Steven. He had been a good friend and an excellent teacher. His interest had also been romantic and he would want to see her socially. He was the kind of man she could be comfortable with, and she realized he might be the man to erase the past. She would take immediate action to determine if the marriage to Brant could be terminated. He was nothing to her and there was no point in continuing the association.

Unbidden thoughts of her husband hovered in her mind. What had happened to him? Was he stuck in a Northern prison living among filth and disease? The conditions would be poor, but Brant was a survivor. He was also resourceful, and she had no doubt that he would find a way to escape.

A thud brought Amber out of her reverie, and she turned toward the door. Hank Rawlins strolled in, stopping abruptly when he saw his niece.

"Amber," he said in stunned surprise. "You're home." He walked toward her, a smile brightening his face. "And you are safe. I have been very worried about you." He put his arm around her shoulders and gave her an affectionate hug.

"Hello, Uncle Hank," she said without returning the embrace. "I didn't mean to cause you worry."

Frowning, Hank led her to the settee. After making themselves comfortable, he turned to her. "Amber, I was furious when I learned you had deceived me. What made you think you could successfully rescue your brother?" He scowled. "I hadn't been able to do anything."

182

Amber straightened her back. "I had to try. I couldn't let him die."

Hank shook his head. "I know you are very close to Andy and I understand his capture was hard on you, but your actions were foolish." Amber didn't agree. "Myra said you posed as a harlot to get inside." He paused, his fingers drumming one of the plush cushions. "A whore. Amber, you are a respectable young woman. How could you compromise yourself that way? I demand to know if anything happened." His face reddened. "Between you and a man."

Amber smiled at his discomfort. "You mean did I go to bed with one?" she asked bluntly and saw his color deepen.

"Amber," he said sternly. "You are my responsibility. I am concerned for you."

"Despite what you think I value my maidenhood. I am not going to carelessly toss it away." She took a deep breath. "Of course I didn't go to bed with a man." Several times it had been close, but her relationship with Brant was private and she didn't want to share her deepest thoughts.

Hank's sigh of relief seemed to calm his tension. "What happened after you got inside?"

"I saw Andy," she said simply.

Hank's eyes widened in interest. "How is Andrew? Is he here with you? How did you get him out of prison?"

"One question at a time," she cautioned. "Andy is not with me." Her shoulders sagged with the remembrance of seeing his body thrown into a wagon to be taken out and buried. "Andy got typhoid fever and died."

Hank paled. "Andy died of the fever."

Amber shook her head, sorry she had to give him the tragic news. Hank put his hands against his temples, his grief evident.

"I have failed your father. His son . . . my only male kin is dead."

He had taken the news harder than she expected, and she laid a hand on his arm. "Don't be tough on yourself. Andy believed in the Northern cause and wanted to fight for freedom. You must never blame yourself."

"How did you get free?" he asked.

"I was being transferred to Confederate headquarters when Union troops captured me." Amber remained firm in her decision not to mention Brant. She didn't want her uncle to know anything about him. "The Union soldiers arranged transportation to Washington."

Hank slid his arm around her shoulders. "I am so glad you're back." His expression sobered. "From now on I am going to keep a close eye on you. You are going to listen to me and do as I say. I won't have any more of your foolishness."

"I went after Andy because I loved him. There aren't any other schemes you have to worry about."

Hank put his hands on her upper arms. "Don't you think I loved Andrew? I wanted to do something to free him, but there wasn't anything I could do. When I learned you hadn't arrived at the plantation, I was scared to death. You are never to leave like that again."

Amber pulled away. "I already told you I wouldn't."

Hank ran his hand through his graying hair. "I wish I could believe you." He looked up. "What are your plans now?"

"I intend to resume my old work."

"Amber," he said sternly. "Didn't you just promise not to get involved in any more schemes?"

"What are you talking about?" she asked uncertainly. She didn't consider her hospital work a scheme, but she clearly remembered his disapproval. "I want to help."

"You know how I feel about your work there," he argued. "It is not proper for you to work on men's bodies."

Amber sighed. This was going to be a difficult battle, but one she had to win. "Papa taught me medicine and let me work in the hospital. He recognized my skills."

Hank shook his head. "It was fine for Andrew, but you should not have been involved in medicine. Your duties are in the home."

"I hate sewing, cooking and afternoon teas, but I can run a house as well as any female. I enjoy helping the sick and injured. Why should my skills be wasted? You know the army is short on help."

Hank could not disagree. Many were dying before they could get medical care. He had learned from the doctors at the hospital that Amber was highly skilled. Hank knew the only way he could keep her out of the hospital was to restrict her to the house and put a twenty-four hour guard on her. He didn't like the idea of making his home Amber's prison. He raised his eyes to his niece. Assuming the role of her guardian had not been something he wanted. He didn't know

185

what to do with her.

"I am concerned about your reputation."

"It has not been tarnished," she said smugly. Her work had always been conducted discreetly, preferring not to flaunt her activities. Gossip would not bother her, but it might embarrass her uncle. "I promise to be careful. Look how long I got away with it before you found out."

"Amber," Hank snapped, his voice rising. "I didn't like being made a fool of, and I won't let it happen again."

"Papa and Andrew are dead. I have to do something to help us gain victory. It is important to me." She smiled sweetly and lightly touched his arm. "Please let me continue my work."

Hank scowled. "I don't like it, but you're right, we do need help. I will agree but only if you follow my rules."

Amber pouted. She didn't want restrictions placed on her movements. "What are they?"

"You must be discreet. No more than five hours a day."

"But Uncle," she protested. "It is not long enough. I have put in many ten hour days."

"No more than five hours," he insisted. "If I find out you are cheating, I'll forbid you to leave the house."

Amber's shoulders slumped. Eventually, she would figure out a way to get around his rule. He couldn't watch her all the time.

"I also plan to check on you at the hospital." He studied her frown. Catching her chin, he raised her face until she looked into his eyes. "Amber, you only have yourself to blame for my decision. You are a young lady, yet you gallivant around the country and work a man's job. You are too impulsive and I intend to keep my eye on you."

"I guess it is something," she muttered, and he released her chin.

"I expect dinner is about ready. Would you like to join me?" he asked, holding out his arm.

Amber had not been given the liberties she had hoped for, but at least her work would continue at the hospital. She suspected her uncle was going to become more involved in her life, and she hoped he would not try to force too many adverse things on her. Her worst fears were realized at dinner. Hank put down his fork and looked at his niece.

"Amber, there is going to be a ball in one week. I expect you to attend it with me."

She groaned, "Oh, Uncle Hank. You know I hate those parties." They were boring social functions and she tried to get out of them whenever she could.

"Nevertheless, I expect you to attend. I warned you before that I am going to supervise your life. I told you the day you left town that you needed a man in your life. I think it is time you found someone to take care of you."

A man had entered her life and she had married him and lost her innocence. She was not free to make a commitment to anyone else. "I won't be pushed into something I am not ready for."

"Before you left Dr. Monroe expressed interest in you. I thought you wanted to see him socially."

"I—I'm not sure it would work anymore."

"Why? Has something happened to change your

feelings for him?"

She moistened her lips. "I have just been through a very difficult time. I am still grieving for my brother. I need some time."

"I just want you to know I approve of Steven. He has an excellent background and I believe a man in medicine might be best for you." He looked at his niece. Though she was careful to hide her feelings, Hank knew she was upset about the direction in which he was trying to push her life. "It is going to be a special party, so buy yourself a new gown. You will want to look your best."

"I will see the dressmaker tomorrow," she said, rising. "I'm tired from the trip. I think I'll go upstairs."

In her room Amber threw herself across the bed. Her uncle was keeping firm control of her life, and she felt smothered by his concern. He could never make her do anything she didn't want to do and at least she still had her work at the hospital. Amber rolled to her back. Tomorrow she would visit the dressmaker. A new gown might be what she needed to boost her spirits and she decided to select something very special.

Amber was up at dawn, dressed and at the breakfast table when her uncle came down. "Did you rest well?" he inquired, joining her.

"It is good to be home."

"I'm glad you feel that way. I hope you don't think I was too hard on you yesterday. You are all I have and I want what is best for you."

"I know you do," she responded, genuinely

touched by his concern. It hadn't been easy for him to accept the care of a young woman when he had been a bachelor all his life. "I'm going to the dressmaker this morning."

"Are you going to the hospital this afternoon?" She nodded. "Yesterday when we talked about Steven I forgot to mention that he is on temporary assignment in Gettysburg."

"I heard casualties were high," she said. Steven would be a valuable asset, but he would find the conditions very different from what he had known in Washington.

Her uncle silently finished his breakfast, then pushed his chair back and rose. "I'll drop you at the dressmaker and pick you up at the hospital late this afternoon."

Amber frowned. It was clear he intended to live up to his promise to limit her time at the hospital. "That will be fine," she said, determined not to start a fight. She was fortunate to be allowed to work at all.

Some of her apprehension over the ball vanished when she studied the fabrics and designs. Her measurements were unchanged, and the dressmaker sighed when she made note of the tiny waist and flat abdomen.

"You have a beautifully proportioned body. I wish all my patrons were as fortunate as you."

Amber laughed. "When can I come for a fitting?"

"Thursday. That will still give me time to complete the final touches. I wish they would plan more balls. My business is picking up."

Amber left the shop and strolled down the sidewalk. She was anxious to get to the hospital, but something else tugged at her mind and she knew it had to be taken care of. Changing directions, she went into a building where she could get legal advice. Using a false name, she explained the circumstances of her marriage and learned a divorce was possible but would take months.

She felt nothing when she said goodbye to the lawyer and left the office. She was not trying to end a marriage that was based on love. She had been tricked into marrying Brant, and there had been no emotional ties. It had been a farce from the beginning, and she wanted it pushed to the back of her life.

The hospital was crowded and wounded soldiers filled every available space. Amber covered her dress and went to the surgery. The smell of blood and infected flesh assailed her nostrils, but she ignored the stench and joined one of the doctors at the operating table.

He glanced up, his eyes widening in surprise. "What are you doing here?" Jerome Bennett asked, finishing the bandage on his patient.

"I came to offer my assistance," she said brightly.

Jerome wiped his hands on a towel and watched them put a new patient on the table. "Does Hank know you are here?"

Amber smiled at the doctor's uncertainty. He was the oldest physician in the hospital and did excellent work. "He gave his permission. I can spend several hours a day helping."

"I'm glad to see you back. We received some of the injured from Gettysburg. Steven is there now." He turned to the table. "Let's get to work."

They were in the middle of surgery on a young

man's chest when Hank stepped inside. Leaning against the wall, he watched the operation, his admiration for his niece's work increasing. His brother had been skilled and Hank could see that some of his talent had passed to his daughter. Amber's knowledge would be a definite asset to the hospital and everything would be fine as long as she was careful not to cause gossip.

He silently renewed his vow to get her interested in a man. She had voiced disapproval on the idea, but he wasn't going to give up. It was time she found a man to take care of her.

Amber stepped back from the table and wiped her hands. The operation had been a success, but the patient's life rested on keeping infection away. There were more soldiers that needed immediate care, but Amber knew Hank expected her to leave. Bidding Jerome farewell, she followed her uncle outside.

"You are very good at what you do," he praised when they were in the carriage on their way home.

Amber's eyes widened. "Thank you."

"It is not work for a woman, but you are talented. Have you ever thought of becoming a physician?"

"I know Papa was pleased that Andrew became a doctor, but I don't think he expected it of me. When the war is over, I will make my decision."

"Would you rather be a wife and mother?" he queried, bringing them back to their conversation about finding Amber a man.

She was already a wife, but there was no chance of a child coming from the union. "Uncle Hank, I have ordered a gown for the ball. Please let my social life work itself out."

Hank remained silent, but Amber knew he still harbored plans for finding her a husband and getting rid of his responsibility toward her.

Amber's work continued at the hospital, and every day Hank made sure he was free to escort her home. She hoped his constant attention would diminish as time passed. She didn't like feeling smothered.

On Thursday morning Hank escorted her to the dressmaker and voiced his approval on the gown. Amber delighted in the way it molded to her curves. Yards of fabric had been used in the skirt and would necessitate the use of the cumbersome hoop to highlight the detail.

"You are going to be beautiful," he praised.

Amber caught the sparkle in his eyes and knew he was hoping she would find a male interest. His desire to find her a man was going to cause problems.

Fifteen

The day of the party was warm and sunny. Amber went to the hospital in the morning so she could spend the afternoon getting ready. It was almost one o'clock when she removed her apron to go home.

Myra had a hot bath waiting, and Amber undressed and sank into the heated water. Twenty minutes later, her hair dripping and her body scrubbed to a healthy pink, she stepped from the tub and dried herself. After putting on knickers and white cotton stockings, she sat before a mirrored table and combed her hair. When it had dried, Myra twisted it up in the back and let thick curls spiral to her neck. Ribbons were woven through the silky strands to highlight the color and accent her eyes. Rising, she let Myra strap the steel cage in place to hold the crinoline away from her body. Amber hated the cumbersome cage, but everyone would be wearing one this evening, and she wanted to look her best.

The gown parted down the back by a series of tiny buttons, opening enough for her to slip her head through without disturbing her hair. The dress was cut low across her bust to highlight her femininity. Standing before the mirror, Amber turned to catch her reflection. The aquamarine color was perfect for her blue-green eyes, and Amber knew she had never looked lovelier.

"You are going to be the most beautiful woman there," Myra applauded, studying the younger woman. "Dressing for anyone special?" Myra asked, remembering that she had mentioned interest in a doctor from the hospital.

Amber knew there was a strong possibility that Steven would be at the party that night, but instead of thinking of him, she thought of Brant. He was her husband, and the man she should be interested in pleasing. What would he think of the beautiful gown and the way it molded to her figure? Would the passion he had thus far been able to maintain be shattered in a moment of heart-throbbing desire? Amber refused to admit she missed the tiny caresses and feather-like kisses. It was part of her memory, and she had to remember to keep the passionate introduction of her body tucked in a safe, emotionless part of her thoughts.

Amber didn't answer her question. Instead she asked, "Do you think Papa wanted me to marry?"

Myra looked at Amber curiously, wondering what had spurred the question. "Your papa always wanted you to be happy . . . Amber, are you trying to tell me something? Is there someone special?" Myra sensed that Amber was troubled. She didn't want to pry, but it was important that she knew a woman was ready and eager to help.

"There was a man, but he is out of my life. . . . I wonder if Uncle Hank is ready," she said, and Myra knew Amber had said all she was going to say on the subject.

Myra watched Amber waltz from the room and her brows came together thoughtfully. A man had definitely touched Amber's life and she would never be the same.

Hank smiled when Amber joined him. "You look lovely." He took her elbow. "The carriage is waiting."

The streets near the hall were jammed with carriages, and it took several minutes before they could stop at the door and go inside. The hall was the largest in Washington, its size being necessary to accommodate the voluminous dresses. Musicians played at the far end of the room while couples danced on the polished floor. Tables of food lined one wall, and doors to the outside were open to permit an evening stroll and privacy among the shadows. It promised to be a grand event and Amber looked forward to the evening.

Hank was drawn into conversation with other officers and Amber left his side to wander through the hall. She nodded to acquaintances, but did not stop to speak to any of them. She accepted her first dance with a prominent city official, and they glided across the floor with ease. Colonel Giles Broadmore claimed her second dance. He had been to dinner on occasion and worked with her uncle in the War Department. When they finished the waltz, they stopped along the side to converse.

"Colonel, can I steal this lady for a dance?"

Amber turned. "Steven," she said, smiling. "It is

wonderful to see you." He rarely wore his full uniform at the hospital and she was impressed by the way he looked in it.

"Of course," Giles said and walked away.

Steven pulled Amber into his arms. "You look beautiful."

They danced three dances. Neither of them spoke and Amber enjoyed the close silence they shared. It was the first opportunity in a long time that she felt completely relaxed and able to be herself. Steven was not the kind of man to dominate her, and she could let her defenses down.

"Would you like to walk through the garden?" he asked.

"I would enjoy that," she said, slipping her arm through his.

"The fresh air feels wonderful," he said, guiding her down one of the paths. "I was hoping you would be here this evening, but I wasn't sure if you were back in town. Was your business a success?"

"Oh, Steven," she moaned, suddenly anxious to confide in someone. "It didn't work out the way I had hoped."

Sensing the anxiety in her voice, he stopped and drew her into his arms. His fingers lightly teased the curls hanging against her neck. "Would you like to talk about it?"

Amber's fingers curled into the fabric on his jacket. Their bodies were not close because the hooped gown prohibited intimate contact, but Amber found it comforting.

"Several weeks ago my brother was taken prisoner. I won't go into details, but I got into the camp to see

196

him. He was sick. . . ." She looked at him, anguish filling her blue-green eyes. "Steven, he died. . . . My brother is dead."

Raising his hand, he lightly stroked her cheek. "I'm very sorry. I know how much he meant to you."

She took a deep breath. Eventually, she would have to tell Steven about Brant, but this wasn't the time. "I managed to get out of the compound and returned to Washington."

"You have been hurt very deeply. I would like to help you through this difficult time."

Amber smiled at Steven. This was the kind of man she wanted to spend her life with, and she wished he would pull her against his body and sweep her into the vortex of sensual delight. She wanted to experience from another man the exciting sensations Brant had shown her. She wanted to be freed from his memory.

Steven lightly ran his palm along the sleeve of her gown to the naked flesh at her shoulder. His finger traced the line of her collarbone. The caress was gentle and Amber waited for the same leaping flame of passion she had experienced when Brant touched her. The low murmur of voices alerted Steven that they were not alone and his hand fell.

Amber was disappointed. She wanted a whirlwind courtship in the hope of erasing her past. Even though she didn't recognize the marriage to Brant it was legally binding and she had no right to entice another man.

Steven tucked her arm through his and they walked back toward the hall. "Would you like something to eat?"

"Sounds wonderful. I will wait for you by those empty chairs," she said, motioning to the corner.

"I won't be long," he promised, frowning when he saw the long line at the tables.

Amber scanned the crowd for her uncle and spotted him on the far side of the room talking with local businessmen. Turning to walk to the corner, Amber found herself against a man's chest. For a minute she could only stare dumbfounded at the buttons on the civilian dress.

"Excuse me," she said, looking up.

Further words lodged in her throat. She wanted to deny the man before her, but the familiar brown eyes, the strong jaw, and especially the sensuous lips parted in a mocking smile made it impossible.

"Brant," she whispered.

His arms rose to steady her. "My dear wife, I am so glad you remember me," he chuckled softly. "But then I think we both know you could never forget me."

"You arrogant Rebel. Remove your hands or I will scream."

"No, you won't. You're not prone to hysteria." He smiled at the change in her eyes. The calm blue-green color became a stormy blue with green flecks of turmoil. "I believe this is our dance."

Before Amber had time to escape, Brant pulled her into his arms. His hands held her firmly as they glided around the dance floor.

"Relax," he whispered. "You are too tense."

Amber's movements were mechanical, her body struggling to recover from the shock. Brant's unexpected arrival had thrown her smooth balance into chaos. The man she was trying to put out of her mind had returned and shattered her careful defenses. A remembered awareness crept through her limbs, forcing her to rely on Brant for support. Her nails dug into the fine fabric of his jacket, wishing instead that she could curve her talons against his face, but knowing if she released her hold she would crumble helplessly against him.

Amber's mind was whirling with uncertainty. She had never doubted that Brant would escape the Union soldiers, but she never expected him to appear in Washington. He was a Confederate officer out of uniform, and his presence in the Union capital could only be interpreted one way. Brant was in Washington to gather information that would result in the Union downfall.

Rage boiled in Amber. She would never let his mission succeed. She would expose him as a spy and hope they hanged him for his traitorous activity.

Brant deftly guided them out of the path of another couple, and Amber had a brief glimpse of her uncle watching her through narrowed eyes. She had no time to wonder at his reaction because Brant swept them into the midst of the dancers, and he was lost from sight.

Taking a deep breath, Amber looked into Brant's eyes. The color darkened with desire and he responded by pulling her closer. His gaze dropped to the curving swell of her breasts, amply displayed for his view. Fire licked through her veins, her body warming with remembered caresses. She struggled for the final hold on her sanity.

"Take your hands off me, you Rebel spy," she

barked.

Brant tipped his face toward hers. "Keep your voice down. I don't want anyone to hear your accusations."

It was on the tip of her tongue to speak again, but Brant whirled her around and out the doors before she knew what was happening. Keeping a firm hold on her wrist, he pulled her into the shadows and away from the festivities.

When Amber realized his intent, she swung at his back with her fist. Brant stopped in the shelter of a tree and dragged her into the bushes. Amber stumbled against his chest and he caught her tightly against his body. The breath was forced from her lungs as much from the contact as from her uncertainty. She looked into his face half-hidden by the darkness. She wanted him to know she was not afraid.

Brant's brown eyes wandered over her delicate features. When his gaze dropped to her lips, an awareness shot through her limbs. She recalled the feel of his mouth against her body, teasing her flesh, yet never satisfying what she craved. Brant knew the effect he was having on her, and her gaze centered on his lips, curving to show a glimpse of his white teeth. The hand against her back pressed her closer, renewing her need for the Rebel's passion.

"Your silence is essential," he said in a husky whisper.

Amber looked at her husband. He believed he could make her physically dependent on him, and she would remain silent. It was an arrogant opinion and one she would prove wrong. Raising her arms, she pushed against his chest.

"You can wipe the smirk off your face," she said smugly. "Nothing can make me keep quiet about you. I am going to tell everyone exactly who you are." She smiled. "I am going to enjoy watching you hang."

"I don't think you'll say anything," he said, unruffled by her warning.

"That is where you are wrong." She pushed out of his arms. "I am going to tell my uncle."

She turned to walk away, but Brant grabbed her shoulder and spun her around. "Amber, there are ways to stop you. Don't make me use them. I will not let you spoil months of careful planning just because you hate the South."

"My dislike is well founded. I lost my father and brother, and I have seen hundreds of men lose limbs and suffer torturous deaths. I would never let you spy on the North . . . Never."

"Then I will have to persuade you that it would not be in my best interest."

His head dropped unexpectedly to her neck, his warm lips roaming over the soft flesh. Amber's pulse beat erratically as his lips nuzzled the lobe of her ear. His hands pressed against her lower body, forcing her into a position of remembered intimacy. Her limbs, weakened and pliant by his caresses, melted against his, and her head fell back to allow him greater access to her neck and shoulders. His teeth nibbled lightly against her exposed neck, his tongue darting out to tease her collarbone. Brant bent her body over his arm, and his mouth trailed along the line of her dress.

When his lips touched the top of her breasts, Amber's breath became ragged. Her hands rose to curl against the fabric of his jacket, and she couldn't let go for fear of falling weakly to the ground. This man's power over her was shattering. She had no defense. He had sparked the sensuous fire in her body and knew the fuel to help keep that feeling alive. Steven had never made her feel this way.

Steven. She had forgotten about him. Pulling together the last shreds of her sanity, she grabbed Brant's head and pushed him away. Her hooped skirt once again settled in even balance around her body.

"Don't ever touch me again," she ordered. "I don't want the hands of a filthy Rebel on my body."

"I am not *just* a filthy Rebel. I am your husband."

"Not by choice," she argued. "I have already taken steps to terminate our distasteful relationship."

"What are you talking about?" he asked, his eyes narrowing suspiciously.

"I have seen legal counsel about dissolving this marriage."

"You didn't waste any time," he drawled.

"I know what I don't want, and I don't want to be married to you. You will always be the enemy."

"I suppose you have designs on the man you were with in the garden." His voice was hard.

Brant had witnessed the exchange between Amber and the young soldier and was bitterly resentful. She had shown another man her sensitivity over her brother's death. She had displayed her vulnerability and he had succumbed to her charms.

"You saw me with Steven?"

"Why didn't you tell him you were married? The man is practically in love with you. You are not free to have a liaison with him."

"Of course I may not need to go through the trouble of having this marriage terminated legally. Once I tell my uncle who you are, you'll hang for spying and I will be a widow."

Brant's grip tightened and his face had a threatening glare. "If you tell anyone who I am, your uncle and boyfriend are dead men."

Amber had not expected Brant to counter her threat with one of his own, and it left her groping uncertainly. Could she betray Brant at the cost of Steven and Hank? It was not a decision she could make without careful thought.

"Amber . . . Amber, are you out here?" She recognized Hank's voice.

"Amber." She heard Steven call.

After a swift kiss of possession, Brant pushed Amber back onto the path and guided her toward the house. "Over here," he called, surprising Amber that he would give away their location.

They were almost back at the building when Steven and Hank found them. "Amber, are you all right?" Steven asked, regarding Brant warily.

"Forgive me," Brant said swiftly. "I asked Amber to dance then we stepped outside for some fresh air. There was no cause for alarm."

"My niece has a mind of her own and I like to keep my eye on her," Hank said to Amber's embarrassment. "I don't believe I know you. I'm Amber's uncle, Hank Rawlins."

Brant extended his hand. "Brant Faulkner."

Steven introduced himself and Brant clasped his hand firmly, commenting casually on his profession.

Amber wanted to get away from Brant. "Steven,

could we go back inside." Oblivious to her husband's presence, she tucked her arm through Steven's and they walked inside.

Steven had left their filled plates on two empty seats, and they sat down to sample the food. Once again she found the full skirt an inconvenience and wished they weren't so fashionable. She preferred the loose skirt or pants.

"I think the party is a success."

"I'm sure the committee responsible for organizing it is pleased with itself," Amber said, thinking how boring the activity would be. Arranging social events did not provide enough action.

"The food is good," Steven commented, tasting one of the fancy tarts.

Amber didn't want Brant's unexpected arrival to spoil her fun, but she no longer felt the carefree gaiety she had experienced upon arrival. Steven noticed it and offered to take her home. In the carriage Amber sagged against the seat.

"Tired?" Steven whispered. "Or is something else troubling you? Your mood changed after you talked to Brant Faulkner."

Amber looked into Steven's eyes, and his mouth curved until dimples marked each cheek. He had an appealing boyish attractiveness and lacked the aggressive masculinity evident in Brant's chiseled features.

"The man upset you. Did you know him before tonight?" he asked cautiously.

This was Amber's chance to tell him the truth, but she was strangely reluctant to confide in him. "Yes, I did. Our relationship was a stormy one and I need time to put it in proper perspective."

When the carriage stopped at the house, Steven asked the driver to wait while he walked Amber to the door. On the tiny front porch, sheltered on both sides by bushes, he drew her into his arms.

"I don't know what Faulkner is to you, but I want you to know I am here for you." Slowly, his head descended and Amber raised her mouth to meet his lips. She responded eagerly to the brief kiss, trying unsuccessfully to blot out the touch of Brant's mouth.

"I think I'd better go. I will see you in the morning."

Amber remained on the porch and watched the carriage leave. She sighed. Steven was a considerate man and she was comfortable with him. Why did Brant have to arrive and spoil things?

The bush to her right rustled and Amber turned her head, a startled, "Oh," escaping her lips as a dark form stepped from the thick foliage.

"Very touching scene," Brant scoffed, a smirk curving his lips.

"How dare you spy on me! What I do is my private business."

"It is my business," he said, leaning against a post and crossing his arms over his chest. "Have you forgotten you are my wife?"

Amber threw her hands on her hips. "I told you I'm taking steps to end our marriage. It was a farce anyway."

"I agree our meeting wasn't the norm, but that does not lessen the fact that we are married. You are bound to me and no other man. You belong in no man's arms but mine." The possessive quality of his voice rocked Amber.

"You don't offer me anything I can't get from any male," she flung back.

"Your boyfriend does not appear to be a very passionate man, and I know your desires run hot."

Amber's cheeks reddened. "You have no right passing judgment on my relationship with Steven. I would much rather be in his arms than yours."

Brant chuckled. "We both know that is not true."

Amber turned to go inside, but Brant swung her back around. "We have nothing more to say to each other. Let me go."

"No," he said abruptly and pulled her closer. "You are my wife. I want you with me."

Amber laughed. "You can't expect me to go with you," she argued, but saw the answer in his eyes. "You are a Rebel. I despise you for not helping my brother. Had you saved his life I would have owed you something. Now there can be nothing. He will always be between us."

"It was my job," he said, his fingers toying with the curls at the back of her neck. "You didn't mention your father. Do you finally believe I had nothing to do with his death?"

Amber had given it serious thought. Brant was guilty of being at the meeting place the night he was wounded. She didn't know if he intended to capture or kill her papa, but nothing had happened. Brant's wounds had been serious, and while he may have wanted to find her papa at Antietam and kill him, she didn't believe he had been strong enough to make the journey.

"Yes," she answered, "but that doesn't excuse what you did to my brother."

"Amber, my work isn't finished. I need you."

Her eyes widened. "I am not going to help you spy against the North. It would be unthinkable."

"I didn't come here to spy."

"I don't believe you. You came to Washington for information to give the Rebels."

"Would you believe I came back for you?"

Amber swallowed thickly. Brant had been forced into the marriage, but accepted it because it blended easily with his desire for her. His position as a Confederate officer had been threatened when he shielded her attempt to save her brother. Brant had made huge sacrifices for her, and he wanted her in exchange. His passion and determination were powerful motivators and made Amber feel weak.

"There are other women," she offered.

"You are my wife." He paused. "When Mason dispatched his report to headquarters about your brother's death, he mentioned my marriage. My superiors will expect to see my wife with me when I return."

Amber believed his story. Edgar had resented Brant's authority and was strongly suspicious of Amber's presence in the compound. He had used their marriage to try and expose their lie. He had been thwarted and hadn't liked it.

"I cannot risk having my credibility as a Confederate officer tested."

Amber shrugged. "I won't help you."

The steady beat of horse's hoofs signaled someone's arrival. "You may not approve of my tactics, but I will get you back. We will talk again soon." With that promise he disappeared into the bushes.

The rider was her uncle and Amber stepped off the porch to greet him. "Amber, what are you doing outside?"

"Enjoying the beautiful night."

He took her arm and ushered her toward the house. "I am glad you are still up. We have to talk." He pushed the door open. "Come to my study," he said, and Amber knew it had to be important. He rarely let anyone into his office because of the secrecy of his work. Amber sank against the cool leather cushions and straightened her gown.

"What is the matter?" she asked as he sat on the edge of his desk."

"I want to know about Brant Faulkner," he said crisply.

Her only outward show of emotion was the tightening of her fingers against the chair. Did Hank already know about Brant's allegiance to the South? Hank's contact with the War Department probably gave him information on many of the Southern officers.

"He asked me to dance, then we walked in the garden. Why do you ask?"

"Is he loyal to the North?"

Amber had the perfect opportunity to tell Hank who Brant really was, but she remembered Brant's threat to have Hank and Steven killed if she revealed his identity.

"That was not one of our topics of discussion."

Hank scowled. "I suppose not. He said he is in

208

Washington on business, but I have reason to suspect otherwise."

"Who do you think he is?" she asked curiously.

"Some of what I suspect is confidential, but I can tell you I think he has ties to the South." Hank's eyes narrowed. "What did you talk about?"

Amber shrugged. "Nothing important."

Hank chuckled, his eyes suddenly brightening. "You made quite an impression on the man. He is captivated by you."

A dryness crept into her throat. "He is," she croaked uncertainly. Was this the tactic Brant intended to use to get her back?

"I tried to steer the conversation to his business, but it kept getting back to you."

"I don't know what to say."

"Faulkner is only going to be in town a short time, but he wants to see more of you."

"What did you say?" she asked, hiding her anxiety.

Brant had known she would refuse to go with him and had cunningly made her uncle think he was interested in her as a woman. He could not outwardly claim her as his wife because Hank would instantly know he was a Confederate. But by playing the suitor he could achieve the same thing. What frightened Amber about his plan was that it would probably work. Hank wanted to be free of his responsibility to her and had hinted that it was time she married. He might use Brant's interest to achieve that goal. She smiled. What he didn't know was that he would be arranging a wedding that had already occurred.

Hank ran his hand through his graying hair. "My first thought was not to let you get involved with a man suspected of having Southern loyalties." He jammed his hand into his pocket and smiled. "Then I realized the possible potential of having you associate with him." Hank became excited as the idea continued to form in his mind. "Socialize with him, get him interested in you as a woman. I have got to know if he is with the Confederacy," he said in a tone that warned of his determination and earnestness to learn the man's loyalty.

Amber didn't like the direction of the conversation. She wanted as little to do with Brant as possible and definitely did not want him back in her life.

"Will you do it, Amber?" He saw the disapproving set of her shoulders and noted the frown. "This is your chance to help the country you love."

"You are asking me to spy."

Hank knew exactly what he was requesting. He had already lost a brother and nephew to the war and found himself in a position of asking his niece to help. He didn't want her involved, but it was absolutely imperative that he learn where Brant's loyalties belonged. If he was a Confederate he had to know why he was in Washington.

"Yes, I am. I can't guarantee that it won't be dangerous because I don't know how Faulkner would act if he learned the truth. In this case I have to step outside my protective authority as your uncle and ask your help."

Amber nibbled her lip. This was her chance to

avenge her father's and brother's deaths. She already knew Brant was a Southern spy, but would have to wait for the right moment to reveal the truth. In the meantime it might be a good idea to keep an eye on him. Getting him interested in her would be easy, and when he was at her feet groveling helplessly in his desire, she would expose him and make him pay for his traitorous actions against the North.

Sixteen

Amber did not sleep that night. She was constantly haunted by the reminder of Brant's caresses, the teasing pressure of his mouth, the mocking smile, and the fiery desire in the dark brown eyes.

She was grateful that she could actively participate in the war, but wished her involvement did not include Brant. She would have to come to terms with the tremulous excitement Brant had taught her and learn to ignore the nearness of his body and the touch of his hand. She could not let the man throw her emotions into turmoil.

Throwing aside the covers, Amber rose and dressed. She had just finished securing the ribbon in her hair when Myra slid quietly into the room.

"Morning," she said quickly. "Your uncle wants you to join him for breakfast."

"I'm almost finished," she said, stepping back to check her dress.

Myra stepped forward and brushed a piece of fuzz from her shoulder. "You'll want to look your best.

Your uncle has a guest."

"A guest?" Amber repeated, her body stiffening suddenly in warning. She was certain she knew who it was.

"A businessman I believe. He is very attractive."

Amber's heart pounded erratically for several seconds. Had Hank arranged the meeting or had Brant begun his attempt to pursue her?

"I don't think I'll have breakfast this morning," she excused. "I wanted to get to the hospital early."

Myra looked at Amber oddly. She rarely skipped breakfast when she was going to work. It was too hard to tell when she would get a break for lunch.

"Your uncle said you are to get downstairs, or he will be up after you."

Reluctantly, Amber walked toward the door. Her first instinct was to rebel and sneak out of the house. She didn't feel obligated to her husband, but she was committed to a Northern victory and that meant enduring his company and learning what he did while in Washington.

Amber's uneasiness had vanished when she joined the men at the dining room table. Other than an acknowledgement of her arrival, Brant said very little to her, and Amber was able to eat without interruption. When she rose to leave, however, he pushed back his chair and stood.

"Brant asked permission to escort you to work," Hank said smoothly. The sly look he passed her warned that she should start arousing his interest.

"That was very kind," she said, keeping all spite from her voice.

Amber stepped into the sunshine, and the sight of

213

the enclosed carriage brought an immediate frown to her lips. Brant would not have any physical contact with her in public, but he wouldn't hesitate in private.

"Frightened?" he asked, reading her thoughts.

Amber's blue-green eyes darkened in fury. "Not of you," she spat and climbed inside. She sat down and spread her skirt over the seat so Brant would be forced to sit opposite her. The carriage dipped as he climbed in, and Amber tensed when he brushed the fabric off the seat and sat next to her.

"You didn't expect me to sit there did you?" he asked, pointing to the opposite cushion.

"Yes," she snarled. Brant's gaze dropped to her lips, thinned in stern disapproval. "What do you want from me?"

His mouth curved in a smile, his body turning sideways. "I think you already know. I want my wife with me."

"Get out of Washington and out of my life."

Raising his hand, he brushed a loose strand of hair from her cheek. The touch of his knuckles over her flesh sent goose bumps down her spine. "I am staying in your life." His hand curved along the back of her neck and his upper body pressed her against the cushions.

"No," she croaked. "I despise you. Your actions against the Union are sus—." She stopped, horrified at what she was about to admit. She was supposed to seduce information out of him and not vice versa.

"Suspicious," he finished. His brown eyes narrowed. "Who does your uncle think I am?" He leaned closer, his mouth inches from hers. "You better speak."

"He thinks you are a spy," she blurted out when his breath fanned her trembling mouth. One touch from his lips would spark the passion she feared.

Brant leaned back and laughed. "Are you supposed to practice your feminine charms on me to get information?" The expression on her face gave him the answer. "You would make a terrible spy," he accused. "I'll be able to get more information out of you than you will out of me."

Amber glared at him. "You are more experienced."

Brant ran his finger along her lips. "You are learning fast." Amber brushed his hand away, but Brant caught the fingers and pulled them to his mouth. "It is nice to know your uncle has encouraged you to get my attention," he said, kissing the fingers. "It makes my job of winning you much easier. Why didn't you tell him I was a Confederate?" His teeth caught the tip of one finger, and his tongue caressed the edge. "Loyalty to me?" he asked, the light of hope in his eyes.

Amber jerked her hand free. Her insides were a knot of unfulfilled tension. His intimate touch was creating havoc with her senses.

"You will never get loyalty from me. You threatened the lives of Steven and Hank. I don't want to be responsible for their deaths."

"A wise choice," he praised. "My capture right now would cause dangerous repercussions and throw the Union government into turmoil." He grinned lazily. "Why don't you try and seduce me into revealing my Washington contacts? It might be fun."

Learning the identity of the men was enticing bait, but she could not learn the truth though seduction.

She would end up in bed without the information.

"You might find out how much I mean to you."

"Brant Faulkner, you are nothing to me but a Rebel spy."

He chuckled softly. "I am everything to you, Amber Faulkner. When are you going to admit it?"

She stared into his brown eyes. She could never believe his words, but they held a power that frightened her. Brant was a very sensuous man and had every intention of being the victor.

Brant's hand curved around her waist, drawing her against his chest. His lips glided into her hair, teasing the silky strands. Remembered passion licked through her veins as her hands feebly pressed against his chest.

The carriage jerked to a stop and Brant straightened. "I believe this is your stop." He regarded her flushed face with amusement. "I promise there will be another time." He helped her out of the carriage.

Amber ran up the steps to the hospital, her legs barely able to support her. She was putting on her apron when Steven joined her.

"Ready for surgery?" he asked. Amber glanced at him and nodded, unaware of the excited flush on her cheeks and the sultry glow in her eyes.

"What has you so anxious?" he quizzed. "I have never seen you look more beautiful."

She smiled. "It is nothing. . . . Do we have a full schedule?"

"Yes. Let's get started."

They were in surgery for several hours, and Amber wasn't aware of the audience until Steven put his equipment aside and reached for a towel.

Amber glanced up, the uncertain throb of her heart returning at the sight of Brant standing with Hank. "Very nice job," he commended, stepping forward.

"Do you know something about medicine?" Steven asked, not sure he liked this man's interruption. He had been jealous to find him with Amber the night before.

"A little," he acknowledged. "I recently spent some time watching a skilled person work." His gaze flickered to Amber, and she was surprised he would praise her work.

"Are you ready to leave?" Hank asked Amber. "I want to have an early dinner."

"I will see you tomorrow, Steven," she said, following the men outside. Amber and Hank climbed into the carriage.

"I will call on you later this evening," Brant said swiftly. He lifted Amber's hand and looked into her eyes. "Will you be home?" She wanted to snicker at the formal request, but the intentness of his gaze stole her breath and brought a rosy color to her cheeks.

Hank smiled. Things were progressing between his niece and Brant very nicely. "Amber will be there," he replied in her silence and instructed the driver to take them home.

"You seem to be on excellent terms with him today," Amber praised.

"But I don't know much about him. He has a way of twisting the conversation away from himself. I must learn why he is in Washington and who he contacts." He looked at his niece. "Did you learn anything this morning?"

"As you said he is very secretive." She thought of

the morning carriage ride and how he had aroused and confused her. It had been obvious that she would never get anything from him and would only put herself in a suggestive position. There had to be another way Hank could get information.

"How far do you expect me to go to get what you want?" she asked.

"I'm not sure I understand."

"Do you want me to climb into his bed?"

"Amber," he said aghast. His cheeks colored. "Has he made improper advances?" She didn't respond. "I've seen you flirt with men and still hold them at a distance. Play the same game with this man."

Brant was not a man to play games with. He wanted a physical and emotional relationship with her and wouldn't settle for less. Amber couldn't tangle with him physically.

"The man speaks very highly of you. It is hard to believe he would compromise you." He stroked his jaw. "Perhaps I'd better have a word with him about this."

Amber turned to stare at the scenery. She didn't know what her uncle had planned, but knew it wouldn't work. Brant would never agree to keep his hands off her body.

Amber didn't join Hank for dinner, but he later found her in the drawing room reading a medical book. She looked past him for Brant.

"Are you alone?"

"Brant was here earlier, but he left. He will call again in an hour."

She wrinkled her nose in confusion. "Why is he coming back?"

Hank shrugged. "He had something to do. . . . We had a long talk. I don't think Brant will be in town much longer."

It was the best news she had heard. "Won't you be glad to get him out of the city?"

"Once he leaves Washington it will be difficult to follow him. The ideal thing would be to send someone with him and have that person tell me where he goes and what hc does."

Amber didn't like the direction of the conversation. Hank suspected Brant's loyalty and believed it was important to follow his actions. Was he planning to involve her in the next phase of his scheme?

Hank studied his niece's thoughtful expression, wishing he could understand her emotions. He often had to make difficult decisions and the one he made tonight had involved her. When he posed his request, would she understand he was not asking her as an uncle, but as an officer in the Union Army? The war had demanded personal decisions and sacrifices, and he had endured the pain because he believed in what he was doing. He hoped his niece would understand.

"Are you asking me to do it?"

"You are the best person for the job. Brant's interest in you is more than a passing fancy. He wants to marry you."

Amber almost laughed aloud. The men didn't realize it, but they were using each other to get what they wanted, and she was trapped in the middle.

"I know it is a huge sacrifice to make, but — ."

"I'll do it," she said flatly. It was no sacrifice to

marry the man who was already her husband. Her goal was to see him exposed as a traitor.

Brant arrived a short time later and Hank greeted him warmly. He looked at Amber, noting that she had changed into a beautiful emerald-colored gown and hoped she had done it for him.

"Won't you sit down?" she asked, indicating the empty place at her side. She had agreed to the marriage and was determined to use it to expose him as a spy.

"Thank you." There was a gleam in his eyes. "Did your uncle speak to you?"

"I have agreed to marry you."

His brown eyes twinkled in victory. "On the chance that Amber would accept my proposal I brought the preacher with me," he said, standing. "He is waiting in the hall."

"You want the wedding now," Hank said, marveling at the speed at which this man moved.

"Yes. I will be leaving town soon and I want Amber with me as my wife."

She rose. "Shall we get started?"

Brant smiled his amusement, but Hank stared at his niece in surprise. He had expected her rebellion, not calm acceptance. Perhaps she saw it as her chance to avenge her father and brother.

Myra was summoned to act as a witness. She was puzzled by the rapid change about to take place in Amber's life, but there was nothing she could do.

Brant stepped to Amber's side and slid his arm around her waist. "Try and look happy," he whispered. "Not every woman gets to remarry her husband."

"My misfortune," she argued, smiling with false sweetness.

This ceremony was easier than the first one, and Amber spoke the words accepting Brant as her husband loudly and clearly. She was not going to allow the second ceremony to change things between them and planned to stay as far from him as possible.

Brant's words were clear, crisp and positive in their acceptance of her as his wife. When he pulled her into his arms for a kiss, his eyes lingered on the soft swell of her lips. She had been denied their touch since the prison, and he knew they held a special fascination for her. Unknowingly, anticipation leaped into her eyes and Brant smiled in victory. Leaning forward, he touched his lips against her cheek. He would wait just a little longer before giving her what she craved.

Congratulations were given and Hank toasted the married couple. Brant kept his arm around Amber's waist, marking her as his possession. She hoped the North would be victorious and her sacrifices would not be too great.

As soon as she could break free Amber went upstairs. Myra followed her, and Amber responded to her questions by admitting the marriage was what she wanted. When Myra left the room a few minutes later, she was shaking her head uncertainly.

Amber removed her dress and threw herself across the bed. Her undergarments still needed to be removed, but she decided to do it when she put on her nightgown. Her immediate problem was what to do if Brant came to her bedroom. There was no lock on the door, but a chair propped against the knob might keep him out. Pushing against the mattress, she rose.

At the sound of her door opening, she turned and stared in horror as Brant joined her. His gaze swept her half clad figure appreciatively.

"Very nice," he said, his eyes resting on her half exposed bosom.

"Get out," she said when he started toward her.

"I have every right to be here. You are my wife . . . and a very beautiful one."

"The second ceremony changed nothing between us. I still have no intention of making this marriage real."

He raised his finger to run it along the top of her undergarment. Her flesh burned where he touched. "No?" he asked, his brow arching. "I think otherwise."

She stepped back. "Get out of my room."

"I will leave when I'm ready," he said casually. Turning, he walked toward the closet. "Do you have anything suitable for riding astride?"

"Why?" she asked puzzled.

"We are going out." He flicked the door open and inspected the contents.

"Won't my uncle think it strange?"

"He has gone to headquarters. When I asked to wed you, your uncle seemed very pleased. I suppose he expects you to be the link between him and me. Considering that he didn't know about our previous liaison, don't you think he was asking a lot of you?"

Hank had made the request as an officer and not an uncle. He wanted information on Brant and she was the tool to get it. "That is none of your business."

Brant shrugged. "What will Doctor Monroe think of the marriage?"

Amber frowned. Steven would be disappointed. "He is a very kind, considerate, gentle person, and is the type of man I wanted for a husband."

"Quite a list of qualities, but you forgot predictable and boring."

Reluctantly, Amber recognized the truth of his words. She was too fiery for a man with Steven's quietness. "I want as little to do with you as possible."

Brant chuckled. "This marriage is going to be a challenge." He paused. "Do you have anything suitable to wear? The horses are waiting."

She walked to the closet and pulled out a pair of men's pants. "Where are we going?" she asked, sliding them over her hips.

"You will know when we get there."

Amber added a shirt and a pair of stout boots. It was wonderful to dress in the clothes she had used with her father and brother. She looked up to find Brant studying her. She did not miss the light of appreciation glowing in the brown eyes.

"Very nice," he drawled. "Why is it that I am not surprised to learn you have male clothing?"

His question did not demand an answer and Amber remained silent. Standing before the mirror, she pulled the pins from her hair and secured it at the back of her neck with a ribbon. Turning, she met Brant's eyes squarely.

"I am ready, but I want to know where we are going."

He touched the tip of her nose. "You'll know soon. Be patient."

"Is this something my uncle will be interested in?"

Brant's eyes narrowed. "Don't play games with me.

My work is very dangerous and I will not let you interfere." His words held a sharp warning.

Hiding her uncertainty, she walked past Brant. Outside, she freed the reins of her horse and mounted. Brant swung into his saddle and they rode into the darkness. When they were away from the houses, they cut across the open countryside and urged the animals to a gallop. It was a beautiful night, but the moon seemed to cause Brant some concern, and he kept to the shadows as much as possible. Amber's mind was alive with curiosity, and she sensed an edge of excitement to their deed.

They had been riding for more than an hour when Amber realized they were making a full circle back toward Washington. Their destination must be near the city, but they had detoured to make sure they weren't followed. The action made her suspicious of what they were doing.

"Are you ready to tell me what we're doing?" Amber asked a short time later when they stopped beneath a cluster of trees.

"We came to see someone," he remarked, his eyes scanning the surrounding woods.

"Does this have anything to do with your spy activities?" He flicked her an impatient glance. "Answer me," she demanded. "Are you meeting a contact?"

Brant's eyes narrowed. "You are obsessed with spies. I am not going to have you continually doubting me."

"You're a Rebel. You'll never get my trust."

"I am in Washington to meet someone and to take you back to headquarters with me."

"I hate you, Brant Faulkner."

"I'm hoping you won't hate me after . . ."

"After what?" she prompted, curious about what Brant believed could change her feelings for him.

Ignoring her question, he pointed into the darkness. "We are headed for that shack."

Amber had not noticed the building. The soft light from the moon gave it a sinister appearance, and she doubted it got used very often.

Brant edged his horse forward, picking a quiet path to the front of the small house. Dismounting, he secured the animal's reins to a bush and waited for Amber to join him. When she slid from the horse, she found herself against Brant's chest. His hands spanned her tiny waist to turn her around and keep her from backing away. His brown eyes gazed into her shadowed blue-green ones.

"Are we really here to meet someone? Or did you just want to get me away from the house?"

"I wouldn't bring you all this distance when I could have had everything I wanted from you right in the comforts of your bed."

"Is that all you ever think about?" she snapped, wishing she was free of his touch. "Have you forgotten your loyalties and my family will always stand between us?"

"I had nothing to do with your father's death, and I didn't make your brother sick," he said softly. "I tried to help him."

"So you could hang him," she spat.

"It was my job. When I was assigned to oversee his execution, I had no idea I would meet someone like you." He sighed. "You complicated things and put my life and credibility as an officer in danger."

"You can blame your troubles on your lust."

"Perhaps," he agreed. "But I got what I wanted. I got you. . . . I am a man first and a Confederate second. When are you going to look past the differences between us? I see you as a woman and not the Union enemy." He touched her elbow. "Let's go inside. We are expected."

Amber jerked free of the contact and walked toward the building. Brant pushed the door open without knocking, and they stepped into the dimly lighted, sparsely furnished room.

Suddenly, Amber felt Brant's hand curve around her waist in a supportive gesture, and the move immediately put her senses on alert. A shuffling sound came from the corner and a figure stepped into the light. Amber was grateful for his support. Had it not been offered, she would have fallen beneath the crumbling weight of her knees.

Gathering her strength and smiling her joy, she ran into the man's arms. "Andy," she said elated. "You are alive." She pulled out of his embrace to look at the face so much like her own. His beard and moustache were gone and there was color in his cheeks. He looked weak but healthy. "I can't believe it. I thought you were dead." She hugged him tightly. When her body finally ceased its joyous trembling, she stepped back. "I don't understand any of this. I saw your dead body."

"You saw what Brant wanted everyone to see. He gave me a potion to simulate death."

"Why?" she quizzed, puzzled that a Rebel would help a Union spy.

"You'll have to ask Brant," Andy said. "He surprised me too."

Amber turned to her husband. "Why?" she repeated.

His eyes slowly caressed her face. "I did it for you," he said softly. "I didn't want the obstacle of Andy's death between us. You wanted him alive and I wanted you."

Amber quickly turned back to her brother to hide her emotions from Brant. Shock, disbelief, and confusion twisted her features uncertainly. The sensitive understanding and sacrifice he had made spoke of a man driven by strong desire.

Andy silently watched the confusion on his sister's face. He didn't completely know what was going on, but something had strongly affected her. Amber usually kept her turmoil locked inside, but this incident had forced an outward showing. He noticed, however, that she was hiding her reaction from Brant, and knew it was reminiscent of her refusal to show a strong man weakness.

Amber finally gained her composure and looked at her brother. "How did you get here?"

"Brant made the arrangements."

She hugged her brother. "It is wonderful news. Who else knows you are alive?"

"Just the three of us."

"Uncle Hank will be thrilled. Why are you here instead of at the house?"

Brant turned up the lamp. "No one can know he is alive. If someone recognized him and Confederate headquarters learned of the incident, I would be accused of treason. I cannot risk it." He looked at the twins. "You owe me your silence."

Andy put his hands on his sister's shoulders. "Brant is right. He may be a Rebel, but I owe him my life. I won't betray him."

"Andy, what about Papa? You must know Brant was at the meeting place to kill him."

Andy nodded. "I suspect he was, but his wounds made it impossible." His hands fell.

Amber desperately wanted to destroy her brother's faith in her husband. "Maybe not then, but what about the meeting at Antietam. Brant disappeared the same night as Papa. He could have killed him."

Andy looked over her shoulder at Brant and knew he had to make a decision. Amber wanted him to believe Brant was guilty. In the past they had always stood together, but this was a time to be his own man.

"I don't think he killed Papa."

Amber's eyes flashed her betrayal, but knew Andy was probably right. Brant had also denied the killing and said his wounds had been too serious to travel any distance.

"Are you going to keep quiet about me?" Andy asked.

Her face twisted in confusion. "I don't know," she whispered. If she couldn't use Papa's death to discredit Brant, she had to try something else. "He is the enemy and probably came here to spy on the North. We can't let that happen."

"Brant came to Washington to bring us together. He plans to return to Confederate headquarters." He paused. "Why all the suspicion?" he quizzed. "You should be grateful to him for saving my life."

"He can't be trusted. I won't keep quiet about this."

"Amber," Andy said sharply. "Where is your sense

of honor? Papa taught us loyalty and dedication. Would you betray a man who helped us?"

"Amber," Brant said from behind, and she turned to find him holding a gun on her brother. "If you do not swear to secrecy, he is a dead man."

Amber did not like being pinned by this man and had to look hard at her reaction. She was an honorable person and under usual circumstances would never think of betraying the man who helped them. Brant inspired something that made her constantly turn against him. The time would come when she would have to examine why she reacted the way she did, but until then she had to remember the values Papa had taught her.

"Put the gun away," she ordered. "You have my silence."

"Do I have your word on it?" She nodded, but Brant wanted more insurance. "If you break your promise, I'll hunt him down and kill him." Brant reholstered the pistol. "You better get things together. It is almost time to leave."

"Where are you going?"

"San Francisco, California."

"Why there? It is so far."

"I have to go where I won't be recognized. There have been Union-Confederate confrontations in the west, and I hope to get back into the war. They might need a good doctor." Andy hugged his sister. "Promise you'll take care of yourself and not try anything foolish."

She knew he was referring to her attempt to free him from the prison. "I thought you would understand."

Andy chuckled. "I also want to say thank you. I would have done the same for you."

Amber wrapped her arms around his neck and hugged him. "I'll miss you. Maybe I should come with you," she whispered.

"No," Brant said.

"Now that I know Andy is alive I would rather be with him," she said.

"I need you with me at Confederate headquarters."

Amber stepped away from Andy, her hands resting against her hips, and her sea green eyes narrowed in challenge. "You don't matter," she said bluntly. Amber knew it was a harsh thing to say, but Brant wasn't going to force her into going south with him. One of her reasons for agreeing had been to avenge her brother's death.

Brant stiffened at the slur against his character. His eyes narrowed and his hands clenched together at his sides.

"Amber," Andy scolded sharply. "Where are your manners? Brant saved our lives at the prison." He turned to Brant. "Why do you want Amber at Confederate headquarters?" It was a dangerous place for a Rebel hater.

"When I told Edgar Mason that Amber was my fiance, he became suspicious of us and tried to discredit our actions. One of the things he did was force us to marry. He notified my superiors of the marriage, and they will expect her to be with me when I return. If she isn't, Edgar's accusations may be taken as more than suspicion."

"The marriage is off," she shouted in defiance.

"You have a problem," Andy agreed, looking at his

230

obstinate sister. Her hostile look warned him that she wasn't happy about the arrangement. Brant didn't seem to share her reluctance, and Andy extended his hand to congratulate his brother-in-law.

"Does Uncle Hank know any of this?"

"He thinks we met for the first time a few nights ago," Brant explained. "He encouraged our relationship and engineered a marriage between us." He smiled. "I had no objection to marrying my wife again."

"I can't believe Hank would force something like this on Amber."

"Your uncle suspects me of being a spy and has instructed Amber to report on my activities."

He looked at Amber. "He asked you to spy?" He ran his hand through his amber hair. This was a touchy situation. "What are you going to do?" he asked Brant.

"Why don't you ask me?" she quizzed. "I am going to find out how he gets his information."

"No. It is too dangerous," Andy forbid.

"Leave your sister to me. I proved once I was capable of protecting her, and I will do it again if necessary."

"The man doesn't care about me. He is full of lust."

Andy arched his brow. Her bluntness didn't surprise him, and the amused smile on Brant's lips said the same thing. Brant was on the opposite of the war, but Andy liked and trusted the man. Whatever his reasons, he had risked his life to help them.

Andy had never seen his sister react so strongly to a man, and he didn't know what it meant. He could not deny that Brant might be the person to curb Amber's impulsiveness. It was time she learned she was a woman and started acting like one. Amber accused Brant of lust, but Andy wondered if there was another emotion involved—one Amber didn't recognize.

Andy looked at the Confederate soldier and Brant met his gaze without flinching. The silent communication that passed between them erased any apprehension he might have had. Brant would keep Amber safe.

"I better get going," he said to Brant. "Take good care of my sister. She wasn't given enough of the female comforts when she was growing up, and she has a wild nature for a woman."

He chuckled. "I rise to the challenge. Have you got your disguise ready?"

Nodding, Andy went to the corner of the room. After a few minutes he returned wearing a large hat, a patch over his eye, and a cane to cover a false limp. "I'm ready."

Brant handed him some papers. "There should be enough cash to last you several months."

Andy shook his hand. "I owe you." He turned to his sister, smiling at the look of surprise on her face.

"You are just going to leave me with him," Amber accused.

"I have no choice. I have to travel fast. You'll be safe with Brant." He lightly caressed her cheek. "I'm going to miss you. Take care of yourself and don't give Brant too much trouble."

Amber wrinkled her nose. "I promise to take care, but I won't promise the second thing."

Andy shook his head. "Then you are in for a

stormy marriage." He kissed her lightly on the forehead, then turned to Brant. "I'm ready."

The men walked outside to a horse hidden at the side and Amber stood in the doorway. Brant talked to Andy for fifteen minutes. Amber wished she could hear what was being said and that the shadows had not hidden her husband's expression. When their discussion was over, Andy glanced at Amber and waved. He mounted the horse and rode into the darkness.

"No tears for your brother's departure?" Brant asked, returning to her side.

Amber turned her cold gaze on his face. "No," she said flatly.

"Does the iceberg ever melt?" he asked softly.

"Never when you are around," she said without thinking.

"I know. You are afraid I will see that you are soft and vulnerable."

His perception of her character was disturbing and she turned to the horses. "I would like to get back to the house. I'm eager to get to bed."

"So am I," Brant said suggestively. "I'm glad you are finally anxious to share my bed. This could be the wedding night I promised you."

Amber turned, her arms flying out in anger. "I do not want to share your bed. You might as well understand that from the beginning."

"If you don't, it will look suspicious."

Brant was right and there was nothing she could say. Turning, she mounted and rode toward home.

He caught her within seconds. "You can't run away from me," he said. "Despite any ideas you may get about not leaving with me, you will go! You better take your brother's advice and behave yourself. If anyone finds out you're a Northerner, your life will be in danger."

"I'm not afraid," she said with a shrug.

"I know you're not," he said, his expression one of admiration. "I've never met a woman like you."

Amber cast him a sideways glance. She didn't know if he meant it as a compliment, but it made her sit straighter in the saddle and lift her chin with pride. She didn't like the direction of her life, but she would fulfill her obligation to Brant and return south with him. When her duty was over, she would find a way to expose him as a spy.

Seventeen

Amber left the horses in Brant's care and went to her room. She was exhausted as much from the physical activity as the emotional shock she had endured at learning Andy was alive. Amber smiled. It had been wonderful news.

After changing into a high-necked nightgown, she climbed into bed and lowered the lamp. For the first time in weeks it was easy to fall into the relaxed world of sleep.

Night still darkened the sky when Amber's peaceful rest ended, and she slowly woke. Reluctant to open her eyes, she snuggled against the pillow and thought about her brother. He was alive and on his way to California, a part of the country she had always wanted to visit.

Suddenly, her pleasant thoughts were disturbed by the reminder of the part Brant would play in her life. He was her husband, but could she keep the marriage free of physical commitment and keep him out of her bed? Thus far she had been lucky.

Shifting her hips, she became aware of a funny weight against her back. Wiggling, she tried to shake off the heaviness, but instead of moving away, it pressed closer. Amber's eyes opened to stare at the wall opposite her bed. There was definitely something different about her bed this morning, and the possibility made her heart race.

Moving slowly, she rolled to her back and turned her head to the side. Her breath lodged in her throat and her stomach somersaulted. Her luck had ended. Brant was in bed with her. She was grateful his eyes were closed and unable to witness her first confusing seconds. He was her husband and had every right to be where he was.

Amber's eyes roamed over his features, and she reluctantly had to admit he was an attractive man. His light brown hair lay against her white pillow, and his nostrils flared with each breath. The long line of his lips stirred, and she was reminded of the sensuous way they aroused her flesh. They held a fascination she couldn't understand.

Her eyes dropped to his neck and bare shoulders, and she realized he wore few if any clothes. The possibility of having a naked man in her bed brought on a renewed fluttering and a dryness to her mouth. The naked male body was not new to her, but there was a confused excitement when the man shared her bed and wanted to make love to her.

An uncertain gasp erupted from Amber's throat, and Brant's eyes fluttered and opened. Her blue-green eyes were a storm of confusion.

"Good morning," he whispered, and she felt his breath against her cheek. "Did you sleep well?"

"Ye—yes, I did," she replied, still stunned to find him in her bed. "What are you doing here?"

"I was sleeping," he replied calmly, his hand easing from beneath the covers to curve up her arm.

"You know what I mean," she snapped, fighting the feeling his touch aroused. "What are you doing in my bed? You have no business being here."

"Have you forgotten I'm your husband?" he asked, a smile curving his sensuous lips.

"But I haven't given you rights into my bed."

"Consent was given when you said your vows." His gaze dropped to her mouth. "I belong here."

Amber's tongue slid out to moisten her lips, and Brant raised his finger to trace the tip. The contact was electrifying and a shot of delightful sensations flooded her limbs.

"No, Brant. I don't want this." Raising her hands, she pushed against his shoulders. "Let me go."

Shifting, he threw his leg across her thighs and leveled his body above hers. There was a tightness in her throat as she looked into his desire-filled eyes. His gaze slowly dropped over her face, caressing every inch of her flesh. His eyes hovered on her lips, and his fingers slid through the silky amber strands.

"You are very beautiful in the morning," he said in a husky tone. "It is going to be a pleasure to wake up to you every morning."

Amber pushed against his shoulders. "Let me go or I'll scream."

"Go ahead," he said casually. "You are the one who will be embarrassed. Your uncle approved of our marriage and wouldn't do anything to interfere."

"I could always tell him you're a brutal man."

237

Brant dropped his head to bury his lips against her neck. "Both of us know that isn't true," he said in a muffled voice. "Your body is trembling beneath mine. You want this as much as I do."

"I'm not trembling from desire," she said, letting her head roll to the side so he could gain access to her neck. "You— ," she moaned as his mouth eased along her shoulder.

"Don't be frightened," he said, shifting his position so she took more of his weight. The movement pinned her to the bed and forced her to awareness of his nakedness.

Why didn't he have the decency to wear clothes? she thought, biting her lip to ward off the sensations he was arousing.

Amber's nails dug into his shoulders, her body totally aware of the man making love to her. Brant's hand slid beneath the bed clothes to run along the curve of her body. The gown did little to protect her from feeling the warmth of his hand as it slid up her thigh to touch the soft flesh.

"Brant," she said, trying to twist out of his grasp. "I have to get to the hospital. I'm expected in surgery."

His hand curved over her hip and stopped on her midriff. This time when he shifted, her bare thigh pressed against his in the most intimate position they had shared since the consummation of their marriage.

"Do you still hate me?" he asked, his lips gliding down her jaw. "Can you feel differently now that you know I saved your brother's life?"

Brant had saved Andy, but he was still the enemy. Even if she could excuse his loyalties he was a man

238

and that posed the biggest threat. He had confused her feelings about herself, shattered her control and thrown her world into turmoil by introducing new emotions. She could not trust him as the enemy and was afraid of him as a man.

"I know you want me. Don't be frightened."

"I'm not scared," she mumbled, refusing to admit her inner fear. "I'm repelled by you."

Brant pushed aside the top of her gown to expose the rounding swell of her breast. Dropping his head, his mouth glided over the gentle swell toward the aroused peak. Amber nearly panicked when he took the tip between his teeth and created an irrefutable hunger in her body. It was becoming increasingly difficult to keep her hands on his shoulders and her mouth away from his.

"I want you," he moaned against her skin.

Amber turned her head, her lips suddenly finding themselves against his neck. His masculine scent filled her nostrils and acted like an aphrodisiac. Her lips parted to taste the salty flesh, and she felt the throbbing pulse in his neck, beating in tempo with hers.

Brant drew back suddenly, his eyes locking with hers. The desire was in his eyes for her to see, and Amber was shocked by the intensity of his need. She responded by wrapping her arms around his neck and dropping her gaze to his lips. He had been teasing and tormenting her body long enough. She had not felt his mouth against hers since the time at the prison, though he had repeatedly aroused her body to the point of fevered desire. She wanted him. Grabbing his head between her hands, she pulled his head down. The sharp knock on the door stopped the descent, and Brant turned his head.

"What is it?" he called impatiently.

"Mr. Faulkner, your carriage is ready."

"I'll be right there." His face darkened with a scowl. He had forgotten his appointment. "Timing couldn't be worse." His eyes roamed over Amber's face and she noticed the glimmer of disappointment.

Amber knew where their intimacy had been leading and was relieved to get the reprieve. "Timing couldn't be better," she mocked, pushing against him to roll away. "You have a very early appointment."

Brant threw his legs over the side of the bed. "Business," he said curtly. He rose and Amber turned from his nakedness. "I wouldn't think the sight of the male body would embarrass you."

"It doesn't," she said with a casual shrug.

"Then why aren't you looking at me?" he teased.

Brant was baiting her and she wasn't going to let him bully her. Raising her head, she tossed her amber hair out of her eyes. Fortunately, he was securing his pants and some of her uneasiness disappeared. Though his lower body was covered, the upper was bared to her gaze and her eyes were drawn to the flat stomach just above the belt. Brant was a fine specimen of a man.

Finally, she raised her eyes and found him watching her hungrily. Tearing her gaze away, she rose and strolled to the window. "How do you think Andy is doing?"

"He'll be fine once he gets out of this area."

Amber swallowed the thick lump in her throat. "Th—thank you for helping him."

"I've never seen two people so dedicated to each other." Brant came up behind her. "Don't you think I've earned the same consideration?"

His hands rose to her shoulders, and she was pulled against his chest. Amber started to move away, but his grip tightened, and she felt every muscle of his body against her back.

"I want an answer," he demanded.

"What do you want from me?"

"I want you to stop hating me. I thought saving Andy's life would make you soften toward me. We are going into Confederate territory. I need to know I can trust you."

"You are a Rebel. We are on opposite sides of the war."

Brant released her suddenly and walked toward the door. Amber glanced at him over her shoulder and noticed the rigid set of his body. He was not a man to cross. Jerking the door open, he stepped into the hall and slammed it closed.

Amber pulled her nightgown over her head and poured water into a basin. After washing she put on fresh undergarments and dressed. She didn't know how long Brant would be gone, but she didn't want to be in the house when he returned. She was married now, and Hank no longer had a say over the hours she spent at the hospital.

She took the carriage to town and stopped at the rear of the building. Climbing from the seat, she walked toward the back door. It was very early and most people were still in their homes. A movement near the alley down the street caught her attention. The pre-dawn light made it difficult to see, and she was about to shrug it off as poor eyesight when a man stepped into view and climbed into an enclosed carriage. His action was not unusual except that she recognized him as Colonel Giles Broadmore, a man with high connections in the War Department.

A frown marred her lips. Why was he out of uniform? Why wasn't he using his usual carriage? She was pondering the strangeness of his actions when she stepped inside the hospital and turned to close the door. Suddenly, she froze. There was a shadowy form of a second man in the alley. Driven by curiosity, she eased the door around so she could watch undetected. The man hovered in the shadows for several minutes before stepping into the light.

Amber gasped aloud. Brant . . . Her husband had been having a secret meeting with a colonel in the Union Army. The implications of her discovery were staggering. Was the colonel her husband's contact to Northern secrets? She had known Giles for a long time and had danced with him at the ball. She didn't want to believe he was a traitor.

Uncle Hank had to be told. He would know what to do. The door was suddenly ripped from her fingers.

"Amber," Steven said. "I'm glad you are here early. There is an emergency. I will need your help."

After seeing her husband with a Union colonel she didn't want to stay. She had to warn Hank.

"Are you all right?" he asked for the first time, noticing she was not her usual self. "I need you at the table." He started down the hall talking about the operation. Amber recognized the seriousness of the case and decided her news could wait until she got home.

The next three hours passed quickly. It was difficult surgery, and Steven was tired when the man was taken off the table.

"I am glad I didn't have to tackle that alone," he said, placing his hands on her shoulders. "I think you are ready to try a simple surgery."

"I don't know," she answered uncertainly.

There was a sudden change in him. His fingers caught her chin and tilted it up. "I care very much about you," he whispered and a dryness crept into her throat.

"No, Steven. You can't."

"What is the matter? I thought you were beginning to feel the same."

Amber's marriage had ended anything she had hoped to share with Steven. He would be hurt when he learned the truth.

"Steven, something has happened to change our relationship." She took a deep breath. This was much harder than she thought it would be. "Last night I — ."

"Take your hands off my wife," Brant ordered crisply.

Steven's head jerked up and he met Brant's angry brown eyes. "What did you say?" he asked, his hands falling to his side.

"I told you to take your hands off my wife."

Puzzled, Steven said, "Amber?"

She took his hand, wishing Brant would leave them alone so she could tell him in her own way. "I was starting to tell you that Brant and I were — ah — ."

"Amber and I were married last night," Brant said coolly, and possessively curved his hand around her waist.

"I am sorry Steven. It was a sudden decision."

"Amber, we have a train to catch," Brant warned. Dropping his hand, he walked to the door.

Amber was grateful for the few seconds of privacy. "I'm sorry I can't explain."

"Do you love him?" he asked softly, and she saw the pain in his eyes.

"No," she said quickly. "All I can tell you is that the marriage was necessary."

"I'll be here if you ever need me."

Smiling regretfully, Amber turned and strolled toward Brant. She glared at him in icy contempt as she walked past him and out the door. He caught up with her outside.

"We have a train to catch," he said crisply. He took her elbow and guided her toward a waiting carriage.

"Where are we going?" she asked tartly.

"We are expected at Confederate headquarters in four days."

"I'm not going," she said smugly, sitting back against the cushions. She couldn't leave town. She had to tell Hank about the meeting between Brant and Colonel Broadmore.

Brant threw himself on the opposite seat. "What do you mean you are not going?"

"I have changed my mind. I would rather stay here."

Brant leaned across the seat and grabbed her arms. "Why?"

Amber had to be careful not to let him suspect she had seen him with the Union officer. "I don't like you."

"Help me and I will give you your freedom at the

244

end of a month."

Amber stared into his brown eyes. Thirty days wasn't long, and she could use the time to get information on the Rebels. The news about Colonel Broadmore could wait until she got home.

"I'll have to get my clothes."

He released her arms and leaned back. "Myra packed and sent them to the train station." His lids drooped to hide his eyes. "I'm glad you took care of your boyfriend."

"What is that supposed to mean?" she asked, stung by the cruel way he had told Steven.

"I mean for the next month you are to devote yourself to me totally. You will not flirt or associate in a brazen manner with any man but me. I am to be the center of your attention. You are to be the adoring wife." His eyes narrowed. "Is that clear?"

"Will you guarantee my freedom at the end of one month?" He nodded. "Can I resume my association with other men?"

A muscle tightened in his cheek. "It won't matter what you do."

Amber turned to look out the window, grateful they were in an enclosed carriage and the driver was unable to hear their conversation. In a month she would be free to resume her life. Thirty days in Brant's company would be hard to endure. He was a forceful man and had aroused her to physical awareness while spurring her hate. She would have to constantly stay on guard.

Looking across at him, she held out her hand. "It's a deal."

Brant's fingers clasped around hers. "I think I

would have preferred a kiss," he said, a mocking curve to his lips.

"This is a business arrangement. Anything else will not be acceptable."

Brant chuckled softly, and the husky tone sent a shiver down her spine. "We will see."

Eighteen

Amber scanned the surrounding area with interest. Three days had passed since their departure from Washington and they had almost reached Confederate headquarters. She was constantly aware that she was in enemy territory and remained alert to everything around her.

Travel arrangements had not given them time to be alone, and she was grateful they had never been forced to argue over sleeping arrangements. Conversation between them had been limited, and she had adopted a cool manner toward her husband. He found her amusing and chuckled at her scowling expression.

The latter part of the trip was completed with a troop of Confederate soldiers and Brant put on his uniform. He rode next to the other officers, but Amber preferred to hang behind with the enlisted men. Her questions and careful probings would not be as obvious with the men of lower rank. She would have to leave her real spying for the main compound.

Brant rode into headquarters at Amber's side. He dismounted, then looked at her. "Smile," he said smugly. "We are supposed to be newlyweds. If anyone sees the look on your face, they will think you hate me." He raised his hands and deftly lifted her from the horse. There was very little room between the horse and Brant's body, and Amber found herself pressed snugly between them. "We both know that isn't true," he said, lifting a finger to stroke her cheek.

"We," she emphasized, "know nothing of the kind." She arched one of her brows. "Have you forgotten how I loathe you?"

Brant was unconcerned by her negative reaction toward him, and his finger returned to caress her cheek. His touch was the first intimate contact they had shared in days, and she reluctantly remembered how easily he could arouse her desire.

"You don't really loathe me," he said in a positive voice. He chuckled softly. "Perhaps you are frustrated because we haven't been able to have the wedding night I promised you. There is plenty of time. Tonight we'll be alone." The suggestive tone of his deep voice made Amber shiver. "It has exciting possibilities, doesn't it?"

Her mouth suddenly felt dry. Brant was already beginning his slow sensual love-making, and she felt the quickening fire in her blood. He knew how to make her respond, and his slow expert arousal made her body beg for the promise of passion. She hated her weakness and hated Brant more for creating the aching need.

"No . . . no," she rasped. "It sounds like a very boring night." Brant's brown eyes darkened. "I think

I would enjoy reading a medical book more."

She had intended her statement to be a slur on his character, but Brant didn't take it that way. It only offered him more of a challenge.

"We'll have to take things very slowly." His fingers curved against her thigh, and his gaze dropped to her lips. "We will go very . . . very . . . very . . . slowly."

Despite the heated blood surging through her veins, Amber trembled. She was already familiar with his expertise in making her aware of his manliness.

"Are you chilled?" he asked in a mocking tone. The day's heat was already unbearable. "Or is there some other reason you are trembling?"

"Of course not," she answered smugly. "You are crushing me against the horse."

Brant shrugged. "Against the horse or against the bed. It doesn't matter. You are going to feel the full weight of my body in a very intimate way."

Color flooded Amber's cheeks. Didn't Brant have any shame talking like this to her? "Shut your mouth."

Chuckling softly, he said, "Are you curious about what should have come after the consummation? There is more . . . much, much more."

"I don't want to know," she conceded, totally shattered by his words.

"Are you surprised by my bluntness? I don't think either of us would want it any other way."

Amber eyed him suspiciously. "Does that include your activities here?" she asked with wide-eyed innocence. "Are you going to tell me everything?"

Brant scanned the area. Fortunately, no one was within hearing distance. His hand rose to her shoul-

249

ders and his fingers dug into her shirt.

"Watch what you say. Your statements might be misunderstood. I have no desire to be shot as a spy."

"I am the one who would be killed." She arched her brow. "I believe you would walk away without a scratch. You are in this rotten army . . . *Major Faulkner.*"

"I would never betray you," he scowled.

"Never?" she asked, meeting his gaze directly.

There was a suspicious light in Brant's eye. "What are you planning?"

Her lip curved in a sneer. "It just occurred to me that you might not have married me out of lust." She kept her voice low. "When you arrived at the prison camp to kill Andy, you probably knew he had strong connections in Washington. You didn't expect to find me there, but when you did, you fit it into your plans. I was an excellent link to my uncle. I despised you on sight, but you pursued me. By saving my brother you figured I would soften toward you and ease up on my hate of the Confederacy."

"You have an inflated idea of your value, don't you?" he scoffed.

Amber's mouth twisted in dislike, but she was spared a response.

"Major Faulkner," a man called. "The general wants to see you."

Glancing up, Brant nodded to the enlisted man. His hands fell from Amber's shoulders. "We will finish this discussion later. In the meantime for both our sakes, pretend to be a love-smitten wife. Do you think you can manage?"

"I won't make any promises," she said and was satisfied to receive a snarl from Brant's lips.

Turning, he walked toward one of the buildings. Amber wished she could join him. There was little chance he would confide in her when they were alone. Brant knew her loyalty to the Union was strong. He would not be foolish enough to trust her with anything, and he was too careful a man to let something important slip.

"Ma'am," an officer spoke from her side. "I would like to take you to your quarters. The major will be busy for some time."

While they walked toward her temporary home, Amber noted the surroundings. Ammunition supplies were stacked in an area away from the living quarters, and a prisoner compound blocked off a large section of the camp. The sight of the medical building brought an instant reminder that she would need something to help pass the time, and wondered if Brant would consent to her working with the injured. Suddenly, she shook her head. What was she thinking? She didn't need his approval for anything. She would do what she wanted.

The young man took her to one of the small buildings and pushed the door open. "I hope you'll be comfortable. If there is anything you need, ask someone."

After thanking him Amber stepped inside. It offered the minimal comforts and no luxury. The bed, though large enough for two people, was narrow and would force close sleeping arrangements. She quickly searched the room for something else that could be substituted, but found nothing adequate. Frowning, she plopped down on one of the two straight backed chairs.

She had come with him to aid the North, and he wanted the rights of a husband. Amber's opinion on the subject would make no difference. He would push aside her rebellion and persuade her to cooperate. Brant was an expert on love-making and knew how to coax her body into betrayal. Would tonight truly be their wedding night—the night he claimed her as his own? In a month the marriage would be over and she didn't want her life complicated by his passion. It would be easier to get him out of her thoughts if she didn't have his caresses to remember.

Rising, Amber walked to the small satchel she had brought and withdrew a dress. She quickly discarded her dusty clothes and put on the blue print frock. After folding her clothes and putting them neatly aside, she stepped outside.

She looked at the building where Brant had been taken, happy that she didn't have to see him. The longer she could avoid his company the easier it would be.

Walking away from the building, she strolled toward the hospital. When it came to medicine, Amber made no distinction between Union and Confederate soldiers. Both were victims of war. The color of their uniforms was different, but their pain was the same. The doors to the building were open to provide relief from the stifling temperatures and to maintain a fresh stream of air. When she stepped inside, she was greeted by tortured cries of agony.

The room was lighted by windows on opposite walls. Three male attendants moved among the sick and wounded. Scanning the back of the building, she spotted the area set aside for surgery where two physicians were working unassisted. Thrusting her chin forward in determination, Amber found a path through the maze of beds and bodies to the doctors. Their patients were suffering from fresh wounds, and Amber guessed there had recently been a battle.

The doctor on her right swore under his breath, and Amber directed her attention to the man on the table. He was bleeding profusely from wounds on his hip and arm. The physician was working on his leg, the more serious of the injuries, but the blood was draining from his arm too fast. If it wasn't closed the soldier would bleed to death. The doctor was so engrossed in his work that he didn't see Amber until she stopped at his table.

"I have had training in surgery. Can I close the arm wound?"

He threw her an impatient look before returning to his work. "I don't have time for games. This man will be dead in less than one hour if I don't get to work."

"Precisely," she agreed. "I can stop the bleeding in his arm."

The doctor was middle-aged, and his black moustache already showed signs of gray. "Women don't know anything about medicine."

Amber stiffened at the prejudiced slur. "That isn't true in my case."

"Where have you worked?"

She started to say Washington, then caught herself. "Field hospitals. I can assure you I know what I'm doing."

He cast her another doubtful look, but Amber was used to skepticism. Few women were involved in medicine and his reaction was understandable.

This time she didn't wait for his response. She reached for a cloth and was glad to find it clean and not soiled from the patient before. She had seen too many men operated on with dirty utensils and soiled bandages. Amber had adopted Steven's belief that things needed to be sanitary.

It was a large wound but not a difficult one to close. She worked quickly, completely forgetting the doctor who doubted her ability. When the wound was repaired, she helped the doctor complete the amputation. The patient was alive when he left the table, but Amber knew the next few hours would be crucial.

"I'm shocked," the physician admitted. "Are you a doctor?"

"No," she assured him. "But I have received some medical training."

"Judging from what I have just seen you've had excellent teachers." The man's dull blue eyes studied her. "I'm Doctor Benjamin Thomas."

"Amber," he said, refusing to tag on Brant's last name.

"I don't know what you are doing here, but will you be in camp a while? I'm short of personnel."

"I will do whatever I can to help." She turned and scanned the ward. "Are they all Confederate soldiers or do you have Union men also?"

Benjamin pointed to a second room. "We keep them separate. I take care of them when I get finisheds with our men."

His statement caused Amber to bristle and she had to remember not to show her animosity. "Of course," she said. "Perhaps I could help in both areas."

254

"Aren't you afraid of the enemy?" he questioned, running his hand through his hair.

"They can't hurt me if they are sick," she said lightly, hiding her real urge to help the men who fought against the gray uniforms.

Another man was placed on the opposite table. "Looks like this will be a long day," Benjamin said, turning and lifting his knife.

The next few hours flew by rapidly. Amber assisted in two surgeries then spent time changing bandages. It wasn't until dusk had fallen that she went to the Union side. Their moans and sobs for help tore at her heart, and she did everything she could to make them more comfortable. Pain medicine was saved for the Confederate soldiers, and their agony was much more prevalent.

The hunger pains in her stomach were forgotten, but the ache down her spine was persistent. Standing, she pushed her hands against the small of her back.

"I thought I would find you here," Brant said.

Amber turned. She had completely forgotten about her husband. "Do you object?"

"Would it matter if I did?" His eyes roamed over her exhausted features. The past few days of travel had been demanding, but Amber had not let it stop her from offering her skills to the wounded. "Have you been helping both sides?" His eyes were guarded.

"Do you think I'm a fool?" she barked in a low voice. "If I only helped the Northerners people would immediately become suspicious."

"I am glad you were smart enough to realize that."

His concession was given as an insult and Amber's blood boiled. "I am sure you can find something better to do."

His mouth curved in a lazy smile. "That is a good idea. I'm glad you are so agreeable."

"What does it have to do with me?" she asked suspiciously.

"It is late and time for bed."

Her mouth went dry. "I didn't realize the time," she said, shrugging. "I'm not tired."

Brant raised his hand to her cheek. "You are exhausted."

"These men still need my help."

"You can't do it all yourself. Another group of workers will be here soon."

"Brant," Benjamin said, joining them. "I just heard you were back." The men shook hands.

"We got here this afternoon. I see you've already met my wife."

Benjamin's eyes widened. "She didn't tell me she was your wife." He grinned. "You never mentioned a special woman. I won't pretend I'm not surprised, but you both have my best wishes."

"Thank you," Amber muttered, aware of Brant's gaze.

"Your wife has excellent medical skills. I hope you intend to let her continue her work here."

"I doubt if Amber would have it any other way." He put his arm around her shoulders in a possessive gesture. "However, I'll have to make sure she knows when to quit. I suspect I will have to drag her away every night." He guided her to the door. "It has been a long day. We'll say good night."

"I will see you in the morning," Amber said, resenting the way Brant was directing her life.

"Come whenever you can," Benjamin suggested.

When they stepped into the darkness, Amber was relieved to feel the cool air across her cheeks. An involuntary sigh escaped her lips.

"Tired?" Brant questioned softly.

"I lost track of time," she admitted. "There are so many who need help."

"True," he agreed. "I want you to understand that you can't care for all of them yourself."

"I know," she conceded. "I always take one more and time slips away. It hurts to see them suffering and know I'm helpless."

Brant wondered if Amber realized she had let her defenses down and given him a glimpse of her tenderness. He guided her away from the building. "I am glad you worked on Confederates and Union men."

Amber snapped, "I am not going to make an obvious mistake." She thought of her near admission that she had worked in a Washington hospital. It would have been disastrous. She was living with the enemy and no one could be trusted, not even her husband. "How did your day go?" she asked casually.

"I spent the day in meetings, planning strategies and learning the troop locations."

"Really? What are you going to do with this new information?"

"Do you have any suggestions?"

"I might have, but I doubt you would listen."

"Why don't you try me?" he prodded.

"Tell me what you learned."

Brant chuckled. "Do you take me for a fool? You would try and pass the information back to your uncle."

"How would I get it out of here?"

"You would find a way and probably get yourself caught."

"How much of what you learned in Washington did you pass along?"

"I told you I was in the city to get you and see Andy."

"Is that all?" she asked, remembering his meeting with the Union colonel.

They eyed each other warily. "That is all. . . . Why do you ask?"

She shrugged. "Just curious." Amber opened the door to their home and tried to slam it in Brant's face. He easily caught the wood against his palm.

"Don't every try that again," he said, slamming the door. "You are going to have to learn to trust me."

She whirled around to face him. "Never."

Brant's brown eyes narrowed. "I am worried you are going to try something foolish." He pointed to the table. "The food is for you."

"I'm not hungry," she said, consumed by anger.

Brant shrugged. "Fine. We might as well go to bed. I have to be up early."

He walked across the room, unbuttoned his gray coat and placed it over the nearest chair. Amber's breath lodged in her throat at the sight of his naked torso. He was firmly muscled and very much a man. The muscles through his shoulders and upper arms flexed and relaxed as he bent to remove his boots. Amber reached out and clutched the edge of the table.

Straightening, Brant turned and his brown eyes locked on her blue-green ones. Their gaze held, then

Amber's involuntarily dropped to his chest. Brant was a tall man, but there was nothing large or bulky about his chest. Muscles bunched on his upper chest and forearms, reminding Amber of a man who was forced to rely often on his own strength. He was not overly hairy, but the mat of hair covering his chest extended down the center of his chest and disappeared into the band of his pants. She was totally unprepared for the tightening in her chest and the shallowness of her breath.

"Amber," Brant said in a whisper-like voice that was deep and coaxing. The tone sent a shot of fire through her veins, and she had to tear her eyes from the sight of his naked chest. "Are you ready to come to bed?" She opened her mouth to speak, but her lips moved without a sound. "Amber," he said again, his eyes moving down her gown and stripping her naked. "I feel the same way. I have waited all day to be with you. I want to feel your nakedness against mine."

His words increased her anxiety and panic. Brant was speaking his thoughts, but Amber couldn't accept his drive for satisfaction. She couldn't deny her physical desire, but that didn't mean she was ready to jump into his bed. Brant crossed the room and reached for the buttons on her dress.

Amber pulled back. "I'm not ready. I want something to eat."

Brant scowled. "I thought you weren't hungry."

Amber twisted her hands in her lap. "I haven't eaten since this morning. I'm starving."

"So am I," Brant said, "but not for food. I'm hungry for you."

Amber refused to be put into a suggestive position

259

with him. "I'm *only* hungry for food."

"You are kidding yourself." He turned and walked back to the bed. "I can wait." He looked over his shoulder. "For a while."

Nineteen

Amber forced her breathing to slow as she sat down to eat the meal she didn't really want. She swallowed thickly, forcing the food past the knot in her throat. Without looking she knew Brant was in bed waiting for her. She had grown up learning to accept challenges and not be afraid. This time, however, she found herself in conflict, torn apart by feelings of uncertainty. The intimate relationship he wanted left her exposed and vulnerable. When his hands touched her flesh, all reasoning fled and she didn't know how to deal with it.

She pushed the last morsel of food around with her fork, then threw a quick glance at the bed. Brant was on his back, his forearm resting across his eyes. A sheet was draped across his lower limbs, but it left his chest bare. Dropping the fork, Amber moistened her lips. She couldn't spend the night in the chair, and she was exhausted from the work at the hospital. Rising, she tiptoed across the room and lowered the lamp.

Amber's heart was thumping loudly in her chest. She hated herself for being afraid. Her father would not be

261

proud of her fear, and she must never show that weakness to Brant.

Sighing, she glanced at the bed. Did she dare lie next to him? His even breathing told her he was asleep. Moving cautiously, she sat on the mattress. Brant didn't move and some of her tension eased. Staying as close to the edge as possible, she stretched out and laid her head on the pillow. Her breathing slowed, and she rolled her head to the side to study the dark profile of her husband. He was a virile, attractive man, but she could not let him complicate her life. She refused to think of him as anything but a Confederate spy. Rolling to her side, she closed her eyes. Brant was asleep; she was safe for the night. Slowly, she let herself relax. Everything was going to be all right.

In the next minute her certainties vanished. Brant's hand ran down her side to curve against her hip.

"What are you doing in your dress?" he exploded, rising on his elbows.

"Trying to go to sleep," she said smugly. She struggled to wiggle out of his grasp, but was dangerously close to the edge of the bed and didn't want to fall on the floor.

"You'll never sleep in that dress. The heat is stifling." His hand ran up her back for the fasteners.

"Don't, Brant," she protested when his warm fingers brushed her flesh. He didn't stop and she rolled to her back to stop the movement of his hands. His fingers were pinned beneath her. "I don't want you undressing me," she insisted, studying the dark profile above her.

"I'm only thinking of your comfort." He grinned. "And mine. Do you think I want to cuddle up to a woman in a dress?"

"I am not asking you to 'cuddle up' to me and I

would prefer it if you didn't."

Brant pulled one of his hands free and the other opened against her back, his palm against her naked flesh. His gaze dropped to her lips while his free hand caught the mattress on the far side of Amber.

"You are my wife. You belong in this bed at my side."

"I don't want to be here," she said hastily. "There wasn't any place else to sleep."

"Why are you fighting me?" he asked in a deep voice. "We haven't had our wedding night."

"I don't want one," she said flatly, wishing he would move away from her. Brant caught the hem of her gown and pulled it up. "What are you doing?" she screamed in outrage.

She twisted, trying to trap the fabric with her legs and prevent him from exposing her undergarments. Even if he got the dress off she would be adequately covered, but the thought of being partially clothed sent a trembling through her body.

"You are too warm. It is going to be hot enough tonight without you throwing off more body heat." He continued tugging at the fabric until it had reached her hips. "Sit up and I can pull it over your head."

Amber didn't move and Brant grabbed her shoulders and forced her to a sitting position. Quickly, he freed her from the gown and tossed it to the foot of the bed. Amber threw her hands over her semi-exposed breasts, suddenly wishing her underclothes weren't cut so low. The touch of Brant's hand against the small of her back forced a sharp breath from her lips.

"Relax," he said in a coaxing voice. "You are so stiff."

It was his touch that caused the stiffness, but she could never admit it. She wanted to run from the bed and at the same time remain and learn the joys his hands could teach.

"Slip off your bodice and let me massage your back."

"No," she protested, but his hands were already freeing the laces and slipping the garment from her shoulders. When he cast it aside, she felt exposed and vulnerable. She hugged her arms against her chest and felt a crimson flush steal over her cheeks.

"You're beautiful," Brant whispered. "You have no reason to hide yourself." He chuckled softly. "This is the first time I have ever seen you meek and submissive. Are you afraid of me?"

Tossing her amber hair over her shoulder, she turned to Brant. His dark eyes, though in the shadows, were marked by alertness.

"I am not afraid of you Brant. I'm not afraid of anyone."

Brant raised his hand to stroke her cheek. "I have never met a woman with such boldness. You try to hide your fears by being hard, but I think you're soft and vulnerable."

No one had ever praised her and at the same time made her feel like a woman. She found herself at a loss for words. His nearness had sparked every nerve in her body, and she held her breath in anticipation. Was Brant going to try and make love to her?

His hand curved down her naked shoulder and along the line of her arm. His finger caught the edge of one of her breasts and her heart throbbed against his palm. Grabbing her shoulders, he pulled her back against the mattress.

"Why don't you relax?" he coaxed. Seizing her wrists, he pushed her hands to her sides. Amber flinched in embarrassment then soared in excitement as his eyes dropped to her naked chest. "So beautiful," he muttered.

Amber slid her tongue along her lips to moisten her dry mouth. The tingling in her limbs made her feel light-headed. Brant raised his hand and traced a line between her breasts. Amber's stomach dropped sharply as his hand stopped above the waistband of her undergarments, his fingers searching beneath the band.

"Brant," she said in a voice that sounded like a whisper. Suddenly, she found herself at a loss for words. What did she want to ask him?

"I know, Amber," he answered in soft understanding. "I know."

She looked into his eyes, finding them hooded and noncommittal. Was there a sensitivity to this man she didn't know about? Brant pulled her against his chest and his lips lightly touched her cheek. It expressed tender affection without frightening her. He gazed into her eyes and smiled.

"You're exhausted. Try and relax." Holding her possessively, he laid his head on the pillow next to her.

Amber was surprised he wasn't trying to force the sexual act between them. Sighing her relief, her body eased into a state of relaxation. She didn't know if Brant was just being kind because she was exhausted. He had given every indication that he wanted her, but he was making no move to coax her into responding. What game was he playing at now? Why did he arouse her then leave her alone? It was definitely something to consider.

She glanced at the man beside her. His eyes were closed, and his nostrils flared with each breath. His fingers were warm and possessive on her body, yet he did not demand what she was reluctant to give. Amber wrinkled her nose in confusion. Was she disappointed or glad?

Exhaustion finally claimed her and Amber welcomed the secure hold of the man at her side. It was one of the most restful nights she had ever spent, and she woke slowly, reluctant to surrender the feelings she found calming. Warm breath against her cheek was the catalyst that spurred her eyes open. She found herself looking into Brant's brown eyes.

"Good morning," he said, a quick smile coming to his lips. "I trust you slept well."

She found herself unable to stop the responding smile. "Yes, I did."

"When are you expected at the hospital?"

"As soon as I can get there," she responded quickly. Benjamin had told her to come anytime, but she didn't want Brant to think she had time to spend in bed.

"Still uncertain, aren't you?" he said huskily. "I don't want to hurt you. I only want to make love to you. I think your body wants it too."

"No. It will only complicate things. At the end of a month I am going my own way."

"What if I don't want you to?" His voice was husky.

Amber didn't know how to respond. Did he want something permanent? The thought almost threw her into panic. She wanted to get away from him as soon as possible.

"It wouldn't work," she said quickly. "We would always be on opposite sides."

"I am not letting that bother me."

"It makes it impossible for me."

His eyes darkened. "Your animosity toward me makes my next request a little difficult. I want you to trust me. I don't want you to do anything to jeopardize my position."

"I don't know if I can." She hesitated. "I will promise not to do anything rash. I am not a fool. I was taught to be levelheaded."

"You are a surprising young woman." His gaze dropped to her mouth. "And a very beautiful one."

Amber's heart pounded against her breast and forced her to realize Brant was cupping the soft mound of her breast with his large hand. A jolt of pleasant surprise shot along her spine. She had accepted the intimate contact without realizing what was happening.

Amber scanned his face. His dark hair, slightly ruffled from sleep, was thick. His wide mouth was parted to display the full lower lip and thin upper lip. Long lashes fanned his cheeks as his eyes wandered over her half-naked state. He was a breathlessly attractive man. Why did he have to be the enemy? Why couldn't she trust him?

His tongue was a shot of erotic excitement when it flicked over the skin between her breasts. His hand moved to knead and tease the flesh already aroused to his touch. Her breath quickened as he nuzzled her neck. Her hands glided to his shoulders to push him away, but when she came into contact with his warm flesh, her palms slid over the smooth skin, involuntarily drawing him closer. Brant took advantage of her invitation to lay his body over hers, his chest flattening her ripe breasts. His leg tangled in the sheet and was unable to find its way across her thighs. Groaning his exasperation, he freed one of his arms, ripped the sheet away, and pressed his lower body against hers. His naked arousal was a surprise, but Amber, protected by the light linen undergarments, found the feel of him new and exciting.

He buried his face in her hair, and the soft, wet scent of her filled his nostrils and pushed his body to the edge of need. His desire for her engulfed him like a ravenous hunger, and he found himself aching with the urge to possess her quickly. There was something about her that created an excited passion. Perhaps it was her timid exploration of his shoulders or the bashful way she responded to his love-making. Though he had not arranged their marriage, this woman was everything he could ask for in a mate, and he suspected their desire would never be equaled. She had unleashed a hunger he never knew he could feel.

Turning her head, Amber gave Brant access to the throbbing pulse in her neck, gasping quickly when his tongue darted over her fevered flesh. She felt confused by the new feelings he aroused, and at the same time welcomed the gentle teaching he was offering. Thoughts of him being the enemy fled and she was aware only of the slow excitement he was creating in her limbs. There was a pounding in her ears that matched the rapid thud of her heart as he pressed her into the mattress. The undergarments over her lower limbs felt thin, yet they weren't thin enough to feel his flesh against her body, and she was appalled that she wanted to explore the sensation. Running her hands up his back, she felt every muscle taut with the uncoiled passion he had yet to release. His lips found her ear and she buried her face against his shoulder, involuntarily and unknowingly sinking her teeth into his flesh. Salty skin tickled her tongue and she ran it over his skin to his neck. Amber could no longer control her emotions. She moved on her own, eager to please.

Brant's hand slid down her side and his weight shifted. His hand dipped beneath the band of her undergarments to cup her buttocks and press her against his lower body. His fingers tugged at the fabric, slowly easing them over her hips. Amber did nothing in protest. She ached for what came beyond their brief consummation; she ached for what had been promised but never given. He had aroused her body many times, but never with this intensity and never when she knew there would be no turning back. Enemy or not, she was his for the taking, and she was willing to make the offering.

Brant was just about to ease the fabric over the most intimate part of her body when he stopped and drew back. His hunger was in his eyes for her to see, and she let her blue-green eyes reflect the passion she was feeling. The tightness in her chest was real, and the trembling in her limbs made her weak. Her mouth parted, her gaze dropping to his lips. He teased her flesh with his mouth, but kept his lips from hers, purposefully heightening her anticipation. Amber was seized by the need to have him plunder the recesses of her mouth. Raising her hands, she caught the sides of his head in her palms.

"Amber," he said softly and his voice mirrored question.

There was a sudden shortness of breath. Brant was asking permission to continue, and the request was surprising. As her husband he had every right to take her, and his question had been asked out of tender consideration. Once again she wondered if she was wrong about him.

There was a tenseness in his body as he waited for her answer. He was coiled, ready to resume his attention and at the same time frightened that she might refuse entrance to the most personal part of her life. He was ready for more than consummation; he wanted the full union of their bodies in driving satisfaction. This woman was in his life and he wanted her to stay. He ached to put his brand of possession on her so no other man could arouse her the way he could. He wanted to block out the men from her past and bring himself to the forefront of her thoughts.

The clanging bell outside brought him out of his thoughtful reverie. When would things start to work for him? The war and all its complications were making a mess out of his life. The woman he wanted was beneath him and he was reminded of a meeting with high officials. Scowling, he met her eyes.

Amber's verbal response hovered on the tip of her tongue. Yes, she wanted this man. He had aroused her to such a fevered pitch, she couldn't refuse. She was ready to explore the unknown.

She was shocked out of her lethargic feeling by the scowl on her husband's face. It was obvious he was displeased with her, and she realized her lack of response had been taken as rejection.

"Well, my beautiful wife," he said drawing back. "You've been saved from my possession."

"But I—," she started to say, wanting him to know she was ready to accept him.

He drew back, his face distant and cold. "One day you will be my wife in every way." Pushing free of her body, he sat. "I have a meeting to attend and can't be late."

Feeling vulnerable and exposed, Amber grabbed the sheet and pulled it to her breast. Beneath the covers she quickly adjusted her undergarments. Completely oblivious to his nakedness, Brant rose and reached for his pants. Amber, shocked by the strength of him, found herself unable to look away. He was a superb male, his thighs and buttocks tight with muscles. He didn't turn to face her until his pants were secured at the waist, and Amber was glad he had maintained a little modesty.

"Disappointed?" he mocked.

"Brant," she said, fumbling for the right words. "I'm not responsible for your leaving this bed." When she had finished speaking, she was shocked at her boldness. She had practically told him she was disappointed.

Brant stopped his dressing and looked at her. "Does that mean you want me to rejoin you?"

Amber's cheeks colored. "Are you deliberately making it hard for me?"

He put his hands on his lean hips and took a breath that strained the muscles in his chest. "Are you ashamed to admit that you want me? I am your husband." His brown eyes bored into her green eyes, darkened by blue flecks of confusion.

Amber didn't know what to say. Could she maintain her outward show of strength to this powerful man like Papa had demanded when she was soft and vulnerable beneath?

He reached for his shirt and pushed his arms into the sleeves. "Why are you afraid to admit that you desire me? I thought you were a woman with courage."

There was nothing Amber could say. She was frightened of the new feelings and more afraid to have sentiment for a man she couldn't trust. She had been raised to be independent. Needing this man didn't fit into her life. Could she maintain her freedom and still need someone else? She had been careful not to let anyone into her life but her father and brother. Was it possible she didn't know how?

"I think you are confused," she said, denying the earlier passion and feelings he had aroused. "You think every woman should fall at your feet. I am not interested."

Brant's face darkened with a scowl. "From the moment I met you I was captivated by your ability to tackle anything that gets in your path. What I didn't recognize is that your ability to feel has crippled you. You are afraid to admit your true feelings because you think I will see it as weakness." He turned to the door. "I have an important meeting to attend."

"What is it about?" she asked casually.

Brant's eyes narrowed. "It is a secret meeting."

"Are you going to tell me about it?"

"No," he said flatly.

"Just as I suspected," she flung at him. "You want me to trust you, but you won't trust me."

Amber saw Brant's jaw tense. "You have made your feelings against the Confederacy well known. I would be a fool to tell you what goes on here." Turning, he left the cabin, slamming the door behind him.

She frowned. Things were not going the way she had planned. Throwing aside the covers, she rose, washed, and dressed. Pulling the door open, she watched the confusion in the complex. More officers had arrived during the night and their appearance hinted at something very important. This might be her chance to gather information for the North. It would be dangerous, but a risk she was determined to take. She would spend time at the hospital, then try to learn what was going on at the meeting.

She didn't want to eat, but knew she needed food to sustain her. Walking to the food building, she got her breakfast and carried it to the shade beneath a cluster of trees. Being discreet, she focused her attention on the building where the meeting was to be held. Many high-ranking officials stood in groups waiting for things to begin. She caught sight of Brant deep in conversation with a Confederate general and wondered what important Union secrets he was giving away. Amber fought back a surge of resentment toward the man she had married. She hated him for his loyalty to the South, refusing to accept that he had a right to his own beliefs.

The men were still standing outside when Amber went to the hospital. No new casualties had arrived so Amber started changing bandages. As expected the Confederate soldiers were getting the preferred treatment, and she ached to help the soldiers who fought for the cause she supported.

Just before noon, she rose from a soldier's bedside and wiped the perspiration from her brow. The heat was stifling and the poor ventilation created stagnant air. Rubbing her hands on her skirt, she walked toward the door. All morning she had been thinking about the meeting and wondering how she could find out what was going on.

Benjamin came up behind her. "You've worked hard. Why don't you get something to eat?"

It was the opportunity Amber needed to get away from the hospital. "Thank you. I think the rest would do me good. I'll be back later."

She tried to formulate a plan as she walked toward the meeting place. There were no guards outside the building, but that didn't mean she would be allowed to enter. Deciding it would be dangerous to walk inside, she went to get her meal.

At breakfast she had recognized the scant portions and knew the South was hurting for supplies. After thanking the young private for her food, she walked toward the shade provided by the meeting hall building with the hope of finding an open window.

There weren't any and she scowled. Strolling casually toward the back, she turned and ducked behind the building. A small alley ran the entire length, and Amber walked toward the sound of voices, her heart thumping wildly in her breast. It was the sound of her husband's voice that froze her motion, and his words forced a lump into Amber's throat. He spoke in a clear tone as he gave precise information on the North's plans for attack against the Southern States. He detailed the North's strength and expounded on its weaknesses. Despite the heat, the words chilled her to her bones. Brant's meeting with Colonel Broadmore had proven fruitful for the South and dangerous for the North.

Amber raised her trembling hand to her forehead. It was too late to block his deceit. The only option open was to expose him as a traitor if they returned to Union territory. Her lips curled in a sneer. Brant had used Andy's rescue to try and gain Amber's trust. It hurt to know she had been used.

Suddenly, Amber felt alone and isolated in the middle of enemy territory. She had been burdened with a heavy responsibility, but she could not shirk her duty to the North. When she returned to Washington, she would have the evidence to expose her husband as a spy and watch him hang.

Amber realized it was dangerous and stupid to remain and listen to Brant. If she were caught eavesdropping, he would be suspicious of everything she did. Still clutching her food plate, she crept along the building. Work would help occupy her thoughts, and she was determined to do all she could to aid the Union soldiers. She started around the corner, oblivious to the obstacle in her path. Seconds too late, she saw the dull buttons on the gray Confederate uniform. Uttering a startled, "Oh," the plate of food fell to the ground.

Amber's blue-green eyes rose to meet the cool gray ones of Captain Edgar Mason. The rigid way he held his body and the pursed lips put Amber on immediate guard. She had not trusted nor liked the man when she had met him at the prison, and it was unfortunate to find him here.

"Well, well," he drawled in a Southern accent. "Fancy meeting you." Amber didn't like the way he was looking at her. His expression was hostile and merciless. "What are you doing here?"

"I am here with my husband," she said easily, relying on her marriage to Brant to ease her unexplained tension.

"Ah, yes," he said, shaking his head. "You never did thank me for arranging your wedding," he sneered. "But perhaps the engagement had been a lie and you never really intended to marry."

"We are very happy," she lied.

His gaze narrowed. "Why are you behind this building?"

Amber moistened her lips and let a reddish tinge of color brighten her cheeks. "I am afraid you caught me returning from my—ah—tending my female necessities."

"Why here?" he argued. "I suppose you know there is a highly classified meeting in progress."

"Really," she said, arching one of her brows. "Brant said something about a meeting. Why aren't you there?"

Her comment was intended as a snub and Edgar's scowl darkened his face. "That is none of your business."

Amber smiled sweetly. "Weren't you invited?"

Mason was angry before, but her statement made him bristle. "I have been given another assignment."

She knew toying with Edgar was dangerous, but she couldn't resist the opportunity to try and learn something. He was so enraged he might spill something important.

"Is it cleaning slop?" she mocked innocently.

"My job is highly classified," he snarled.

Amber cast him a doubtful look. "Sorry Captain, but I don't believe anyone would trust you with anything of importance. You blundered your job at the prison camp."

"The blunder you speak of might prove important to the Confederacy. . . . So will your being here."

His words sparked the warning of trouble, and she threw her hands on her hips. "I don't know what you are getting at," she said briskly, "but I don't like your insinuation. We made a fool out of you and you didn't like it."

"No, I didn't. Funny thing about your plan to disgrace me. No one here knew anything about the scheme." Edgar chuckled wickedly. "Do you have anything to say?"

"Talk to Brant. I have work to do."

Tossing her head, she stepped around Edgar and walked away. She didn't even glance at the meeting hall when she stepped into the central complex, and walked to the hospital. Only when she was inside and out of view did she turn to search for Edgar. He was standing next to the meeting hall watching the hospital. He was a dangerous adversary and she had to take steps to protect herself.

Twenty

Benjamin ran to Amber's side. "I'm glad you're back."

"What is wrong?" she asked, noticing the man's heightened anxiety. "Has something happened?"

"There was a battle. We received word that casualties will arrive in less than two hours. We are probably going to run short of supplies."

"Will any doctors arrive with them?"

Benjamin shook his head. "No. Can we count on your assistance?"

"Of course. Where do you want me?"

"We have finished with the men here. Why don't you go back with the Union men until our soldiers arrive?"

Amber was thrilled with his request. It was what she had wanted to do all morning, but was afraid of being obvious. Turning, she went to the back room. The low moans of the men tore at her heart. Kneeling at their bedsides, she whispered soothing words and gave them tender care. The medicine went to the Confederates and nothing was given to the Union soldiers for pain. She wanted to sneak some medicine to them, but knew the supplies were being prepared for the incoming injured.

The time passed rapidly and she was soon given the signal that the wagons had arrived. Amber ran outside, knowing immediate attention was crucial for the men wounded hours before. The injured were removed on stretchers and carried into the already crowded building.

Work began immediately. The serious cases went directly to surgery. Amber worked with Benjamin, anticipating his needs before he asked. They lost the first man because his wounds were too serious to repair. Amber saw the hopelessness on the doctor's face and wondered if he ever got used to the sight of death, knowing there was nothing he could do to prevent it. Amputations were done on the next two men. Both would probably die of gangrene.

It was well after dusk when the last man was moved from the surgery table, and they could attend the less seriously injured. Medical supplies were dangerously low, but they hoped to have a new shipment within the next few days.

Amber had tied her hair at the nape of her neck when they started work, but it was beginning to stray from its ribbon. Sighing in exhaustion, she pushed the stray curls behind her ear. There was so much to do, but she was finding it increasingly difficult to stay awake. She heard one of the workers say morning was only a few hours away. Sighing, she returned to her patient and hoped things would begin to slow down. There wasn't anyone to ease the work load, and everyone would soon need sleep.

"Am I gonna live?" the young soldier she was attending asked.

She finished securing the bandage in place. "You'll be fine. It was a flesh wound and not serious."

"I guess I am one of the lucky ones."

Amber smiled at him. He couldn't be more than sixteen. "Yes, you are." She lightly patted his arm. "Try and get some rest."

Amber walked to the supply room to retrieve a fresh supply of bandages. Squatting, she selected several sizes. Sighing, she rested her back against the wall and slid to the floor. She was so tired she didn't know how much longer she could continue. It was becoming more difficult to keep her eyes open. Everything fled her thoughts as she dropped her chin to her chest, willingly surrendering the fight she had waged against her exhaustion. Her sleep was deep and she felt surrounded by comfort and security.

"Amber, Amber," Brant said and she stirred.

"Mmmm," she sighed.

"It is time I took you home." Brant lifted her, and she wrapped her arms around his neck, her head rolling against his broad chest. He left the hospital and crossed the distance to their home. Kicking the door open, he entered and shoved it closed with his boot. Crossing the room, he gently laid Amber on the bed. She moaned softly, her green eyes opening to mark her state of confusion.

"Where am I?" she asked sleepily.

"In our room. Go to sleep," he said, turning up the lamp.

"I'm so tired," she moaned. Her head rolled to the

side, her lashes fanning softly against her creamy cheeks.

Looking down at her, Brant sighed. She was so beautiful and desirable. He wanted her more than he had ever wanted any woman, and he intended having her one time before—. He shook his head, determined to shake off the grim reminder of his future. There would be plenty of time later to think about that. Right now he wanted to give all his attention to the beautiful woman in his bed. Her state of sleepiness only made her more alluring, and he suspected she would be more cooperative when she didn't have her wits about her. He would make love to her, and she would respond with the passion he knew she was capable of. He would awaken her slowly and finally take her when she was too aroused to stop him. It was one victory he intended having.

Quickly unfastening the buttons of his shirt, he removed it and tossed the garment over a chair. His pants and boots followed, and he stood proud and naked at the bedside. Amber's dress opened down the front and Brant's supple fingers gently eased the buttons free. The fabric parted and he pulled the gown from her body. Amber stirred, but her sleep was still too deep to awaken passion in her limbs. He smiled. It would come and he looked forward to it.

Her underwear was made from fine fabric, and it clung to her skin, molding her lush curves. She was a beautiful, well-proportioned woman and in a few minutes she would be his. The marriage had been consummated, but this would be their wedding night. He wanted it to be so special that it would burn in her mind forever. He wanted her to remember tomorrow after—. He shook his head. He didn't want to think of that now.

Slowly, he raised his hand to stroke her creamy white cheek, and her lips involuntarily parted in a soft sigh. Brant's finger followed the curve of her soft lower lip. He ached to feel their touch against his, promising the passion she had never given. Tonight would be his night.

His fingers strayed to the laces on her underclothes, his fingers fumbling in his excitement. Her clothes were carefully removed and tossed to the floor. His eyes devoured her beauty.

Amber's eyes fluttered and opened, the hazy light of sleep still clouding their depths. Brant watched her, the smoldering light of passion sharpening the brown in his eyes. Suddenly, Amber sucked in her breath, and her eyes widened to run over the naked chest covered by soft hair. Her eyes traveled to the narrowing of hair at his flat stomach, and her hand rose to her lips.

Brant climbed over her to the far side of the bed, and Amber turned her head to follow his progress. He wasn't going to give her the chance to protest and awake fully. He didn't want a fighting lioness in his bed, but a soft kitten, still drugged by her sleepiness. Moving swiftly, his fingers curved up her side to stop just below her breast. His gaze met hers, their eyes locking to each others—hers reflecting uncertainty and his mirroring passion and need. Rising to one elbow, his mouth sought the rise of her right breast, and his lips parted to rain a series of kisses along her flesh. His hand moved swiftly to cover the crested peak taut with desire. His lips glided to her neck, and

Amber rolled her head to the side to allow him greater access to the sensitive points. Brant accepted the invitation like a starved man given food, and he greedily caressed the flesh. His teeth nibbled, and his tongue slid over her sweat-dampened skin.

"Brant," she whispered uncertainly. "What are you doing?"

His teeth nipped her ear. "I am making love to my wife. This is our wedding night."

His words added to the fire already building in her body and she twisted, her head turning to find itself against his shoulder. Brant threw his leg between her thighs to halt her wiggling. His fingers glided down her back and across her buttocks, not yet ready to press her nakedness against his. She wasn't willing enough; she had not begun to respond.

His lips glided down her jawline, seeking, but not able to find her mouth. His hand returned to her breast, and his palm claimed the mound with possession. Amber moaned deep in her throat, her senses heightened by his caresses and the vulnerability of sleep. She wanted to flee, but she wasn't certain if it was a deep-seated desire.

Brant's palm was creating an exciting tingle wherever he touched. His lips were promising and teasing without giving her the reward of their touch against hers. Amber eagerly pressed her upper body to his, her mouth leaving his shoulder so she could look into his eyes. The smoldering passion she saw took the breath from her lungs.

"Brant," she said uncertainly. Her confusion between letting him continue and forcing him to stop had surfaced. Her body wanted his touch, but her mind had remembered who he really was.

Brant sensed the change coming over her. Her sleepy state was vanishing, and she knew where she was and what was happening. He couldn't let something ruin this night with his wife. Pulling her hands from the dormant state between them, he laid them on his shoulders. With his hands against her back, he propelled her length against his.

The shock of his naked male body pressed against hers threw Amber's senses into turmoil and made her head spin. Her fingers dug into his shoulders, the tips burning from the heat of his skin. There wasn't a part of her body that wasn't throbbing with awareness. Her breath escaped her chest in a sigh of pleasure. There was not an inch of space between them — every part of her belonged to every part of him. His desire throbbed against her, filling her with a new height of uncertainty. There was no response in the smoldering brown eyes, and she saw only the promise of conquering and being the victor. Her gaze dropped to the hard lips, her eyes lingering on the full lower lip. She was hungry for their feel.

"Brant," she whispered. "Please."

Her plea went unheeded though she wasn't certain what she was asking for. Did she want him to stop or continue? A puff of air came from Brant's parted lips to tease hers with feather softness. His fingers twisted in her amber hair to force her head against the pillow. Air rushed between their bodies, and Amber felt exposed and vulnerable without the pinning weight of his. Clutching his shoulders tightly, she pulled him toward her, her mouth parting in hopeful expectation Brant's eyes flickered over her face, his body eager

284

and willing to be against hers. She took his weight easily and his large frame pinned her against the bed. With his leg wedged between her thighs he ran his fingers across her lower abdomen, forcing her to draw a sharp breath. Her stomach fell like water off a cliff, and she was so aware of Brant's manliness that she no longer felt in control of her destiny.

"Amber, you are so beautiful. I want you," he muttered against her lips. "I want to feel your softness . . . just once."

There was nothing Amber could say or do. Brant had made her powerless to the quaking need he had aroused in her body. He had created a passion in her that could not be denied. Fears she had held in her thoughts were drowned by the overpowering awareness he had created. Exhaustion blocked even the simplest contemplation.

Brant dropped his head and his lips glided along her jawline. Amber threaded her fingers through his thick, soft hair. Brant's hand opened along her thigh and she moved toward the touch. Amber moaned, her head turning toward Brant. His mouth caught the edge of her lips, and his tongue edged out to cautiously taste their sweetness. She opened her mouth, waiting and wanting to feel his possession, but he ignored her offering and plundered the opposite corner. She twisted beneath him, her body pressing intimately against his. Brant's hands were everywhere carefully drawing her into a world she had never fully visited. Her fingers gripped his shoulder blades and her nails dug into his flesh. Amber no longer wanted to be a visitor. She wanted to belong in the world that gave such pleasurable sensations and created an excitement she had never thought possible.

Brant's tongue rolled across the edge of her lips. He drew back and looked into her eyes. "Amber," he said softly. "You are mine," he said and claimed her mouth with a drugging kiss that swept her into the surging heat of passion. Every inch of her body trembled as he plundered her lips.

Unable to remain dormant, she eagerly moved her mouth against his, her fingers running the length of his broad back. She was drawn to a height she never thought possible, held and suspended by the continuous motion of his mouth and body. Brant shifted, his manhood searching for the hidden place in her body. He found her softness and hesitated. He tore his mouth from hers to kiss her cheeks.

"Oh, Amber," he called and slowly joined their bodies.

The pain had been erased the night of their consummation, and on her "wedding night" she was filled with his whole being. If Amber expected she had experienced everything, she was surprised when Brant continued the teasing caresses and drew from her lips a kiss that spiraled them to soaring heights while his body brought an explosion of passion.

Trembling, they held each other gently and returned to the sane realities of life. Brant buried his face in her amber hair and sighed. She had been everything he had expected and more. Why did their first time have to be the last? He still had the night and he would savor her nearness. It would be the memory he would carry with him, but a memory he was sure would haunt him the rest of his life.

Amber stirred, her body still accepting the weight

of his. Exhaustion beckoned, but she did not want to surrender the luxurious feeling her limbs had experienced for the first time. It was too wonderful and exciting. Brant had taken her across the threshold of becoming a woman and introduced a new series of feelings. She thought of this man as her husband and the reasons she was in his bed. He was the enemy and she had responded. She felt like a traitor to the Union Army and her father. Their relationship had passed into one of intimacy. Would there be other times like this — other demands from Brant?

Looking down, he saw the confusion on her face. "It is all right," he whispered. "Try and get some sleep."

"Why Brant?" she asked, remembering that she had fallen asleep in the hospital and knowing he must have carried her to their cabin. "Why did you arouse my body when I was asleep?"

"You were too frightened to accept me any other way," he said simply. "It had to be tonight." He lightly stroked her hair. "You are brave in many ways, but you were scared of this kind of relationship. You have always been afraid to show me the soft, vulnerable woman." He pulled her head against his shoulder. "I wish I had time to teach you to depend on me — trust me . . . I wanted this and it had to be tonight."

There was a maze of questions in her thoughts, but she was unable to fight the exhaustion that was claiming her body. She sighed. Tomorrow would be soon enough to ponder the uncertainties he had introduced into her thoughts. Still clutching his shoulders, she closed her eyes and let sleep overtake her.

Twenty-one

Amber woke slowly, a delicious warmth spreading through her limbs. She felt completely rested, her exhaustion from the day before gone. She didn't know why, but she felt wonderful this morning. Slowly, she opened her eyes and saw the sun streaming through the curtained windows. Its brightness told her the early morning hours had long since passed, and Amber knew they would be expecting her at the hospital. Frowning, she remembered the sick, helpless victims of the battle. The casualty rate had been high. How many Union soldiers had lost their lives?

Brant would be able to tell her more about the battle. He might even know who had been victorious. Scanning the cabin, she wondered where he was. They had very few possessions in the room, and it didn't surprise her not to see anything of his. Amber started to throw back the sheet and froze, the memory of the night before flooding over her.

Brant had carried her from the hospital and placed her in bed. She did not remember losing her clothes, but vaguely recalled waking and finding him standing over her, his body naked and wanting hers. She flushed at the memory of his hands caressing her flesh, teasing her skin until her body begged to become his possession. He had been a master in arousing her need, taking her slowly to the height of passion and making her a woman. He had forced his attentions on her when she was too exhausted to fight, and she had responded wantonly, giving her body freely to him.

Had she given him pleasure or had she merely received? He had satisfied his lust, but had it been pleasurable for him? Would he come to their bed again with the intention of making love to her? He had called her name and admitted his desire, but had once been enough for him? Or would tonight bring more love-making?

Amber remembered Brant's accusation that he had to excite her body when she was too tired to refuse because she was afraid to do it any other way. Clutching the sheet across her naked chest, she wrinkled her nose. Was she scared of having their relationship on a one to one basis? Had she been frightened of the physical relationship because it meant she had to give of herself? By the time she had realized what was happening last night she was too drugged by passion to stop. Would things change now that she had become part of him? Would she cower in fear or let him make his advances and satisfy his lust?

Brant was a strong Confederate. He had given away the Union's secrets. How could she have responded so wantonly to a man who wanted to destroy everything she believed in? Brant had accused her of being a coward and afraid of him as a man. Was it true? Frowning her uncertainty, she tossed aside the sheet and reached for her undergarments.

Her questions would not be answered until Brant made another attempt to seduce her. It would happen, but what would she do? Could she deny the longing he had aroused? Could she ignore the touch of his hands and the feel of his body? If she denied her fears and became involved with Brant it would only complicate things. He was the enemy—a man she had vowed to hate. Making love to him would be a betrayal of her real feelings. Why couldn't she have married a man she liked?

Amber dropped her dress over her head and buttoned the front. Her stomach rumbled in protest of the lack of food, and she remembered she hadn't eaten since breakfast yesterday. She had decided to speak to Brant about Edgar Mason. He posed a dangerous threat to her safety, and she did not want to live with the uncertainty that he might accuse her of spying.

Amber turned and a paper propped on the table caught her attention. Curious, she crossed the room and picked it up. Her name scrawled across the top in bold lettering made her heart pound. Her eyes dropped to the bottom, and Brant's signature created a tightening in her chest. Her eyes flew back to the top and she read:

Amber, by the time you read this message I will be gone from your life. It is probably better this way. Your hatred toward me is obvious, but last night you proved you could respond to me as a man. I'm sorry I had to deceive you and force you into a state of desire while you slept, but I knew you would not come to me any other way.

You are afraid of our marriage—afraid of me—afraid to trust. You are a coward because you are scared to be a woman. Perhaps you never learned how. Return to your uncle and your empty existence. Affectionately, Brant.

Amber crumpled the paper in her hand and let her fist fall to the table. Brant was gone from her life—gone almost as fast as he had entered it. Everything between them was over, but this note had been cruel, poking at her uncertainties and calling her a coward. Amber had never thought herself to be one. Papa had never wanted her to whimper in fear of anything. He had taught the twins to meet their challenges and think clearly. Her father had praised her cunning, bravery and demanded strength, but he had never called her a coward.

Brant's accusation stung and she experienced a burst of anger. She wasn't afraid of anything, and it rankled her to know Brant had convicted her of something she disbelieved. If he were here, how would she disprove his charges? Would she climb into his bed and become a wanton in his arms? Would she surrender her mind and body to a man she couldn't trust? He wanted her dependence, but she had been taught to rely on herself. Why had he put doubts in her mind, then left before she could prove he was wrong?

Brant had played her for a fool and she didn't like

it. Scowling, she smoothed out the paper, folded it into a tiny square and pushed it into her undergarments. It would help remind her of the Rebel who had turned her life upside down.

There was a brisk knock on the door and Amber hurried to open it. A private, his face flush with uncertainty, stood in the entrance holding a plate of food and cup of coffee.

"I brought you something to eat. You should be preparing to leave within the hour."

Amber accepted the meal. "Leave?" she said dumbfounded.

"Yes. Major Faulkner made the necessary arrangements."

"Yes, of course," she said, smiling. It wouldn't be wise to show the young man her confusion. Thanking him, she kicked the door shut and sat at the table. She stared in silence at the food. Brant had left without warning, but he had taken the time to make arrangements to get her out of Confederate headquarters. Any thoughts of remaining to gather information for the North fled her mind. With Edgar Mason at the camp it would be too dangerous.

She ate quickly, then walked to the small traveling case containing her clothes. Opening it, she inspected the contents and was surprised to find a sack of money that would adequately cover her expenses.

Certain her hour was almost up, Amber opened the door and stepped outside. The air was humid and promised to make travel uncomfortable. She scanned the headquarters and wondered if she could give the Union Army its layout for possible attack. Leaving her case at the door, she crossed to the hospital. Benjamin had been kind to her and she wanted to say goodbye. She found him between operations.

"Amber," he said, forcing a smile. "I was wondering when you would be here."

"Is something wrong?" she asked, noticing the droop of his mouth.

"We have fallen behind and I just used the last of the medicine. It is going to be hard on the men."

"Maybe you'll get that shipment today."

"I hope so," he agreed. "Are you ready to work?"

"I'm leaving today," she said flatly. "My husband has been sent — ." She fumbled uncertainly. She had no idea where Brant had gone or what he was doing. "Away from headquarters," she finished. "He made arrangements for me to leave."

Benjamin frowned. "We'll certainly miss you."

Amber smiled and stepped outside. She was temporarily blinded by the sun and paused to shield her eyes.

"Well, well," a voice drawled and Amber swung around.

"What do you want?" she snapped, hating the sight of Edgar Mason.

He was leaning against the building, but he straightened and strolled toward her. "I was following you."

"Really," she said innocently. "Why?"

"I think we both know the answer." His gray eyes narrowed. "I heard your husband left the camp." He waited for confirmation, but Amber remained noncommittal. "I understand you are leaving also."

In a few minutes she would be gone and there was no point in denying her departure. "Yes, I am."

"Why?" he quizzed bluntly.

"There is no reason for me to stay."

"Just because your husband is gone is no reason for you to disappear. I understand you are quite good at the hospital."

His statement warned Amber that he had been checking up on her activities and she didn't like it. "I would think a man in your *position* would have more important things to do than follow me around."

Her slur on his rank forced a narrowing of his gray eyes. "I believe I have good reason to watch you . . . and your husband."

"Then why aren't you following him around?" she baited. "You might become a big hero, or—" she dared, "you might make a complete fool of yourself." She smiled sweetly. "I believe the latter would happen."

"I'll see you both hang."

Amber didn't let him see how nervous his words made her. Turning, she walked toward her room where she found a soldier waiting. Her case was placed in the back of a wagon, and she joined the private on the seat.

Amber experienced relief as they left headquarters and started down the road. Soon she would be back in Washington and this episode of her life could be forgotten. Her fingers absently pressed the part of her dress hiding Brant's letter and knew all of it could not be forgotten. Too many things lay between them.

When they arrived at the train station, Amber thanked the soldier and watched him drive away.

Unfortunately, she could not travel toward Washington and had to be content to stay with the train until she could buy private transportation to the nearest Union depot. After days of dusty travel, she purchased a ticket on a train going to Washington.

She tried to block Brant from her memory, but it wasn't easy. He was constantly in her thoughts, and she vividly remembered the feel of his hands, the touch of his lips, and the tickle of his tongue.

The train jerked to a stop and Amber reached for her traveling case. She had not notified anyone of her arrival, so she hired a coach and gave her uncle's address. She had many things to tell Hank, but wanted the conversation in the privacy of their home.

Myra's squeal of delight brought a quick smile to Amber's lips. "What are you doing home?" she asked, taking Amber's case and giving her a big hug.

"It is a long story," she answered, returning the embrace. "It is good to see you."

"You look wonderful."

Amber saw the questions on her friend's face. "Don't ask me anything. Just be glad I am home."

"Hank will be surprised."

"Is he here?"

"No, but I expect him soon."

"I think I'll change," she said and went upstairs.

On Brant's orders Amber's clothes had remained behind, and she wondered if he had known their time together would be short. Brant had used her to reinforce his credibility with his superiors, then deserted her.

Because of Brant's ties to the South, she felt no

295

loyalty to him. Her father had died fighting for the North and Andy had been forced to flee. Commitment to a man who had betrayed their cause would be like treason, and she knew it was time to warn Hank of Brant's connection with the Rebels.

Sighing, Amber thought of Andy. Had he reached California? Had he continued his service with the Union Army? Details on the West were sketchy because the papers devoted their space to the battle-front news. It hurt to know everyone believed he was dead, but she had promised to be silent. Had the time come to break that vow? Admitting that Brant was a Confederate officer opened the door to acknowledging that Andy was alive.

Amber reached for the note hidden in her under-clothes. Opening it, she stared at Brant's bold writing. It was a good thing she hadn't been fooled and trusted him.

The sound of a horse took Amber to the window. Pushing aside the curtain, she saw her uncle. She quickly finished dressing, hid the note in one of her drawers and ran downstairs. She reached the entranceway at the same time the door opened.

"Amber," he said affectionately. "I'm glad you finally arrived. I was starting to get worried."

She stopped. "You knew I was coming?"

"Of course," he stated flatly and walked toward the drawing room.

"But how did you know?" she demanded, joining him.

Hank looked at her in surprise. "Brant told me. He said you were stopping at the plantation for a few days."

"Brant." His name came from her lips in a whisper. "He told you that?" she muttered in disbelief. "When did he tell you?"

"A few days ago," he answered, dropping his hat in a chair.

"Brant is here . . . in Washington."

"Yes," he said, his gaze narrowing uncertainly. "Didn't you know? He has been staying in your room."

Amber could not explain the tightness in her chest. She thought Brant was out of her life and had not expected to find him in Washington waiting for her arrival. He had left her at Confederate headquarters to give him time alone in her uncle's home.

"Where is he now?"

His expression sobered. "I hoped you could tell me." He watched his niece carefully. "I want to know where he has been and what he has done. There is reason to believe there is a spy operating out of Washington. Several of us at headquarters believe that person has access to important information."

"Has something happened?"

"The Confederates have known our plans for battles and troop locations. They are certain to have scouts in the field, but I believe this information is coming out of Washington."

"How long has this been going on?" she asked, thinking that Brant might not be the source. He had not been seen in town before the night of the ball.

"Months," he answered. "But activity has recently increased. I believe Brant is involved. Can you confirm my suspicions?"

Amber turned and walked toward the window.

This was the chance she had been waiting for. It was time to expose Brant's spying. He had threatened Steven's and Hank's lives and it frightened her. She could not be responsible for someone getting hurt.

"Amber, why are you so quiet? I must know the answer." He came up behind her and lightly touched her shoulder. "Did you fall in love with your husband?" he asked, wondering if her feelings for Brant kept her from betraying him. It would definitely complicate things.

She backed away until his hand dropped. "I could never love Brant Faulkner."

"You are reluctant to discuss the man. I can only draw the obvious conclusion."

"You'd better sit down, Uncle Hank. This might take some time to explain."

He cast her a puzzled look and pulled out his pocket watch. "I don't have much time. I didn't know you would be here, and I already set up a meeting."

"Social or military?" she quizzed.

"Military." He smiled. "And very important. You will be interested to know part of it since you were instrumental in spurring my suspicions."

Hank seemed to have forgotten Brant for the time, and Amber was anxious to learn where he would be going. He rarely involved her in the military operations, and she knew this must be something important.

"We have located William Boone."

"Is he in Washington?" she asked quickly.

"Yes. He is supposed to meet with me this evening. I hope to get some answers to a few very important questions."

"Do you think he is spying for the Rebels?"

"He might be part of it, but there is someone else involved. Willy does not have access to the kind of information being passed, but he might be the key to the leader."

This was exciting news. There was a strong possibility that William could tell her what had really happened to her father. She wanted to know for sure that Brant had not been involved.

"This is important," she agreed.

"If a connection can be made between the two men, we will be able to stop one of the most dangerous spy networks.

Amber could sense Hank's excitement. It would be a valuable discovery. "I will tell you about Brant, but you first have to know that he threatened you and Steven if I told the truth. Can you guarantee protection for both of you?"

His eyes widened at her statement. "Brant threatened us?" She nodded. "Of course I will take the necessary precautions."

Taking a deep breath, she looked into her uncle's eyes. "Brant is a major in the Confederate Army." She expected surprise or shock, but she hadn't expected anger.

"A major!" he bellowed. "How dare they send a major to Washington for information! When I think of the things he could have learned living in this house." He raised his hand to his forehead. "We have been used, Amber. The scum used us. I thought he desired you. You're a beautiful woman. All he wanted was information."

Amber could vow for Brant's passion, but she wasn't going to argue the fact with her uncle. "When we left here, he took me to Confederate headquarters. I heard him giving away Union secrets."

Hank's skin had taken on a grayish tinge. "I can't believe this. I'll see him hung for spying against the Union." His gaze softened as he looked at Amber. "When I think that I subjected you to this man and encouraged your marriage, I find it hard to look you in the eye. The Rebels were responsible for the deaths of two people very near to you. I have ruined your life by tying you to a man you couldn't feel anything for but hate." He stared hopefully at his niece. "Can you forgive me?"

Amber smiled to relieve some of her uncle's tension. "There is nothing to forgive. I knew what I was getting into when I married Brant."

His mouth twisted in confusion. "You knew. How?"

"I knew who he was when I married him. I had met him before." She wasn't going to get into the details of their first wedding ceremony. It would only confuse things.

"I don't understand. You didn't mention it to me."

"I was afraid he would hurt you and Steven."

"Where did you meet him? I don't remember seeing him at any of the parties."

Amber moistened her lips. "It was at the Confederate prison camp where Andy was being held. . . . He was the man the Rebels sent to hang your nephew."

Hank's face darkened with rage. "And he had the nerve to come to Washington to try and deceive me.

Does the man take me for a fool?"

"He doesn't take anyone for a fool. He is a very cunning man."

Hank's hand curled into a fist. "I'll see him hanged for what he has done. I will not let any man trick me. He must be exposed."

"Do you think he is here to meet Willy?"

"It is possible. We'll get Willy to confess his loyalty to the South and use him to set a trap for Brant." Hank checked his watch. "Amber, I know we should talk more, but I have to leave. Colonel Broadmore is expecting me."

"Colonel Broadmore," Amber repeated.

Hank walked toward the door. Over his shoulder he said, "You remember Giles Broadmore. He has been following my suspicions about William and asked to be included in this meeting. I will talk to you later."

Amber's stomach tightened. She already knew Giles Broadmore was passing information to Brant. He was the man she should have warned her uncle about. If Willy was involved in the conspiracy, there were three men working out of Washington who had to be stopped. Suddenly, Amber sprang to her feet. There was a strong possibility that Brant would be at the meeting and she wanted to trap him.

Lifting her skirt, Amber raced up the steps to her room. Her fingers tore at the fastenings on her dress and it dropped in a heap on the floor. Throwing open the closet, she rummaged through the back for her pants and shirt. Dressing quickly, she pulled on her boots and secured her amber hair with a ribbon. Opening the door, she tiptoed to the back stairway and crept outside.

Hank had taken the time to saddle a fresh mount, and he was just riding away from the house. Amber ran to the barn and put a bridle on her mare. Without bothering to add a saddle, she jumped on the horse's back and urged the animal forward.

It only took a few minutes for Amber to realize that Hank wasn't riding toward town. He turned off the main road and galloped across a field. Amber followed, her heart racing. She was reminded of the times she had ridden through the woods with her father and brother. It had been wonderful, wild and exciting.

The moon gave her enough light to make travel easy, but when Hank plunged into the woods, Amber had to slow her pace to avoid detection. It became increasingly difficult to keep her uncle in sight, and she had to stop twice because of noise in the brush. It was only animals, but she had lost valuable time and Hank was gone. She continued on the same path, but recognized the hopelessness of ever finding him.

The undergrowth to her right rustled and Amber reined in her horse. She tensed at the sight of the rider coming toward her. It was too late to run and hide, and she wished she had brought a gun.

The rider was too small to be Brant or Hank, and Amber looked at the shadowy figure with uncertainty. The rider stopped and his head turned toward Amber.

A bubble rose in her throat. "Willy," she said. "William Boone."

"Amber Rawlins?" He edged the horse closer. "I

don't believe it's you."

She stared at the man she believed had had a hand in her father's death and Andy's capture.

"What are you doing out here?" he asked, astonished to find her riding through the woods after dark.

"Can I ask you the same thing?" she queried, remaining noncommittal.

"I have a meeting with your uncle."

"Why here? Why not at headquarters?"

Willy ran his fingers along his jaw. "I never go to headquarters. We always meet in isolated areas. . . . I just got back to town. There was a message that your uncle wanted to see me out here." He shook his head. "Somethin' is happenin', and I'm not sure I like it." He met Amber's eyes. "Are you goin' to the meetin'?"

"No, but I knew my uncle was going to see you and I followed him. I wanted to speak to you."

Willy edged his horse closer. "That is funny. I wanted to talk to you."

"Did you know Andy was captured?"

Willy nodded. "Everythin' was set up for us to meet, but somethin' went wrong. I think someone knew about the meetin' and betrayed us. I sneaked back to Washington to talk to you, but you were gone." He looked at Amber intently. "I heard you married Brant Faulkner."

"I did. Do you know him?" Her limbs tensed. His answer was going to be very important. If he knew her husband, then Willy was a Rebel.

"Do *you* know who he is?"

"Are you asking if I know he is a Rebel?" He remained silent. "I spent some time with him at Confederate headquarters."

William's surprise was genuine. "Confederate headquarters. What were you doin' there?"

"It's a long story," she answered, reluctant to confide in him without being certain of his loyalties.

"Where is Brant now? I would like to see him."

Amber shrugged. "I'm not sure, but I strongly suspect he is close by." Amber didn't want to talk about her husband. She needed to learn about her father's death and Andy's capture. "Do you know why my uncle wants to meet with you?"

William shook his head. "I assume it is related to a new assignment."

"He suspects that you are working for the South." Willy remained silent, but his body stiffened, and he shifted uneasily in the saddle. "There is a Southern-influenced spy organization working out of Washington. Papa and Andy were trying to expose the traitor when the Confederates captured them. You were their contact the night they were taken prisoner. Evidence points to your involvement and Hank is suspicious of you."

William was trying to remain cool, but Amber sensed his agitation. "Andy," he muttered, "never doubted me. I am sorry that you do."

"William, we have been friends for a long time. I don't want to believe you betrayed my father and brother, but you were involved each time one of them was captured. If you are not guilty of working for the South, then who else knew Papa's and Andy's meeting places?"

William gazed into the darkness. "I have to go. It

isn't safe for me here."

"You are guilty," she accused, edging her horse forward to block his retreat. "Are you working with Brant?"

"I am involved with your husband." There was pain in his eyes. "You must let me go. I am a dead man if your uncle finds me."

"Willy, did Brant know you were meeting Andy and my father?"

"He knew about—"

A shot shattered the quiet of the night and the rest of William's answer gurgled in his throat. He slumped across the horse's mane and fell to the dirt. Amber dismounted, dropped to his side and pushed him to his back. He had taken the shot in the head. There would be no more answers from William Boone.

Amber had no intention of being the next victim. Pulling the pistol from his belt, she grabbed the reins of her mare and ran through the woods. She was two hundred feet from Willy's body when she was grabbed and hauled into the bushes.

The handle of the pistol became her weapon as she punched her assailant. She was thrown to her back, and the breath left her lungs in a painful burst of air. The weight of the body held her helplessly immobile. Her arms were pinned above her head, and the gun was successfully wrestled from her hands. Amber looked at her captor and met her husband's eyes.

"Get off me, you murderer," she screamed. "You killed Willy to keep him quiet about the part you played in Papa's death and Andy's capture."

"Shut up," he warned, but she continued her verbal assault.

Brant's hands were busy holding her body still, so he fastened his lips against hers to still her accusations. Her mouth had been open and the attack was an intimate strike against her senses. His lips ground against hers sending first rays of pain then feelings of uncertainty through her limbs. His kisses softened until he was playing with her lips, and small whimpers rolled from her throat. His long hard length pressed her into the soft brush, her body completely taking the weight of his.

Amber trembled as he ravished her mouth and glided to her eyes, cheeks and neck, his hunger for her steadily growing. Her fingers curled against his and her nails bit into his flesh. Her heart pounded unsteadily against her breast as his lips pushed aside the shirt to find the valley of her breasts.

One hand was enough to hold her now unresisting fingers, and his free hand glided the length of her side, his palm curving over her hip and up to her breast. Brant shifted, his body taking some of his weight. Breath returned to her lungs, but it didn't remain long when he tore the buttons from her shirt and fastened on the mounds of flesh.

His fingers expertly explored every curve of her chest and flat stomach. His mouth continually returned to hers to maintain her state of euphoria. His free hand quickly dealt with the fasteners on her pants and pushed aside the offending barrier, leaving her ready for his body. A cool breeze floated across her naked limbs when Brant rolled to his side to remove his clothes. When he returned to cover her, his nakedness pressed her into the ground. His knee eased between her thighs and his hands cupped her head, his lips dropping to tease a series of kisses on her flesh.

Brant had weakened her defenses, taken command of her body, and she surrendered. She smelled the masculine scent of him and felt the warmth of his flesh against hers. Her arms lost the will to battle the enemy, and her fingers, no longer weapons to destroy, caught his shoulders to hug him close.

Brant took her with the gentleness of a lover—a man who cared. His hunger was great, his body ready, but he went slowly, building for her an eruption of pleasure. Amber arched against him, her body so high on his that she gripped him to her and started to cry out his name. Brant silenced her with the hungry touch of his mouth. She was still trembling and sated with desire when he rolled to the side and dressed. Amber opened her eyes to find him buttoning his shirt.

"Why?" she whispered. It was a question for so many of her uncertainties. Why had he killed Willy? Why had he used her? Why had he made love to her? Why? Why? Why?

Brant regarded her thoughtfully. "That could cover many questions."

"It does," she responded.

"If you want to know why I just made love to you, it is simple. You are my wife and I wanted you. Your state of confusion over seeing that young man shot made you very—." He wanted to say vulnerable, then decided she would despise that reference. "Desirable," he finished.

"Why did you kill him?"

He jammed his shirt into his pants. "Would you believe me if I told you I hadn't?"

"No," she answered flatly.

Brant dropped to his knees, his eyes locking with hers. "Why can't you trust me? Are you afraid you'll lose your independence? That you'll be less of a woman? Women are supposed to be soft, sympathetic and able to shed a few tears. You are like a rock. You guard your independence and refuse to trust anyone. You are even scared to feel something when we make love. If I walked up to you and said I wanted to love you, you would run like a scared rabbit. To care about someone you must make a commitment and learn to share your life with them." His brown eyes bored into her confused green ones. "You are a coward, Amber. You know how to love your brother and father and maybe even your uncle, but that is because they don't demand anything in return." His gaze wandered over her nakedness. "I want a real woman, not someone who is afraid of passion or fears me because I'm a Rebel." Standing, he grabbed the reins of his horse.

Amber pulled the blouse against her breasts and scrambled to her feet. His words hit hard, drawing attention to the faults of her character. "You Rebel spy." She lunged at him, her fingers tearing at his hair. Brant had attacked her with words, but her battle with him would be physical. "You are a spy for the Confederate Army. You used me to get close to my uncle."

Brant yelped in pain as she pulled on his brown hair. His long fingers caught her hands and pinned them against her sides. His body pressed against hers, his arms becoming bands of steel around her ribs.

"I have heard enough from you," he growled. "Shut your mouth."

"Not as long as I have a breath in my body," she spouted. "Uncle Hank is going to capture and hang you. I told him where your loyalties belong."

His eyes narrowed. "Did you tell him about Andy?"

Yes," she lied without thinking. "I told him everything."

"You are a fool, Amber Faulkner."

"Don't ever call me by your name. I don't want any association with a Southern pig. I hate you for using me."

Brant grinned, his teeth showing white in the darkness. "I don't think you hate me as much as you hate yourself because I have shown you a weakness. . . . I have stirred your physical desire. Your father never intended for you to be so hard."

"My father," she shrieked. "You don't even deserve to mention his name. What do you know about him?"

"Quite a lot," he said, shrugging. "But it doesn't matter because he is dead."

"Did you become his friend before he was killed?"

"He is dead. Leave it at that."

"Did you enjoy seeing your cohort, William Boone, die?"

"No," he snapped. "Willy was an excellent soldier. He believed in what he was doing."

"Willy was about to tell me something important. What were you afraid I would learn?"

"I'm never scared of the truth." His eyes wandered over her face, his lips drooping in regret. "There is nothing more to say." Releasing her, he mounted his horse.

"Where are you going?" she asked, her hand on the animal's neck.

"I have a feeling you are going to make it very difficult for me to stay around here, and I can't afford any negative rumors." He captured a handful of her amber hair, and she saw disappointment reflected in his eyes. "I'm sorry things couldn't work out for us."

Amber was at a loss for words. She wanted him out of her life, but wanted him brought to justice for his crimes against the Northern States.

Dropping over his horse's neck, he lifted her and pressed his mouth to hers. "Maybe we'll meet again sometime. I hope by then you'll have learned how to trust people."

Amber's bare feet hit the ground. "Where are you going?"

"San Francisco, California," he said and was gone.

Brant had walked out of her life a second time, but not before he had accused her of being a coward and afraid of her response to him. Feeling strangely vulnerable, she reached for her clothes. Her head pounded from trying to sort out the questions in her mind. He was the enemy, but at the same time he was her husband. She fought the tingling response he aroused in her because she didn't want it, and Brant accused her of being afraid. Part of her wanted to betray the enemy, and the other part wanted to prove she was not a coward.

Squaring her shoulders, Amber recognized the challenge. She was going to find the man who had called her a coward and learn the truth about herself. She would prove him wrong, then watch him hang as a spy.

She wondered why Brant had chosen San Francisco, California—the same city as Andy. Suddenly, Amber's hand flew to her mouth. In a moment of rage she had lied and admitted telling Hank that her brother was alive. Brant had threatened to kill him if the truth came out. Her trip to California would not only prove she wasn't afraid of him; it would also save her brother's life.

Twenty-two

Amber opened her eyes and stared at the bedroom ceiling. She had spent a restless night, her thoughts continuously on Brant's hard, blunt accusations that she was afraid of the kind of relationship a man and woman shared. It was the kind of commitment her father had never discussed, and for the first time Amber wondered if her papa had been wrong in expecting her to be like him. She was not a man.

Brant had shown her the physical pleasures of her femininity. He accused her of being a coward to her passion, and she was afraid because it conflicted with her independence and forced her to rely on a man. She was supposed to be strong, but the man-woman relationship exposed a vulnerable weakness that went against the high expectation her papa had demanded. She had to face her fears and find out if her passion and Papa's teaching could be blended together in a satisfying harmony. She would find the answers in California and nothing was going to stop her from making the trip.

Tossing aside the lightweight blanket, she rose and dressed. After adding the finishing touches to her hair, she went down for breakfast.

"Good morning," Hank said when she sat across from him. "Did you sleep well?"

"Yes. It is wonderful to be home." She took a sip of juice.

"Were you out last night?" he asked, his eyes studying her carefully.

She smiled sweetly. "I went for a ride. I'm sorry if I disturbed you."

Hank shook his head. "It is not safe for you to be out after dark."

"I'm careful," she argued.

"Just the same," he protested. "I don't think it is a good idea. Where did you go?"

Amber broke off a piece of bread. "I rode toward town." Hank sighed his relief. "Is something wrong?" she quizzed.

"There was some trouble last night—about three miles from here."

"What happened?" she asked, her body attuned to the anxiety she sensed in him. "Did it have any connection to your meeting with William?"

"That is a military matter and not something I can discuss with you."

Resting her elbows on the table, she leaned forward. "I am involved in this war. I have sacrificed a father and brother. My—my husband is a Confederate spy. I have a right to know what is going on."

Hank hesitated. "I don't want to upset you."

Amber frowned. "I'm not the hysterical type," she reminded him. "I can handle the truth."

He watched her carefully. "You are a very unusual female. You have a strength and boldness that is not found in most women. I suppose it is because you were raised like a boy. Your father meant well, but I hope it won't hamper your future happiness."

"Could we talk privately?" she asked.

"Of course," he said, rising. "If something is troubling you I want to help."

Amber rose and walked to the library. Her uncle followed and closed the door behind them. He sat in a straight-backed chair while Amber preferred the softness of the settee.

"I don't want you shielding the truth from me." She met his gaze directly. "I know William Boone was shot."

Hank's brows arched. "How could you know?"

Amber smiled. "I didn't ride to town last night. I followed you."

"Amber," he said aghast. "Why?"

"I wanted to learn the truth about my father and brother. I also needed to know if Willy was loyal to the North. I didn't think you would tell me."

"You should not have followed me. It was too dangerous."

"I was talking to Willy when he was shot."

Hank stiffened. "You could have been killed."

She shook her head. "Brant would not hurt me," she said with certainty. She had been right in her assumption that Brant would be in the area of the meeting.

"Do you believe your husband shot Willy?"

"Yes. When I fled into the bushes he caught me."

"This is damaging evidence against him. I wish we

314

had Willy's side of the story. Did he say anything to you?"

"He admitted that he was working with Brant."

Hank leaped from his chair, his face pale. His tenseness was unmistakable. "Faulkner has to be stopped," he muttered. "He'll destroy . . ." He stopped, his head snapping up to meet Amber's eyes. "Where is he?"

"Gone."

"We've got to find him." Hank ran his fingers through his hair. "This is terrible . . . just terrible. He has to be stopped before he does serious damage."

Amber had never seen Hank so agitated about anything. Brant must have done more damage than she ever thought possible.

"Amber, you are Brant's wife. He must have told you where he was going." His eyes were hopeful.

"He went to California."

"California," he repeated in surprise, but she saw his shoulders sag in relief.

"Is that good news?" she asked.

He sat down, a sigh escaping his lips. "We have some important things coming up and it is better if he is not in Washington."

Amber nodded in agreement. "He was afraid to stay in the city. He knew he would be captured."

"I wonder why he went west instead of south."

Amber became thoughtful. In her anger she had told Brant that Hank knew Andy was alive. It had been a lie, but she believed he had left with the intention of making good his promise to kill her brother.

Hank watched the confusion on his niece's face. There was something troubling her. What did she know? He experienced a tinge of regret for getting Amber involved with Brant, but at the time he believed it was the only way he could learn the truth. The success of his mission depended on exposing Brant as an enemy against the Union.

"Amber, what is troubling you?"

Despite her promise to remain silent, Amber considered telling Hank that his nephew was alive. It would be a wonderful surprise, but months, maybe years would pass before they would meet again. Until she had resolved her feelings toward Brant she would respect Andy's vow of silence.

"Nothing." She smiled to hide her uncertainty. "I was wondering why he had gone west." She wanted to make plans for the trip as soon as possible.

"Faulkner may have left this area, but he is still dangerous to the North. There has been trouble with Confederate sympathizers in California. If he makes the right contacts he could damage our western position." He scowled. "I can't leave Washington, but it is essential that Brant be found." He moved to Amber's side. "I have already asked you to make a sacrifice for the Union when you married Brant. I have to ask again. Would you go to California and try to find him?"

Amber breathed a sigh of relief. Smiling, she said, "Of course I'll go. I was planning to make the trip anyway."

Shaking his head, Hank chuckled. "I should have known. I'll notify our people out west and get you the name of an officer you can ask for help. For the time being I want you to keep the trip a secret. I'll make sure you have all the money you need."

"I'll make the arrangements today." She chuckled. "I am glad you approve. I didn't want to disappear again."

Hank rose. "I have work in my study before I can go to town. You can take the carriage."

Amber went to her room for her reticule. "Going to town?" Myra asked.

"I have a few errands to run."

"Are you stopping at the hospital?"

"I am going there first." She wanted to see Steven and explain about her marriage.

The hospital was always the same. The smell of sickness and death was something she would never forget. Hopefully, supplies were more plentiful here than they had been in the South. Amber nodded to several of the workers as she walked toward the operating room. The doctors were busy, but Steven was not there and she learned he had gone to the field. Amber bit back a sigh of disappointment, but knew it was probably better that she didn't see him. As long as she was Brant's wife she would not encourage his interest in her.

Amber watched the doctors for several minutes, surprised that she didn't feel the usual driving urge to assist. She attributed her lack of interest to her indecision over Brant and the trip west. Turning, she left the building where she had once found great satisfaction.

There were two major forms of transportation west and Amber decided to check both possibilities. She wanted the quickest, most direct route. Money was not a problem, so cost would not influence her decision. She made her first inquiry at the depot. Trains ran with limited regularity to the Missouri River where she would have to change to coach. The thought of traveling fifteen hundred miles in a stagecoach did not appeal to her, but she would use it if necessary. Unfortunately, there wasn't a train heading west for five days and too much time would be lost.

Thirty minutes later Amber was inquiring about ship transportation. "I want to go to San Francisco, California. When can I get passage?"

The clerk checked his records. "You get the train to New York City and take a boat from there."

"Can you arrange it for me?" she asked and he nodded.

"Planning a trip?" a man asked from Amber's side.

She glanced up, carefully masking her surprise. "Good morning, Colonel Broadmore," she said sweetly, hiding her animosity for the man who had given Brant information on the Union. The man was a spy, but it couldn't be proven until Brant was forced to confess the colonel's part. He was the last person she wanted to see. He was probably in contact with Brant and would notify him that she was going west.

"Are you leaving town?" he asked again, his brown eyes sharp with curiosity.

"I was —."

"Everything is arranged," the clerk said, holding out some papers. "Enjoy your trip to San Francisco."

"You are leaving town," Colonel Broadmore remarked, a knowing smile curving his mouth. "That is a very long trip."

"Yes, it is," she admitted. "Excuse me," she said coolly and walked away. Amber glanced back at him before leaving the office. He was involved in a conversation with the clerk, and Amber decided he was getting information for Brant on the ship's arrival. Amber scowled. Why did he have to interfere in her plans? She didn't want her husband to know she would be in California, but she was sure Broadmore would tell him.

Amber only had two hours before the train left for New York City, so she rushed home to pack. As promised Hank had sent money and the name of an officer she could contact in California.

Myra's reaction was as negative as Amber expected. "You can't leave town," she argued. "Look at all the trouble you got yourself into last time." Myra looked at Amber and decided the time had come for a little interference. "How are things between you and Brant?"

Amber averted her eyes. It would be hard to hide the truth from her. "He is away on business," she said, hoping that would satisfy her curiosity.

"That isn't what I meant and you know it," she scolded lightly. "I'm the only mama you have known, and I don't know if I explained things right."

Amber smiled at the older woman's uneasiness. "Everything is fine," she assured her. Unbeknownst to her, a flush stole over her cheeks. Myra had her answer.

"Does your husband know where you will be?"

"He is meeting me," she answered, certain it was the truth.

Amber dragged her trunk from the closet and opened the lid. "Nothing is going to make me change my mind." She placed folded undergarments in the

319

bottom. "Are you going to help me? I can't take much, but I don't want to forget anything."

Scowling, Myra took charge. Amber never packed for herself, and Myra knew things would be forgotten if she did it alone. Amber used the time to change into a beautiful cotton gown, cool, yet comfortable enough for traveling. When she was satisfied with her appearance, she dropped to her knees beside the dresser and rummaged through the bottom drawer. When Myra wasn't looking, she withdrew the small pistol and slipped it into her reticule. It was the only protection she would have, and she wasn't afraid to use it. Myra was just about to close the trunk when Amber tossed a shirt and pants on top.

"What are those for?" she asked, regarding Amber with a frown.

She shrugged. "Just in case I need them. . . . Don't worry so much. You know I prefer to ride horseback without a dress."

Myra stood and put her hands on her hips. "I don't like this."

"I might miss the train." Amber slipped her bonnet over her chignon and secured the strings.

"Let me come with you," Myra pleaded, her brown eyes misting with tears.

"Are you going to cry?" Amber asked impatiently.

"It might do you some good to shed a few tears, too," she sniffed.

"Everything is going to be fine." She hugged her friend, then checked the tiny watch she carried on a chain around her neck. "I have to go. I guess it only takes three weeks for a letter to cross the country. I promise to write."

One of the servants came for the trunk and the women walked downstairs. Myra was unsuccessful in holding back her tears, and she dabbed her eyes with a delicate handkerchief.

Amber felt no sadness over leaving. She would miss her friend, but she was filled with the anticipation of the adventure ahead of her. She would find her brother in San Francisco and convince him that Brant had to be stopped.

The train trip to New York City went smoothly and early the next day she was in her cabin on the side wheel steamer. Reluctant to get involved with the passengers, she spent the day in her cabin. At ten o'clock she stretched out on the narrow bed to rest.

Pictures of Brant floated through her thoughts, and she hated herself for thinking of him. She was glad their time together had been short and no emotional involvement had complicated things. She would feel nothing for the man who had betrayed her and forced her into a loveless marriage. He had used her to help the Confederate States, and she hated him for twisting her life into knots.

She wondered how Brant had gotten to California and wished she had checked to see if a train had left for the Missouri River during the night or early morning. She sat up with a start. What if he was a passenger on the ship? Tomorrow she would have to search for him.

Amber was up early the next morning, dressed and ready to begin looking for Brant. Many of the travelers who could only afford deck passage were still asleep on their make-shift beds. California was an exciting prospect for people who wanted to escape the war and start a new life.

She spent the morning looking for her husband. After a quick lunch in the commonroom, she resumed her search. When darkness descended, Amber was certain he had chosen alternate transportation.

The days passed rapidly. Amber alternated time between her cabin and the deck. She listened to conversations and finally decided to mingle. Most of the people were fed up with the war and anxious to get a new start. Many were businessmen hoping to become involved in the expansion of the western cities.

The steamer missed all water battles and never passed close to another ship. When they reached Panama, everything was unloaded and put on a train. This was the worst part of the trip. The air was hot and fever infested, and her clothes clung to her body. Mosquitoes were heavy and attacked in swarms. Amber was relieved when they finally crossed the Isthmus and boarded the steamer to take them to San Francisco.

They had picked up more passengers in Panama, and Amber began to think seriously about how she would find Brant. California was a Union state, but there were no open confrontations between Union and Confederate troops. Rebel sympathizers, however, did everything in their power to stir up conflict and try to get control of the state. The Indians and Mexicans were their favorite trouble spot and most land travel was dangerous. The Confederate activity was secret and the society was careful to screen its members. Amber didn't know how she was going to get inside, but was sure that was where she would find Brant. Once she located him she would make plans to betray him to Union officials.

Many of the passengers were from the South, and Amber recognized them as possible connections to the organization. After dark she went up on deck, hid in the shadows and eavesdropped on private conversations. Finally, something one of the men said alerted Amber to his Southern connections.

Early the next morning, she rose and dressed in a blue gown decorated with darker trim. As she stood before the mirror and twisted her amber hair into a chignon, she knew it was going to be a special day.

When she went out on deck, she saw the man she wanted to meet standing at the rail. Pretending interest in the ocean, she strolled toward him. When she was almost at his side, she tripped and muttered a startled, "Oh." Reaching out, she clutched the rail, her elbow brushing the stranger's arm as she struggled for balance.

"Let me help you," the young man said smoothly.

Amber looked up and flashed him a brilliant smile. "I am sorry," she said, her long lashes fluttering against her cheeks. "I lost my balance. It was very clumsy of me."

"Nonsense," he assured her. He was an attractive man, his blue eyes sparkling against his sun-bronzed skin. "I don't believe I've seen you before," he said, studying her face.

"I stay in my cabin most of the time. A woman can't be too careful."

He arched one of his brows in interest. "Are you traveling alone?"

She nodded. "Many people warned me against such a venture, but they couldn't change my mind. I have to get to San Francisco."

"You sound like a very determined young lady."

She smiled. "Perhaps."

"Would you join me for breakfast?" he asked, and Amber eagerly accepted.

Taking his arm, they went to the dining area. After being seated, Amber leaned back in her chair and smiled. "It was kind of you to bring me here. I never felt comfortable dining alone."

"A beautiful woman like yourself shouldn't have any trouble finding company."

"Thank you," she said, forcing herself to blush. "Is your home in California?"

"For now," he answered.

"Tell me about the city," she encouraged. "I am excited to see it."

"It is expanding at a rapid pace. Since the war started many of our supplies have been cut off. The people have found it necessary to adapt and make their own items. We are becoming industrialized."

"It sounds exciting."

"San Francisco is a *very* important city," he agreed, and she was certain there was more to his statement than just the possibility of investments.

"I hope I'll be able to find a position when I arrive."

Christopher studied her curiously. This woman was an exquisite beauty, and it was hard to believe she was alone. Most men would fight to get her attention. He was suddenly possessed to find out all he could about this woman, but he didn't want to do it in an obvious or nosy way. Since the war broke out people had become suspicious of each other. He didn't even know which side of the war she favored, and his beliefs

324

were very firmly implanted.

They ate in silence then strolled along the deck. "Forgive me for being so bold," he said, stopping in an isolated area. "But do you have a gentleman, husband, or fiancé?" He saw the surprise on her face and hastened to explain. "I'm only asking because I don't want to infringe on someone else's claim."

Amber lifted her eyes to his, the color green and soft. This was one time she wished she could force tears to her eyes. Her fingers curled tightly against his sleeve and he noted her tension.

"I'm sorry if I have upset you," he apologized quickly.

"You haven't," she said, smiling. "I was married, but my husband was killed in the war. . . . His death was a shock. I worked in the hospitals, trying to help the cause, but I got tired of feeling helpless. There weren't enough supplies and men were dying daily." She watched the swell of water. "I had some money, so I packed my belongings and booked passage on the steamer. I want to start over again."

"Where is your home?" he asked casually.

"I think I'd better go to my room," she said bluntly.

"I'm sorry if I have offended you," Christopher said, frowning. "I was just making conversation."

"Forgive me," she pleaded. "I have enjoyed the day, but I am afraid if we start talking about the war I might find out we're on opposite sides." She met his eyes. "I hate everyone on the other side. I wouldn't want you to be one of them."

They returned to her cabin and Amber said good night. Once in her room she flopped on the bed. Thus far things were working out just as she had planned.

By the time they reached San Francisco Amber wanted to be firmly embedded in Christopher's mind.

Being in Christopher's thoughts was the last thing Amber had to worry about. He paused at the railing and stared at the sea. He had spent an exciting day with a beautiful woman, and he ached to know if her loyalties matched his. If she was a Southern lady, he wanted to enlist her aid in seducing information out of Union officers. There had to be a way to learn which side of the war she favored, and he was determined to find it.

They spent the next two days together and were slipping into a relaxed companionship. Amber didn't know what would happen if he made advances toward her. She had no feelings for her husband, but she was a married woman and that demanded respectable behavior.

The heat was stifling and Amber discarded her dress and stretched out on the bed in her undergarments. She preferred to sleep naked, but decided the lock wasn't strong enough for uninhibited behavior.

Extinguishing the light, she rolled to her side and closed her eyes. Tomorrow she would be in San Francisco and would begin the search for the men in her life. The next thing she remembered was a tiny tickle along her arm, up her neck and over her cheek. She twisted away from the irritation, but it became more persistent as it glided over her lips. Her eyes flew open, her body suddenly attuned to the difference in her bed. When she had fallen asleep, she had been alone in the darkness. Now a candle flickered its brightness and showed her the face of the man at her side.

"Brant," she whispered. "What are you doing here?"

"I came to see my beautiful wife," he said, looking down at her. "I missed you." Amber's heart fluttered. "Did you miss me too?"

She stared at her husband, unable to find an answer to his query. She had not missed his presence, but with him at her side she was acutely aware of her body's need.

"I don't understand," she said softly. "I searched the ship for you. You weren't here."

He smiled. "You didn't look in the right place." He brushed a strand of hair from her cheek. "I thought it was time to talk."

Her eyes widened. "You want to talk?" Her gaze dropped to his broad, naked chest. "If that is true where are your clothes? We would talk better if we were dressed."

She started to rise, but Brant put his arm across her chest to stop her. "We will be more comfortable the way we are." There was a wicked gleam in his eye that told Amber he wasn't only hungry for talk. "What are you doing here? Why aren't you in Washington?"

"Did you expect me to remain there when I knew you were going to California to murder Andy?"

"What made you think that?" he quizzed sharply. "Why would I want to kill your brother?"

"Because you think I told Hank he was alive." She looked deeply into his eyes. "I lied. My uncle doesn't

327

know anything about my brother. There is no need to track him down."

There was a noticeable relaxing of his shoulders. "I am glad you honored your promise and remained quiet."

"For now," she said briskly. "I could always wire the truth to my uncle."

"Don't threaten me, Amber. I won't let you interfere with what I am doing here. Not you or your brother. Do I make myself clear?"

"Is that a warning? Would you kill us?"

"I don't want it to come to that," he said, his hand curving over her shoulder.

Amber flinched from the contact. "We were *only* going to talk, remember?"

Brant chuckled. "Still the frightened woman. You are terrified of the passion I arouse."

"I am not afraid," she denied. "I did not like the things you said about me before you left. I am not afraid of you or of being a woman." Her eyes narrowed. "I don't like you. Have you forgotten you are a Confederate?"

"No, I haven't." His fingers glided over the flesh above the undergarments. "When you are strong enough to recognize your feelings, it won't matter that I am the enemy."

His words sent a tremor through her body. "It will never happen," she vowed. "I came here to prove it to you. You mean nothing to me. My body betrays me, but you will never have my emotions."

He shifted to cover the lower half of her body. "For now I guess I will have to settle for your passion, but someday I intend to have more. You are in my blood and I can't shake you out of my mind."

"You act as though I am your weakness," she said curiously. Did she have some power over this man that she didn't recognize?

His finger lightly caressed her lip. "I am not afraid to tell you that my passion for you makes me weak or that my desire — my feelings — make me vulnerable to the hurt you constantly fling at me." He started unfastening the laces holding her undergarments in place. "If my feelings for you are a weakness, then I won't deny it." He met her eyes. "But you are also my strength. I'm not afraid to share with you."

Amber's blue eyes clouded in confusion. She had never doubted that Brant was a powerful man, and she didn't know what to think of the sensitivity he had shown. How deep were his feelings for her? Was there more than a desire to satisfy his lust? Had he used her to get into Hank's household?

"Have I confused you, Amber?" He gently eased the fabric from her body. "Let your emotions guide you."

She struggled to get hold of her rapidly failing resistance. "The only emotions I feel for you are hate and betrayal," she spat, the angry green color returning to her eyes. "We will never be on the same side. I am going to expose you and Colonel Broadmore for your spying and watch you hang."

Brant stiffened, his hand flying to her neck to force her face still. "What did you say?" he demanded.

"I know where you were getting your information about the North. I saw you with Giles Broadmore before we went to Confederate headquarters. He is the man you are working with."

"Who else knows about this?" His fingers closed tightly around her shoulders. "I want the truth."

Amber saw the anger in his eyes and knew she had stepped into a dangerous area. She glared at him, refusing to show him fear. "Don't play with me," he warned. "A man's life is on the line."

Amber wondered if he was talking about his own. If she lied to him his rage and need for vengeance would probably interfere with her activities. Brant was already suspicious of her actions, and she didn't want him doubting her any more.

"I am going to present both of you to my uncle in one neat package."

"I want you to return to Washington. You are getting involved with dangerous people."

She wondered if he knew she had been seeing Christopher. "What I do or who I do it with is none of your business!"

"I'm making it my business," he barked. "You are to stay out of trouble. I can't be worrying about your safety."

"You don't have to. I can take care of myself."

He chuckled softly. "I know what a fighter you are." His eyes dropped to her lips. "I also know what a lover you are, and right now I am hungry for your body."

His mouth against her lips gave her no time to protest as he expertly plundered the inviting softness. He pulled their bodies together, her naked breasts flattening against his chest. His fingers glided over her hips to pull her beneath him. Brant's desire was strong and Amber was unable to fight the enemy. Her hands curled around his shoulders as they came together in an explosion of urgent passion that cascaded them into the surging world of sated pleasure. Nestled together in their haven of forgotten hate, Amber's defenses temporarily slipped, and she slept peacefully in the arms of her husband.

Twenty-three

Amber woke slowly and unconsciously reached for Brant. The cold bed warned that he had disappeared hours ago. She sighed. His presence complicated things, but she had no intention of letting him interfere with her plans. She was still going to find Andy and ask his help in exposing Brant as a spy.

There was no sign of Brant when Amber came out of her cabin and walked along the deck. She didn't like knowing he was on the ship, but was determined not to change her actions. Her smile was warm when Christopher joined her at the rail to look at the San Francisco harbor.

Amber had already made arrangements for her trunk to be taken off the ship. So when they docked, she took Christopher's arm and walked down the wooden plank. She threw a quick glance over her shoulder for Brant but he wasn't there.

She knew it was time to convince Christopher of her loyalty to the South. When they walked past a group of soldiers holding the Union flag, Amber dug her fingers into his arm and filled her eyes with hate. She felt Christopher's gaze and his hand slid over hers in comfort.

"Is something wrong?" he asked.

Looking up at him, she smiled. "No. I was just reminded of the past. It was a painful memory," she said and turned her attention to the waiting carriage, missing Christopher's smile of satisfaction.

"This is the best hotel in town. I hope you will be comfortable," he said, taking her to one of the upstairs rooms.

"I'm sure it will be fine."

"Could I call for you at dinner? There is a wonderful dining hall downstairs, and there is someone I would like you to meet."

"It sounds wonderful. How can I ever thank you for all your help?"

Christopher grinned. "Sharing your company is all I need."

When he was gone, Amber locked the door and ran to the window. San Francisco was exciting and she was filled with the hope of finding Andy. It would be dangerous because while pretending loyalties to the South to locate her husband, she would also have to gain Union help to find her brother. There had to be a way to make both goals work together.

Her eyes traveled along the plank-paved streets. She was in the fashionable area of town, and the brick and stone buildings were beautiful with their ornamentation. In the distance she saw construction that reinforced stories of the city's rapid expansion.

Turning, she walked to the bed. After removing her shoes, she flopped down on the feather softness and tried to sleep, but thoughts of taking a nap were blocked by the anticipation of the evening ahead. Rising, she removed her gown and opened her trunk. If she was going to go out in the evenings, she would have to think about adding to her wardrobe.

While she dressed, she reflected on the risk of appearing in public. If Brant was going to keep his eye on her activity, she would be making it easy for him. Reminding herself to keep a firm hand on the situation, she applied the finishing touches to her amber hair.

Christopher arrived promptly and they went straight to the dining hall. They were seated with a man and woman he introduced as Miriam and Thomas Crowley. Amber immediately recognized them as passengers on the steamer from Panama. Conversation was light and focused on subjects other than the war. Amber applied all her cunning to draw out their trust in her.

When the evening was over, Christopher escorted her upstairs and bid her a gentlemanly good night. Amber closed the door with a sigh of relief. She undressed quickly, then knelt to retrieve her pants, shirt and boots. It was early, and she intended to learn all she could about San Francisco at night. She jammed her hair into the shirt to hide her femininity, then pushed the small pistol into the band of her pants and walked to the door. Opening it a crack, she made sure the hall was clear, then ran down the back stairs. She was winded when she stepped into the fresh evening air and walked toward the front of the hotel.

She was about to cross the street when Christopher stepped outside. Amber's heart pounded in excitement. If she followed him he might lead her to the Rebel headquarters and eventually Brant.

Christopher signaled a carriage and Amber frowned. How would she keep up with him? She had not brought money to hire a driver for herself. The carriage pulled away with its passenger, and Amber stepped quickly to the sidewalk and followed. Her side ached and one of her boots rubbed a blister, but she dared not stop. She had moved into a poor section of the city and her uneasiness increased. She automatically felt for the pistol in her belt, reminding herself she wasn't afraid to use it.

The carriage stopped and Christopher got out. Amber ducked behind a building and peered around the corner. She tried to get control of her rapid breathing and fight the exhaustion her body tried to claim.

Christopher entered a run-down building, and Amber scanned the blackness for a guard. She spotted one on the far side of the street and frowned because she wouldn't be able to get near the windows. Another carriage arrived, but the buggy blocked the passengers from sight, and she realized her position wasn't very good. She looked for a better location and spotted several wooden barrels about one hundred feet from the house. If she went behind the houses, she could come up near the barrels without being seen.

Rising, she ran down the narrow alley. A noise on her right froze her action and she reached for the gun. Pivoting automatically, she prepared to fire. Instead she grinned at the tomcat digging through the garbage. Returning the gun to her belt, she continued. She was breathing heavily when she reached the barrels. Looking at the house, she was dismayed to find a riderless horse tied to the rail. Someone had arrived and she had missed it. Glowering, she scanned the darkness. The guard was still on the far side, his body little more than a shadow.

With nothing else to do Amber studied the horse. It was a beautiful animal, its golden coloring obvious even in the darkness. A richly tooled leather saddle rested on the animal's back and the bridle was decorated with detail. Why hadn't she stayed in her other position longer? She wanted to know who the animal belonged to.

Time dragged and her body cramped from the uncomfortable position. She decided two hours had passed when the guard came from the far side of the street and untied the horse. Keeping the reins in his hands, he walked away from the house. Amber was certain the animal didn't belong to him, but she was in no position to follow him. She would have to cross an area that would expose her, and she couldn't risk it. Too much was at stake. Angrily, she rose and ran behind the buildings.

She made several wrong turns on the return to the hotel. After successfully sneaking into her room by the back way, she flopped on the bed. Tonight had convinced her that Christopher was part of the secret society, and she was determined to gain his confidence and get into the organization. Once inside she ran the risk of confronting Brant and being accused of spying. It posed a serious problem and one she had to be prepared for.

Rolling to her stomach, she rested her head on her hands. She didn't want to remember Brant and the brief time they had shared together. From the beginning she had despised him and hated his loyalty to a side that fought for slavery. He had used her body, and she felt like a fool for being duped by the touch of his mouth and hands.

Shivers raced up her back as she remembered his caresses against her naked flesh. He had stirred passion she had never experienced and showed her the close control she tried to maintain could be shattered beneath another person's power. Amber had been frightened of the weakness he made her feel. She desperately wished she could ask her father how her strength and independence belonged in a relationship with a man.

She remembered Brant's accusation that she was a coward, afraid to depend on another person and scared to let her real feelings surface. Amber's jaw clamped tightly. She had to prove that wasn't true. With those thoughts she closed her eyes and drifted to sleep.

The sun had barely touched the sky when she rose and dressed in a yellow gown with tiny green flowers. After a quick breakfast she hired a carriage for a thorough tour of the town. She could not afford to get lost again. If there were short cuts to her destination, she had to know them.

She was surprised by the size of the rapidly expanding city. Old buildings were being torn down and replaced by newer ones of stone and brick.

Many of the main streets were being covered by planks to eliminate the mud. At noon she asked the driver to stop in the center of town. After a quick lunch, she purchased a bigger gun, a floppy hat to hide her hair, pants, shirt and newspaper. Instead of hiring a carriage for the return, she walked.

The problem of finding Andy troubled her. Where in a city this size did she look? She was certain he would be working with the Union Army, but she knew contact with the soldiers could end her chances of getting into the Rebel organization.

When she reached the hotel, she found a message from Christopher inviting her to dine with him at eight o'clock. While she waited for his arrival, she scanned the paper. It was strong Union and took a firm stand against the Southern movement.

Christopher arrived promptly at eight and Amber opened the door with a smile. His blue eyes swept her in appreciation.

"I hope this means you are going to accept my invitation."

"I am delighted you made the offer," she said, reaching for her shawl.

His eyes dropped to the table. "What do you think of our leading newspaper?"

His question was very casual, but Amber knew her answer would be important. "I didn't find it very good reading. Some of the views were not to my liking. Is there another paper in town?"

He smiled. "Yes, but you'll find the contents very similar. California is strong Union and anything else is quickly silenced." Heavy lids slid over his blue eyes. "The Northerners hold control of the city and they want to keep it that way."

Amber sighed heavily. It was time to make him believe where her loyalties rested. She raised her green eyes to his face. "Christopher, I enjoy your company, but there is something I think you should understand. I am too proud of my convictions about the war to pretend they don't exist. When I read that paper today I was furious. There was no one standing up for what I believe—the Southern cause. I am proud of my heritage." Amber lifted her chin and tried to read his reaction. "I hope it won't spoil things between us."

Christopher grinned. "I hope your confession has made you feel better. Shall we go downstairs? I have reserved a table."

Amber picked up her reticule and walked toward the door, trying hard not to let her disappointment show. He hadn't seemed overly concerned with her announcement, and he hadn't admitted that he shared the same beliefs. Perhaps she had been wrong about him.

Dinner was a pleasant affair, but Amber had to force herself to be a sparkling companion. Christopher never mentioned her loyalties, and she had to squelch pangs of disappointment. At the door of her room he took her hand.

"Do you have any family?" he asked.

His question seemed to come out of nowhere and put Amber on the alert. She decided it would be foolish to deny the existence of a brother that resembled her so strongly.

"I have a twin, but I don't know where he is." She looked into his face. "Why do you ask?"

"Curiosity," he said, leaving her to wonder if it was the truth.

When he was gone, she went into her room and changed into pants and shirt. The large hat successfully hid her amber hair. After checking the new pistol to make sure it was loaded, she tucked it into the belt of her pants and crept outside by the back stairway. Amber took the short cut she had discovered while riding in the carriage, and she arrived at the house before Christopher. The golden horse was already tied to the rail, and Amber was sure he belonged to an important man in the organization. She wanted to get closer, but was afraid the guard would see her. Christopher arrived a few minutes later and went inside. The pounding in Amber's heart was the only sound in the still night and for a while she feared it would give her away.

She waited almost an hour before Christopher left the building and rode off. The guard disappeared a few minutes later and Amber's gaze returned to the horse waiting outside the house. Her mouth twisted in a frown. Was the owner still inside? Did she dare risk approaching the building?

She was still deciding what to do when she was seized from behind and spun around. Before she had time to utter a warning shout, a hand was clamped over her mouth. Her initial attempt to struggle met with defeat when she was jerked against something hard, and her limbs were rendered helpless. She had picked one of the darkest areas so she could watch undetected, and the man who held her was only a shadow.

Amber felt the pistol press against her stomach as

the man's hold tightened, drawing her even closer to his body. When his warm breath fanned her cheek, her struggles stopped and something else stirred her limbs. His lips touched her just below the ear and ran along her jaw. The hand was pulled from her lips, and his mouth claimed their softness.

Amber did not need the light to tell her whose arms held her. Her nostrils were filled with his scent, her body involuntarily springing to life in betrayal of her emotions. His hold was loose, and she knew she could break free, but her limbs were drugged with the lethargic feeling only Brant was capable of arousing.

Amber heard the gun drop softly to the ground while his hand pushed inside her shirt to cup her breast. Her breath quickened, and her body strained against his. One of his hands tangled in the silky strands of her amber hair while he teased her lips into an electrifying sensation of tingling awareness. Amber moaned softly, her fingers running up his arms to tangle in the thick hair.

Amber knew she should fight this man and recognize the danger he represented to her and Andy, but she felt powerless and incapable of reasoning. For now he was her husband, the man who stirred her body into submission.

His tongue teased the edge of her mouth before his lips claimed hers in a plundering kiss of sensual passion. Amber sagged against him, no longer able to control the weakness that had invaded her limbs. Brant easily took her weight, his own body shifting to gently ease her to the ground. Amber felt the earth against her back, then Brant's weight as he laid his body next to hers. His fingers glided over her buttocks to pull her against his hips while his mouth played havoc with the tiny pulse at her throat.

Her fingers slid down his neck to gently ease the buttons free of his shirt, so her hand could caress the hair-roughened chest. His heart pounded against her palm with increasing steadiness and reinforced his arousal.

His breath was warm as he pushed aside her shirt to kiss the inviting flesh. Loosening the ties holding her undergarments in place, he parted the fabric and glided his mouth over the soft curves.

Amber felt that aching need to find satisfaction with her husband's body and despised herself for it. She did not like the lethargy invading her limbs, but was unable to fight it.

Brant shifted, his mouth gliding back to her neck. "My beautiful wife," he whispered. "What are you doing here?"

Her eyelids drooped as his mouth kissed them. Amber never wanted the floating sensation to end. It felt like a dream she never wanted to wake from.

"What are you doing here?" he asked again.

"Looking for you," she responded swiftly, not even realizing how her statement might be interpreted.

"I am flattered," he said, an edge of satisfaction in the deep husky voice. "Are you ready to admit your desire and surrender the differences between us?"

The words spy, traitor, Rebel, Confederate, and betrayer flooded her thoughts. Brant was those things to her, not lover, husband, friend or trusted companion.

Brant sensed Amber's withdrawal and teased her lips with his, igniting the hunger licking through her limbs. He wanted to maintain her drugged passion a little longer. He wasn't ready to fight the spitting tigress.

"Have you found Andy?" he asked, nuzzling her neck. Her head rolled to the side, allowing him access to the corner of her ear. "Where is your brother?"

"I don't know," she whispered, certain that if she knew the truth she wouldn't tell him. Brant was a threat to Andy's life.

"You can tell me," he persisted. His hand curved over her hip. "Have you seen him?"

"No," she moaned, fighting to control the drugging sensations he was arousing.

"Amber, I don't want you involved in this. It isn't safe. Go back to Washington."

Before she had the chance to tell him she wouldn't leave, his mouth teased hers with tender caresses, building the fire in her veins. Suddenly, it was over and Brant was gone.

Amber lay in the dirt, her body aching, her thoughts drugged by his passion. Minutes passed before the reality of what had happened finally registered on her mind. Somehow Brant had found out where she was and had used his body to try and get information about Andy. Fortunately, she had not found him and there was nothing to tell. He was an expert at making her forget her loyalty, and she scowled at herself. Why was he able to dissolve her strength and will by the touch of his hands?

Feeling disgusted and disappointed with herself,

she pulled her shirt together and secured the buttons. Rising to her knees, she felt along the dirt for her pistol. She located it a few feet in front of her and slid it into her belt. Once on her feet she looked for the golden-colored horse, but it was gone. Had Brant drawn her attention away from the animal so the owner could slip away unnoticed? Or had he ridden away on the stallion himself?

Knowing there was no point in remaining, she returned to the hotel and flung herself across the bed. She was bitterly disappointed in herself and made up her mind not to let Brant have such strong influence over her life. Never again would he be able to use his hands and body to get information from her. She would show him her strength and prove that she was not frightened.

Two days passed without hearing a word from Christopher, and Amber wondered if her declaration about the South had chased him off. She maintained her nightly vigils at the house as soon as it was dark, but watched from a new location to avoid another encounter with Brant.

On the third night the horse was waiting outside, but when everyone left the meeting, the guard led the horse away. Sighing her disappointment, Amber knew she had lost her chance to see who owned the animal and started back to the hotel. She was in the middle of an alley when she was grabbed from behind and pushed against the wall. The roughness of her attacker told her that it wasn't Brant, and her nails became claws to gouge her assailant's flesh. It was too dark to see the man's face, but the heavy smell of rum warned of his drunken state. Raising her knee, she hit the man in the crotch. When he groaned and doubled over, she kicked him in the jaw. His screech of pain told her she had probably broken it. Amber grabbed her gun and ran. She didn't stop until she had reached the hotel and was safely in the room.

When Christopher didn't get in touch with her the next night, Amber began to worry that her plans had failed. No one appeared at the meeting place, and she decided they had changed locations.

One week after her arrival she viewed the success of her trip pessimistically. Her friendship with Christopher had gone astray and there was no sign of her brother. Deciding a stroll through the city might give her a fresh outlook on things, she grabbed her reticule and went downstairs. Christopher was in the lobby and she smiled as he walked toward her.

"Amber, it is wonderful to see you. Are you free this evening?" he asked, taking her arm and guiding her to a settee.

She arched one of her brows. "I am surprised to see you." She boldly met his gaze. "I haven't seen you for days, and I thought my — ah — beliefs had chased you away."

His hand covered hers. "Sweet Amber," he said. "You could never do that. I had some urgent business. I'm sorry if you thought my absence was because of our conversation."

"In that case I am free tonight."

"I will pick you up at eight." He squeezed her hand lightly. "We will go for a long ride. There is something I would like to discuss with you."

Rising, she pulled her hand free. "I'll be ready."

Excusing herself, she returned to her room. Certain this was going to be a special night, she took extra pains with her appearance. She bathed in scented oils, then dressed in a low cut brown gown.

Christopher was punctual. "Amber, you look beautiful," he praised.

"Thank you," she said, batting her eyes. Thus far she had not been forced to fend off any physical advances from him and felt safe to flirt. As far as he was concerned she was a widow.

"Shall we go for a carriage ride?" Nodding, Amber slid her arm through his and went to the enclosed buggy.

Amber settled against the plush cushions. "You have aroused my curiosity. Is everything all right?" she asked when he was seated opposite her.

"I think so." He grinned, the smile brightening his face. "When you made your announcement about supporting the South, I was elated."

"You were?" she said in surprise. "You didn't act it."

He shrugged. "I couldn't. What I am about to tell you is highly classified information." His eyes softened. "Forgive me, but I had to be sure where your loyalties belonged."

Amber shifted in her seat. "Are you sure now? I am a Southerner."

"I know," he said positively. "If I had any doubt I wouldn't be telling you this now." Christopher leaned forward and rested his hands on his knees. "California is a Union state, but I am part of a Confederate organization that wants to change that. The society demands absolute secrecy. I know ten of the members, but I am certain there are hundreds . . . perhaps thousands."

"Why can't you know each other?" she asked, puzzled that so much confidence was required. It might make it harder to locate and expose Brant.

"The leaders think it is safer. If I were captured I could only betray the ten people I know are involved. Everyone else would be free to continue the work."

Amber shivered. "It sounds like a highly efficient operation. Is it successful?"

"Yes. We get Confederate recruits and slip them through the border past the Union patrols. We have also managed to stir up trouble with the Indians. Eventually, we hope to gain control of the entire state."

Amber pretended excitement. "It would be wonderful," she agreed. "I have seen so much evidence of the city's importance." She looked into his eyes. "Christopher, I would like to be part of the organization."

"I was hoping you would suggest that. We are going to a party. It is a small affair, but all the guests are members of the society."

"Will the high officials be there?" she asked, trying not to sound too eager."

"No," he said flatly. "I don't know who they are. The people at the top are carefully guarded."

Amber wanted to frown her disappointment. How could she get the information she needed if things were so secret?

"Will you join us?" he asked eagerly.

"Yes," she agreed. Leaning forward, Amber patted Christopher's hand. "Thank you for letting me be a part of this."

"We can use a beautiful woman in the group. A few nights ago I met a man from another branch of the organization. I think you will be very interested in meeting him."

"Why?" she asked, puzzled. She couldn't imagine whom he knew that she would want to meet. She had mentioned very little about her past, so there was no way he could tie her to anyone. His announcement, however, made her uneasy. She didn't like walking into a situation she was not sure she could control. It might prove to be dangerous.

"I have never liked surprises," she said cautiously. "Could you give me a little hint?"

His blue eyes twinkled. "All I can tell you is that the man joined our group while I was in Atlanta on business. He rides the most beautiful golden stallion that I have ever seen, and I have been trying to convince him to sell the animal. Perhaps you could help me with that." He chuckled. "I can't wait to see the expression on your face."

Amber forced a smile she wasn't feeling. If Brant was the owner of the horse, she would be walking into a trap. Her hand pressed against her reticule, and she was glad she had the derringer.

The carriage slowed to a stop and she took a deep breath. She had to be calm and ready to accept whatever confronted her. Christopher helped her from the carriage, and Amber studied the house with admiration. It was one of the newer homes outside the city and she was impressed by the workmanship.

"The house is beautiful." she complimented.

Christopher took her elbow. "Thank you. I had it built in the tradition of the Southern plantation houses, but left off the white pillars."

"This is your home?"

"It is," he agreed. "I'm glad you like it. You will probably be spending a lot of time here."

The wide entryway spoke of elegance and very plush surroundings, and she recognized Christopher as a man of substantial wealth. If the secret society had strong financial support, the North could be in for trouble.

Amber recognized Miriam and Thomas and Christopher introduced the other guests. Drinks were passed by a maid and dainty sandwiches were placed within reach. Amber was involved in a discussion with Miriam when Christopher tapped her shoulder.

"Excuse me," he said. "Amber, would you like to see the rest of the house?"

She had been on edge ever since Christopher announced that he had a surprise for her. "I would love to," she said and followed him into the hall.

"This is the library," he said, taking her into a room lined with books. "I don't like to have meetings at the house, but if I do, they are conducted here."

"This is a lovely room."

"I am glad you like it." He took her into his study and pushed open a door to a private area. "Whenever I have very personal business I do it here." He moved aside for her to enter. "There is someone waiting for you."

The breath lodged in Amber's throat as she crossed the threshold. She kept her expression blank, determined not to let her apprehension show. She would never let the Confederates see her fear.

"Amber," a voice whispered.

She scanned the room, her green eyes stopping on the man at the far side.

"Andy," she cried, running into her brother's arms. Amber rested her head against his shoulder and hugged him close. "It has been so long," she whispered.

Andy slipped his arm around his sister's shoulders. "We have Christopher to thank for bringing us together." He looked across the room at the smile on the sympathizer's face.

"How did you know?" Amber asked.

Christopher chuckled. "I met Andy when I returned to San Francisco. I only had to look at him to know there was a connection between the two of you."

"Why didn't you tell me before?" she asked, remembering the time he had inquired about her family. "I never expected to find Andy here."

Christopher shifted uneasily. "I've explained the secrecy of the organization. Andy joined us when I was gone. I had to be certain of him . . . and you." He looked at Amber. "I hope you will forgive me for doubting your loyalty."

"I understand," she forgave, and slipped her arm around her brother. "I hope you will accept our help."

"Andy is already involved. Do you want to tell her what you have been doing?"

"Sit down," Andy ordered, pushing her toward a chair.

"But what about the other guests?" she asked, knowing it was rude for the host to be absent.

"They will excuse us," Christopher explained.

Amber raised her hand to her brow. "This is a shock. What have you been doing?" she asked her brother.

Andy sat next to his sister and took her hand. The pressure of his fingers against hers would tell her when he was lying. Finding her brother in the enemy camp had been a shock. She had no doubt that he was acting in the capacity of a spy, and she knew there couldn't be any mistakes. Their lives would depend on it.

"When I left the South, I had names of people in the society. I contacted them as soon as I arrived," he explained briefly.

Amber wondered where he had gotten his information, but knew she couldn't ask. "I'm excited about your work here," she said with genuine interest. "I hope there is something I can do to help."

"There is," Christopher explained.

"What is it?" she asked eagerly.

"I told you once that San Francisco is an important city. The entire state is vital to our victory, but getting control is a problem. We can't attack the harbor because of two Russian ships." He put his hand on his hip. "This valley is the key to the state, and it is invaluable as a water port. Too many goods are going to the North from here. Everything centers around this city. If we can get control of it, the North will have to take the long routes. We *must*

351

acquire this city," he emphasized, "and we need information on the Union's plans, supplies and activities." Christopher crossed his arms over his chest. "We had a massive plan for taking the Northern part of the city, but it was destroyed because information leaked out and we had to cancel everything."

"What can I do?" she asked quickly and wondered if Andy had been involved in ruining their plans.

Christopher stepped forward and sat on the edge of the desk. "We want to put someone inside the Union organization to learn everything they can." He grinned. "We need a cunning, beautiful woman to seduce information from a Union official." He paused. "We need you."

Amber's fingers were squeezed, and her brother's touch told her many things. He warned her they were involved in a dangerous undertaking. It reminded her of their father's death at the hands of the Confederate soldiers. If she agreed she could pass the information that would be least damaging to the Union Army.

"I'll do it," she agreed, a sense of excitement building in her chest. She loved the challenge of adventure and hoped she would be successful in helping Andy destroy the secret society. "Will you give me more details when they are available?"

Christopher nodded. "My superior is working with me on this, and we need to talk more before you get started." His statement told Amber that his "superior" was not her brother. "How about lunch the day after tomorrow?"

"I'll be waiting," she said lightly. She glanced at her brother. "Will you be working on this project also?"

"I'll be involved," he promised.

"We'll find a way to make things work," she vowed, and only Andy knew her words held a hidden meaning of victory for the North.

Christopher rose. "Let's go break up the party. I want to get you back to the hotel before it gets late."

She joined Christopher at the door and turned, surprised to find Andy at the other side of the room. "Aren't you coming?" she asked.

He shook his head. "I'm not known to the people out there. I don't dare show my face. The guests were not told the details of our meeting."

"When will I see you again?" she asked, wanting some private time with her brother.

"We can't risk being seen in public. I'll make the arrangements through Christopher."

Amber carefully hid her disappointment. "Fine . . ." She looked into eyes exactly like her own. "Take care."

After flashing him a smile she turned and stepped through the open door. Leaving her brother was one of the hardest things she had ever had to do, but she suspected there would be more times like this before the war was over.

Most of the guests had already left. Only Miriam and Thomas remained.

"Did everything go as planned?" Thomas asked.

Christopher nodded. "Amber has agreed to help, but her involvement must be kept secret."

"We understand," Miriam answered, bestowing a warm smile on Amber. "Welcome to the society. . . . May we be victorious."

On the return to the hotel Christopher sat at Amber's side rather than opposite her. "I think our evening was successful," he said, twisting in his seat. "We have our eye on victory." He slammed his hand against the cushion. "We must win control of this city."

"Do Thomas and Miriam know Andrew?" she asked. "I know you said no one knew the real purpose of the meeting, but they seem to be close to you."

"I've known them for years, but they are not entitled to confidential information. Andy's identity is being carefully guarded. He is not seen in public and works with men high in the organization."

Amber was pleased to learn her brother was important to the sympathizers. Being near the top would give him more access to vital facts. Between the two of them they would know what information to feed the Confederates while making sure the North maintained the strict control they sought.

At the hotel Christopher kissed Amber's hand and watched her climb the stairs. He was very pleased with the evening's events and knew Amber and her brother would be valuable in helping the Rebel sympathizers get control of the city.

Amber was smiling when she opened the sitting room door and stepped inside. Locking the door behind her, she tossed her reticule and shawl over the nearest chair and turned up the light. Hugging her arms to her chest, she let a bubble of laughter erupt from her throat and fill the room with her joy. She had found Andy; he was safe.

The door to the bedroom opened and Andy joined

her. There was a lazy smile curving his full lips, and his blue-green eyes sparkled.

"Andy," she shouted in happiness and rushed forward to be seized in an affectionate hug. "I knew you would come."

"It is so good to see you," he said, holding her tightly. "I didn't believe Christopher when he told me he had met a woman on the steamer that looked just like me." He held her away from him and glanced at the door. "Did you put the lock on?"

She nodded. "How did you get in here?"

Andy held up a key. "The lock isn't much good, but it will give us warning if someone tries to get in."

"Let's talk over there," she said, pointing to the chairs on the far side of the room. She was glad she had pulled down the curtains before leaving for the party. "Is it safe for you to be here?"

"None of what I am doing is safe," he warned. "I'm right in the middle of the Confederate operations trying to get to the top and find out who is running things."

"I knew you were coming to California, but I never expected you to be involved in something like this. . . . How did you get inside the organization?"

"I had the influence and names to get me there."

"Where did you get them?" she asked curiously.

He shook his head. "It is better if you don't know."

"Do you realize the danger you are in?" she asked, knowing the answer.

He shrugged. "I believe it is a risk worth taking. It was right for Papa and it is right for me. Are you sure you want to get involved?"

"I have a lot of reasons to hate the Rebels," she said, thinking first of her father and then of Brant's treachery. "I'll do everything I can to beat them." She saw the doubtful glance her brother cast her. "Are you afraid for me because I'm a woman?"

Andy chuckled. "I know you are one woman who would never fall back on her femininity. You are more capable than most men, and I know you will rise to the challenge." Leaning forward, he rested his elbows against his knees and let his arms dangle between his legs. "When Christopher suggested you for the plant, I knew you wouldn't refuse. Female or not, I'm glad you're on my side." He grinned. "At least I know I can trust you. . . . Some of the other people I am working with I am not too sure about." He raised his blue-green eyes to hers. "It is dangerous. We could both get caught and hung."

"You can't frighten me," she warned. "We've been in tough scrapes before and always gotten out of them." She shrugged. "It is a risk I'm willing to take."

"We will have to be careful to always keep our stories straight." His eyes roamed over her face. "Why aren't you using your married name?"

Amber tore her eyes from his. Rising, she turned her back. She had forgotten Andy knew about her marriage to Brant. "I decided it would be better if I didn't acknowledge my husband."

"Do you know where Brant is?" he asked, coming to his feet. He had noticed his sister's agitation, and knew her marriage was a very touchy subject.

"We parted company in Washington."

Andy lightly touched her shoulder and turned her

to face him. "Is there a problem in your relationship with him? I don't want to pry, but I am here to help."

"The marriage was forced. I thought you understood that."

He slowly shook his head. "I know that is what you told me," he said hesitantly.

"It was the truth. Brant may have saved my life and yours, but he used me to get what he wanted. When I had served my purpose, he left me at Confederate headquarters." Andy's eyes widened. "I saw him in Washington, but everything between us is over. I am pretending to be a widow."

"Will the two of you get back together?"

"He can't be trusted," she said flatly. "He used me—made me look like a fool. He is a Confederate spy."

Andy's grip tightened on her shoulders. "Amber, whatever you believe he is, he saved our lives."

"I haven't forgotten," she acknowledged. "But he used the camp situation to his advantage. He knew our connection to Uncle Hank and used it to get into my life and our Washington home. By helping us he helped himself; he ensured his position with our uncle."

"Does Hank know I'm alive?"

"No. I thought about telling him, but decided it should come from you."

Andy nodded. "I'm glad you kept your promise. I believe we owe it to Brant to protect his position."

"Why do you have so much loyalty to the enemy?"

"Brant saved my life and that is something I don't take lightly. I will call him a friend and give him my trust."

"You may have to. Brant is in town. He is looking for you."

"Brant is in the city," he said sharply. "Where is he?"

She shrugged her indifference. "I don't know. Have you heard his name mentioned? Is he involved with the sympathizers?"

"He hasn't been involved with me, but that doesn't mean he isn't in another part of the organization." Andy paused. "Brant doesn't worry me."

Amber's eyes widened. "Andy, he knows you are a Union man. If he finds you working for the Confederates, he will expose you."

Andy grinned. "I will just have to be careful."

Amber couldn't believe he was treating this so lightly. "This is serious," she snapped.

"I know it is." His gaze was intent. "Trust me on this and do it the way I say. Your thinking has been clouded by your hate for the man. Brant may be a Confederate, but he is an honorable man and your husband. I'm putting my trust in that."

Amber's eyes glazed in confusion. She had always respected Andy's judgment on things, but how could he trust the enemy? She didn't even like Brant. Who was wrong?

"Amber, it is going to work out," he reassured her. "I am being careful to cover all my tracks."

She remembered the golden horse at the secret meetings and wondered if it belonged to her brother. "The first few nights I was here I followed Christopher to one of the sympathizers' meeting places. I saw a golden colored horse. Were you riding it?"

"I bought the animal when I arrived in the city. He

is a beauty," he said, smiling.

"Get rid of him," Amber ordered.

"Why?" he said, his nose wrinkling in confusion.

"Christopher wants him and the animal is too easily recognizable. It could trip you up."

"I'll sell the horse," he promised. "It is getting late. I'd better leave."

"When will I see you again?"

"I'll contact you after your lunch with Christopher." Stepping forward, he hugged his sister. "Take care of yourself."

When Andy was gone, Amber relocked the door and walked to the bedroom. This had turned out to be a wonderful day. Finding Andy and knowing she would be working with him was very special. The excitement of the future presented a great challenge and Amber was ready to accept whatever happened. Her only uncertainty was meeting Brant in the conflict that would surely occur.

Twenty-four

The day of Amber's luncheon meeting with Christopher arrived quickly, and she smiled warmly when she met him in the hotel lobby.

"It is a beautiful day," he said, taking her to the carriage. "I thought we would have a picnic."

"That sounds wonderful," she said, knowing it would be safer to talk away from the crowds.

They refrained from discussing the Confederate movement until they had reached their picnic area. Leaving the carriage, they walked a short distance to the shade of some large trees. They were safely tucked away in the country and could be assured of having their talk without interruption. Amber spread a blanket on the grass and sat down. Kneeling, Christopher opened the basket and laid out the food.

"Everything is ready," he said, looking up at her.

Amber met his gaze and had the feeling he wasn't talking about the meal. Nevertheless, she reached for a plate. "Are you referring to the meal?" she asked bluntly.

"No." He smiled. "We can talk about it over lunch."

Amber helped herself to the food but kept her portions small. "Are you ready for my help?" she asked, not wanting to wait any longer.

"Yes," he said, breaking off a piece of chicken. "My meeting was very successful." He scanned the trees in a full circle around them. "We can't be too careful. We will have to limit the time we spend together."

"Would it jeopardize the mission?"

"It might. I met with my contact and we decided there is no way to get you into their headquarters. We believe the next best thing is the hospital. One of the officers divides his time between the medical facility and headquarters. We want you to get to know him. His name is Major Charles Danbury."

Amber recognized the name immediately. It was the same man her uncle had told her to notify.

"Can you handle it?"

The thought of returning to the hospital was a brightening prospect. It would certainly revive the use of her skills. They had been dormant too long.

"Do you really believe he is going to give me information?" she asked doubtfully.

"It is up to you to get it." Christopher regarded her thoughtfully. "I don't want to offend you, but your status as a widow makes you an excellent candidate."

"Why? Because you presume I know a man intimately?" she said bluntly.

"Perhaps you were not cut out to do this job," he said doubtfully. "Maybe we'd better find someone else." He regarded her through lowered lids.

"You are wrong," she said with determination. "I'll

361

do whatever is necessary and I intend to prove it to you." Amber would get the information the Confederates wanted without climbing into his bed. "Should I go to the hospital tomorrow?"

"The sooner you get started the better. Many prominent women work at the facility and they are strongly Union connected. You will have to pretend to like the North."

"That won't be hard," she said, smiling sweetly at the irony of her words. "I think I am a pretty convincing actress."

"You're certainly a beautiful one," he said, his eyes roaming over her face.

Amber lowered her gaze and picked at her food. The one thing she didn't want was for Christopher to show a romantic interest in her. She had made the acquaintance out of necessity and had no desire for him at all. He was a Confederate sympathizer and she did not want a physical relationship with him. Images of Brant sprang to her thoughts and Amber forced them back as she began packing the basket.

Amber spent the evening reviewing a current medical book. At ten o'clock she put her reading aside and removed her dress. The bedroom door opened and Andy slipped into the room.

"I'm glad you are alone," he said, sitting on the bed.

"Who did you expect to find?" she asked, throwing her hands on her slim hips. She wasn't embarrassed to be wearing only her underclothes.

Grinning, he said, "A maid. What did *you* think I meant?"

Andy raised his hands in protest. "Just teasing," he

said. "I wondered if I could get under your skin like I did when we were kids."

"You can," she assured him and reached for her robe.

"Seriously," Andy said. "Christopher wants information from Major Danbury and expects you to use every means at your disposal, including inviting the major into your bed."

"How do you know?"

Andy flopped back on the bed. "I was at your meeting this afternoon."

"You were there!" she exclaimed. "Did Christopher know?"

Andy rolled his head side to side. "I didn't think it was important to tell him." He gave her a lazy grin. "But I wanted to be around to protect my sister."

"Christopher was certain we were alone," she said.

Andy chuckled. "That wasn't hard. Papa taught us to move through the woods undetected. I was close enough to hear everything that was said."

"Can I always count on your protection?"

"I'll be there whenever I can, but there will be times when I won't be available. I'll have to believe you can take care of yourself."

Amber beamed under his compliment. "Andy," she said, her eyes distant. "What happened the night you were captured by the Confederates? How did they know where you were?"

"I was always very careful whom I trusted. Someone betrayed me."

"Do you believe it was Willy?"

"I don't want to think so. He knew I was trying to find the leak in Washington and was working with me. We were so close to finding out who was responsible." He slammed his fist against the bed. "I hated to leave Washington when I knew what was going on, but my identity had been exposed and I was no longer useful as a spy. I also owe allegiance to Brant for saving my life."

"You owe him nothing," Amber growled. "He knew about your meeting and conspired with William in your capture."

"Amber, it doesn't make sense."

"I talked to Willy and he admitted that he knew Brant."

Andy's mouth dropped. "Willy admitted that he was working with Brant." She nodded. "I wonder," he said thoughtfully. "Do you know where Brant is? I would like to talk to him."

"You want to talk to the man who is an admitted spy?"

"There are some questions I would like answered. I can't ask Willy until I return to Washington."

"You can't ask him at all. He is dead. Brant shot him because he was about to tell me something important."

"I'm sorry to hear that." His eyes darkened. "I trusted the wrong person."

"I know who is working with Brant." Andy's eyes widened. "It is Colonel Broadmore. Brant had a secret meeting with him before he went to Confederate headquarters and gave out crucial information."

"Giles Broadmore," Andy said, stunned. "Amber, we've got to get our business out here finished and get back to Washington. It is very important."

"Do you know Major Charles Danbury?"

"He is my contact," Andy supplied.

Amber dropped to the bed. "Have you done anything to hurt their organization since you got here?"

"I am responsible for exposing their plans to seize part of the city. They are looking for me, but I covered my tracks. All I need is a little more time. The sympathizers are planning something big and I have to learn what it is. As soon as I know we'll pull out. All my information passes to Charles in a secret code. You'll have to learn it."

"Does he expect me?"

Andy nodded. "Tomorrow. He'll give you the information he wants passed. You can tell Christopher everything he says."

Amber was excited at the prospect of really getting involved in the war and wanted to help break up the organization.

"How often can we meet?" she asked, not wanting to lose track of her brother.

"You and I can't be connected in any way." He grinned. "We look too much alike. If you want to reach me leave a message with Mary Daniels. You'll meet her at the hospital." He took a sheet of paper out of his pocket and opened it.

"What is it?" she asked, puzzled.

"It is a cipher. Every symbol has a different meaning. When you want to send me a message, you'll have to use this code." He looked at his sister. "Learn this immediately and destroy it. This alone could convict you of being a spy."

Amber took the paper. "I understand," she said, realizing for the first time how dangerous her work would be. "Is Mary someone special?" she asked, teasing her brother.

"No," he said, grinning. "I'm too busy to get involved in romance, and if I were, Mary wouldn't be the woman."

He pushed himself off the bed. "I'd better leave. It is risky being here." He pulled his sister to her feet. "Take care of yourself. I'm counting on the things Papa taught us to get both of us through."

"We'll make it," she said, stepping forward to hug her brother.

They walked to the door. "The lock is lousy, but put it on anyway," he ordered. "I don't want any strangers walking into your room."

When he was gone and the door was locked, she returned to the bedroom and flopped on the bed. She spent the next four hours memorizing the code and making sure she understood how to use it. Satisfied she knew what she was doing, she rose and burned the paper, leaving nothing to remind her of the mission but the ashes. Tomorrow would be the beginning of a new adventure.

The next morning Amber dressed in a gown that would not hinder her work. She arranged her hair with a ribbon, then grabbed her reticule and went downstairs to find a carriage. The Union hospital was not one of the newer buildings, but it was large enough to be serviceable to the people who needed it. When the carriage stopped, she counted out the necessary coins and walked inside. A private, wearing the uniform of the Union Army, sat behind the desk where passes were issued.

"Hello," she said, lowering her lashes in a flirtatious manner. "I've come to offer my services to the hospital."

The soldier regarded her with interest. "We have many women who help make bandages and ease the soldiers' pain. I'm sure we could use your help."

She glanced around to make sure no one was within hearing distance. "I've worked at the Washington hospital. I am qualified to assist in surgery," she said modestly.

The young man looked skeptical. "That is hard to believe," he said. "I ain't never heard of a woman wantin' to be a doctor."

"I'm not a physician," she insisted, "but I do have skills that would be wasted folding bandages."

"Just a minute," he said and stepped into another room. He returned within seconds. "Come this way," he said.

Amber was led down a short corridor to an office and asked to wait inside. A short time later the door opened and a man joined her.

"I'm Doctor Kent Williams."

Smiling, she said, "I'm Amber Rawlins. I would like to help in surgery."

The man's doubt was obvious. "I'm ready to perform an operation. Would you like to watch?"

"I would like to assist you," she said. "I can assure you I am qualified."

"Ah, yes, the private said you worked at the Washington hospital." He looked at her curiously. "I'll give you an apron to cover your dress."

Amber was smiling as she followed him to the area set aside for surgery. She put her reticule in a safe place, remembering that she still carried the tiny pistol inside. In the future she decided it would be safer in her undergarments where it would always be available.

The patient had been injured while loading explosives into a wagon. The torn flesh on the right side of his body was not a pretty sight, and she was certain he would lose his leg.

Even though she had been absent from hospital work for weeks, she anticipated the doctor's needs before he asked. She sewed a gaping hole in his arm, then neatly tied off the stitches.

The man pleaded with the doctor not to take his leg, and Kent relented by letting him keep it, but warned that he would probably get an infection in it. Like most men who found themselves in a similar situation, he preferred to be dead than live without a limb.

When the young man was taken away, the doctor looked at Amber. "You are very good," he said, commenting on her work. A man in his early fifties stepped into the room. "Major Danbury, I would like you to meet Amber Rawlins. She is going to be working here with us."

Amber hid her excitement at meeting Andy's contact and nothing in his expression gave him away. "It is a pleasure to meet you. I am surprised to find a lady interested in medicine."

"Most men do," she said, smiling.

"How do you like San Francisco?"

"The city is nice, but I'm afraid I don't know many people here."

Charles smiled. "Perhaps some evening I could give

you a tour of the city, then take you to dinner."

"I would like that," she assured him.

Kent glanced at the man being put on the table. "I have more work to do. This injury doesn't look serious. Why don't you show Amber around the hospital and tell her what will be expected?"

Amber preceded Charles out the door, then waited for him to catch up to her. He took her to the room where the wounded were kept, their number surprisingly low because it wasn't an area where actual fighting occurred. The sick were housed in a separate section in the hope of keeping everything contagious contained in one location. The hospital took not only military personnel, but anyone who needed help. The Washington hospital always had the overpowering smell of death, but this one did not have the same black edge.

When Amber met Mary Daniels, she understood why the woman was not a romantic interest for her brother. She was nearly sixty years old, her brown hair streaked with gray. Her eyes, the warm color of a golden sunset, were still an attractive feature. She held out her hand to Amber and when their flesh met, Amber felt the squeeze of friendship. This woman would be her only link to Andy.

Amber worked until late afternoon, then walked back to the hotel, exhausted and disappointed that Charles had not mentioned the companionship they would share. They had several opportunities to speak of it, but nothing was ever mentioned.

Two days passed before something finally happened. Amber received a message that asked her to walk to the south side of town at eight o'clock. After making sure she had her weapon strapped to her thigh, where she decided it was safest to carry, she strolled along the planked sidewalk. The shadows did not make her uneasy, but she exercised caution whenever she passed an alley. A man passed close enough to brush her shoulder.

"Go inside the dress shop across the street," he whispered.

Amber walked forward without question and pushed the door open. The inside was dimly lighted and she did not move away from the door. She wanted to be ready to flee if necessary.

"Amber," a voice whispered from the far corner. "Step out of the light." She moved and Christopher appeared from the shadows.

"Is this the way we will make contact every time?" she asked, knowing it was dangerous to walk into an unknown situation.

"What have you learned?" he asked without answering.

"Nothing," she said. "He spends hours at the hospital then leaves. I think he goes to headquarters."

"You think," Christopher snarled. "You are supposed to get close to the man."

Amber threw her hands on her hips. "I will when the time is right. He wants to have dinner with me."

"Go with him. I've had word that the North is planning something in this area. I want to know what it is."

"I'll get your information," she said, stung by his attitude. "When I learn something, how do I get in touch with you?"

"Light the lamp in your window. Fifteen minutes

later walk to this shop. I'll be waiting."

"Won't people wonder why I am coming here?"

"It is a dress shop. You are having gowns made. Try to get something for us in the next few days. It is vital." He smiled. "I understand you told them you worked in the Washington hospital. Good thinking," he praised.

"Where did you learn about my work?"

"That isn't important," he said, and Amber knew she would have to be very careful if her movements were being watched. "Go back to your hotel and think about how you're going to interest Charles Danbury."

Amber was furious when she let herself back into her room. Christopher had implied that she hadn't been doing her job, and she knew it was because he needed information. She would have to approach Charles if he didn't say something.

The opportunity presented itself the next afternoon when Charles asked her to have dinner with him. "I think it is time we got better acquainted. Andy told me you had a meeting last night with Christopher. They must want information."

Amber was reassured to know that her brother had been aware of Christopher's actions. Though she hadn't seen him, he had been somewhere watching and ready to help.

"They know the Union is planning something and want to know what it is."

"I'll give you some details tonight. I hope you won't find my company boring."

Amber already liked the man. "I'm sure I won't."

Her work at the hospital kept her busy the rest of

the afternoon. A few minutes before they were to leave Amber removed her apron and fixed her hair. Charles was waiting for her by the door, and they took the first available carriage.

"I thought we would dine at your hotel. I understand you will want to pass the information immediately."

"Yes," she answered. "Is something going on?"

Charles smiled. "For your protection and ours, I'm only going to tell you things I want you to pass. I trust you, but I know how persuasive people can be when they think you have something they want."

Amber knew how to keep a confidence, but there were ways of getting information, and it was safer if she had nothing to tell.

"We have a valuable cargo coming by ship. It contains ammunition and weapons. It will be unloaded in three days. The Confederate sympathizers need guns if they hope to take over the city."

"Where will the merchandise be taken?" she asked.

"There is a large warehouse near the docks. It is empty now, but in a few days it will be loaded with weapons. We are making this big enough to pull the group together and bring out the top men. I'll give you more facts over the next few nights."

They had dinner in the quiet part of the dining hall then returned to Amber's room. Charles said they should build the appearance of a close relationship to lend credibility to her statements on Union activity. He stayed with her for two hours, carefully coaching her on what to say, then left so she could pass the information.

Amber put a lamp in the window and walked out

of the hotel fifteen minutes later. It was really too late for a dress fitting, but the shop was open and she went inside.

Christopher came forward immediately. "I hope you had an enjoyable meeting with the major," he said, his brow arching as to what really passed between them in the privacy of her bedroom.

"I told you I would do whatever necessary to get information," she said, letting him think they had been lovers.

"I'm glad you believe in our cause so strongly."

"I believe very *strongly* in what I am doing," she assured him.

"What did you learn?" he asked eagerly.

"There is a large shipment of weapons coming into the city in the next few days."

"That would explain the increased number of soldiers," he said thoughtfully. "We desperately need weapons." His eyes were hopeful. "Where will they be stored?"

"A warehouse near the docks."

"Excellent," he praised. "I'll have men start watching every ship that comes to port. It shouldn't be too hard to find the building."

"I would like to get back to the hotel. I have had a long day." She strolled to the door. "You'll be happy to know I am having dinner tomorrow evening with the major. Perhaps I will learn something more."

Without waiting for Christopher's response, she stepped outside and closed the door. Her heart was pumping quickly, the excitement of her part in the scheme filling her with satisfaction. She was ready to cross the street when she saw an obvious movement on the far side of the street. It happened quickly, but not before she recognized Andy letting her know he was close and ready to help if she needed it. When this was over, they would return to Washington and expose Giles Broadmore.

Amber had trouble getting her door unlocked, but at last she stepped inside and closed it behind her. She walked straight to the bedroom and threw her reticule on a chair. She turned up the lamp then removed her shoes and gown. She turned to the wardrobe and froze. Her blue-green eyes widened and the tenseness in her limbs held her against movement. Slowly, the color changed to brilliant green daggers of hate.

"What are you doing here?" she rasped.

"I came to see my wife," Brant said, rising from the chair he had positioned where the shadows were the darkest.

"Don't call me that," she snapped. He stopped a few feet from her and she focused on his face. He didn't look much different than when she had last seen him. His dark hair still dipped over his forehead, but it was longer in the back and brushed the collar of his shirt. After the initial appraisal of his face, the first thing that registered was the lack of a uniform. He was dressed as a civilian, nothing marking him as a man of the military.

"You are my wife," he stated firmly, and she noticed the suppressed anger. "In every way," he added to make her furious.

His reminder of the intimate times they had shared threw Amber off balance. She didn't like remembering the times he had held her in his arms and seduced her body until it lost the will to obey. She had not yet come to grips with the power he held over her. She had come to California to prove to him she wasn't afraid, but her limbs felt like jelly.

"Get out," she seethed.

"No," he said flatly. "I'm not leaving."

"There is nothing for you here," she argued, watching him very carefully for unexpected movements.

"You are here." His flat statement forced a dryness into her throat and her stomach tightened like a spring.

"I want nothing to do with you. You are out of my life."

"It is not that simple," Brant said smoothly. "You are the most desirable woman I have ever known. I'm fortunate enough to have you for my wife."

"Fortunate enough," she gasped.

"I think we had a similar discussion once before, but I will review it for you again. I want you, but more than that, I need you." His eyes dropped to her chest, and she clutched the gown against her breasts to shield the swelling flesh displayed above her undergarments. "You're beautiful. For some reason you cannot accept our marriage, nor the responsibilities that go along with it. You are afraid to accept me as your husband—afraid of the dependency you might have on another person."

"That is not true," she argued. "I never wanted to marry you. It was a forced arrangement."

"Perhaps," he conceded, "but one I am very happy with and don't want to change. When Edgar arranged the ceremony I despised his reasons for doing it. As his superior officer I could have refused. I didn't want to. I wanted the wedding."

"Wh—why didn't you rape me the night of our marriage?"

"You are a very special woman. You possess many of the qualities I admire. I consummated the marriage to put my brand on you and make it real. I wasn't trying to hurt you with violence." Amber knew Brant spoke the truth. He had been very gentle. "You were afraid then and you still are. I can see it in your eyes."

"You can see nothing but loathing," she snapped. "My feelings are disgust."

"Why do you hate me so much? When we make love your body begs for mine."

Amber couldn't comment on something she knew was the truth, but didn't have an answer for. She ran her eyes down his civilian clothes. His shirt fit tight over his broad shoulders and the pants hugged his muscular thighs.

"Where is your uniform, Rebel?" she quizzed tartly.

"I am not using it out here."

Her eyes narrowed suspiciously. "Which side are you pretending to favor?"

"The right side," he supplied. "You'll be happy to know I am a wanted man. Thanks to you, your uncle notified the Union headquarters out here that I would be arriving and if seen should be captured and held for spying. I can't even get close to the Union organization."

Amber smiled. "Isn't that too bad," she said sweetly. "I'm sure you didn't have any trouble working your way into the favor of the sympathizers."

"None at all," he agreed.

Something tightened inside Amber. Christopher had told her the secrecy of the Rebel organization rested with the members knowing only those within their small group. Thus far Andy had not run into Brant, but what if he did? Would he be in danger? Amber searched her thoughts for a way to stop Brant from learning about Andy's involvement, but couldn't think of one. She wasn't worried about what her brother would do. He would never betray Brant. She couldn't understand or agree with his loyalty, but she respected it. Andy had been able to look past the enemy and see the man. Amber couldn't do that, not even when the man was her husband. Brant on the other hand couldn't be trusted not to betray her brother.

He noticed the confusion on her face. "What is wrong?" he asked.

"Nothing."

"Why does my working with the sympathizers upset you?"

She could never tell him about Andy's involvement. "Why don't you get out of my life and leave me alone?"

He took a deep breath and the cloth shirt stretched over his chest. "I can't do that."

There was something in his tone that made her meet his eyes. The brown color had darkened with intent and his jaw had hardened with purpose. His nostrils flared and his mouth parted in a whisper of breath. There was a sudden tension in his body that spoke of awareness, and Amber was instantly on the alert.

"You are my wife. I want you."

The spring of tension that had been tightening in her stomach broke free. A hot rush of emotion poured through her body, her breasts swelling against the fine cloth of her undergarments, and her thighs trembling. Dryness crept into her mouth, and her throat tightened as her breath became forced and irregular. Shooting sensations of pleasure traveled along her nerves, making every part of her body alive and aware of the man before her. Against her will Brant had introduced the wanton desire she had tried to suppress, and it created a series of uncertainties. Her body begged her to admit that she wanted the man, but her mind consciously reminded her that he was the enemy — a traitor to all she believed.

He stepped forward, but did not touch her. Amber felt the heat of his body mingle with the heat of her desire until the space between them was a scorching flame of awareness. Raising his arms, Brant trailed his fingers along her upper arms. His touch sent shooting jabs of sensation along her naked flesh, and she clutched her dress closer to her chest.

"Don't, Brant," she pleaded. "Leave me alone."

Even as she warned him to stop, she felt powerless to move. She shook her head, her amber hair tumbling out of its pins to cascade down her back. She forced herself to think of something other than what he was doing to her body, and the words spy and enemy centered on her thoughts. This man represented everything she hated. She would not let him overpower her thinking and weaken her resistance.

Stepping back, she turned toward the door. Dressed as she was there wasn't really any place she could escape, but she had to break free of the desire she felt. She hadn't gotten halfway across the room when Brant grabbed her upper arm and jerked her back across the room. Amber released the grip she had on her gown to beat against his chest. Once she was successful in hitting his jaw and heard his grunt of pain. Brant pinned her arms against her sides, forcing her tightly against his chest.

Amber wished she had left her shoes on because her bare feet were useless against his booted ones. She struggled against the weight holding her arms and when she couldn't free herself, she sank her teeth into his shoulder.

Brant's eruption of pain made her feel victorious and when his grip slackened, she pushed him. What she had not expected was his rapid recovery. He twisted and their arms tangled forcing them to lose their balance. They landed on the soft mattress and Amber was pinned by Brant's weight. Before she could lash out at him, he captured her wrists and held them immobile.

Their eyes locked, his in victory and hers in bitter defeat. His free hand ran up her thigh to curve across her waist.

"You are a fiery temptress. Even now with all the accusations you have flung at me I want you." His voice was husky with emotion. "I can put our differences aside. When will you see me as a man and forget the side I favor in this war?"

There was a tightness in her throat. She had no doubt of his masculinity, but she could never put their differences to the back of her thoughts. He was a Rebel—a man against all her values. She did not want to be in his arms seeking his caresses when her mind screamed hate.

"Never," she whispered.

"If our love must be a continuous war, then I'm willing to meet you in battle. You have drawn the battle lines, but I will be the victor. . . . You are my wife and I will not take my desire with another."

"Our love," she sneered. "All we spawn is hate. There will never be a victor in this war. In time one of us will destroy the other."

"Have you ever heard of two uniting for the common good?"

"We are too far separated in values. We are like the men in battle, quick and ready to draw our weapons. The only difference is that our weapons thus far have been words of hate."

"One day it will be the real thing."

Brant smiled, his eyes dropping to her rapidly rising breasts. "It won't be tonight, my love. It won't be tonight."

His fingers reached for the lacing on her undergarments, pulling them free as his head dropped to rain a line of kisses just above the fabric. His leg held her lower body immobile and Amber's struggles were wasted. When the cloth parted, he slipped his hand inside to the warm flesh eagerly budding against his palm. Brant's mouth traced every inch of her skin, arousing tingling nerves to throbbing awareness. His lips trailed up her neck to tease the lobe of her ear and finally along her jawline toward her lips. He touched their softness tentatively, his lips catching her lower one between his teeth. His warm breath fanned against hers, the heat of their bodies fusing them together.

Amber felt herself sliding into the vortex only he had been able to create, and she was powerless to stop. A whimper of uncertainty rushed from her throat, and Brant seized her mouth in a drugging kiss that stole the breath from her body. She heard a thud and realized he had let his boots fall to the floor.

Her legs were no longer pinned, but she was weighted by an all consuming passion that left her weak. Brant freed her hands, but Amber left them lying helpless above her head, her mind totally fixed on the only part of his body that was touching her — his plundering mouth.

The mattress shifted and then he was totally against her length, his clothes no longer an inhibitor to his body. The touch of his chest against her naked breasts made her head tingle with unexpected awareness. Brant's hand curved down her stomach, and his finger dipped beneath the band of the garments covering her lower body. Slowly, as though to maintain the swirling effect of what was to come, he inched them down her thighs until finally they were gone, and she was naked in his arms.

Rolling her to one side, he pressed his body against the entire length of hers, forcing every part of her to be attuned to his male need. He kissed her eyes, the tip of her nose and claimed her lips, pushing them into a world where only passion existed and knew no bounds. It was a place where there was no war, only the meeting of two bodies. All else between them forgotten, she reached for him, her hands curving over the muscles in his back, her lips returning every playful caress he had given her. Brant pushed her against the mattress and took her to a world where there was no hate, only the passion of their straining bodies seeking peace from their field of battle.

Amber's eyelids were weighted, her body flowing in a lethargic sensation of calm when Brant pulled her back against his stomach and curved his legs around hers.

"Sleep, my beautiful wife. For tonight a truce has been called."

Amber drifted to sleep, her body close to the man she recognized only as the enemy. Tomorrow would be time enough to hate again. Tonight it was impossible.

Twenty-five

Amber woke at the first sign of dawn and stretched her naked body. Suddenly, her eyes flew open to search the room. It was empty; Brant was gone. Scrambling off the bed, she grabbed her robe and threw it around her shoulders before running to the sitting room. The emptiness added a finality to their night of passion, and she was able to review it in the light of the new day.

She refused to allow herself regrets that he had vanished as quickly as he had come. There was no place in her life for the complications he might present. He was legally her husband, but there could never be anything more between them. Her spite was too strong.

Returning to her room, she cast aside the robe and washed. As the cloth touched her body she remembered the feel of his hands caressing her flesh. Infuriated that he had reentered her life and stamped his image in her thoughts, she threw the cloth into the water and toweled herself dry. Why had she fallen prey to his experienced caresses? Why had she let her body disobey her true feelings about the man?

When they had finished making love, Brant had said a truce existed. A truce was only temporary, and they had once again returned to battle. She did not want him complicating her life. He wanted more than she could give. More than once Brant had admitted that he could put her opposing beliefs aside because they had no place in their relationship. Amber couldn't do that. Brant had betrayed the Union and deserved to be hanged.

She dressed, then tied her hair back with a matching blue ribbon. After a quick breakfast, she walked to the hospital and assisted Kent in surgery. Charles was out most of the morning, but he sought her out late in the afternoon.

"Do we still have a date for dinner in your room?"

"Yes," she said, wondering if Brant would decide to show up while the major was there. What would he think if he knew she was entertaining a man in her room? She mentally shrugged. It didn't matter. Whatever she did with her life was her concern and none of his business. Brant was wanted by the Union Army, and Amber had made it clear that she would turn him in.

"I should be ready to leave here by five. Would that be a good time for you?"

"Fine," she agreed.

In the course of the afternoon Amber asked Mary to have Andy contact her. She finished work early and sat in the waiting area for Charles. As hard as she tried, her thoughts constantly strayed to her husband. Why couldn't she forget him? Why had he come to

California if not to kill her brother? He had admitted his connection with the Rebel organization, and she wondered if it was time to speak to Charles about him.

"Are you ready?" he asked, breaking into her thoughts. "You seemed very far away," he said, ushering her outside "Are you having second thoughts about being involved?"

"No, it isn't that. . . ." This was her chance to speak, but something held her back. Once it was said it could not be retracted. "It is a personal matter. I may want to discuss it in the future, but not now."

"Whenever you are ready, I'll be glad to listen."

Amber smiled. Charles Danbury was a very nice man and she felt comfortable with him. "Thank you," she said softly.

Amber had made arrangements for the meal to be brought to the room, and while they dined, they discussed the warehouse and arrival of supplies. She needed more information to pass to Christopher to lend validity to their visits together.

"Have you seen Andy?" she asked, wondering if Mary had passed on her message.

"He has gone north for a few days. We think the Rebels are bringing in guns farther up the coast. He went to find out."

Amber carefully hid her disappointment. If Andy was gone, she would have to deal with Brant's arrival on her own.

Charles stayed late to make it look like their relationship had deepened. Amber placed the lamp in the window and waited the required fifteen minutes before going to meet Christopher. He was pleased with the news she had brought him and asked her to find out how the shipments would be guarded. They intended to steal whatever they could and if that wasn't possible they were prepared to blow up the whole building. Christopher stressed the importance of time. They would need every available minute to get ready.

Knowing Andy was out of town made Amber more cautious on the return to the hotel. Once inside her room, she locked the door and walked toward the bedroom, wondering if Brant would be waiting like he had been the previous night. Satisfied she was alone, she removed her clothes and climbed into bed. It was very late and she dropped into a deep sleep immediately.

Two thumps and a rustling noise were the sounds that warned Amber she was not alone. Struggling out of her deep sleep, she sat up as the mattress bowed beneath Brant's weight. The narrow shaft of moonlight entering through the window gave her a clear look at his face.

"You," she breathed and clutched the blanket against her breast.

"Did you expect someone else?" he asked, his words cold. "I was beginning to wonder if the major was going to spend the night."

Amber's hand flew out to catch the side of his cheek. "How dare you imply that I would sleep with him!"

"I am glad to know you respect my vows." Rubbing his cheek, he gave her a lazy grin. "Perhaps you feel some responsibility toward this marriage."

The only way Amber could shield her confusion

was to attack, and her hands flew to his face. Moving quickly, Brant caught her wrists and imprisoned them against her legs.

"You are playing a dangerous game," he warned.

"I'm not playing any game," she snapped heatedly.

"You are entertaining a Union major in your room, then meeting with a member of the secret Confederate society. You are taking a serious risk."

"I don't know what you are talking about," she denied.

"I know what you have been doing," he said, his grip tightening. "You've been getting information from Charles Danbury and feeding it to Christopher."

"How do you know?" she breathed.

"Do you have to ask?" he said, chuckling. "You should know my position in the Rebel Army gives me contacts here."

"Did Christopher tell you about me?"

"He didn't have to. I saw you with him on the ship and several times after. I warned you to stay out of it."

"I can't. I want to see the organization and you shattered."

Brant sighed. "You need to examine your need for vengeance. It is not me or the Rebels you want to destroy. It is the fear of your own feelings. You think you can accomplish it by getting me out of your life. It won't work." He paused thoughtfully. "I was at your meeting this evening."

"You were there?" she whispered. "Where?"

"It doesn't matter. You are giving the society some very valuable information. Christopher believes you are on the side of the Confederacy, but I know different. You hate the Rebels and want them destroyed. That is why I am finding it difficult to believe the things you've been telling him."

"I'm telling him the truth," she argued.

"You may be telling him part of the truth, but you are only passing along the information Charles wants you to tell." She opened her mouth to deny it, but Brant shook his head. "You would never betray the Union."

"I hate you."

Brant's brown-eyed gaze roamed over her face and finally stopped at her eyes. "Would it make a difference if I were on the same side?"

His question shook her to the soul of her being. It was not something she wanted to ponder. She had used his opposite political values as a protection against the man. Without her spite for him as a Confederate, what would she have as an excuse for hating him? Would there be a difference in their relationship?

"I don't have to answer that," she said, refusing to meet his eyes. "You admitted that you were a Confederate." She took a deep breath and fought down the urge to hope that he was a man from the North. "Can you deny it now?"

"No, I can't."

"Then it doesn't make any difference. It doesn't change anything between us."

Brant's expression darkened. "Why can't you admit your prejudices toward me and accept me as I am?"

"Because you believe in slavery, you possess an arrogant pride, and you are everything I oppose."

"Stop fighting me," he said, his head dropping to her throat. His lips caressed her flesh and Amber felt the flare of passion. "Admit what you are feeling for me. You belong in my life. You have become a part of me." His mouth slid along the hollow of her throat to the valley of her breasts. "Don't be afraid to let me into your life. I'm not going to destroy your independence. I won't mock your vulnerability."

His words hinted at fear and her limbs coiled tightly. This man did disturb her, and she didn't like the confusing thoughts his attention forced.

"No, Brant," she said, twisting to the side. "Leave me alone. I don't want you here."

His fingers released one wrist and his palm glided over her hip. "You want me here, but you're too stubborn . . . or afraid to admit it. You were here, ready and waiting, your body naked. Can you deny that you looked for me when you came back tonight?"

She couldn't because the possibility of finding him had taken the forefront in her thoughts. Had she suppressed her disappointment over his absence? Had she wanted to find him waiting so she could melt into his arms? She didn't like the confusion his presence always stirred. She had been independent for so long, she didn't know how to let him into her life.

"There is no place in my future for you," she breathed, her lips almost touching the flesh on his shoulder.

His hand pressed against her lower back to fit her against his body. "It is not wrong to love and make a life with another."

"I can't," she admitted and hated the words for slipping past her tongue.

389

His fingers traveled along her spine and Amber shivered against him. "You can't be cold, so I know you're feeling something for me. I'm not asking you to give up your freedom. I'm asking you to be a woman and let me see some of your softness and vulnerability."

His words did not calm Amber. Her thoughts were confused, her mind torn between what she believed and what her body wanted. "You are the enemy," she accused. "Anything else you believe is pure fantasy. I never asked you into my life, and I don't want you here complicating things."

Brant smiled. "If I recall correctly, your kiss against a dying man's lips was the beginning."

Amber's cheeks reddened. Something about him had enticed her from the start, and instead of lessening it had grown stronger.

Brant pushed her against the mattress and his hand slid over her stomach. "I am part of you, and while I am here, we might as well enjoy each other's company. We both have a job to do, and it is a pity we can't work for the same cause."

The reminder of the war and Brant's treasonous convictions snapped Amber out of her passive resistance. "No, Brant," she said, twisting free of his body. "I don't want this. Leave me alone."

His jaw hardened. "Not until I do what I came here to do." He reached for her, his body pinning her against the bed. His mouth and hands were suddenly everywhere, and Amber did not have the speed, nor after a while, the inclination to fight him off. She hated him for being a Rebel, but she hated herself even more for responding to a man she could never love.

Her arms clung to him, her lips searching out his mouth for kisses that stole the breath from her body and made her limbs tremble in awareness. This man's power over her was frightening, but there was nothing she could do to stop him. Their limbs entangled, their bodies growing moist from the heat flaming between them.

Amber moaned as Brant buried his face against her hair, his fingers roaming quickly over her sensitive flesh. Their union was the battle of two foes, each struggling to be victorious against the other, but neither able to injure because their only weapons were passion and need. Brant trembled in victory as Amber surrendered to the enemy, her body weakened by his cunning advances. They had met in battle, and once again she had been defeated in the war of their passion.

Brant kept his wife at his side, his fingers stroking through her silky amber hair. Their breathing slowed and languid satisfaction rushed through their bodies. As sanity returned Amber's disappointment in herself surfaced. She felt threatened by Brant and she wanted him out of her life.

"I guess you have done what you came here to do. Now I am telling you to leave." Her words sounded cold after the passion they had shared.

Brant grinned, his teeth glowing against the soft light. "We haven't even done what I came to do. This was a fringe benefit."

"Oh, you insufferable swine," she sputtered, pushing herself up on her arm. "What did you come here for?"

"I want to know what information you haven't passed to Christopher."

"What!" she exploded.

The smile left Brant's face. "I know you are passing only the information you want him to know. What aren't you telling him?"

"How dare you think I would tell you and betray the North!" She pushed out of his grasp. "If I knew anything I would never tell you. I'm not for the society. I'm against them."

"I know that, but Christopher doesn't . . . at least not yet."

"What is that supposed to mean?" she asked, watching him warily.

"I'm saying that it would only take a few words from me for Christopher to learn the truth."

"You wouldn't dare," she whispered, her blue-green eyes flashing in anger.

"No?" he said, arching his brow. "I want that information."

"Get it yourself."

"How?"

"Go to Union headquarters and ask Charles Danbury." She smiled. "Then they can arrest you for spying, and you will be out of my life."

Brant's eyes darkened in anger. "Don't take me for a fool."

Amber pushed her long hair over her shoulder. "Then don't take me for one. Don't come here expecting me to give you information."

"Did you know the search for me has intensified? Your uncle is applying pressure. He wants me back in Washington to hang."

"Maybe I should tell them how to catch you."

Brant sat up and wrapped the sheet around his lower body. "Why haven't you?" he asked, his eyes probing.

It was a question she didn't have an answer for. She had almost mentioned it to Charles, but at the last minute changed her mind. Perhaps deep down she believed he could be useful to her. She wanted to wait and talk to her brother about it.

"I'm not ready."

"Where is Andy?" he asked abruptly.

Amber shook her head. "That is none of your business."

"I saved his life once. Why would I want to take it now? He is your brother and if I had anything to do with his death you would never forgive me. It would destroy every chance of us coming together when this is over. Do you believe me?"

"No." There was no mercy in her tone and she saw him flinch. Her lack of trust for the husband who had just made love to her was a bitter sting.

Brant grabbed her upper arms. "Where is your brother? I have got to see him."

She didn't flinch under his hard gaze. "Why?"

"I have to talk to him."

"What about?" she asked.

"Perhaps I want to warn him to be careful."

"I don't believe you."

Brant's mouth curved in a smile. "I guess it is my turn to be hurtful. I can't talk to you. Your mind is too full of your hate for me. My business will be conducted with your brother."

His words were like a slap. Brant didn't trust her

anymore than she trusted him. "He won't sell out to the Rebels."

"Maybe he already has," Brant said, putting a question into her head.

"You beast," she screamed, lunging at him. Her thrashing limbs were hard to contain, and they were both breathless when Brant finally succeeded in ceasing her movement. "My brother wouldn't do that."

Brant didn't answer and his expression carefully concealed his emotions. His eyes wandered over her face and he saw the raging conflict in her stormy green eyes. "Would you cry for him . . . or yourself . . . if he did?"

She swallowed a lump in her throat. "No," she said, knowing the tears would be hidden inside.

"What does it take to crack through the hard shell you have built around yourself? Why can't you yield? Why can't you stop hiding behind your independence and let me know how you really feel? Why can't you cry and laugh, be soft as well as hard? Why can't you be my wife—the woman in my life prepared to give herself totally and without fear? Why can't some of that hate turn to love and respect? Why can't you step over the boundary that divides us and meet me halfway?" His brown eyes were soft as they gazed into hers. "Why can't you love me like I love you?"

Amber was shocked. His words had held an anguished plea and a hope for the future, but Amber knew there were no answers for his questions. By his own admission he loved her, but she felt only hate and resentment toward him for complicating her life. He had admitted his love while she threw daggers of hate back at him.

As she gazed into his brown eyes she saw the love he had spoken of — a love so strong that he had humbled himself before her. He had sacrificed his pride with the admission and not been afraid of rejection. He was a strong, independent man, and he had offered himself as a commitment to the future.

Amber's head spun with uncertainty. She hated him for using her, confusing her thoughts, and making her body betray her. What was she going to do?

Brant watched the conflicting emotions float over her face, her eyes stormy one minute then calm as the sea the next. Her lips quivered and he dropped his gaze, his brown eyes reflecting her yearning as they caressed hers. She was caught in their depths, her breath struggling to pass her throat. There was question in his eyes, but she had no answers for the yearning desire she saw; no answer for the questions he had raised. She couldn't become a traitor to her country or herself by loving this man. She wouldn't do it.

She swallowed, and her breath passed her throat in a soft gasp. Brant's hair fell loosely over his forehead as his mouth moved toward hers, but stopped to hover above the softness in uncertainty. Their first touch was like the spring breeze rustling over her flesh. When he touched her lips again, his hand glided along her side to make her body aware of him. Finally, the pressure of his mouth against hers was a sweet sensation, flooding her limbs with a tenderness she had never before experienced.

Amber responded, opening her mouth to accept the deepening urgency of his, her hands roaming over his muscled shoulders to draw him close. She needed no coaxing from his hands, and she moved against him until she felt every inch of his masculine flesh.

When his mouth freed itself from hers to nuzzle her neck, she teased the flesh on his shoulders with her tongue. Her fingers ran along his back, and Brant shifted so she could caress his narrow waist, flat stomach and hair-roughened chest.

"Amber," he muttered, his mouth teasing her breasts.

She pulled his lips to hers and greedily drank of their taste. Anticipating her desire, Brant carried her to the satisfying explosion of her pent up passion and left her feeling sated and relaxed. Curled against her husband, his arms holding her tightly, she blocked out Brant's earlier questions, her insecurities and her hate. They slept like lovers.

Amber woke alone and realizing the feeling of satisfaction that she had experienced the night before was gone. She didn't bother to look in the sitting room for Brant because she knew he would be gone.

She dragged her legs over the side of the bed and pulled the sheet around her nakedness. What had happened between them? Last night had not been like the other times. She had sensed something very special in Brant's desire to please her. She remembered his admission of love with a frown. Did he really care? Was it love that brought him to her bed? The possibility frightened her and she felt like a trapped animal. He wanted her to laugh, cry and be soft as well as hard. More than that Brant wanted her love and a place in her life.

Amber shook her head, her amber hair tumbling wildly down her back. She had never felt such a complete sense of uncertainty and perhaps fear. Fear was one word she would not readily accept. Papa had taught her to challenge her fears and overcome her uncertainties, but each time she met Brant she had become more confused. She raised her hand to her forehead. Where would she find the answers?

The reminder of something Brant had said forced her to jerk her head up. He had hinted that Andy might be involved with the Confederates. She couldn't believe it was true of her brother and hated Brant for putting the doubt into her head. She had to see him.

Rising, she put on her underwear and sat at the desk to write a cipher to her brother. She was finishing it when the bedroom door opened and Brant walked in. Amber rose and blocked her work with her body. Why had she been so confident that he would be gone that she hadn't checked the outer room?

"Good morning," he said easily and walked toward her with an easy stride. He smiled. "Did you miss me when you woke?" he asked, stopping before her and drawing her into his arms. His mouth fastened on hers instantly, the passion they had shared the night before exploding and forcing her to waver against him. The paper on the desk was forgotten as her arms entwined around his neck, and her body arched against his. Brant's lips left hers to leisurely explore the line of her neck and shoulders. His hand curved along her spine and dropped toward her buttocks, then left her body completely.

Amber felt him stiffen, and when he drew back he was clutching the paper. He scanned the small symbols and his mouth pulled into a thin line. Amber lunged for the note, but Brant successfully eluded her hand and pushed her aside.

"They changed the code," he said flatly. His eyes locked with hers. "Who are you sending this to?"

"I'm not going to tell you," she flung at him.

"I demand to know," he said, stepping forward. He grabbed her upper arms and his fingers dug into her flesh. "Who are you sending this to?"

"I won't tell you," she said, refusing to flinch under his attack.

"Where is the code to decipher this?" he asked, walking to the wardrobe and searching through her clothes.

"You don't think I'm stupid enough to have it in my room? Everything I know about this is in my head."

Holding his body rigid, he walked toward her. Amber took a step backward, then froze. She wasn't going to run from him.

He held the paper under her nose. "I want to know what this says."

"I won't tell you anything and you can't make me." Brant jerked her against his body. There was none of the love in his eyes that he had spoken of earlier. "What are you going to do, beat it out of the woman you love?"

It was cruel to throw his feelings back at him, and Brant's face mirrored his disgust. Flinging her away from him, he folded the paper and stuffed it into his pocket.

"You can't take that," she said, trying to grab it back.

"I want to figure out what it says."

"You won't be able to break the code."

"It may take some time, but I'll do it. I've had experience with these before." He raised his eyes to hers. "Do you want to make it easier for me and tell me what it says?"

"Never," she vowed.

Brant scowled. "You'd better get dressed or you'll be late for work."

Turning, Amber grabbed her gown and dropped it over her head. "Are you going to spy on me?"

"Unfortunately, you have access to information I need. I am a hunted man and cannot get it myself."

Amber closed the buttons on the gown and secured her hair with a ribbon. "You'd better stop coming here. This is the first place the soldiers will look for you. Uncle Hank sent me out here to find you. I'm the bait."

"You certainly have complicated things for me," he snarled. "I have an appointment."

"Anyone I would be interested in telling Charles about?"

"No," he snapped.

Amber picked up her reticule, determined to be unconcerned by his presence. "Don't come back tonight. It is not safe."

Brant caught her arm and forced her to face him. "Does that mean you care for me a little?"

"It doesn't," she snapped, wrenching her arm free. "I'm sick of you coming in here and using me to satisfy your lust."

"Is that what you thought we were doing last night?"

"Wasn't it?" she tempted.

"If you don't know the difference, then I'm not going to answer that." The rage on his face was mingled with hurt. Brant stormed past her and seconds later the hall door slammed.

Amber should have been elated over his departure, but she wasn't proud of the taunts she had thrown his way. She had mocked his feelings, and if they were sincere, it must have hurt. She didn't know why, but last night had been different.

Stiffening her shoulders, she put Brant to the back of her mind and left for the hospital, completely forgetting to eat breakfast. There was no surgery that morning, so Amber helped make the patients more comfortable. They received a shipment of medicine, and she was able to ease some of their suffering.

Amber was getting ready to leave for the noon meal when Charles approached her. "Can we have lunch? I have to talk to you."

There was urgency in his tone and Amber quickly accepted. He chose a quiet dining hall where they could be assured of privacy. After their orders were placed, he looked at Amber.

"I want to talk about some information we received at headquarters." He cleared his throat and she sensed his anxiety.

"Does it have something to do with the warehouse?" she whispered.

Charles shook his head. "No." He paused. "Though I suppose they could be connected. Several weeks ago we received word to watch for Brant Faulkner. A second message arrived yesterday, and your uncle wants an intensive search conducted for him. Officials in Washington believe he is a spy."

Amber kept her face expressionless. "I was the one who warned my uncle of Brant's activities."

400

"So I understand," he conceded. "I also believe you are married to him."

"I won't deny it, but I was tricked into marrying him. No feelings were involved."

"Have you seen him?"

There was a sudden dryness in her throat. Brant was the enemy, and she had constantly threatened him with exposure. But he was also her husband, and that spoke of a different kind of loyalty. Did she owe him anything?

"Yes," she said softly. "I have seen him."

"What did he want?" Charles asked bluntly, and Amber lowered her eyes. She couldn't admit that he had wanted to make love to his wife.

"He knows I have been giving information to Christopher."

Charles scowled. "Then they know there is reason to suspect what you have told them."

"Not necessarily. I don't think Brant betrayed me to Christopher," she said truthfully. "My husband knows I am not a reliable source, but he is eager for what I can give him. He'll confirm everything I say and fill in the empty spots on his own."

"You might be right. He won't find any fault with the information." He frowned. "You are in a dangerous situation. Can you trust Brant?"

Amber moistened her lips. After the way she had coldly disregarded his feelings she wasn't sure of anything. If his love was real she wanted to believe he would protect her.

"I don't know."

"This complicates things," he said, frowning. "You can't meet Christopher again. It isn't safe."

"I am not afraid," she argued. "If I don't continue they will get suspicious."

"The weapon shipment is real, and we have made it easy for them to confirm it. Because Brant knows your loyalties he'll be on guard for a trap when they try to steal the merchandise."

"Has everything arrived?"

Charles nodded. "It came this morning. The men started unloading at dawn."

"It is early," she said, remembering that she had told Christopher it wouldn't happen until tomorrow.

"We moved things forward."

"What if they attack tonight?"

"We'll be ready for them. Why are you asking?"

"I should get a message to Christopher about the change in plans."

"I can't allow it."

Further argument from Amber was impossible because the food arrived and they ate in silence.

"You seem troubled by my decision," Charles said when they had finished.

"I haven't fulfilled my obligations."

"You have done enough. Anything more is too risky. They have scouts who will know we received the shipment ahead of schedule."

"Charles, I have to see Andy." She wanted to know why Brant had suggested that he was a Rebel.

"Is it important?" he asked, searching her face.

"Brant intercepted a cipher I was sending to him. I wouldn't tell him what it said."

"He'll figure it out. I will have it changed immediately."

"What about my brother?"

"He'll be back in town tonight." He wiped his mouth and put his napkin aside. "For your protection I want you with me all day."

"I can take care of myself," she argued in her behalf. She was perfectly capable of protecting herself and felt for the gun strapped to her thigh. "I am not afraid."

"I know you aren't. We'll spend the afternoon at the hospital, then go to the hotel. As a precaution I am going to assign men to watch you."

Amber sighed. There was no point in trying to talk him out of it. As promised Charles stayed close to her during the afternoon. Amber didn't like being under his constant observation and when the opportunity arose, she went to the back to get supplies. There were two doors in the room, one from the hospital and one to the outside. The latter was open and Amber went to close it. Suddenly, she was pushed outside and forced against the building.

She looked into the angry eyes of her husband. "What are you doing here?"

"Aren't you glad to see me?" he sneered. "I want to know what is happening with the weapon shipment."

"How should I know," she said, shrugging.

Brant shook her. "This is important. Something has changed and I have got to know about it. Did it arrive early?"

"You can't expect me to answer that," she argued.

"I do expect it. You got yourself involved in this and it isn't safe to quit now."

"Safe?" she asked, her nose wrinkling in confusion.

"That is right," he snapped. "You have been giving Christopher information. What is he going to think

403

when you don't tell him about the change in delivery?"

"How do you know I'm not going to tell him?"

"Because there are guards around the hospital. I had to take care of the one back here so I could get inside." Amber was horror-stricken. "I didn't kill him, but he'll have a headache."

"You brute." She tried to push him away.

"I'm trying to save your neck. If Christopher doesn't learn about this, he'll get wise to your loyalty. The man will kill you if he suspects you have lied to him."

Amber's struggles stopped. "I didn't ask you to protect me," she said scathingly. "Am I supposed to believe it was your love that brought you here to warn me?"

Brant's eyes narrowed. "Don't mock my love with cruelty. I don't want to see you killed."

The sincerity of his voice made her wonder if she had misjudged him. "I am sorry if my sharp tongue stings. I don't know what to think of your feelings for me, but I am certain you would do or say anything to get information from me."

"I want to know what is going on because I want to save your life. . . . Now, I want answers."

Charles had told Amber that Christopher's organization had ways of finding things out for themselves. If that was true she had no reason to hide the facts from Brant.

"It will be in the warehouse tonight."

"Knowing your loyalty to the North and how readily you gave the information to Christopher, I'm certain there will be a trap. I don't suppose you would like to confirm that." Amber glared at him. "No desire to save your husband's life?" Brant released her in disgust.

She looked at him and the words unexpectedly tumbled from her lips. "Stay away from the warehouse."

He grinned. "You give me reason to hope." After kissing her soundly on the mouth he disappeared.

Amber's fingers pressed against her lips. Why had she warned Brant about the danger? Puzzled and horrified by her actions, she went to find Charles.

"I'm not happy this happened," he said, "but I think it takes the pressure off you. Brant will take the information to Christopher, and he'll have no reason to doubt your part in this."

"Did you find the man Brant knocked out?"

"He is doing fine," he assured.

When it was time to leave, they took a carriage to the hotel, had dinner in the dining hall and went to her room. They were beginning a discussion on the hospital when the bedroom door opened. Charles jumped to his feet and reached for his gun.

Amber held her breath. Had Brant come while she was gone? "Andy," she said, not knowing her voice held relief.

He embraced his sister, then stepped aside to salute the major. "I understand you wanted to see me. Has something urgent happened?"

"It was your sister's request. You'll have to ask her."

Andy looked at Amber. "What is wrong?"

"Could we talk privately?" She looked at Charles. "Would you excuse us?"

"Of course," he said agreeably.

When they got to the bedroom, Amber turned to her brother. "I've seen Brant. He came to my room." She took a deep breath. "He is wanted by the Union Army for treason."

Andy's brows came together. "Didn't you expect it? You are the one who told Uncle Hank about him."

"I know," she whispered. "He intercepted a cipher I was sending to you and he wanted to know what it said."

"Did you tell him?"

She shook her head and looked into his eyes. "He hasn't been satisfied with ruining my life, now he is out to destroy yours."

There was a deafening explosion and the twins ran to the outer room. Charles was standing at the window staring into the darkness.

"The Rebels have attacked."

"Were we ready for this?" Andy asked, stopping at his side.

Charles nodded. "Yes. If we are lucky we will catch the leaders and disrupt the organization."

"What exploded?" Amber asked.

"It was a signal for our men to move in." They were close enough to hear the rapid succession of gunfire. "I have to get down there," Charles said, walking to the door.

"Can we come along?" Amber asked, not wanting to be left out of the excitement.

"It will be dangerous," Charles warned, "but no more dangerous than being here. By now they know it was a trap and that you betrayed them."

"Give me a minute," she called and ran to the bedroom. She emerged in a shirt and pants and carried her pistol. "I am ready," she called.

Charles looked shocked and Andy grinned. "Just like old times," he called.

Carriages were available, but they walked the short distance. A fire had started in one building and the air was clouded with the thick smell of smoke. A continuous barrage of gunfire told of the heated confrontation. When they neared the fighting, Charles disappeared to consult with the men in charge of the operation. Andy and Amber ran between buildings to reach the heavy fighting. Union soldiers were firing rapidly against the trapped Rebels.

Andy pulled his sister behind a pile of crates. "It will be safer to watch from here," he said, seeing Union soldiers advancing on the warehouse.

The Rebel sympathizers had barricaded themselves in the building and refused to surrender. Amber felt a tightness in her throat as she watched a man torch the building to force their exit.

"What is he doing?" she shrieked. "There are explosives inside."

Andy's hand clamped on her shoulder. "Take it easy. The building is full of worthless junk."

"No one told me that," she offered.

Andy grinned. "You were only given information we wanted the Rebels to know. There was no chance of anyone getting more out of you. The real shipment arrives in two days."

Amber was relieved the truth had been kept from her. Brant was too skilled in getting details from her.

Flames licked at the wooden structure. "Do you think Brant is one of the trapped men?" she asked.

Andy turned his green eyed gaze on his sister.

"Does it matter if he is?"

She didn't answer his question. "Andy, Brant hinted that you were working for the Confederates."

"Did you believe him?" he asked, giving her a searching look.

"I didn't want to," she said, her throat tight in fear.

Andy put his arm around his sister's shoulder and pulled her against his chest. "What exactly did he say?"

Amber searched her thoughts for the correct words. "He wanted to see you. He said he had business with you. I told him you wouldn't have anything to do with the Rebels and would never sell out the Union. Brant said, 'Maybe he already has'."

The statement hovered in the air. She refused to admit how much was resting on Andy's denial.

"I wish I had gotten to see him," he said, scowling.

"Andy," Amber said aghast. "Was Brant telling the truth?"

"No." He gently cupped her face and kissed her forehead. "Brant probably said that to make you mad. Were the two of you fighting at the time?"

She nodded. "Then why do the two of you want to see each other?"

"I wanted to tell him to stay out of the way. Perhaps he wanted the same."

"I warned him this afternoon."

"I'm glad to hear that," he said, hope entering his eyes. "Brant is a decent man and is fighting for the cause he believes in—just like you. His spying is no different than Papa's and mine." He caught her chin and forced her to look at him. "Amber, Papa always expected us to be strong. He did not like weakness in himself or those around him and tried to get us to suppress our feelings of uncertainty. He was harder on you because you are a female, and I don't think you were able to keep a firm grasp on what he wanted and what was real. Amber, I have many sensitivities that he would call weakness, but I am not ashamed of them. Brant and Papa—."

"Don't compare Brant to our father. They are not the same."

Andy grinned. "That is right, they aren't. Some of their strengths and qualities might be the same, but that is where it ends. . . . Think about what I have said."

They were so involved in their discussion that they hadn't realized the Union soldiers were gathering people together. There was an isolated shot, but for the most part it was over. Amber scanned the faces of the captured, searching for Brant. A golden flash caught her eye and she turned her head to see the horse Andy had sold to Christopher coming toward them.

Amber grabbed Andy's arm and pointed at the horse and rider. "Look," she shouted. "Christopher is trying to get away."

Andy climbed the pile of crates to give him the height he needed. When Christopher rode past Andy, he lunged at him and knocked him off the horse. Amber drew her gun and aimed it at Christopher.

"Don't move," she warned.

Christopher's expression mirrored his surprise. "You," he shouted, rising from the dirt. "You are both lying traitors."

"Let's go," Andy said, pushing him toward the prisoners. "Your days of causing trouble in California are over."

When he had safely been delivered to the soldiers, Andy put his arm around his sister's shoulders. "Let's go back to your room."

"I'm ready to go home," she said and realized she meant Washington.

"I wonder what Uncle Hank's reaction will be when he sees me."

"Let's find out."

Twenty-six

There was little activity around the hotel when they returned, and Amber decided the commotion had forced people off the street. Inside her room she put her gun on the table and shook her hair to free it from the collar of the shirt.

"It is good to wear pants again," she said.

Andy chuckled. "Did you see the expression on Charles's face? You shocked him."

Amber wrinkled her nose. "Be glad you don't have to wear dresses," she scoffed.

"I don't have the body for one," he said, stretching out on the settee.

Amber laughed, but the sound died on her lips when the door opened. Brant slid inside and kicked the door shut. His hair fell carelessly over his forehead, and his brown eyes had an intent look. His arms were crossed over his chest and one hand rested on his shoulder.

"I—I am glad you are both here." He looked at Andy. "I wa—wanted to see you."

Amber looked at her husband in confusion. Why was he stumbling over his words? Why were there beads of sweat on his lip and forehead?

Brant fell against the wall and Andy sprang to his feet. "Help me get him to the settee," he yelled to his sister, but she was too shocked to move. He slid his arm around Brant's waist and helped him across the room. "What happened?" Andy asked, opening his shirt. He carefully pulled the fabric free and exposed the bloody shoulder.

"I got caught in the crossfire," he explained, wincing when Andy began a skilled exploration of the injury. "I don't think it is serious," Brant said, but Amber saw the sweat rolling down his forehead.

"You are lucky," Andy said. He looked at his sister, his expression impatient. She was trained to respond to injury. What was wrong with her? Why was she standing as though nothing had happened? "Amber," he snapped. "Get me something to use as a bandage." She ran to the bedroom. "I'll also need scissors, needle and thread," he called after her.

Amber tore a petticoat for the bandages, then pulled the other things from her trunk. When she returned to the sitting room, she put the items next to her brother and stepped back.

"I've never seen you so unresponsive in the face of injury," Brant said, his eyes locking with hers. "Is it because I am hurt? Are you hoping I'll bleed to death?"

"Why did you come here?"

The pain in his eyes was not from the wound. "You are my wife. Where else would I be safe?"

His statement dangled in the air. The denial was on

her lips, but nothing came forth.

"Amber," Andy barked. "Don't just stand there. I need fresh water." She had to go downstairs for it, but she was back within minutes. "We have to get the lead out. I'll need your help."

Amber's motions were mechanical, and she had to force herself to pretend he wasn't her husband. When Andy probed the wound, Brant's jaw clamped so tightly against the pain that the muscles along his jaw flexed. Amber's stomach rolled in tempo with his agony.

Brant's eyes opened to lock on her face. "What, no tears for my pain?" he said with sarcasm.

Confused, Amber looked away. She remembered the turmoil the night Brant had entered her life. He had been near death, and she had experienced compassion, pain and heightened awareness of him. She had been unable to treat him until her father reprimanded her for the emotions he had interpreted as weakness. He had seen her confusion and warned her to squelch her feelings. It had been the only time he had had to remind her of her responsibility for the injured. The situation had duplicated itself and she had experienced the same feelings.

"You should be a full time doctor and give up spying," Brant admonished.

"That," Andy said pointedly, "is an excellent idea."

Brant looked at his wife. "Are you going to make your career in medicine?"

Amber couldn't think that far ahead. Did Brant care what she did with her life? She shrugged. "I don't know."

"I am glad you were here tonight, Andy. I think

413

your sister would just as soon stick those scissors into my heart."

Shaking his head, Andy glanced at Amber. He had never seen her this uncooperative and didn't know what was wrong with her. Rising, he pushed the bloody cloths into a neat pile.

"You should take it easy for a few days," Andy recommended.

"A few days in bed might be a good idea," he agreed, his gaze floating to Amber. When the implications of his statement registered, her eyes widened.

Smiling, Brant threw his feet over the edge of the settee and pushed himself to a sitting position. Luckily, the wound was not serious and it would heal in a few weeks. He stood and took a deep breath, his chest bronze and hard in the light cast from the lamp. Amber moistened her lips.

"I think I'll go rest," he said. "Andy, I would like to talk to you."

"Sure," he agreed.

Brant had almost reached the bedroom when the door to the hallway burst open and four men rushed into the room and lowered their guns. Amber's initial fear eased when she recognized Union uniforms.

Charles stepped forward and looked at Brant. "I see you got shot," he said, indicating the injury. "Under orders from Washington you are under arrest for spying against the United States. You will be returned to Washington, questioned and hanged as a spy."

Brant turned his hard gaze on Amber, and his face was tight with anger and disbelief. Slowly, he crossed the room and stopped before her. "You betrayed me.

414

When you went for the water you told them I was here." The disbelief turned to hate.

It wasn't the truth, but the denial caught in her throat. She had warned Brant that morning it wasn't safe for him to come back. Did he think she would offer him safety?

"Where are your loyalties to me?" he whispered, so only she could hear. "You have loyalty to your country, but what about to your husband? Were you so afraid of the love I offered that you want me dead? Do you think seeing me hanged will ease your emotional turmoil?" Raising his uninjured arm, his fingers caught her chin and his thumb gently stroked her lips. "We could have had so much, yet you were afraid to share with me, and afraid to love and trust. You hid your fear and lost all softness of your femininity. You are afraid to be a woman. You have been with your brother too long and were raised by a man's standards." He teased her lips, sending rays of remembered pleasure through her body. She stared at the rise and fall of his chest. "My love for you was pure and genuine. It had nothing to do with this war. Why did you want to turn it to hate?"

She raised her eyes, stunned to find a single tear rolling down his cheek. Without knowing what she was doing, she reached up and caught it. It was warm to the touch and alien to her. Could he really love her that much?

The momentary warmth she had witnessed vanished. Using his good arm, Brant jerked her against his body, and his mouth plundered hers. His words had already weakened her, and now she found herself helplessly caught in her churning emotions. He released her just as quickly and flung her aside. Turning, he straightened his shoulders and looked at Charles.

"I'm ready," he said and followed the guards into the hall.

"What happens now?" Andy asked the major.

"I will tell you tomorrow. I have to make the arrangements."

"How did you know Brant was here?" Amber asked softly.

"This morning when you said he had been to see you I assigned men to watch the hotel. I want to thank you both for your help."

"Were the Rebels put in jail?"

"Yes. The mission was a success. We know some escaped, but we've inflicted serious damage to their organization. I recommend that both of you leave the city as soon as possible," he said, walking to the door. "I'll see you tomorrow."

When the door closed, Amber sank into a chair. "Are you all right?" Andy asked, dropping to her side.

"Brant believes I turned him in to the army. He thinks I betrayed him. I warned him this morning to stay away."

"Does it bother you that he has been captured?"

Amber ran her hand across her forehead. Her head pounded in confusion. "I don't know." Andy saw his sister's confusion for the second time that night. "Why did he come here?" she asked.

"You are his wife. He thought he would be safe with you." Smiling, he patted her arm. "Try and get some rest. I'll sleep on the settee. If I am gone when you wake, I went to see the major."

Amber went to her room. Listlessly, she dropped her clothes to the floor and climbed into bed. Sleep eluded her. She was constantly confronted by Brant's accusations. Was she really a failure as a woman? Had she mocked his love and made it something cheap? Had she been afraid of the relationship he offered? She buried her face in the pillow. Why couldn't she sort things out? As she drifted to sleep she kept seeing the single tear running down Brant's cheek. He was a powerful man—strong and masculine—yet he had shed a tear for her.

Amber woke late and Andy was already back from the major's office. "Do you want coffee?" he offered.

"No," she said, flopping on the settee. "What did you learn?"

"Brant spent the night in chains. Physically he is fine. They tried to question him, but he refuses to speak."

Amber looked at her brother. Had she taken Brant's spunk and destroyed the man? "What happens now?" she asked.

"Uncle Hank has ordered his return to Washington. He leaves on a ship this afternoon." He took a sip of coffee. "We have some unfinished business in Washington."

"Do you mean Colonel Broadmore?"

Andy nodded. "Let's go home and get the spy out of the capital. I got two tickets on the same ship. We leave at two o'clock."

Amber rose. "I will go pack."

Andy caught her wrist. "It is what you want, isn't it?"

"I don't know any more what I want," she remarked and left the room.

Brant was taken to the ship under guard and heavily chained. Amber stood at the rail and watched the soldiers push him across the deck. The conflicting emotions that tore through Amber's body were something she would never forget. Brant had never looked her way, but if he had he might have seen a glimmer of regret in her blue-green eyes.

She was constantly troubled by the events that had occurred in California. She would never forget the look in his eyes when he accused her of betrayal. In her dreams she heard his barbed accusations against her character and realized she had no answers.

Andy tended his wound and reported that it was healing nicely. Amber's guilt over the way Brant had been captured finally forced her to ask permission to see him. It was important that he know she had not betrayed him. The officer in charge agreed to the meeting, but Brant refused to see her. Amber felt that a door in her life had slammed shut.

The trip by steamer was uneventful, making the crossing in Panama and the short stop in Havana without difficulty. Security on Brant was strong when they left New York City for the journey to Washington.

"Amber," Andy said for the second time. "We are almost home." Passively, she glanced out the window and noted the familiar sights. "Do you want to go to the house immediately?"

"Where else would I want to go?" she asked, wondering if Andy thought she should be with Brant. "Are you going home?"

"Depends on Uncle Hank. No one told him that I am alive. When my meeting with him is over, I want to see what happens to Brant."

Amber looked at her brother. "You care about him, don't you?" It was more of a statement than a question.

"Yes." He ran his fingers through his amber hair. "I might as well tell you that I am going to speak in his behalf at the trial."

"Did he ask you to?" she quizzed, stunned that Andy would even consider doing it. "Won't it damage your reputation in the Union Army? The man is an admitted Confederate."

"He is a man, Amber, not an animal. He deserves a fair chance at life. Brant may be a Rebel, but he put his life on the line when he freed me. Do you think the Confederates would welcome him if they knew he had arranged my freedom? He would be hunted by them too. He hasn't any place to go." Reaching forward, he caught his sister's hands. "He set me free because of you."

"Did he tell you that?" she whispered.

"Brant loves you and has for a very long time. I knew it the night we met at the cabin. That is why it was so easy to leave you behind when I went to California. I knew he would watch over you."

Andy's words created more anxiety for her already troubled thoughts. She pretended to ignore his comment. "I think we are home."

419

They waited until all the passengers had left the train, then got out and stood on the platform. Andy carried a case in each hand. "Wait here. I'll get a carriage."

Amber watched a group of Union soldiers approach the depot. She knew what they wanted and she turned to look at the train. Brant had been carried in an enclosed car, and when the door opened, he raised his hands to shield his eyes from the brightness. A guard pushed him and Brant stumbled out of the car. Another man poked him in the ribs with his gun.

Brant shook him off and stood. He started to step forward, but stopped at the sight of Amber standing alone on the platform. Contempt marked the handsome lines of his face and there was a sneer on his lips. He pushed past the guards and approached her.

"Have you waited so you can see me pushed around and abused?"

Her eyes dropped to his chained wrists and ankles. As a prisoner his treatment was no better than her brother had received. She had despised the cruelty toward Andy, and now she was witnessing it against her husband. She had viewed one man with love and the other with hate.

His gaze locked with hers. "Are you going to come to my hanging? I'm sure your uncle can get you a front row seat."

A bubble of nausea lodged in her throat and she gulped it down. "Brant," she whispered, unable to tear her eyes from his face. She couldn't explain the trembling in her limbs or the emptiness she felt in her stomach.

He looked at her gown, and his brown eyes devoured the pale flesh displayed by the low-cut design. Brant had made love to her on other occasions with his eyes, and it wasn't having any less effect this time. He may despise her, but he still wanted her. Amber tried to force herself not to respond to the sensuous light in his eyes as they roamed over her figure, but she felt that he was stripping the gown from her body; and he was feasting his eyes on her nakedness.

Unconsciously, her arms rose to cross at the waist. The slight lift of Brant's mouth warned that he recognized her shaky composure, but he didn't look at her. Taking a deep breath, she studied his sun-bronzed face. Her gaze wandered to his mouth, and she stared at the sensual lower lip that was capable of introducing all kinds of pleasure. She had been drawn to it from the beginning, and it had not ceased to captivate her.

"It will never be the same with any other man," he said in a husky tone and Amber gasped. Pulling together the remnants of her composure, she turned and smiled at her uncle.

"Amber," he said fondly. "It is good to have you home." Knowing she wouldn't appreciate the physical contact, he didn't welcome her with an embrace. "I understand you were instrumental in his capture," he said, looking at Brant. "You are to be commended for your fine work."

Fear clutched at Amber. Her uncle had just confirmed something she wanted to deny. She had not purposefully forced Brant into a trap, and had not been an active participant in his capture. The contempt was back in his eyes when she turned and met his gaze. Denial was on her lips, but she knew Brant would not believe her.

"Men," Hank said to the guards. "Get him out of here. I'll be along to question him."

Guards seized Brant's arms and he was dragged away. Amber did not turn to watch. She felt sickened by what had just happened.

She looked past her uncle and saw her brother approaching. "Uncle Hank, there is something about Andy I never told you."

He looked at her curiously. "What else could there be about him? Andy is dead."

"No, he isn't." Hank's lips quivered uncertainly and his eyes narrowed. "When I left the prison I thought the fever had killed him. I found out the night of my marriage to Brant that he was alive."

"Uncle Hank," Andy said and he turned.

All color washed from his face and there was a noticeable trembling in his body. Amber read confusion, horror and finally relief on his face. Smiling, Hank pulled his nephew into his embrace. Amber watched silently, refusing to admit that she regretted not receiving the same kind of welcome.

"This is a shock. . . . I can't believe it." He rubbed his forehead. "Why did Amber think you were dead?"

Andy hesitated and she could see him mulling over his words. It was obvious he wanted to be very careful with what he said.

"When Brant met Amber at the prison camp he was hot with desire. Amber hated him because he was a Rebel and refused to fall into his bed."

Hank turned red. His niece and nephew had a way

of embarrassing him without causing themselves any discomfort. When would he get used to it?

"Brant knew the only way he would get Amber's physical response was to save my life. She learned I was alive the night of her sec—wedding." Andy had started to make reference to Amber's double marriage and decided not to confuse the issue. "I respected Brant for what he did and agreed to leave the area. I went to California."

"Weren't you aware of the danger of leaving a Rebel in Washington?"

"Brant was going south and I knew Amber would keep track of his activity."

Hank turned his narrowed-eyed gaze on his niece. "Your cooperation in this becomes more clear. But why didn't you tell me Andy was alive?"

Amber was sick of hashing over the past. Seeing Brant had only sparked anxiety, and she wanted to get away from everything. "It is over Uncle Hank. I don't want to talk about it." She looked at her brother. "Is the carriage ready? I want to go home."

Hank scowled at his niece, but decided to leave things alone. He had Brant Faulkner and would make sure the man was convicted as the Rebel spy working out of Washington.

Andy helped Amber into the carriage. "I am going to headquarters with Uncle Hank. I'll talk to you later."

On the ride home Amber felt alone and left out. She couldn't explain the restless feeling and wasn't even content to watch the passing scenery. When she arrived at the house, she went straight to her room. She was sitting on the bed when Myra came in.

"Amber," she said. "You're home."

"Hello," she answered and forced a smile.

Myra made a quick appraisal of Amber, immediately noting the changes in the woman she had known since infancy. Something had had a very strong impact on her life, and it was reflected in her dull green eyes and frowning lips.

"Do you want to tell me about the trip?" she asked.

"Not really," she replied listlessly.

"I'll have a bath prepared and food sent up. I imagine you are tired from the traveling." Amber didn't respond and Myra silently crept from the room to make the arrangements.

Amber sat in the scented tub for almost an hour, then rose and toweled herself dry. Sitting on the bed, she combed her amber hair. Her mind unwillingly remembered the way Brant's hands had threaded through the thick tresses. Suddenly, she threw her brush against the bed and frowned. What was wrong with her anyway?

Hearing voices downstairs, she quickly tossed aside the towel, dressed in nightwear and robe and ran down the steps. She found Hank and Andy in the study.

"Amber," Hank said when she joined them. "I thought you would be asleep by now."

"I wasn't tired," she offered, sitting in a chair and curling her legs beneath her. She was certain to hear something about Brant and wanted to be sitting. On several occasions it had been a chore to control her emotions, and she didn't know why.

Andy sat on the settee and rested one foot over his knee. He looked at his sister, his eyes carefully hooded beneath his lids. Amber shifted under the close appraisal and nervously ran her fingers through her hair.

"I'm going to the hospital tomorrow," she said to break the silence. "Care to join me?"

"I've temporarily been assigned to the facility."

"Are you giving up your spy activities?" she asked.

"I'm needed in Washington for a while, and Uncle Hank thinks it is too risky for me to get involved in the undercover work. I might be recognized."

"I agree," she said, smiling. "I hope you won't find the hospital boring."

Andy grinned. "When I worked on Brant's shoulder, it was the first time I had done medical work in months. I have missed it."

Amber didn't flinch at the mention of her husband's name, but she couldn't control the dryness in her throat. "Should we go early?" she asked.

"I would like to be there by eight," he said.

"Doctor Steven Monroe is back at the hospital," her uncle supplied.

"He is a fine doctor. I think Andy will benefit from working with him."

A tense silence descended in the room. Andy's head dropped against the back of the settee, and Hank walked to the window and pushed aside the curtains.

Taking a deep breath, she said, "I suppose you are waiting for me to ask you about Brant. I'm not afraid to discuss him. I want to know what happens to him."

Hank turned and walked across the room. "He is under guard. We are afraid he might try to break free, or that the Confederates might try and rescue him."

Amber shook her head. "I don't think you have to

worry about that. They would hang him for helping Andy."

Hank shrugged. "Perhaps you're right"

"When is the trial?"

"It will be the day after tomorrow—in the afternoon."

"I want to be there," she said softly and was surprised by the sound of her request.

Andy's head jerked up to look at his sister. Hank shook his head. "I'm not sure it is a good idea."

"Have you forgotten I'm his wife?"

"No," he said quickly. "You told me when you left for California that you hated the man. Does that still hold true?"

"I could never love a Rebel."

Andy's head fell back against the couch and the droop of his mouth indicated his disappointment. "I've told Uncle Hank that I am going to speak in his behalf. He says Brant has a right to a fair trial and doesn't think it will hurt my reputation."

"What will happen to him?" she asked.

Hank shrugged. "I can't say for sure. Colonel Broadmore and I questioned him, but he refuses to speak."

"Colonel Broadmore?" she repeated and caught the negative shake of her brother's head. Andy didn't want the colonel's spy activities revealed and until she knew why it was best to remain silent.

"Yes. He is one of the men working with me."

"Do you think Brant will refuse to speak in his own behalf at the trial?"

"I would say it is a good possibility. We believe there was someone involved with him. We offered him his life in exchange for the names of his contacts, and he still refused to talk. I don't think he cares what happens to him."

"I'm going to bed," Amber said abruptly. Rising, she said, "Good night."

Andy and Hank exchanged glances as Amber walked out of the room. "Something is different about your sister," Hank said. "Do you know what it is?"

Andy grinned. "I might. I think I'll go to sleep myself."

Amber lay in her bed and stared at the ceiling. In two days she would face Brant and she had to get hold of herself. Tomorrow she would shake off the heaviness she had been feeling and put her energy into her work. It had always been a help; perhaps it would be again.

Andy was back in Union uniform when she arrived downstairs the next morning. Her eyes widened when she sat next to him. "You've been promoted," she said. "Congratulations."

He looked at the new stripes on his uniform. "Looks pretty good, doesn't it?"

"Papa would be proud of you."

Andy nodded. "I guess he would."

"Why didn't you want me to tell Hank about Colonel Broadmore?"

"It should come from Brant. It is the only thing that will save his life. If he doesn't say anything at the trial, I'll take care of the matter. Will you trust me?"

"Of course."

Andy drove the carriage to the hospital and left it behind the building. "Nervous?" Amber asked when they entered the building.

"A little," he admitted.

Amber introduced her brother to several people, but Steven had not arrived. Andy shed his coat and went to assist a doctor with a serious operation. Amber put on an apron and helped with a simple procedure.

She was between operations when Steven arrived. "Amber," he said, his lips parting in a warming smile.

She had forgotten how attractive he was with his blond hair falling over his forehead and his blue eyes sparkling. The dimples she remembered so well creased each cheek.

"Do you mind having me back?"

"Not at all," he said, taking his place at the table.

"I brought my brother with me this time," she said, indicating Andy at the next table.

"But I thought —" he began.

"It is a long story. I'll tell you about it later."

A patient was carried in and placed on the table. This was not going to be a simple case. The man's leg was swollen and rotten from gangrene.

Steven worked with his usual competency, but Amber was slow to react to his needs. Andy's surgery finished and he walked to his sister's side. Steven was working on one side of the man's leg and Amber on the other. After dropping her tool twice, she looked at her brother.

"Will you finish up? I can't do it." Steven glanced up quickly, a puzzled light coming into his eyes. "I'm sorry," she apologized and left the room.

Sagging against the wall, she tried to steady her trembling nerves. What was wrong with her? She had lost her concentration and interest in the operation. Knowing she could not return to the operating room, she walked to the patient ward and changed bandages. It was almost four o'clock when a shadow passed over her work, and she looked up.

"Are you almost finished?" Steven asked.

Amber knew he would seek her out. "Give me five more minutes."

When she was done, Amber washed her hands and joined Steven. "We can talk in here," he said, indicating a private room.

He was a striking man and she remembered that she had once hoped for a romantic interest with him. "I suppose you want to scold me for my failure during the operation."

Steven smiled and his eyes softened. "Andy told me you have been under a serious strain. I understand. It happens to all of us at some time."

Amber lightly patted his arm. "Thank you for understanding."

"Your brother is very good at the operating table."

"I'm glad Andy is going to be in Washington for a while. I don't think I could stand to have him in any more danger."

"He told me what happened." Steven put his hands on her shoulders and turned her to face him. "I know about Brant. I am sorry things didn't work out between you."

Amber sighed. "Our relationship was doomed from the beginning. I was forced into the marriage." She took a painful breath. "He goes on trial tomorrow. Uncle Hank says he will hang. . . . I'll probably be a widow soon." There was a tightness in her chest she couldn't understand.

Steven gently drew her against his body, his fingers curving around her back. "I'm sorry this had to happen to you." He tipped her chin up. "You are a very beautiful woman."

Amber stared into his blue eyes and recognized the light of desire. Slowly, his mouth dropped to hers and he gently tasted the sweetness of her lips. Amber submitted to the pressure, her mind trying to force off reminders of Brant, but his words, "It will never be the same with any other man," echoed in her thoughts. Amber waited for the whirling sensation she experienced when Brant kissed her, but it didn't come. She stepped back.

"I'm sorry Steven," she said, her voice calm. "It was wrong of me to let that happen."

Steven's disappointment was evident. "I think I understand." He smiled. "Andy is still in surgery. Would you like to have dinner with me?"

"Not tonight. Would you tell Andy I went home? I'll leave the carriage for him."

Steven nodded. "Will I see you tomorrow?"

"Probably, but not necessarily in the operating room. It might be better if I did something else for a while."

Amber walked outside, stopping to feel the sun on her face. It was late afternoon, but still very hot. There were carriages available for hire, but Amber started to walk, her destination not really clear. It was some time before she realized the direction she was headed. Stopping, she stared at the Union headquarters, her eyes scanning the buildings until she saw the one where prisoners were kept. She spoke to the guard at the gate and he admitted her to the complex. The jail did not have many windows and the ones that existed were covered by heavy bars. Two guards stood by the door and she was sure there were more around back. She stopped and stared at the building. Why had she come to the jail? Did she want to see Brant? One of the guards walked toward her, his actions cautious.

"Can I help you?" he queried.

"I—I would like to see one of the prisoners."

"Which one?"

"Brant Faulkner." She forced past the lump in her throat.

The guard shook his head. "That man is in chains, and there ain't nobody allowed to see him except Captain Rawlins."

"But I'm his wife," she protested.

"His wife," the guard repeated in surprise. "You married a Rebel."

The words caused Amber to bristle. "Yes, and I'm also Captain Rawlins's niece."

"Then you better take it up with him. I ain't lettin' you in."

Holding back her anger, Amber turned and left the compound. She hired the first carriage she found and went home. Once inside she slammed the door behind her.

Andy ran out of the library. "What is the matter?"

Hours must have passed since she left the hospital. "Nothing," she said, brushing past him.

"Not so fast," he said, grabbing her arm. "What happened?"

"I went to see Brant. They wouldn't let me in."

"Why did you want to see him?" he asked, his eyes narrowing on her face.

"I don't know. Leave me alone," she said, shaking free.

"We have always talked before. Why can't we talk now?"

"There isn't anything to say."

She started up the stairs. "You know what I think," he called from below. "I think you care more for the man than you are willing to admit."

Her only answer was the slamming of her bedroom door. Running across the room, she fell on the bed. Why couldn't she forget him? Why wouldn't he stay out of her thoughts? His accusations came back to haunt her, and she threw her hands over her ears as though to block out the sound. Would she ever be free of him? Did she want to be?

The last question clung to her mind, but she refused to acknowledge the possibility. Closing her eyes, she pictured him as the wounded man she had cared for with her father, and the man she had battled in the prison. Brant had worn a Confederate uniform, arrived in Washington, married her twice, and looked at her with contempt when he believed she had betrayed him. But more than anything she remembered the lingering tear of his shattered love.

Rolling her head to the side, she tried to block out the feel of his hands on her flesh as they tenderly aroused and introduced a desire she had never experienced. Brant had brought her body alive and made it tingle with awareness. She had wanted Steven's brief embrace to be earth-shattering, but it had not moved her. She had been branded by one man—a man who

432

had whispered words of love.

Brant had made changes in her life. He had confused her thoughts and made her feel things that were alien to her. Even her work at the hospital had begun to suffer. She wasn't able to concentrate, and didn't find it as fulfilling as it once had been. Closing her eyes, she willed herself to sleep, but the pressure of her thoughts kept her awake until the early hours when she finally fell into a restless slumber.

Twenty-seven

Amber woke and flew off the bed. She was still in the gown she had worn yesterday. Quickly removing it, she washed and put on fresh clothes. Before going to sleep last night she had made a decision and wanted to talk to Uncle Hank. Unfortunately, he was already gone and Andy was getting ready to go to the hospital.

"You don't look like you slept," he commented, putting on his hat.

"Does that mean I look terrible?" she teased.

"You are always beautiful."

"I guess that makes you handsome," she bantered, and he wrinkled his nose in confusion. "Have you forgotten how much we look alike? If I am beautiful then you are handsome," she giggled, "or beautiful."

"I'll take handsome. I'm glad you're in a better humor this morning."

"I am spending the morning at the hospital, but I am returning home at noon. I still plan to go to the trial."

"It is at three o'clock. I'm not sure Uncle Hank thinks you should attend, but he is going to permit it."

Andy drove the carriage and left it at the back of the hospital. "You take the buggy home at noon. I'll walk to headquarters." He caught her chin and tilted her face up. "Are you going to be all right?"

She forced a smile. "I don't know."

Amber stayed out of surgery and worked with the wounded patients. One man died while she was changing his bandage, and she was shaking when he was carried out of the room. He had only been nineteen. Amber hugged her arms across her stomach. Why was she falling to pieces?

When twelve o'clock came, she went home, bathed and let Myra fix her hair. She dressed in one of her prettiest gowns, a deep yellow that accented her tiny waist and full breasts. She ignored the hat in favor of a parasol.

Less than an hour later she approached headquarters. One of the guards took the carriage and Amber walked to the building where the trial would be held. The room was smaller than she expected, and the first person she recognized was Colonel Broadmore.

Hank walked toward her, his eyes roaming over her exquisite beauty. As usual her expression was icy, and she did not seem troubled by the forthcoming events.

"Are you sure you want to be here?"

"Even though our marriage is a farce I feel I have a responsibility."

"If this involved any other woman I would be worried, but I know you can handle it."

435

Amber wasn't sure his statement was a compliment or a slur. A group of men filed into the room and sat in the high backed chairs. Excusing himself, Hank went to the front and sat next to Giles Broadmore. Amber took one of the two remaining chairs, and Andy joined her minutes later.

"Does Brant have anyone to speak for him?"

Andy shook his head. "He refused. Perhaps he doesn't trust the Union's choice."

"I don't blame him," she said, surprised by her comment. "Could he trust a Union man to represent him fairly?"

Andy looked at his sister, but she wasn't aware of his scrutiny. Her attention was centered on the front of the room. Two guards shoved Brant toward a chair that faced the spectators. He started to sit, then froze, his eyes locking on Amber. Her body felt limp and her breath left her body. Slowly, he lowered himself to the chair, his eyes never leaving her face.

The trial began and Brant kept his attention on his wife. The charges against him were very serious. He was accused of getting information for the South and working with the sympathizers. Hank presented information against him she hadn't even known existed. Andy spoke in his behalf, but his words seemed unimportant in view of the damaging evidence already given.

They didn't ask Amber to speak and she doubted words would pass her lips. She didn't feel like she was in a courtroom. Voices faded and she saw only the man at the front accused of being a traitor. Once she would have found victory in seeing him tried for treason. Now she felt empty. This was not a victory. Her battles with him had always ended in the truce of passion.

Her hostilities warred in her mind: passion versus apathy, independence versus reliance, and companionship versus loneliness. They struck out at each other trying to beat the other down. She was fighting the hardness she had always shown and wondering if she could or should break free. Her fingers rose to her face.

"Would you name your contacts in the city?" Brant was asked.

"No," he said. "Nothing is going to make any difference. My fate has been sealed. It doesn't matter anymore."

The room became quiet as the judges whispered among themselves to decide Brant's innocence or guilt. Slowly, Amber lowered her trembling fingers and stared at the man who had murmured words of love. Brant's eyes were locked on her, carefully watching her emotions.

"It is the decision of this court that Brant Faulkner be sentenced to hang. The execution is to be carried out tomorrow at dawn."

The room swayed and Amber clutched at Andy's leg, her mouth opening to gulp breaths of fresh air in an attempt to steady herself. It took several seconds to regain her composure.

"Are you all right?" Andy whispered.

Turning her head, she smiled at her brother. "I am now."

A puzzled light entered her brother's eyes. "I will take you home."

"Would you get the carriage and wait for me outside? There is something I have to do."

Rising, Amber walked toward the front of the room. Most of the men had left and Brant was being pushed through the door to another area. She stopped at her uncle's side, her control complete; her hard exterior shell was firmly in place.

"Uncle Hank, I want to see Brant."

"Amber, you're not serious."

Out of the corner of her eyes she saw Giles listening to their conversation. "The man is my husband. He made a fool of me. He got the sentence he deserved. I want to be at his hanging, but in the meantime I want to see him privately."

Hank shook his head. "It is not possible."

"Make it possible," she said in a firm voice. "I want to see him."

Hank recognized the determined set of her jaw and knew she would not be deterred from her objective. If he didn't allow it he wouldn't have a moment's peace.

"Your niece is a very determined young woman," Colonel Broadmore said smoothly. "She was very helpful in securing Faulkner's capture. Give her a few minutes with him."

Amber looked into his eyes, carefully keeping her animosity hidden. Brant had said nothing to expose the colonel's spying. It was now up to Andy.

The man held a higher rank than her uncle. "All right," he was forced to concede. "You can see him, but only for fifteen minutes. As for attending his hanging, we will talk about it when I get home. It is not something for a lady to witness."

Amber's blue-green eyes narrowed. "I've probably seen worse in the hospital."

438

Hank shook his head. "We will discuss it later." Taking her arm, he showed her where she could wait. The room didn't have any windows, and she had her back to the door when Brant was brought in. She turned slowly and frowned at the sight of the guards.

"I said alone," she argued, but the soldiers didn't move. Throwing her hands on her hips, she said, "The man is heavily chained. He cannot escape." She glanced at the men. "Perhaps you would like to search me for concealed weapons. I have more reason to hate this man than anyone. I get fifteen minutes with him. Now get out and don't come back until the time is up."

Shocked by her outburst, the guards stumbled out of the room and closed the door behind them. Amber didn't move, but her body was alert and cautious. Brant shifted and the chains rattled against the floor.

"Why did you want to see me? Did you want to gloat over the Union victory or your personal triumph?"

"What if I said it wasn't a victory?"

Brant's eyes narrowed. "It is what you wanted, isn't it? You arranged my capture in California."

She shook her head. "No, it wasn't me. I didn't know there were men waiting for you."

Doubt showed on his face. "Are you going to deny that you wanted to see the Confederacy destroyed? You have told me countless times that you want to watch me hang for betraying the North."

Amber couldn't deny it. "I did."

Brant snorted. "I knew you would be happy with the results, but I didn't expect you to come and gloat." There was pain in his brown eyes, and

439

Amber's throat tightened. "Are you going to have a front row seat at my hanging? It should be a grand event for you."

They were cruel words and Amber's head dropped to her chest. Tomorrow Brant would be dead and she would be free to start over. She would never again experience the tender moments, laugh with him, fight with him, love with him. There was a strangled cry in her throat. Slowly, she raised her head, her eyes no longer clear to focus on the man of her dreams. They were filled with the tears of her love.

"Amber," Brant whispered hoarsely as the moisture splashed down her cheeks. He walked toward her uncertainly. "You are crying," he breathed in wonderment. His finger caught one of the tears.

Amber didn't know what Brant was feeling toward her, and she knew he had every right to throw his contempt in her face. He had exposed himself to her when he had admitted his love, and she had cruelly mocked his feelings. It was Brant's turn to humiliate her, but Amber knew whatever happened it was time for truth.

She looked into his brown eyes. "I love you Brant."

"Oh, Amber," he whispered, pulling her against his body. "I had given up hope of ever hearing that." He kissed away the tears. "You have found the woman in you."

"I need you Brant," she sobbed. "I want you in my life."

His mouth dropped to hers, and her lips parted to still the guns of war and welcome the peace of their love. Amber wrapped her arms around his neck and hungrily arched her body against his. Brant responded instantly and he ravaged her lips in an explosion of their love.

"Why couldn't we have found our love before it had to end?" he whispered against her hair. His words reminded Amber of the execution to be held the next morning. "I don't want you there. You have got to resurrect your hate and stay away."

Amber cupped his head between her hands. "We haven't had a chance together. I want to show you how much I care."

Brant held her tightly. "I wish I could feel your naked body against mine." He brushed away the last traces of her tears. "I decided I wanted you in my life when you soothed my pain with the touch of your lips. Finding you at the prison camp was a surprise, and you had so many qualities I admired. It was easy to fall in love."

Amber was so wrapped up in the emotion showing in his eyes that she didn't hear the guards open the door. Brant flung her away from him. "Get out of my life," he barked. "I never want to see you again."

Amber's flinch was real, the shock on her face a convincing reality. The guards grabbed Brant and dragged him out of the room. He never looked back at his wife even though her eyes followed him down the hall.

Breathing deeply to regain her composure, Amber squared her shoulders. Brant's final reaction to her had been for the benefit of the guards, and she knew his love had not faltered. Keeping her head down to hide the moistness in her eyes, she went outside. Andy was waiting in the carriage and Amber sat at his side.

441

"Let's go home," she said in a choked voice.

Andy caught her chin and turned her face. His blue-green gaze roamed over her red-rimmed eyes, and a smile slowly spread across his lips. Dropping his hand, he urged the team forward.

"What is so funny?" she asked.

"Just glad to know my sister has found her feelings."

"I'm happy too," she said and lifted her chin proudly.

The carriage left the military complex, and Amber's gaze wandered over the activity in the street. Suddenly, she grabbed her brother's arm.

"Stop Andy."

He slowed the horses. "What is wrong?" he asked.

"Over there," she pointed. "The man with the blue shirt and brown hat. He is from the Confederate prison."

Edgar Mason saw the twins and his eyes widened in surprise. He was too far to hear what Amber was saying, but the accusing finger warned him of her intent. He quickly disappeared around the corner.

"The swine," Andy yelled, jumping down and taking pursuit.

Amber followed, but her skirt hampered progress and she couldn't keep up. Two streets over Andy stopped and waited for his sister to catch up.

"He is gone," he mumbled in defeat.

"What do you think he is doing here?"

Turning, they walked back to the carriage. "Maybe he is here to free Brant."

Amber shook her head. "Mason hated us and did everything in his power to prove I was an imposter.

He was suspicious of Brant's reasons for supporting my presence."

"He saw us together and probably guessed our relationship. He knows I am not dead." Andy helped her into the carriage. "Let's go home."

Amber's thoughts focused on her meeting with Brant, and her surprise at finding Edgar Mason in Washington. He was not in town to help her husband and would probably be glad to see him hang. His reasons for being in the city suddenly became clear.

"Andy, Mason must be here to meet with Colonel Broadmore."

He ran his fingers through his amber hair. "He probably has a definite connection to the spy."

"I was enraged to see Colonel Broadmore at Brant's trial. I felt like exposing him for his connection to Brant."

"Did you say anything?" Andy asked, glancing at her.

"No. When are you going to tell Uncle Hank?"

"I'm working on a trap to catch the traitor."

"I want to help."

Andy grinned. "I wouldn't think of excluding you."

They had almost reached the house when Amber asked Andy to stop the wagon. "What is wrong?" he asked, slowing the animals. "I'm not ready to give you the details of my plan."

"It isn't about that. It is a private matter."

"Does it concern Brant?"

She nodded. "I love him. Andy, I've been a fool. I was afraid to feel anything for him. Papa always wanted to see my strength, and I thought I had to show Brant the same thing. I can't do it any more. I have feelings and I need to express them. I want my husband to know how much I care."

"I am glad you made that decision. You are a woman and your emotions are different. They should not have been squelched by male values."

"Papa worked on Brant's injuries, but I wish he could have known him. . . . I have strong Union allegiance and didn't want anything to do with a man who believed everything I was against. Andy, it doesn't matter that he is on the opposite side." She looked into her brother's eyes. "I believe he is a good man. I want to share my life with him."

"I am glad you finally see the man for what he is. I tried to tell you how I felt about him."

"But I wasn't ready to listen," she finished.

"It is too late now."

Amber took a deep breath and felt like she was falling back in time. "Andy, I am going to get Brant out of jail."

She didn't expect him to chuckle. "I wondered when the solution would dawn on you."

Amber's eyes widened. "You expected me to try and free him?"

"You tried to get me out, didn't you? I knew once you realized how you felt about Brant you would try and free him." He touched the tip of her nose. "You are a predictable young woman."

Amber frowned. "If I am then Uncle Hank will suspect me."

Andy shook his head. "I guessed because I know you and everything that has been going on. Uncle Hank will never be suspicious of you. You made your animosity toward Brant very clear at the trial."

"I haven't worked out a plan, but I want you to cover for me at the house tonight."

"Can't do it," he said, shaking his head. "You are not going to do this alone."

Amber knew he would offer to help, but she couldn't let him. "I can't let you do it. You are in the Union Army. If you are caught you would be discharged and possibly branded a traitor."

"It is a risk I am willing to take," he said. "You must know you won't come out of this unscathed if you are caught."

She stuck her chin forward in determination. "It is going to work," she said positively. "We will have to think of a plan."

Andy urged the team forward. "Getting into the fort won't be a problem," he said, chuckling. "There is a way I can protect myself."

She sensed his excitement. "Going to tell me about it?"

"I need to clear up a few things in my mind first."

"I don't want anyone killed."

"I agree." He looked over his shoulder. "We'll talk about this later. Uncle Hank is behind us." Andy stopped the carriage at the house and helped Amber down.

Hank dismounted and walked toward the twins. "Are you all right Amber?" he asked.

"Fine," she said, preceding the men into the house.

"Let's go to the library. I want to talk to you." He looked at his nephew. "You better come along too. I might need your help convincing Amber she shouldn't be at the hanging tomorrow."

Amber heard what he had said and set her jaw in

445

determination. "Uncle Hank, you know I am not prone to hysteria. I can handle whatever happens. I despise the man." She threw her hands on her slim hips. "He used me and I hate him. I want to see him dead."

"You might as well admit defeat," Andy said, grinning. "Amber is experiencing one of her stubborn streaks."

Hank glowered at his nephew. He wanted his help and not his casual acceptance of his sister's behavior. "Amber, do you have any idea what a hanging is like?"

Unknowingly, her hand crept to her neck. "It was explained to me once in vivid detail," she said, remembering how Brant's hand had tightened around her throat.

"Learned anything from Brant?" Andy asked.

"Nothing. Colonel Broadmore and I tried, but he refuses to tell us what he knows. With William Boone dead, Brant is our only link to the traitor."

Myra summoned them to the dining room for the meal. When they were seated at the table, Amber looked at her brother and uncle. "Let's have the meal without a discussion of Brant or what is going to happen tomorrow. I'm sick of the whole business."

The men nodded and conversation was focused on the war. When they had finished eating, Andy announced his intention of returning to the hospital.

"I think I'll spend the evening in my room," Amber added. "What are you going to do, Uncle Hank?"

"I have paper work." Rising, he walked toward the hall. "I'll be in my study."

Smiling in conspiracy, Amber and Andy went upstairs. When the door to Andy's room was closed and locked, he walked to the wardrobe and pulled out a uniform.

"We have to get you inside the compound. Security is tighter at night and no nonmilitary personnel are allowed inside. You'll have to pretend to be me."

"Are you suggesting I wear this?"

Andy nodded. "I am taller than you, but lean enough that it shouldn't be too baggy." He pulled her to a mirror and wrapped his arm around her shoulder. "We bear a strong resemblance. Let's hope the darkness will conceal the difference." He pulled her hair up. "I think you can pass for me."

Amber unfastened the buttons on her dress and slipped out of it. "I'll have to bind my breasts to flatten me."

"What do you need?" he asked.

"A piece of cloth cut in a wide strip."

Andy rummaged through his closet for something he could use, then cut it to size. He left the room while Amber wrapped the cloth around her body and slipped into the jacket. The sleeves were too long, so she rolled the fabric under and secured it with a pin. She made the same adjustments to the pants.

Andy returned with her boots and dropped them on the floor. "I just saw Myra. I told her you want to be alone for the rest of the night."

"Good," she said, pulling on the boots. "I had forgotten about her." She straightened. "What do you think?"

"We've got to do something with the hair."

"Cut it off," she said simply.

"Let's try tucking it under the hat."

447

She pulled the hair up and shoved it under the hat. "I think we can fool them," Andy said, grinning. "The guard changes at nine o'clock. I'll go inside fifteen minutes before the hour and you'll follow at fifteen minutes after. You must remember to salute the man at the gate." He stepped back and showed her how to do it. "Keep you hand stiffer," he said in response to her attempt. She tried again. "Perfect," he praised.

"Where do we meet once we're inside?"

"If you don't walk toward the main office it will look suspicious. When you are out of sight of the guard, duck between the buildings and you'll come up near the jail. I'll meet you there."

"Where do we keep the horses?"

"Behind the hospital. I'm headed there now and will have an extra one for Brant. I don't have to tell you to be careful."

"Thank you for helping me."

He grinned. "I enjoy the excitement. It reminds me of old times."

"Before you leave would you get the pistol out of my top drawer. I don't want to be unarmed."

He opened a cabinet and withdrew a gun and belt that matched the one he wore. "It needs to be loaded. I will see you at nine fifteen. Good luck."

Andy left and Amber locked the door against surprise intruders. She quickly loaded the weapon and put the belt around her waist. When it was time to leave she unlocked the door. With Hank in the house it was impossible to leave by the front door, so she pushed the window open. Bracing herself on the sill, she lunged for the thick branch that almost touched the house. Pausing to make sure she had a firm grip, she climbed along it until she could drop to the ground. She saddled the horse and walked him away from the house before mounting and riding toward town.

She stayed on the back streets and stopped in the shadows near the hospital. When she was certain no one was around, she tied her horse next to the others and strolled toward headquarters. She wasn't worried that her walk would be too feminine. She had had enough wild years with her brother to remedy that. Hiding near the front, she watched Andy go inside. Time passed slowly, and she knew the success of getting inside rested with the change of the guard.

Amber's excitement mounted when the clock struck the time for her to act. Squaring her shoulders, she stepped from the cover of the buildings and walked toward the entrance to headquarters. She reached the gate and her arm rose to salute the young guard.

"Evening," he said.

Amber nodded instead of speaking. She walked to the place Andy had indicated and ducked between the buildings. He was waiting.

"Everything went as planned," she whispered, looking at her double.

He pointed at the building where Brant was a prisoner, and she saw the guard. "Walk around the side and get his attention. I'll come up from behind him and knock him unconscious."

Nodding, she walked around the building. A fake stumble successfully got the attention of the soldier. Amber stayed in the shadows so he wouldn't get a clear look at her face.

"Good evening, Lieutenant Rawlins."

"How is the prisoner?" she asked in her deepest voice.

"I expect he is worryin' about his hangin'."

Andy moved quickly and a soft blow landed against the guard's head. Andy caught him before he hit the ground.

"Get the keys," he whispered.

Amber grabbed the metal ring from his uniform and ran to the door. She was trembling and unable to get the key to work. Chuckling, Andy took them and unlocked the first door. Inside was a series of rooms. Andy pointed to one of the cells and ran toward it. He released the lock and pushed the door open. Amber quickly stepped inside and Andy shut the door behind them.

A flickering candle was the only light in the room. Brant had been sleeping, but he woke instantly. Andy dropped to his side and searched for the key to free him from the chains.

At last he stood and Amber floated into his arms. His lips hungrily ground against hers and she clung to him in fevered desire.

"You will have to save the romance for later," Andy warned with a grin. "We still have to get you out of here."

"It is good to see you," he whispered to his wife.

"You didn't expect me to let them hang you in the morning."

"I was beginning to wonder," he teased and followed Andy to the door. "You both took a big chance."

"We think you are worth it," Andy supplied. "I owed you for getting me out of the Rebel prison." He jerked his finger toward Amber. "She is just crazy about you."

Andy made sure the corridor was empty before they left the cell. They stopped at the door to the outside. "Getting you out should not be hard," he explained. "There is only one guard at the gate. Once you get past him you can go to the horses . . . . Take care of her," he said to Brant.

They stepped outside. "Aren't you coming?" she asked.

"I'll follow later. The guard I knocked unconscious thought you were me. I've got to be here or suspicion will be thrown in my direction." He squeezed his sister's hand. "I'll meet you at the little shack," he said, referring to the building where they had met before he went to California.

He walked back to the unconscious guard and stood in front of him. Andy looked at Brant and he left Amber's side. Seconds later Andy slumped to the ground.

Amber opened her mouth in protest, but Brant grabbed her arm. "He isn't hurt. I had to make it convincing."

They stayed in the shadows until they reached the front gate. Picking up a large rock, Brant threw it against a building about twenty feet in front of the man. The thud forced the guard to step away from the building. Brant rushed forward and hit him in the head. The man dropped in an unconscious heap. Amber and Brant slipped outside.

"Meet me behind the hospital," she told Brant and

they separated to lessen the risk of discovery.

Amber reached the hospital first and had the horses ready. When Brant joined her, she wanted to rush into his arms, but he shoved her toward her horse. They stayed on the back streets until they were out of the city, then galloped down the main road. They approached the shack cautiously, and when Brant was sure it was safe, they dismounted and hid the horses in the woods.

Hand in hand they went inside and Brant lighted a lamp. Amber pulled her hat off and her hair tumbled to her shoulders.

"You look wonderful in uniform," he said. A mischievous light entered his eyes. "But you look better without it." Raising his fingers, he slowly unfastened the buttons. Amber stood motionless as the coat gapped open, and Brant pushed it from her shoulders. "What is this?" he quizzed.

Amber looked down at the cloth she had wrapped to flatten her breasts. "I had to look like a man."

"Not anymore," he said, releasing the ties and slowly unwrapping the cloth.

It floated to the floor, and Brant ran his finger between her breasts. The familiar fire was back and this time it was welcome. Amber quickly unfastened the buttons on his shirt, and Brant threw it aside. He pulled them together, their upper bodies blending together in a firm commitment of their love. The light covering of hair on his chest tickled her breasts in a sensitive arousal of her nerves.

Wrapping her arms around his neck, Amber offered her mouth to his. His lips teased and tantalized their softness while his hands slid over her back to hold her close. It wasn't enough and Amber reached for the buckle on his pants. When they were both naked, Brant lifted her and carried her to the narrow cot in the corner. Placing her on the blanket, Brant looked at her lovely, young body. Amber pulled him to her side and slid her arms to his shoulders to hold him close. Their mouths fused and their hands explored. Brant rediscovered every part of her flesh using his love to guide him. Amber renewed the feel of his hard muscled body with a tenderness that expressed her deep feelings. Finally, the closeness they had been seeking brought them together, and they found the union of their hearts.

"You're so beautiful," he whispered. "I love you."

"Brant, you are my life," she breathed, her mouth continuously plying his neck with kisses.

"You realize what you've just done, don't you?" he asked, pushing her back so he could see her face.

"Yes, I have made love with my husband."

"Have you forgotten I'm the enemy—a man you had sworn to hate?"

"The war between us is over and my weapon of hate is gone." She chuckled. "I better warn you I won't give up my principles."

"Why is that funny?" he teased, running his hand over her abdomen.

"I don't know where we will spend most of our time, but when we are in the North I will wonder if you are stealing information, and you will wonder the same of me when we are in Rebel territory."

"We'll work things out." He dropped a swift kiss on her lips. "How about a truce based on love?"

"That is fine as long as we are together."

"You don't know how long I have waited to hear that."

Amber pulled his head down and kissed him long and fully, her hands sliding up his back to pull him against her. They welcomed the renewal of their love and the exploding ecstasy that brought them closer together.

Sated, Amber snuggled against her husband. "Mmm," she whispered. "I could stay like this for the rest of the night."

"So could I," Brant agreed. "But our time together is almost at an end."

"We've only been here two hours."

"That is right," he agreed. "Your brother should be arriving soon. Do you want him to find us like this?"

Amber blushed. "No," she said and slid off the cot. Crossing the room, she reached for her uniform.

"Here," Brant called and threw her a shirt and pants. "Wear these instead."

"My clothes," she said in surprise.

"Andy brought them here this morning."

"This morning," she echoed. "You hadn't been convicted, and I hadn't decided to free you."

"My conviction was a sure thing. I saved Andy's life once and he wanted to do the same for me." Brant smiled warmly. "He believed you would recognize your feelings and want to help."

Amber smiled at her husband. "I'm glad I decided what I wanted before I lost it."

"So am I," he said, reaching for his pants.

They were dressed for at least twenty minutes before Andy rode up. "No one suspects a thing," he said, joining them. "The knock on the head kept me in the clear." He touched the tender spot. "The officers at the fort believe you were rescued by the Confederates."

"Excellent," Brant said.

"What is the plan now?" Amber asked, knowing Brant had to get out of the city.

"You and Andy will go home," Brant said. "I'll stay here."

She shook her head. "Not without me," she claimed firmly.

"Did Amber tell you we saw Captain Edgar Mason?" Andy asked.

"Mason," Brant said thoughtfully, his gaze locking with Andy. Something passed between the men Amber didn't understand. "His presence complicates things. We'll have to move with extra caution." Brant ran his hand through his brown hair. "Andy, the man is trouble to me, but more important he is a threat to your sister. He hates her for what happened at the prison. You've got to devise a way to get Hank to initiate a search for him."

Andy stroked his clean-shaven jaw. "Amber, go back to the house and get inside without being seen. Tell Hank you saw Edgar Mason in town and suspect he is a spy."

"But why?"

"For the reasons Brant said. If anyone can find him, he can."

"How do you know he is home? Don't you think headquarters notified him about Brant's escape?"

Andy shook his head. "I'm supposed to tell him what happened when I get home."

"What are you going to do?" she quizzed Brant.

"I can't be seen in public, but I'll be available if I'm needed as bait. I'll work with Andy from the background."

"Brant," Amber said suddenly. "When I saw Mason at Confederate headquarters, he said he was on a special assignment. I think it had something to do with us."

"That makes it even more imperative that we find him. I have to know what Edgar told my superiors. If he falsely cast doubt on my loyalty, it will never be safe for me to return to the South."

Amber nodded. No one had to tell her that Edgar Mason was a threat to their security. The man had sent chills up her spine.

"I'll bring the uniform later," Andy said when she started to pick it up.

Brant walked Amber outside. "What is going to happen?" she asked, despising the way their lives were being twisted.

"I wish I had an answer, but there is a good possibility I won't have a place to call home. I am a wanted man in the North, and if Mason cast doubt on my southern loyalty, I can't return there."

Raising her hands, she caught the sides of his face and looked him in the eye. "It doesn't matter."

"You are a very special lady." Drawing her against his chest, he lowered his lips to hers in grinding urgency. "Be careful," he whispered. We'll be together soon. Remember that I love you."

Twenty-eight

Amber mounted and rode into the darkness. It was hard to leave Brant behind and at one time she would not have trusted him. That wasn't true anymore. He had saved her life and proved his devotion for her. Because they were on opposite sides of the war their life wouldn't be easy, but Amber was determined to make it work. She loved him very much; no matter where they spent their lives she would be happy.

Thinking of what might happen in the attempt to find Edgar Mason, Amber trembled. The two people she loved most in the world were getting involved in something dangerous, and she was scared.

Amber wondered how Papa would have felt about her actions. Would she believe she had betrayed the North by falling in love with a Rebel? She was ready to accept that marriage would change her independence. She would still be free, but there would be shared responsibility on decisions.

Amber thought back to the discussion she had had with her father the night he had brought Brant to the battlefield hospital. Her confused response to the wounded man had been obvious and Papa had seen it. He had reprimanded her for showing emotion and acting weak. As she reflected back on it Amber realized Papa hadn't known what to do with her feminine feelings, so he had pretended they didn't exist. He had apologized for not being able to smooth out the "rough spots" in her upbringing and explained it was something a mother would have done. Amber finally realized that her relationship with men was the "rough spot", and Amber finally felt free to show the woman in her. Papa would not have despised her tears when he realized she was still the strong woman he had taught her to be.

Leaving the horse behind the house, she climbed the tree to Andy's room. Letting herself in the window, she walked to the door and checked the hall. She stopped at her bedroom to cover her clothes with a long robe. Kicking off her boots and ruffling her hair, Amber decided she was ready to approach her uncle.

"I thought you were asleep," he said when she entered the study.

"I was," she admitted, stifling a yawn. "I remembered something I saw in town today and decided I'd better tell you."

"What is it?"

"When I was at Confederate headquarters with Brant, I met Captain Edgar Mason. I saw him in town this afternoon."

Hank jumped to his feet. "You saw him here . . . in Washington?"

She nodded. "He was dressed in civilian clothes.

Andy and I tried to catch him, but he eluded us. It can't be good having him in the city."

"You're right. He is either in town to receive information from the spy we haven't been able to find, or he plans to free Brant. I'm meeting Colonel Broadmore in about thirty minutes. We'll discuss plans to try and find him."

Amber didn't know if Andy had told Hank about Broadmore's Rebel loyalty. Brant would never condone his betrayal, but that was because they worked for the same cause. Amber would be loyal to her Rebel husband, but never to another Confederate.

"Uncle Hank, did Andy talk to you about the Southern infiltrator?"

"No, but he did tell me there was something important he wanted to discuss."

"Have you found the betrayer in the Union Army?"

He shook his head. "Amber, do you know something about the person responsible?"

"I think I know who he is."

Hank walked to her side and put his hands on her shoulders. "This is very important. I must know what you learned."

"Before I left for Confederate headquarters with Brant I saw him having a secret meeting with Giles Broadmore. When we reached the Rebel camp, he gave them very important Northern plans."

There was a gleam of satisfaction in Hank's eyes. "Giles Broadmore," he said, smiling. "Excellent work," he praised. "If I watch Giles, I'll probably catch Edgar Mason also. He might be at the meeting, so I'll have to be extra cautious." Hank's hands fell.

459

"This could be very important to the Union."

"Promise to be careful," Amber pleaded. Mason was a dangerous man, and she suspected Broadmore would fight when confronted and accused of being a spy.

"I will. What are you going to do?"

"Probably go back to bed."

"Would you ride to the hospital and tell Andy the meeting is in the clearing by the big oak? I might need backup."

"I'll do it," she said and went upstairs to change. In her room she threw off her robe and pulled on her boots. Grabbing the pistol, she tucked it into her pants. Hank knew she was going out, so she left the house using the front door. After mounting her horse, she rode in the direction of town. When she was out of sight of the house, she changed course and headed toward the shack.

Amber didn't know how Brant would take the news that Broadmore was going to be taken as a spy, but it was a risk she had to take. As it turned out there was no reason for concern. The shack was empty and Amber had no idea where the men had gone. Hank's meeting place was nearby, and Amber decided to go in her brother's place. When she was a safe distance away, Amber dismounted and went the remaining distance on foot. Reaching the clearing, Amber hunkered in the bushes and watched her uncle.

He was alone. Fortunately, there was a moon and the tenseness on his face was clearly visible. Amber watched him check his gun, glad that he was exercising the precaution he had promised. She didn't want anything to happen to him.

Amber heard the rider before she saw him, and she crouched lower in the brush. Colonel Giles Broadmore rode into the clearing and dismounted.

"Hank," he said. "We have trouble."

Hank was instantly on the alert. "What happened?"

"Brant Faulkner escaped."

"What!" Hank shouted. "How did it happen?"

Giles shook his head. "It was a very clean operation. Someone got into the compound, knocked out the guards and freed him. Your nephew was there at the time and got a nasty bump on the head." He paused. "We don't know who is responsible."

"I have an idea," Hank offered. "I talked to my niece this evening. She saw Edgar Mason, a Confederate captain, in town this afternoon. He might have done it."

Broadmore shook his head. "It looks like the Rebels are closing in on the city. With Faulkner loose there is no telling what will happen. The people in the War Department want answers. The spy in the Union organization must be exposed."

Amber was engrossed in the men's conversation and didn't hear the quiet tread of boots on the soft earth. Suddenly, a hand clamped around her mouth, and her neck was jerked to a threatening angle that made it impossible to move. Her gun uselessly dropped to the dirt.

She was pushed into the clearing and both men turned their heads. Hank's eyes widened in surprise at the sight of his niece in a man's arms. He reached for his pistol, but stopped when he saw the gun Amber's captor held against her side.

"What is the meaning of this?" Hank demanded. "Let go of my niece." The man's hold slackened slightly, but she was still not free to move away.

"Who are you?" Giles asked.

"Edgar Mason, captain in the Confederate Army," he explained. "Would you care to tell me your names?" he ordered and the men answered.

Amber felt Edgar relax, and she was certain he had recognized Broadmore's name as the Washington contact. Without warning, she was pushed free of his body. She stumbled, then got her footing and turned to look at the man who had frightened her on more than one occasion. Amber had not bowed to him on those meetings and had no intention of doing so again.

"What are you doing in town?" she asked, her hands on her hips.

"Still the smart female I see?" he snarled. "I'm here to take care of you and your husband."

"Did you free Faulkner tonight?" Giles demanded.

"Free him," he sneered. "I would never save that man from the gallows. I want to see him hang." His gun leveled at Amber. "And I want to see you dead."

Amber's throat tightened, but there was no outward show of her fear. She had found the soft, vulnerable female and become a fuller, better woman, but Papa's teachings were still there whenever she needed them. She would always be the woman he wanted.

"Mason," she called. "You are a piece of Rebel slime just like my husband." She wanted everyone to think she despised Brant.

Edgar laughed. "So now the truth comes out. I

never believed you cared about him. I guess I was right." His eyes narrowed. "What were you doing at the Rebel camp that day?"

"I was there to rescue my brother."

The hand holding the gun trembled. "I saw you with him in town today. I was tricked into believing he had died of the fever." Edgar's gray eyes roamed down her body. "Faulkner was so obsessed with you — your body — that he put his entire position as an officer in jeopardy. As far as I'm concerned he betrayed the Confederacy and deserves to die."

For Brant's sake she wanted to know how much the Rebels knew about his activity. He could never return to his homeland if it wasn't safe. "What does headquarters know about this?"

"Nothing. I wanted to make sure I wasn't being made a fool of again."

"You are a fool, Mason," she baited, uncaring that he held the gun.

"Never again," he vowed. "I'm in town to meet the contact in the Northern organization. I'll replace Brant and the important work against the Union will continue."

Amber looked at her uncle and their eyes locked. He had known her long enough to suspect she was planning something. He would be ready to back her up. Her eyes darted to Giles in a look of contempt. He had betrayed the country she loved and she wanted to see him destroyed.

She glanced at Edgar, but he was staring at Giles. Knowing it was time to act, Amber dove for his knees. She hit his body hard, knocking him off balance. His gun discharged as they landed on the hard earth. Amber landed on top of him, and it was easy to push free and give Hank the freedom to take control. She had rolled once when she heard the deafening explosion of a weapon.

Hank had fired at Mason and the bloodstain on his shirt looked serious. He was the enemy, but her medical training took control, and she crawled to his side. There was no heartbeat.

"He is dead," she said, rising and walking toward her uncle.

"Amber," he scolded. "I'll never be ready for your impulsiveness, but in this case I thank you. He was determined to kill us."

"I'll add my thanks for your quick work," Giles praised, walking closer. "That man had to be stopped. I wish we could have questioned him about the spy. We have got to learn his identity."

Hank pulled his niece to his side. "That won't be too hard," he said, raising his gun in the colonel's direction. "I already know who is responsible."

Broadmore's eyes widened in surprise and he came to an abrupt halt. "What is the meaning of this?"

"I am arresting you for being a traitor against the United States Government. Amber saw you with Faulkner and knows you were giving him information on the Union Army. I am going to enjoy seeing you hang." He glanced at his niece. "Amber hates her husband, but Brant wants her. She will help me capture him."

Amber knew she wouldn't do it, but wasn't ready to expose the fact. As far as everyone was concerned Brant was the enemy.

"Amber," Hank ordered, "get his gun."

She walked toward him. When she was directly in front of him, she stopped and looked him in the eye. "I didn't want to believe it when I saw you with Brant. Why did you betray your country?" There was no answer, and Amber carefully eased the gun from the holster on his hip. When it was in her hand, she stepped to the side.

There was an angry intent in Hank's eyes. "Maybe I should kill you now and save the Union Army the trouble of giving you a trial."

"I have a right to a trial," Giles argued.

"You have no rights. With Faulkner loose it would be better if you were dead."

"Don't kill him," a deep voice demanded from the far side of the clearing.

Amber's eyes widened in confusion as Brant stepped forward. His gun was pointed at Hank, and she knew he would not let his Rebel associate die. Was Brant's loyalty to the Rebels so strong that he would risk his life? What had happened to their future together?

"Keep Broadmore covered," Hank ordered Amber. His gun turned in Brant's direction.

Every muscle in her body tensed. The men held guns on each other. Who was going to shoot first?

"You are not taking him to jail," Brant warned. "He is coming with me."

"Drop it, Faulkner. It is over. You are both going to hang."

"Somebody will hang, but it isn't going to be me," he promised with a smile.

Hank fumed at the man's insolence. "I made a mistake letting my niece get involved with you. Giles has been giving you information, and you have been feeding it to the Confederates." His gaze flickered to Amber. "I might as well tell you that Brant was responsible for your father's death. He was waiting at the meeting place with a group of soldiers. Richard's contact arrived in time to witness the fight between Brant and your father. They were both badly beaten when it was over. One of the times your father was in the dirt Brant pulled a gun and shot him. Faulkner then carried the information to his superiors."

Hank's words were a shock and Amber stared at her husband in dumbfounded confusion. She sifted through the painful thoughts for an answer to what had just been said. Grasping hold of what she believed was reality, she walked toward Brant. Stopping a few feet from him, she raised her gun.

"You killed my father," her voice and eyes accused. "Drop it or I'll kill you where you stand." Her voice was emotionless and hard. She was drawing from the strength she knew she had to maintain. She cocked the hammer on the weapon. "Don't make me kill you."

Amber met his gaze without quivering. She saw something in his eyes she couldn't recognize. She waited, her hand steady, but her emotions beginning to break down. This was the hardest thing she had ever had to do. She expected a comment or argument from him and was surprised when he lowered the weapon and dropped it to the dirt. Defenseless, he stood before her as a proud man.

A low sob erupted from her throat when she took a final look at his face. Slowly lowering her gun, she walked toward her uncle. Reaching him, she raised her tear-filled eyes to his.

"Amber," he said gently. "You are crying."

"It hurts when you learn people you love have deceived your trust." She choked back a sob. "Brant couldn't have fought my father. He was near death himself. Papa and I treated Brant for serious wounds just before he left on his final assignment. Brant wasn't strong enough to make it to Antietam. He didn't kill my father." Her eyes were filled with pain as she searched Hank's face for an answer. "Why, Uncle Hank? Why did you betray the Union? Why did you have your brother killed? Why did you try to destroy your nephew? You used all of us for your own gain."

"I don't know what you are talking about," he said. "We have the two guilty men right here. They are responsible for the betrayal."

"I don't know how I am going to prove it, but you are responsible. I won't let you hurt Brant. He is my husband and I love him."

"You are the traitor," Hank snarled angrily.

He moved swiftly, hitting Amber in the shoulder and knocking her off balance. The gun fell from her hand as she dropped to the dirt. Stunned, she pushed herself to a sitting position.

"Now you'll all have to die."

"Drop the gun, Uncle Hank," Andy said, stepping out of the bushes, and Amber wondered how he had known about the meeting. "It is over. There is no escape. We have all the evidence we need against you. Brant knew about Papa's meeting, but he was too weak to reach him. Papa's location was exposed by the man who stood to lose the most."

The gun was still in Hank's hand, and it was obvious he would not surrender it without a fight. "William Boone would have told you the truth if Brant had not killed him," he sneered, looking at Brant.

"You killed him," Brant accused.

"That is right," Andy agreed. "He was going to name the people who knew about our meeting places. You couldn't risk being identified. You had your brother killed and sent men to capture me. Papa was smart. He knew you wanted slaves to make your plantation work. When you enlisted, he doubted your choice of sides and was upset when you were stationed in Washington. He made contact with one of the higher officers and convinced him you should be watched. You have been suspected for months."

His gun lowered to his side in defeat, but Amber saw his hand tighten on the weapon. "That is right," Hank claimed. "I am a Southerner, dedicated to their beliefs. I've worked hard to make them victorious, and I won't let you destroy my work. All of you will have to die to protect my position."

Like a madman, he raised his gun and lunged at his nephew. The gun exploded as they hit the dirt, but neither of them appeared to be hurt as they struggled. Brant and Giles ran forward to drag them apart.

Brant took hold of Hank and twisted his arm behind his back. "It is over Hank. You are finished," Brant declared.

"We are Rebels, Faulkner."

"I don't want any connection with scum like you."

"You don't have a home," Hank sneered at Brant. "The North wants you for spying and you won't be welcome in the South when they learn you freed my nephew. You have no place to go." His eyes glared hate. "Why did Confederate headquarters send you to Washington? I was doing my job."

"They didn't. I came on my own." Brant smiled. "For your information I do have a home. Gray was never my color."

Hank's face reddened with rage and he tried to break free. "You lying cheat. I suspected there was something strange about your arrival in the city, but I couldn't be sure, so I convinced my niece to get involved with you."

"You used her to advance your own purpose. You didn't care anything about Amber when you suggested that she marry me."

Hank sneered, "She agreed to it without any qualms."

Amber looked at her uncle, her eyes flashing. "I never told you about our first marriage."

Hank's eyes narrowed in confusion. "What first marriage?"

"Brant and I were married at the Confederate prison. I didn't tell you about it because I considered it a private matter. When you asked me to marry him, it was easy to agree."

"You never did want to trust other people," he accused. "You were always too independent. Richard —."

"Stop," Andy said abruptly. "I don't ever want to hear our father's name from your lips. You betrayed your family."

Hank's hard gray eyes looked at his nephew. "I should have killed you when you got back from California, but I thought Brant's execution would detract

469

from the focus on the spy."

Andy shook his head. "I was already cautious of you. By the time I got back from San Francisco, I had inside information and answers to many questions. I wasn't going to let you make a fool of me again."

Hank tried to wiggle out of Brant's grasp, but his arm was twisted painfully against his back.

"Giles," Brant said. "I think it is time to take the prisoner."

Colonel Broadmore nodded. "I won't pretend I wasn't nervous. We put our lives on the line by not giving Amber all the facts." He looked at her. "You have a very clear head. Your husband said we could count on you."

She didn't have an answer. Everything had happened so fast that she was still trying to put it together.

Six Union soldiers rode into the clearing and tied Mason's body to a horse. One of the men secured her uncle's wrists and dragged him away.

"Andy," Brant called just before everyone else rode away. "I'll need you here."

Amber turned to her husband. "Whose side are you on?"

"The only one I have ever been on." He stepped back and saluted her. "Colonel Brant Faulkner of the United States Army."

Amber's mouth dropped. "You are not a Rebel?" He shook his head. "Why did you tell me you were?"

Brant looked at Amber and chuckled. "When you treated my injuries, I was a man without political preference. At the prison compound you saw me in the Confederate uniform and naturally assumed I was the enemy."

"What else could I think? You had been sent to kill Andy."

"William Boone arrived at the meeting place to get information from your brother and saw Andy being taken away by the Rebels. Your uncle had given away the location of their meeting. Willy contacted Giles who in turn got in touch with me. I used my Confederate position to get the job of hanging Andy. I never had any intention of killing him; I was there to rescue him."

"Andy, when did you learn Brant was a Union officer?" she asked, wondering how much her brother had to do with the deception. "Did you know he was going to save your life?"

"No. I was sick, but the medicine he gave me was really a drug to simulate death. When I regained consciousness, I was outside the prison. I thought he had saved my life because of his feelings for you. Brant gave me instructions and money to get me back to Washington." It explained why Brant had refused to show her a grave. "I didn't suspect he was working for the Union until I was on my way to California. Something he said before I left should have alerted me, but I didn't put it together until I looked at the papers he had given me. They were full of information on the Rebel activity in California."

"Why didn't you tell me?" she asked both of them.

"Brant asked me not to," Andy explained.

She looked at her husband for an answer. "I wanted you to like me for who I am. Had I confessed to being a Union man you would have felt threatened. You needed to come to terms with your feelings and it wasn't easy for you."

"It wasn't," she admitted, but knew she had worked out the emotional turmoil to a satisfactory ending.

"I didn't tell you after you helped me escape because I wanted you to believe I was a Rebel and Broadmore was the infiltrator." He grinned. "Andy and I counted on you telling Hank about Giles. He was the man your father went to when he suspected your uncle of treason. I was a Union man working in the Rebel organization."

"What about the information you gave them?"

"Some of it was valid. It had to be real, but the Union officers always knew when they should expect trouble. We were very careful with what we told them. I brought a lot of Rebel plans to Giles."

Amber wearily shook her head. "This is almost too much to take in."

Brant slid his arm around her shoulders and held her against his side. "Neither of us ever meant to deceive you."

"I still have so many questions," she whispered. "What about California? Why didn't you work with the Union?"

Brant grinned. "You made that impossible by telling your uncle about me. I was a wanted man and couldn't contact anyone in the Union organization. Since I couldn't contact anyone in the Union openly, I decided to use my Rebel influence to get into the society and monitor their actions. I was Christopher's contact and made sure he did what would benefit the North."

Brant's constant probing of Northern activity suddenly became clear to Amber.

"I would have confirmed everything with Andy, but he was in another part of the society, and you wouldn't tell me where he was."

She looked at her brother. "You always wanted to talk to Brant."

"I suspected he was a Union man and wanted to confirm it. He told me the truth when we were on the ship headed for Washington. At the same time I learned about Giles and Uncle Hank."

"Your trial and sentence were all fake," she accused.

"We wanted Hank to think he was safe to continue his spying," Brant explained.

"Did Giles work with you on arranging Brant's escape?" she asked Andy.

"He made sure there weren't many guards." He looked at his sister and brother-in-law and decided it was time to leave them alone. "I want to go to town and find out about Hank." There was sadness in his blue-green eyes. "I'm sorry Papa had to die because of his brother."

"What will happen to him?"

"If he cooperates and gives us the information we want, he might live," Brant supplied.

Amber pulled free of Brant and put her arms around her brother. She had acknowledged her marriage to Brant, but the bond with Andy would always be strong.

"It has been quite an adventure, hasn't it?" she asked, looking into his blue-green eyes.

Andy grinned. "There will be more," he said positively. "The war is far from over, and I'm sure the two of you will get involved in something else. I hope you'll let me be part of it."

Amber threw a sideways glance at her husband. "As long as we *all* know everything that is going on, we'll make a good team."

Andy kissed her on the forehead and disappeared into the brush. A few minutes later they heard him ride away.

"I should be angry at you for not trusting me," she teased, pushing her lip forward in a pout.

Brant grabbed Amber's wrist and pulled her into his arms. "I trusted you with the most important thing I have—my life. When Hank told you I had killed your father, I didn't know what to expect. I wasn't sure if the gun aimed at my stomach had real intent or not."

Her fingers rested against his chest. "In the beginning I believed you were responsible for Papa's death, but I came to realize your wounds were too serious. You were almost dead. No one makes a rapid recovery from that kind of injury." She smiled at him. "I was afraid Hank was going to kill you. Blocking you from his gun was the only way I could think to save your life."

Brant threaded his fingers through her long hair. "Giles and I had learned your father was going to be killed. He was supposed to die by the field hospital, but I got there first and got rid of the men waiting for him. That is how I got my wounds." Brant sighed. "I have wished a hundred times that I had regained consciousness earlier and been able to stop him from going. I left the hospital with the intention of warning him, but I was too weak."

"Why didn't you tell me?" she wondered.

"I talked to one of the workers, but he thought the head wound had made me crazy. I wanted to tell you, but you ran away before I had a chance." He pulled her hand to his lips and kissed each finger.

"I'll never flee again," she said in a sultry tone.

"I'm glad you are no longer afraid. I love you deeply."

Amber's gaze dropped to the sensual line of his lips. Slowly, she raised her finger and caressed their fullness. She had been attracted to his mouth from the beginning, and it still held fascination for her.

"I love you," she said softly. "I never believed I could open myself to another person, but you have made my life fuller and more complete."

"What do you want to do with our lives now? My work in the South is done. Would you like to stay in Washington? You could help at the hospital."

"I might give it some of my time, but it no longer holds the same fascination it once did. I have my thoughts on other things," she said wickedly.

"I hope it involves me," he said, his mouth dropping to her neck.

"It most certainly does."

"Care to tell me what it is?"

Amber reached for the buttons on his shirt, and her palms opened against his naked chest. "It might be better to show you."

"Please do," he murmured, removing her shirt and pulling their upper bodies together.

"I thought my passion for you made me a traitor," she said as he slowly lowered her to the ground.

Brant held her close while he studied her face. "You are so beautiful," he said softly. She had all the qualities he admired: courage, intelligence, spunk, independence, beauty and passion. "I've searched for you all my life. I'll never let you go."

Brant's possessive declaration made her feel needed, and she wrapped her arms around his neck. "Kiss me Brant."

He was happy to accommodate her request, and she knew that Brant was the only man who could ignite Amber's flame.

THE BEST IN HISTORICAL ROMANCE
by Elizabeth Fritch

TIDES OF RAPTURE   (1245, $3.75)
When honey-haired Mandy encounters a handsome Yankee major,
she's enchanted by the fires of passion in his eyes, bewitched by the
stolen moments in his arms, and determined not to betray her loyalties! But this Yankee rogue has other things in mind!

CALIFORNIA, BOOK ONE: (1229, $3.50)
PASSION'S TRAIL
Before Sarah would give Toby her innocence, she was determined
to make his destiny her own. And as they journeyed across the vast
mountains and prairies, battling blizzards, drought and Indians,
the two young lovers held the promise of riches and glory in their
hearts—and the strength to shape a new frontier in the blazing,
bountiful land of CALIFORNIA.

CALIFORNIA, BOOK TWO: (1309, $3.50)
GOLDEN FIRES
The passion Clint Rawlins stirred in Samantha's heart was wilder
than the town he had come to tame. And though they fought
against each other's independence and their own desires—they
knew they were destined to share in the creation of the west, the
lush, green land of California.

CALIFORNIA, BOOK THREE: (1439, $3.50)
A HEART DIVIDED
Awestruck by the wealth and power of the fabled Rawlins family
in the San Francisco of 1906, Felicity was swept off her feet by the
two Rawlins brothers. Unlike his upstanding brother Bryce, Hunt
Rawlins thrived on the money, women, and danger of the Barbary
Coast, but Felicity was drawn to him even though she realized his
unscrupulous heart would never give her the lasting love offered
by his brother.

*Available wherever paperbacks are sold, or order direct from the
Publisher. Send cover price plus 50¢ per copy for mailing and
handling to Zebra Books, 475 Park Avenue South, New York,
N.Y. 10016. DO NOT SEND CASH.*

EXCITING BESTSELLERS FROM ZEBRA

HEIRLOOM (1200, $3.95)
by Eleanora Brownleigh
The surge of desire Thea felt for Charles was powerful enough to convince her that, even though they were strangers and their marriage was a fake, fate was playing a most subtle trick on them both: Were they on a mission for President Teddy Roosevelt—or on a crusade to realize their own passionate desire?

A WOMAN OF THE CENTURY (1409, $3.95)
by Eleanora Brownleigh
At a time when women were being forced into marriage, Alicia Turner had achieved a difficult and successful career as a doctor. Wealthy, sensuous, beautiful, ambitious and determined—Alicia was every man's challenge and dream. Yet, try as they might, no man was able to capture her heart—until she met Henry Thorpe, who was as unattainable as she!

PASSION'S REIGN (1177, $3.95)
by Karen Harper
Golden-haired Mary Bullen was wealthy, lovely and refined—and lusty King Henry VIII's prize gem! But her passion for the handsome Lord William Stafford put her at odds with the Royal Court. Mary and Stafford lived by a lovers' vow: one day they would be ruled by only the crown of PASSION'S REIGN.

LOVESTONE (1202, $3.50)
by Deanna James
After just one night of torrid passion and tender need, the dark-haired, rugged lord could not deny that Moira, with her precious beauty, was born to be a princess. But how could he grant her freedom when he himself was a prisoner of her love?

Available wherever paperbacks are sold, or order direct from the Publisher. Send cover price plus 50¢ per copy for mailing and handling to Zebra Books, 475 Park Avenue South, New York, N.Y. 10016. DO NOT SEND CASH.

ZEBRA HAS IT ALL!